HE WAS DECEIVED

HE WAS DECEIVED

ZACHARY GOLDMAN MYSTERIES
BOOK EIGHTEEN

P.D. WORKMAN

PD WORKMAN

ISBN: 9781774687055 (KDP Paperback)
ISBN: 9781774687086 (KDP Hardcover)
ISBN: 9781774687048 (Large Print)
ISBN: 9781774687079 (Lulu Paperback)
ISBN: 9781774687062 (ePub)
ISBN: 9781774687338 (Accessible Audio)

ALSO BY P.D. WORKMAN

FIND MORE BOOKS AT PDWORKMAN.COM

MYSTERY/SUSPENSE:

Zachary Goldman Mysteries
Private Investigator
She Wore Mourning
His Hands Were Quiet
She Was Dying Anyway
He Was Walking Alone
They Thought He was Safe
He Was Not There
Her Work Was Everything
She Told a Lie
He Never Forgot
She Was At Risk
He Drowned in Memory
Their Walls Were Empty
They Came for Him
They Sought Vengeance
She Was Their Target
His Fear Was Real
She Was Out of Reach
He Was Deceived
She Once Vanished

Kenzie Kirsch Medical Thrillers

Unlawful Harvest

Doctored Death

Dosed to Death

Gentle Angel

Rushin' Death

Posed for Death

Death of a Corpse

Endowed with Death

Shattered to Death

Captured in Death

Currying Death (Coming Soon)

Healed to Death (Coming Soon)

Death's Charm (Coming Soon)

A Bleeding Hearts Valley Thriller

An Abrupt Departure (Coming Soon)

High-Tech Crime Solvers Series

Virtually Harmless

Stand Alone Suspense Novels

Looking Over Your Shoulder

Lion Within

Pursued by the Past

In the Tick of Time

Loose the Dogs

AND MORE AT PDWORKMAN.COM

*To those whose lives
went in a different direction*

Zachary gazed out the front window at a delivery truck moving slowly down the street. He couldn't help but feel anxious when he saw a courier. The last package that had been delivered to him had not been what he had expected. It would be a while before he could feel the same excitement and anticipation opening a box or envelope left on his doorstep.

"You okay?" Kenzie asked.

Zachary swallowed. He nodded and forced a smile. "Yeah, sure. I'm good."

She evaluated him, her dark eyes serious and her bright red lips pursed. She nodded slowly, her dark curls bouncing a little, a movement that always made him want to touch it and wind the curls around his fingers. But he refrained, turning his attention to the breakfast preparations.

"Coffee is on," he told her, though he wasn't sure whether he had turned on the machine or she had. "I'll pop some toast in for you…" He noticed the smell of the toasting bread mixing with that of the coffee. Obviously one of them had already done that job too. He got out plates and cutlery and found her marmalade in the fridge.

"Where are you going this morning?" Kenzie asked.

He hadn't told her he was going out anywhere, but she could tell from his shirt—a button-up shirt rather than just a t-shirt or polo—that he was planning to meet with someone today. He didn't dress up for computer work, going for a walk, or running errands. Or for a surveillance job, unless he was positioning himself in an office building or somewhere such an outfit would blend better than his usual work "uniform."

"Meeting with a potential client. Not sure yet what kind of a case it is," he anticipated her next question. "He didn't want to discuss anything over the phone. And I like to meet with possible clients face-to-face in the beginning. Remote work and communicating electronically are fine, a convenient way to run a case, but I like to get a read on a person before I accept the job."

"You never know what you might be getting into otherwise," Kenzie suggested.

"Yeah. Surveilling a possibly adulterous spouse is one thing, if the guy is just looking for information. But if he's lying and is really an abuser trying to find an ex who is hiding from him…"

Kenzie nodded, understanding, as she poured each of them a cup of fresh coffee.

"Can you always tell, though?"

"I'm pretty good at reading people. That doesn't mean that I don't ever make mistakes… but if I'm not sure, I'll turn them down, say I'm too busy to give their case the attention it needs right now."

"So someone else gets the job?"

"Well…" Zachary didn't like to think that he was only delaying the abusive husband finding his runaway wife. Still, it wasn't like he could do anything to keep the man from hiring a private investigator who didn't have the same scruples or intuition as Zachary. If he were determined to find his wife, there wasn't much Zachary could do other than refuse the work himself.

"Hopefully, he's so disappointed by my refusal that he can't bring himself to approach another PI," he told Kenzie. "You can see how crushing that would be."

2

Kenzie chuckled. She took a sip of her coffee. The toast popped and Zachary buttered it before putting it on Kenzie's plate and grabbing a yogurt cup for himself.

"Yes, that would definitely be a consideration," Kenzie agreed. "I can't imagine what it would be like to be turned down by you."

Zachary tried to figure out whether there was any secondary meaning to her statement, but decided just to take it at face value. He sat down across from Kenzie and opened his yogurt cup. He usually had a yogurt cup or a granola bar for his breakfast with Kenzie. He was more in the mood for a granola bar today but didn't want to unwrap one with Kenzie watching him. The noise of the crinkling wrapper was like fingernails on the blackboard, and he wouldn't be able to hide his grimace from her. She was already watching him closely enough without his giving her something else to worry about.

"Do you think it's wise?" Kenzie asked.

Zachary looked at her, uncertain. He had probably missed something else she had said and lost the thread of the conversation.

"Taking on a new client right now," Kenzie said slowly. "I mean… this time of year…"

So close to Christmas. She tried to avoid saying it, but they both knew what she meant. At this time of year, when he might shut down completely and not be able to do any work.

"No… I'll check him out and see whether it is a case I want to take on. And I'll warn him I might need to take a few days off around the holiday. People are usually pretty good about it if you let them know… set expectations."

He was doing really well this year on the new med protocol. At this time last year, he had been in the hospital psych ward, unable to deal with the depression and control the thoughts of self-harm without professional help.

But that was last year. He was much better this year. The anniversary of the fire, that Christmas Eve disaster, was quickly approaching. It was a struggle to keep his spirits up and function at the same level as he did the rest of the year and he dreaded slipping further into the abyss. But he was functional. The work, especially the novelty of a new case, would help him to stay focused on something other than traumatic memories.

If he had to take a few days off, he could do that. It wasn't unusual for someone to take a few days off work for family around Christmas. His client would think nothing of it.

"I just don't want you to be overwhelmed," Kenzie said. "It might be better if you didn't take too much on until after... maybe in the new year."

"It isn't too much," he assured her. "I mean... depending on what it is. If it's too big and he needs answers in two days, that's another story, but most people are not in a big hurry."

"You'll be careful?"

"Of course. Yes, I will."

Kenzie nibbled her marmalade toast and studied him a little too closely. Zachary's face warmed.

"Did I miss a spot shaving?" he asked, brushing his hand over his face to break the eye contact and allow him to look away. "Or are you just admiring my manly scars?"

The numerous small cuts from the explosion were healing, but it would be a while before they were all gone. One or two of the deeper ones that had needed stitches might leave scars. Nothing that bad. They would blend in with his other scars. And when he let his whiskers grow for a few days, as he usually did, they would be camouflaged.

Kenzie smiled and shook her head. "It must be the manly scars," she said lightly. "I just can't seem to tear my eyes away."

He blushed further, even knowing she was teasing him. His ears burned and were probably bright red.

She dropped the conversation thread and didn't insist that she knew better than he did about managing his business at this difficult time of year.

She was having her own difficulties this year, and Zachary wondered whether that was one reason she was so concerned about his state of mind and traumatic memories. Either empathizing with him because of her own feelings or trying to distract herself by focusing on someone else's problems.

Zachary needed to pay attention to Kenzie's mood and stress levels, not just his own. She needed his support just as much as he needed hers.

2

Zachary had agreed to meet Oliver Dwayne at a coffee shop. Neutral ground. They were past the morning rush, so the venue was not too busy. But it wasn't empty, either. People came and went, both individually and in pairs or small groups. Zachary and Oliver would not stand out.

Zachary ordered a pot of coffee, and the waitress placed a couple of mugs on the table for him. He kept an eye on the door, watching for the man he was to meet.

Most people who walked into the coffee shop went directly to the counter or a table and ordered what they wanted. They either settled in to work on a computer or tablet or left with a "to go" cup as soon as they were served. They didn't look around to try to find the person they were to be meeting with.

Then, a man walked in, stopped, and looked at the other customers. Tall and distinguished, dark hair with streaks of gray at the temples. A short, carefully shaped mustache and beard. His cheeks were prominent, face narrow. He looked like someone who had been through a lot, but he was strong and confident. Well-dressed, but a little weatherworn and vulnerable, too.

Zachary stood partway up from his seat, and the man's eyes met his. He walked over. He put out a hand and raised his brows. "Mr. Goldman?"

"Zachary, please. Mr. Dwayne?"

"Oliver."

"Have a seat," Zachary motioned to the table, and Oliver sat down. He poured himself a full mug of coffee and drank it immediately, no cream or sugar. He gulped it so fast it must have burned his throat.

"This is difficult," Oliver said. He put his cup down and dabbed his lips with a napkin. "I suppose we do all of the usual small talk first."

"Sometimes it puts people at ease," Zachary told him, smiling slightly. "But we don't have to. Whatever you're most comfortable with. If you want to jump straight into the case, you can."

"I just want to get on with it. It's hard enough without having to deal with social conventions. I have no idea what the usual protocol is for something like this."

"There really isn't one. Everyone approaches it differently."

Some people wanted to get to know Zachary and build that relationship first. Some of them beat around the bush, hoping Zachary would guess what they were there about. Some blurted it out and then cowered back, waiting for the fallout of having spilled their guts and made themselves so vulnerable.

Oliver seemed to need some questions to get closer to the issue. Zachary evaluated him. Not married, he didn't think. He didn't wear a ring. Didn't have that "cared for" look, the confidence that he was going back to someone who was waiting faithfully for him. So there was probably not an unfaithful spouse to tail. That was a relief because he really didn't like those jobs.

A business deal gone bad? Industrial espionage? It didn't feel like it.

Maybe a missing person? Maybe someone he had lost touch with long ago and wanted to reconnect with?

"This is a personal matter?" Zachary guessed.

Oliver nodded. "Yes. It's personal."

"Family? Someone you've lost touch with?"

An expression of sadness settled over Oliver's face. An expression that was clearly natural for him. Profound sadness. But not a sadness that he shared with others. He put on a different face to deal with Zachary—his public face.

Not a missing person. A loss, yes, but not someone he had lost touch with or fallen out with.

"Someone you lost?" he amended.

Oliver nodded. "Yes... I don't even know why I am here. I dealt with this a long time ago. I put it behind me."

Cold cases were difficult. Evidence disappeared. Witnesses forgot what they had seen and heard. Alibis were almost impossible to establish. And the longer ago it was, the harder it was to get any traction.

"How long ago?"

"Ten years."

Zachary nodded. Better than twenty or fifty, but still difficult.

"Who? What happened?"

Oliver gave a long sigh. He turned his coffee cup in place on the table, rotating it in a circle once, twice, and a third time before he could get anything out.

"My wife."

So he had been married. But ten years ago. Long enough to lose the look of a married man.

Oliver didn't answer the "what happened" immediately. He swallowed, considering how to tell Zachary about it.

"She was shot," he said finally.

Zachary nodded and waited.

"The police said that it was accidental. Just a freak thing. I accepted that and moved on. It was... so tragic. I couldn't spend time wallowing, mourning her, questioning their findings. I had children. They needed me. I had to be the strong one, the one to move everyone forward. We couldn't stay focused on the past, the 'why' of it all. It was an accident... so we went on."

"How old were your kids?"

"Nine, thirteen, and fifteen."

Zachary had been ten when he lost his family. He knew what it

8

was like to lose a mother at that age. Though his mother had not been shot. And she had not been the loving, caring parent he had craved.

"Tough time to lose your mother," he sympathized, staying focused on Oliver's situation and not his own.

"I think any age is a difficult time to lose your mother. Especially so suddenly and violently. But yes, it was terrible for them. We had to draw closer together, help each other through it."

"They were lucky to have you. It sounds like you were there for them."

"I thought I was. Now… I wonder if I was or if I just went through the motions. I had work to do. I still had to support them financially as well as emotionally, and I wonder how well I did. I want to say that I didn't bury myself in my work. But I did to a certain extent."

"It's natural," Zachary said. "Trying to distract yourself. To focus on what you can do rather than… spinning your wheels. The police told you it was an accident, so what else could you do?"

Oliver spread his hands apart. "What I'm doing now. Hiring someone. Digging down deeper into it. Not just taking things at face value."

"Well… you are now. Maybe this will bring you some peace."

Certainly, Oliver didn't look like he was at peace now. More like he was haunted. Zachary didn't know if he could help him find that peace, but he liked Oliver and what he had seen of him so far. He wanted to do what he could, though he didn't know how much that would be after the passing of ten years.

"How did it happen?"

He hoped that it hadn't had anything to do with the children. He could only imagine what *that* would do to the family.

"She was in her car. Out for a drive. The bullet went through the window and struck her. She was found hours later. There was nothing that could be done by then. The police said it was probably a hunter, kids playing with a gun, or someone doing target practice. Something like that. Just a freak accident that couldn't have been predicted. Out in the country… people think they can fire off their guns whenever they like. They think they're alone, so... why not?"

"Did they talk to anyone who had heard the shots? Had anyone been out target shooting?"

"They never found anyone who had been out that way with a gun. Maybe kids. Kids who never even knew that they had ended up killing a woman with their carelessness."

"How hard did the police try?"

It wasn't a very tactful question. But Zachary would need to know. If there had been an extensive search and investigation, there might be nothing more for Zachary to do. Was there a chance that he might find something ten years later that the police had overlooked?

"I don't think... I don't think they did much investigating at all. I think they just assumed they knew the story. We weren't looking for someone to blame. If it was an accident, I certainly didn't want some kid to go to jail for it. Ruin another life for no reason."

Zachary could understand that. He sipped his coffee. In ten years, Oliver's kids had all grown to adulthood. One or two of them might still be at home with him. They might know other kids in the neighborhood who had been old enough back then to find some witnesses. Or to identify any borderline "bad apples" who might have been experimenting then.

"So... if you didn't want any kid being sent to jail for it back then, what has changed your mind?"

"It's the blasted phone calls."

3

Zachary raised his brows.

"I've been getting phone calls," Oliver explained. "Someone who... seems to know something about what happened."

Zachary sat back and looked at Oliver, considering this idea.

"Someone who wants you to know what really happened?"

"I don't know. I don't know what his purpose is. Why would he want to bring it to my attention now, so many years later? Whatever happened, they got away with it ten years ago. It's buried in the past."

"What does the caller say in the phone calls?"

"He says... he knows who killed her. He knows what happened."

Zachary considered the wording. "Who killed her. That sounds like intent. Like he's not just saying he knows who was fooling around with a gun that day and accidentally shot her."

Oliver stared at him, a silence settling between them as he considered Zachary's words. Then, finally, he nodded. "Yes. That's what it sounds like. He sounds... malicious. Like he enjoys calling me. Like he enjoys making me squirm."

"Why would he? Why would someone want to hurt you?"

Oliver shrugged and shook his head. "I'm the most boring person in the world. I do bookkeeping for a warehouse. Do you think anyone cares about that? I've spent the last ten years raising my kids. I haven't committed any crime. I don't use drugs or gamble. I don't have any work rivalries or romantic entanglements. I go to work and fill in spreadsheets. I go home and help with homework and studying. Why would anyone want to hurt me?"

"Are your kids still at home? The youngest still lives with you?"

"He took an extra year to finish high school. He's just started college, away from home. I'm an empty nester. All alone in the nest." He stared grimly into space. He had once assumed that he would be an empty nester with his wife. Maybe they'd had plans for all the things they would do when the kids were gone. Travel. Go to wine tastings. Take up bowling. Broken dreams.

"When did these calls start?"

"On the tenth anniversary of her death."

Where had the caller been for those ten years? In prison? Biding his time? What triggered him to call Oliver, other than just the date? Did it have anything to do with the last child going away to school? With Oliver being alone?

"Have you gone to the police?"

Oliver looked away, pretending to be watching the deft movements of the barista while she made a tall, complicated coffee for a girl who didn't look old enough to be out of high school.

"I tried," he admitted. "Not at first. At first, I thought it was just the one call and that it was just some cruel prank. Some sicko who saw in a newspaper or something that it was the anniversary of my wife's death and thought they were clever. I thought that it would just be once. But then he called again. And again. I just don't know what to do."

"What did the police say about it? Were they able to trace the calls?"

"They didn't even try. They said it isn't threatening and wouldn't be worth anyone's time to track him down and charge him. Putting too many resources into something that's so low-level..." Oliver sighed. "I get it. I understand we're not talking about a celebrity stalking here. It's not murder or drug dealing or a gang war. No threats were made. So what do the police care? They said the easiest thing would be for me to change my number and not give it to anyone."

That wouldn't stop someone from sending letters. Or showing up on Oliver's doorstep. And how was Oliver supposed to conduct his business or carry on with his life without giving anyone his phone number? He would have to give it to his employer, his kids, to the utility companies, the bank, and a dozen other companies. Phones were the key to unlocking most any account these days. How was he supposed to prevent everyone he gave it to from sharing it with someone else? Vermont was small; everybody was connected somehow.

"What about your wife's death? If that was something other than an accident, shouldn't they be investigating it? Looking into the allegations?"

"They already determined that it was an accident. It isn't up for discussion. Looking into it again would be a waste of time and resources." Oliver put his coffee cup down too hard, expressing his frustration. But he had drunk most of the beverage already, so it didn't make a big mess—just one splash over the edge of the rim that was easy to wipe up with a napkin.

"What do *you* think?" Zachary asked. Obviously, if Oliver was willing to hire a private investigator about it, he felt that there was something there. Something they had missed in the initial investigation. The caller had left him with enough doubts that he was willing to put his own money into finding out. His own resources.

"Back then... there was no time to think about it. There was no reason to dig any further. It looked like just an accidental shooting on a lonely road. Something that was just... fate. Tragic. I had three motherless children to take care of. I was just... weighed down with grief and the responsibility of having to be Mom and Dad to my kids. Taking care of them and getting them through this horrible thing... I really... for years, I haven't dealt with it, but it has never been off my mind."

He started turning his cup again, the small puddle of coffee being spread in a circle. Zachary stared down at it while Oliver thought through what he had been asked.

"It didn't make any sense at the time. I mean. The thing that made the most sense was that it was just a random accident. So even though I hated to think about such a terrible thing happening to her out in the middle of nowhere... it was easier than trying to make sense of it. If I thought that it had been targeted, that she had been killed for a reason... I think that would have been too much. I couldn't have handled it."

And maybe that was part of why the police hadn't looked any further than they had, figuring they were doing the family a mercy by not raising any additional questions.

"So the police are not interested in looking at it now."

Oliver shook his head. "They just want me to go home and keep quiet about it. Go back to sleep. Pretend that nothing has changed."

"*Has* anything changed?"

Oliver opened his mouth to answer, then stopped and thought about it.

"Now that I've 'woken up,' I don't think I can go back to sleep," he admitted. "I wish that he had just kept quiet and not started to bother me. I want to go back to that place where I didn't have to think about it. Where it was just something that had happened years ago for no reason."

Zachary had been in that same situation himself when something from his past had resurfaced and refused to leave him alone. Refused to let him go back to sleep and ignore it again.

"So you think there's something to these allegations? You think that someone *did* kill her intentionally?"

4

"No," Oliver said immediately. "No, it doesn't make any sense that anyone would want to kill her. There was no reason for it. There was no more reason for someone to want her dead than there was for someone to want to upset me by making me think that they did. Neither of us was involved in anything sketchy. We didn't break the law. We didn't have friends who broke the law. We didn't have enemies. She was a mother. She did some work when the kids were at school, stuffing envelopes, filing, and doing administrative work. There is nothing dangerous about that! There is no reason for someone to single her out and to… *hurt* her."

And yet, if the unknown caller was right, someone had done just that. But why?

"Was this an isolated event? There were no other accidents or threats? Nothing that would suggest this was part of a pattern? It just came out of the blue?"

"Out of the blue," Oliver echoed. "Exactly."

"She didn't get any strange phone calls? She wasn't worried about anything? Behaving strangely?"

"Well…" The other man scratched behind his ear thoughtfully. "Well… not that I knew of."

"Threats? Concerns?"

"It's just that... She *was* jumpy. I don't know how else to describe it. And I don't remember a lot of details. I remember her being sort of jumpy. Worrying when the phone rang. Thinking that someone might be outside the house or following her. But she would laugh it off and say it wasn't anything. That she... was tired or had just been reading a spooky book. I was concerned... I agreed with the suggestion that she wasn't getting enough sleep. What mom ever does? But I was getting a little worried at her... changes in behavior."

"What did you think was going on?"

"Only that she wasn't getting enough sleep. I don't know... I guess I thought she was getting burned out, trying to do too much. That she was a little loopy from lack of sleep."

"She was jumpy and worried about people calling her or following her, but she didn't tell you why?"

"No, she just brushed it off. And I thought... I don't know what I thought. I was worried for her mental health, I guess, but not for her physical health. I didn't think that anyone was after her."

"And now...?"

"I guess now I'm wondering for the first time. I didn't think anything of it when it was happening. I didn't think it was related when she died. That was just a random, accidental shooting. But now, for the first time... I can't help wondering."

"Do you remember any specific times? What happened? How did she react, and what did she say?"

He shook his head slowly. "I remember the phone ringing and her just about jumping out of her skin... when I went to answer it, she wouldn't let me. Said she wanted a quiet night with me with no interruptions. Which was silly because the kids were around and we were constantly being interrupted." He gave a wistful smile. Those were the days. He missed the happy family days, even if he had been irritated by the children's interruptions at the time.

"She wouldn't let you answer it? Was that her phone or yours?"

"The house phone. We still had a landline. Still do, actually. It's a rural area and I am paranoid about the cell phones not having adequate reception one day when we really need it." He paused, a look of pain crossing his features. "When I need it," he amended. He was alone. There was no "we."

"Your anonymous caller is calling on the landline?"

"Yes. Do you think that is significant?"

"I don't know yet. It may just be that it is the only number listed in directories. Cell phones tend not to be."

"Right. Of course."

But Zachary was unsure if that were the reason. The anonymous caller might have been the same person who had been calling ten years earlier—the caller Oliver's wife had not wanted him to talk to.

"What was your wife's name?"

"Edie. It's an old-fashioned name for an old-fashioned girl. She used to say that because she liked being a stay-at-home mom with the kids and other things that weren't valued anymore by the 'modern' woman."

"Edie. Do you want to give me the details about... her death?"

"You're going to take the case?" Oliver sounded surprised. Zachary raised his brows. He had done nothing to suggest he would not take the case.

But Oliver had perhaps expected to be turned down after encountering obstacles with the police department.

"Yes. I would be happy to take it on. I can't promise you that I will be able to solve it. But I will look into it if you want me to."

Oliver could be having second thoughts too. He might have decided, upon seeing Zachary, that he didn't want him to take it. Or he might have decided he didn't want the answers and would prefer to leave it alone and hope the anonymous caller would stop calling. Maybe he would change his landline phone number. Only a few people needed to have it. His children. Emergency services. He could use his cell phone for everything else.

Oliver looked uncertain. Wanting to forge ahead and, at the same time, worried about where the investigation would take him

—worried about what Zachary might find out and how it would affect the lives of Oliver and his children.

Zachary took out his rate card and put it on the table in front of Oliver.

"You don't have to decide now. Sleep on it. Think about it some more. If you want me to take it on, give me a call and we'll arrange for an initial retainer. If I don't hear from you, I'll assume you changed your mind. I won't call and demand to know why. That's your business. Okay? Shall we leave it at that?"

"Okay," Oliver agreed. "I might… want to talk it over with my daughter first. See what she thinks."

"Sure. I'll wait to hear back from you. No pressure. You do it when you're ready."

"Thank you." Oliver stood up and held out his hand. Zachary got to his feet and they shook hands warmly. "I really appreciate you hearing me out. This is helping me to sort out my feelings about the whole thing. I'll let you know one way or the other."

Zachary nodded his thanks. "Good luck."

5

When he got home, Zachary called his older sister, Heather, who helped him out with some of the administrative work for Goldman Investigations. He called to let her know about the possibility of the new case, even though they hadn't been retained yet.

But she didn't need to know that ahead of time. That wasn't actually why he was calling. In truth, the reason he was calling was to follow up on her thoughts on their recent family dinner. The first time all the Goldman siblings had gotten together to break bread since the family had been broken up decades earlier, when Zachary had been ten and had unintentionally burned down the house, resulting in devastating and far-reaching consequences.

He told Heather about the new case, but didn't need anything set up yet. Heather was silent for a few long seconds. "So... other than that, how are things going, Zach...?"

"Things are okay. I'm just... you know... taking one day at a time."

She didn't say anything.

"It was nice meeting Michael," Zachary said.

"I wasn't sure whether to bring him," Heather said with a self-conscious laugh. The birth son nobody had met. "Nothing like throwing a new wrench in the works, just as we're trying to get to know each other again."

"What did he think about it? Did he run away screaming once we went our different directions?"

"He was really good about it. But a bit quiet. I had warned him that it would not be your typical TV family reunion. But I think he was still expecting a lot of hugs and happy reminiscing."

There had been some tentative hugs. But not a lot. Nothing like Zachary had seen on old episodes of *Unsolved Mysteries* or one of the many reunion programs that were popular. No squeals of delight and explanations of how exciting it was to see everyone together in one place. Zachary had met all the siblings previously at least once, though Michael had been new to the mix. But it had been the first time all six of the siblings had been in one room in decades and none of them had known what to expect.

"How did you feel about it?" Heather asked tentatively. "Was it too much?"

Since Zachary was the one who had put the reunion dinner together, he couldn't very well complain that he hadn't wanted to do it. He could complain that it hadn't worked out the way he had wanted but, since he had gone in with a very low bar, that wasn't really a problem either.

"It was okay," he said. "I was glad to get all of us together. But it's going to be a while before we feel like one big happy family. It was a start. We needed to start somewhere."

"Yeah. I hoped you were okay with it. I know you were probably disappointed over the way things went, but…"

"It worked out about how I expected," Zachary countered. "I wasn't expecting any fairytale story."

"Well… that's good. It *was* nice to get everyone together."

"Yeah."

"I'm going to talk to Joss. She really needs to… chill. To back off and just let you be. I hate the way she treats you. I get that she's… prickly. And she has a right to be. But good grief… you were ten. You weren't trying to do anything wrong. You couldn't have predicted what was going to happen. How long is she going to go on punishing you for it?"

"You don't have any resentments about it?" Zachary asked. "Even little ones? I don't think Joss is the only one who blames me for what happened to the family and the way their lives turned out. She's just the most open about it."

"I don't blame you for all of the bad things that ever happened to me."

Zachary noted that she hadn't denied having any resentments at all. She hadn't said that she didn't blame him for burning the house down and the family being separated. Just that she didn't blame him for *everything*.

"And you can put aside the other things and just take me as I am now," Zachary said, grateful for Heather's ability to do that. "But it isn't the same for Joss."

"Well, it isn't very fair of her," Heather said. "She should be able to leave the past behind and to separate what you did as a little boy from what happened to her after that. It isn't your fault that she was sent to another family or that she got addicted or trafficked. That had nothing to do with you."

"But none of that would have happened if I hadn't done what I did," Zachary pointed out.

"Wouldn't it?" Heather challenged. "Our family was already in trouble. The fire might have been the last straw for Mom but, if it hadn't happened, something else would have had the same effect. She wasn't going to keep us, Zachary. She was done being a mom."

Zachary swallowed. He'd heard similar things from Heather and Tyrrell in the past. And he'd talked about it with Dr. Boyle, his therapist, and Kenzie. They all told him that it wasn't all because of him. That if the fire hadn't split his parents up and prompted her to relinquish the children, something else would have. After the big blowout they'd had the night of the fire, maybe it was over anyway. Maybe in the morning his mother would have called DCF anyway, even without the fire.

But as much as they tried to reassure him on these points, Zachary couldn't believe what they told him. He'd been told his fault and he had believed it. He had repeated it to himself for years. It was ingrained in his psyche.

"Anyway, you don't need to get on Joss's case about it," Zachary told Heather, trying to do an end run around all the self-examination and the argument over whether everything that had happened to Joss was truly his fault. "You can't argue with her feelings, and I wouldn't want her to pretend she feels any differently than she does. I'd rather she was honest about it and didn't put on a fake front."

"Well, if you want the cold, unvarnished feelings about something, Joss is the one to ask. But I think there's a difference between telling the truth and trying to hurt someone, and I think Joss goes too far. She could be nicer about it. She could watch what she says and be open to listening to others and sharing her feelings in a... less hurtful way."

"I don't want to change her. I don't care if she's prickly. That's who Joss is. I'm not going to ask her to be someone different. I want people to take me as I am. I don't want her masking who she is for my comfort."

"You think you deserve to be punished," Heather said, "I think you like her how she is because it makes you feel better to have someone echoing those feelings and being mean to you. Maybe because Mom and Dad were abusive, you are looking for that in someone else."

Zachary didn't want to hear that. And he didn't want to think about Bridget, his ex-wife, and how abusive she had been. Dr. B had suggested on other occasions that perhaps Bridget had been a substitute for his mother. Both had been verbally abusive, constantly criticizing him and trying to change him. He was with Kenzie now, and she was different. She treated him fairly, even when he screwed up. She didn't swear and scream and rail at him. So he had moved past that. He wasn't seeking someone who hurt him anymore.

"I just want Joss to be able to be who she is," he told Heather sensibly. "Don't get on her case for my benefit. Just let her be."

Heather sighed. "Maybe we can talk about it another time. I don't think she should be that way. She needs to get over it."

"Leave her to deal with it her own way. Maybe if she can express her emotions and feels like she is being heard, she'll be able to move on. I still love her and I'm not going to stop seeing her and talking to her. In time, maybe things will change and she won't be so bitter. But for now..." Zachary shrugged helplessly. "Let's just accept her as she is. That's all any of us want."

6

"How were things at the morgue today?" Zachary asked Kenzie. It had been more than twenty-four hours since he had talked to Oliver, and he wasn't sure whether the new client was actually going to be a new client. But he'd had plenty of other work to keep him busy in the meantime. There was always a stack of skip traces, insurance files, and other work on hand. Those jobs never dried up.

"Pretty dead," Kenzie told him.

Zachary laughed. "I would hope so. I don't think you would want any of your patients suddenly waking up."

"That would be rather awkward," Kenzie agreed.

"So, nothing particularly interesting this week?"

"No, all pretty routine. Accidents and natural causes. Nothing too disturbing or shocking."

Zachary was always interested in anything particularly interesting Kenzie encountered, and she was happy to have someone to share it with who didn't gross out at hearing the details.

Zachary started to set the table, putting out the plates and cutlery while Kenzie worked on the cooking. His phone vibrated in his pocket. He pulled it out to see whether it was a call, calendar alarm, or other alert. He saw Oliver's name on the screen.

"Oh, this is my new client. Maybe. I'll be right back."

Kenzie made a noise of agreement. Zachary returned to his computer in the living room. He sat on the couch and touched the keyboard to wake it up.

"Oliver," he greeted, answering the call.

"Oh, hello," Oliver greeted, sounding surprised Zachary had answered the call. "I'm sorry, you're probably having dinner…"

Maybe he had intentionally called over the dinner hour in the hopes that he could leave Zachary a message instead of talking to him directly. Zachary had done the same thing himself, though he usually chose lunchtime, since noon was pretty universally accepted as the lunch hour and dinner could be anywhere between five and nine.

"No, it's okay," Zachary said. "We haven't started yet. How can I help you?"

If Oliver was hoping to reach him during supper in order to leave a message, then he had probably decided not to give Zachary the case, whether it was because he hadn't clicked with Zachary or because he had decided not to pursue it any further.

"Well, I talked to my daughter. Marissa. About the case. Her mother's death."

"She didn't want you to pursue it?" Zachary guessed.

"Oh, no," Oliver sounded surprised. "She was supportive. She doesn't really think there is anything to it, but she said that we might as well look into it while there may still be people who remember what happened. Easier now than in another ten years. And then we'll be able to… be at peace about it. Whatever the results."

"So you want me to take on the case?"

"Uh… yes."

"Great. I'd be happy to see what I can find. As I told you, there's no guarantee that I'll get anywhere with it or that the results will be what you hope, but I'll do my best. I'll need to get as much information from you as I can. There's no point in paying me to look up stuff you already know."

"Sure, of course."

"If you know who was assigned to the case at the police department and if they're still around, that would be great. The date and any of the circumstances surrounding it. Contact information for your kids."

"The kids?"

"I'll need to talk to them and see what their recollections are about the events surrounding her death."

"They don't know anything. They were just children when it happened."

"You'd be surprised what kids can remember or what they were aware of. They may not have felt like they could talk to you about it back then. Or there might be things that were connected, but they didn't realize it at the time."

"They don't know anything," Oliver repeated.

"I'll still need to talk to them to verify that."

Oliver sighed loudly but then conceded and gave Zachary their names and contact details. Marissa, Terry, and Jeff. They were fifteen, thirteen, and nine when Edie Dwayne had been killed. Not that different in age from Zachary and his two older sisters at the time of the fire and the dissolution of their family. And Zachary could remember a lot about the family dynamics even as a ten-year-old. As he'd told Kenzie, he was good at reading people. That had been a necessary skill for him to develop in the family he had grown up in. Without being able to read people and predict what they would do next, he might not have survived. And it had been a vital skill as he moved from home to home in foster care as well.

People didn't always say what they meant or tell him what he needed to know. He needed to be able to figure it out somehow.

Oliver had suggested that the person Zachary should talk to first was Marissa. Or maybe she was the only one he needed to talk to. She had been the oldest and the other two really wouldn't know anything that she didn't. And she was the only one who knew anything about the investigation yet. He would have to give the others a heads-up before Zachary called them.

So Zachary looked at the information he had for Marissa and tapped her number into his phone.

He wasn't sure whether she would answer his call right away. People—especially young people—didn't like to answer unknown callers. Older folks who had grown up without caller ID were more likely to answer without knowing who was calling.

"Hello?"

"Hi. Is this Marissa? My name is Zachary Goldman, and I've been talking to your dad."

"Oh, yeah." Marissa had a pleasant voice. "He said something about that. I'm not sure what exactly he expects to be able to find, but… I don't think it hurts to look. What else is he going to spend his money on?"

Zachary could think of a lot of things that he could have spent his money on rather than looking for the possible murderer of his wife from ten years ago. A lot more sure things that might make him happy, when this venture might only lead to pain and more loneliness.

"He's lucky to have your support," Zachary told her in a warm tone. "Now, I realize we could do this over the phone, but I would prefer to meet face-to-face, if possible. Do you think we could meet?"

Her tone was more hesitant when she replied. Answering the phone to a stranger was one thing. Agreeing to meet him somewhere was quite different.

"You can pick the venue," Zachary told her. "I like a coffee shop that is busy but not too noisy. If you have a meeting room where you work, that's another possibility. A library. I'm not going to ask you to meet me somewhere isolated."

"Oh, well, I guess that doesn't sound too bad." She would be surrounded by people and would be able to leave if she ended up not liking Zachary or if he were asking intrusive questions or putting the moves on her. He could hear it all in her voice. Women learned early in life how cautious they had to be of male attention.

"Where are you located?" Zachary asked. "Do you have a favorite hangout or somewhere you would like to meet?"

27

"I'm in Burlington. When do you want to meet? Like, tomorrow? I'm not sure I can find a time that would work for you."

"I'm flexible. So, if you have a break in your schedule, I'll make it work. I'm not that far away so, as long as it's not within the next couple of hours, I can be there whenever it suits you."

"Oh, well, I don't want to take you away from your dinner and whatever other plans you might have," she said doubtfully. Oliver had raised a very polite daughter. "Maybe it's best to wait another day. Or maybe put it off until the new year."

"I don't want to wait that long. I'd like to make inroads before… the holidays. If you don't have any time today, I understand. It is a busy season, but I'm happy to defer to your schedule and find a time that works for you."

"Hmm. Well. I could meet around six tomorrow. Maybe we could have dinner if you don't have any other plans. I know this great pizza place."

"Just point me to it," Zachary told her. "I love pizza."

7

Highway travel was one of Zachary's favorite things. He was rarely able to leave the chatter of his brain behind and be focused and calm. No restlessness, no anxiety, his brain staying focused on one thing rather than jumping like a rabid squirrel from one thing to another. Highway travel was one of the few times he was able to enter that state of Zen, to become what he imagined it must be like to be an ordinary, neurotypical human being. So he had not been at all upset by the prospect of taking a couple of hours to drive out and meet with Marissa, and then to drive back home again afterward. He didn't see it as wasted time but as one of the few times he could think clearly and calmly without being so hyperfocused that he forgot the rest of the world around him.

He wondered what he would be able to uncover in the case of Edie Dwayne's death. Would he be able to prove that it was something more than just a tragic accident? Or were he and Oliver looking for something that didn't exist? Was the mysterious caller someone who was "in the know" or someone who wanted to hurt and unsettle the grieving widower? If the caller just wanted to hurt Oliver, why had he waited ten years to do it? What had provoked his renewed attention in the case?

Oliver thought that his wife had been jumpy in the days before her death. Had there really been something going on, or was he just seeing that as he looked back over the years with the whispered words of the anonymous caller worming their way beneath the surface and coloring his memories?

If she had been jumpy, then what had it been about? Why hadn't she told her partner about it? Or hadn't told him clearly enough for him to remember? She might have made some passing comment about being afraid or something going on at the office that had just gone over his head, as he was wrapped up in his own daily life and work worries.

Oliver had undoubtedly forgotten many details over the past ten years, focused on raising his children. There must have been a lot for him to worry about during that time. How the loss of their mother affected the kids. Grades and homework. Their after-school sports and activities. The kids probably bickered with each other, as siblings did. He couldn't be with them during the day but had tried to be there for them after school and during the evening. Tried to make things as normal for them as possible.

Almost before Zachary knew it, he was pulling past the Burlington city limits sign. The time had flown by. He checked the time to see just how fast he had been traveling on the highway. Kenzie did not like the way he sped. But he'd never been in an accident due to speed and had rarely been pulled over by the police. When he was, he could usually apologize and get off with a warning.

He had a bit of time to kill before meeting with Marissa. He pulled into the parking lot of one of Burlington's many parks. As usual, he had a camera in his pocket, and the snow blanketing the scenery was enchanting. He had not been able to walk as much in the winter as in the warmer months and did not have a lot of nature pictures on his camera's SD card. It would be good for him to get some fresh air and exercise. Too much sitting was not good for his physical or mental health, and he needed to take care of himself, especially at this time of year.

· · ·

Zachary nearly lost track of time taking pictures, but his numb fingers and toes eventually prompted him to check the time. He needed to get to the pizza place quickly if he didn't want to keep Marissa waiting. She would not be impressed if, after assuring her he could meet with her any time it fit into her schedule, he failed to show up or was an hour late.

He reached the restaurant only five minutes before their agreed-upon time, which in Kenzie's books would be a fail. Her family believed in being at an event well before it began. Only five minutes early was late.

The smell of freshly baked bread, spices, and cheese filled the air. Zachary's stomach growled in anticipation. He breathed in the air as if drinking it down. His stomach would have to wait a few more minutes.

He looked around for the young woman. She had described herself, but he feared he wouldn't recognize her. In the hip pizza joint, she was more likely to recognize him as an outlier than he was to differentiate her from the dozens of other young people there for pizza or company.

A young woman with brown hair and glasses was looking toward him. She cocked an eyebrow questioningly. She was a match for the description, but so were a dozen other young women. He walked toward her, not wanting to scare her if she were not Marissa. He cocked his head slightly, stopping a few feet away from her, not crowding her personal space.

"Marissa?"

"Yes." Marissa motioned for him to sit down in the booth she had staked out. She didn't try to hide her scrutiny. "You're actually not what I expected."

Zachary smiled. "Not a hard-fisted, gun-totin' cowboy?"

She laughed and nodded. "Yeah, I guess so."

"Most private investigators are just regular people. Nothing special about us other than an abnormal interest in other people's lives."

"Yeah? Maybe I could be a PI."

"I'm sure you could. My sister has actually just started doing some investigations work. Just computer searches and that kind of thing. If a forty-year-old mom can do it, why not you?"

"I have to admit, it isn't a profession I have ever considered." Zachary sat down, getting comfortable. "What is it you do?"

"I'm an optometrist."

Zachary noted the stylish eyeglasses. Did she have a dozen more at home? One for every occasion?

"So the two of us are both into spying, in different ways."

She chuckled at that. "I guess we are."

They ordered soft drinks from the waitress, who came over to inquire, and then browsed the menus. Zachary wasn't too concerned about what was on the menu. Pizza was the same all over. He could order the kind of crust and toppings he wanted and have a great experience every time.

"Do they have a specialty here?" he asked Marissa. Some places had unique takes or were known for a particular twist on an old favorite.

"Deep dish. I wouldn't bother with stuffed crust or anything like that. Their sauce is really nice, a little bit sweet and peppery. No weird toppings, unless you count things like pineapple, chicken, or shrimp."

"Sounds great. Do you want to share a pie or get individual ones?"

"Are you an anchovy person?"

Zachary shook his head. "Afraid not."

"Then we can share a pie. I won't have any fish on my pizza pie, even if it is divided into halves."

"Fair enough," Zachary agreed. In a few minutes, they had run through their preferences for the various toppings and settled on a pepperoni, Italian sausage, and mushroom pie. Zachary's mouth watered in anticipation.

"And garlic bread?" Marissa suggested. "I love garlic bread."

"Oh, we're going to get along great," Zachary assured her. "Garlic bread is one of my favorite foods."

They included a couple of dipping sauces, though Zachary knew that he wouldn't end up using them. He would taste each one, but he just loved garlic bread, without anything else to adulterate the experience.

8

Zachary and Marissa kept up the small talk while they waited for their pizza and chowed down on garlic bread. When the pizza arrived and they'd had a few bites, Zachary decided it was time to get down to business. There shouldn't be any more interruptions.

"So, how old were you when your mother passed?"

"I was fifteen." Marissa took a bite of her pizza and shook her head. "I was devastated; I'm sure you can imagine what it would be like to lose your mom at that age. I was at an age that I really needed her, as a friend and a parent, and then suddenly she was gone."

"I lost my family quite young."

"Your whole family?"

Zachary nodded, not giving her all the details, just the little that she needed to know that they had something in common, having lost their mothers as children.

"That sucks," Marissa said. "It was bad for me, and it's hard to say who it was the worst for, but Jeff was so young... not even a teenager yet. I felt so bad for him. I had to step forward and be the mom, since I was the only girl. But I was way too young to be a real mom, you know? I did my best, but I don't know if I can say that I was a good mom. I wasn't ready for it. I didn't have any experience or training. I was thrown into it and tried to make sure that he was looked after and not forgotten."

Zachary had helped to look after his younger siblings when he was still with his biological family and had done the best he could to protect younger children in the foster homes and institutions he had been in, to make sure that they were not abused or neglected. But he had never been a parent. That was different. He'd never had *all* the responsibility.

"You two must be pretty close."

"We are," Marissa agreed. "We didn't fight very much like siblings do. I saved that for Terry. We were close in age and we argued and got on each other's cases all the time. But me and Jeff never did. He might have argued when I said he had to do his homework or study, but he knew I was just trying to do what Mom would have wanted me to. And he was a pretty good kid. He tried to do the things he was supposed to."

"It must have been hard to look after him without your mom around."

"It was. But at least it was something to do. I couldn't just sit around grieving for my mom and saying what an unfair world it is. I had a job to do, so I just focused on that."

"Not much of a childhood."

"I was almost an adult anyway. It wasn't like I was… twelve or something."

Zachary raised his brows. "Fifteen isn't quite an adult. And most young adults—eighteen, nineteen, twenty-year-olds—are not raising teenagers."

Marissa gave a small smile and nod. "True," she admitted. "It wasn't exactly the pathway that any of my friends were on."

Zachary paid attention to his pizza for a few minutes, then started the conversation again. "You know your father is having some second thoughts about your mother's death. What really happened. Why it happened."

Marissa nodded. "I don't quite get why… but he said he wanted to look into it. That he never really felt like it was properly investigated at the time." She shrugged and picked toppings off her pizza. "I don't remember any investigation at all. I remember them coming to talk to my dad, to let him know that she had died... and that's it. I don't remember them asking any questions. It wasn't ever treated as anything other than just an accident. I didn't even know that she was shot. For years, I just thought it was a car accident. I never even knew she'd been shot."

"Is that what your dad told you?"

"I don't know if he told me that, or just said something to make me think it. Maybe he wasn't even trying to mislead me. Maybe I didn't want to hear it. I don't remember what he told me or about what anyone else was saying. People in town must have known that she was shot, but no one ever said anything to me. It's kind of weird."

"People don't like talking about death. Maybe they were just avoiding the subject. Or they thought that it would be too painful for you."

"Maybe, yeah."

"What can you remember from the days or weeks before her accident?"

"I don't know. Not much. That was 'before' and there's a big bright line in my life between 'before' and 'after.' 'Before' is all sort of fuzzy. An idealized time. I feel like I made it all up."

Zachary tried to find a way to make it more concrete. Just asking whether anything unusual had happened during that time or mentioning the phone calls that Oliver had described probably wouldn't get him anywhere. He didn't want to lead her answers or implant memories.

"What was your mom's schedule like back then?"

"Well, she would get up early in the morning to work out, have her breakfast, and get our lunches ready. She was all showered and dressed when it was time to get us off to school. I had friends with cars, so I would get a ride to school with one of them. Terry took the school bus. Mom would drive Jeff into town and drop him off at school. He was the baby, you know. We all thought he was spoiled."

"And then where would she go while you were all at school? Back home?"

"No. She had a job in town. I guess that's why she could drop Jeff off. She would go there, spend a few hours... I don't know what her schedule was every day. Some days, it was just the morning, and she would do errands in the afternoon, and other days, she would go until Jeff let out of school, pick him up, and drive him home. Help him with any homework or school projects. Terry and I would get home sometime before supper or would call to say where we were going to be if we weren't going to be home in time. After seven or eight, we were supposed to be home to do homework unless it was a weekend."

"Where did she work? What did she do?"

"Didn't Dad tell you this stuff? She worked for... what was his name...? It was his campaign office. Uh, Neufeld, when he was running for the Senate. Mom was one of the campaign ladies. I don't know if she had an actual position like campaign manager or file clerk. She just went and did whatever needed to be done. And I don't think she was paid very much. Most of them were there on a volunteer basis. But she got paid for some stuff."

Zachary pictured a campaign office, buzzing with activity, people stuffing envelopes, making posters, running copies, yelling across a room crowded with long tables. Was that what it looked like? Or just something he had seen on TV?

"She wasn't the only one who worked there?"

"No. There were other ladies coming and going. And maybe a guy or two, but it was always 'the campaign ladies' when Mom or Dad talked about it."

Zachary imagined them all wearing blue ribbons with the words "campaign ladies" stenciled on them.

"Some of the other school moms? Neighbors that she knew from around town? I gather you guys lived on a property outside of town."

"Yeah. It's not a working farm. More like... an acreage. Neither of them was really into animals or crops or anything outdoorsy, but they liked not living in the middle of all the noise and traffic. And they liked us being able to go and play outside, without having to worry about kidnappers or drive-bys or whatever other dangers they worried about in town or in the big city."

She and Zachary both smiled over Burlington being considered a big city. But it was bigger than an acreage, bigger than the town that Marissa had grown up near or Roxboro. And there were gangs and other dangers that parents tried to protect their children from.

"Did your mom like the work?"

"She loved it. She liked being a stay-at-home mom, but I think she got tired of it after a few years, especially as we were getting older. She didn't feel like she had to be at home all the time anymore. Especially once we were all old enough to go to school. She'd have to be in an empty house all day. And I think she preferred working to being at home. And feeling like she was contributing to something important."

"And the people she worked with? What did she think of the campaign ladies? And the candidate?"

"I really think she liked it. Being at the center of things. Maybe I'm idealizing it, imagining it was better than it was, but I think she really did like it. And she could still be home every night and get on our cases about doing our homework." She smiled fondly.

What would it have been like to grow up in a home like that? Where the mother liked her kids and wanted to spend time with them? Where she sat them down every night to make sure that they understood their homework and got it done? It was so far removed from what Zachary had gone through that it was like something that happened on another planet. He'd fought with plenty of foster parents about getting his homework done. Between rebounding from his ADHD meds and his learning disabilities, homework was torture—a never-ceasing source of contention and shame.

He would never have mentioned homework with that fond smile that Marissa had on her face.

"And then I guess it was bedtime. Maybe some time to relax before sleep," Zachary suggested.

"Yeah. We were allowed to watch some TV if everything was done. Jeff had an early bedtime. I think Terry and I both had a ten o'clock bedtime. Something like that. Mom and Dad would have a drink before bed, read the newspaper, do a crossword. Then they were off to bed at eleven or twelve, depending on the day of the week."

"Rinse and repeat."

She nodded. "Yeah. I don't know how she could fit everything in, but she did. And she usually made supper; we didn't just order in or fend for ourselves. She must have been pretty organized. I wasn't that good at getting dinner on the table after she died. It was too much for me. Dad helped. And I got Terry to do some stuff. Making mac and cheese. Vacuuming. Whatever I could get him to do."

"But you were just his sister and he didn't see you as an authority over him."

"Pretty much," Marissa agreed. "I don't think he listened that well to Mom, and he definitely didn't listen to me. He was always... on his computer. Playing games and chatting with his friends. Shutting the rest of the world out. He'd yell at me that he'd do whatever I was telling him to do. And then he wouldn't."

Zachary smiled and nodded. He'd been that kid. Telling the adults what they wanted to hear and then bailing on whatever he'd agreed to do. He just wanted them to get off his case.

9

"Was there anything that broke the routine the last few days or weeks before she died? Something that you thought was out of the ordinary?"

Marissa frowned. "I don't know. I guess... things were always changing. She had to take us to different activities... soccer ended and baseball started, or I started taking voice lessons..."

"Uh-huh. And what about her own stuff? Her work schedule? Things around the house?"

Marissa bit her lip. She removed her glasses and fiddled with them, pressing the earpieces outward as if they had been squeezing her head too hard.

"Do you mean the phone calls?"

"What phone calls?" Zachary was careful not to feed her any information.

"She was getting these calls... they upset her. But I don't think we were supposed to know about them. She didn't talk about them and if I asked her what was wrong or who it was, she would brush it off. I thought... I wondered at first if she was having an affair because I knew she didn't want Dad to know about the calls. But she didn't talk lovey-dovey or anything like that. She would hang up right away. She didn't have any conversations with this guy."

"You're sure it was a guy? Not one of the school moms or campaign ladies?"

"Well... it isn't like she talked to me about it. Maybe she was getting calls from more than one person. She could be, I guess. I just know that..."

Zachary waited for her to finish the thought.

"I picked up the phone once," Marissa admitted. "I knew I wasn't supposed to. Mom would not have been happy. But I wanted to know what was going on, and it was the house phone. Not her personal cell phone. So anyone could answer the house phone, right? Especially if she wasn't home. I wouldn't just let it ring."

"So, who was it on the phone?" Zachary asked. "What did you hear?"

"It was a man's voice, but electronically altered so I couldn't recognize it if I heard it again. I wouldn't know if I ran into the guy in real life. I just picked it up and said hello. He couldn't tell that it wasn't my mom. We sounded alike on the phone; even Dad couldn't tell us apart."

"What did the man say?"

"He said... he called her names. Like, swore at her. Said he knew where she lived and he was going to come after her. That he would come after her and... her kids. If she knew what was good for her, she wouldn't get in his way. He could do whatever he wanted, and no one would ever know it was him."

Marissa sat looking down at her hands. Zachary waited for anything else she could provide, not prompting her. He wanted whatever came out of her mouth to be unadulterated. Not influenced by any question he put to her.

"I just hung up," Marissa's voice shook. "I was so shocked and scared by what he said and I just hung up the phone—slammed it down—and wouldn't answer it again. I wouldn't let Terry answer it either."

Zachary nodded sympathetically. She continued to sit there, swallowing, trying to control her emotions.

"I felt so bad about answering it. I knew Mom wouldn't have wanted me to. I just felt sick over what I had heard. Like he'd hit me in the face or something; I felt like I'd been assaulted. I went to bed. Mom found me there when she came home. It was like six o'clock or something. I don't remember where she was and why she got home so late. Maybe parent-teacher interviews at the school. She thought I had the flu. I just pulled the blankets over my head and went to sleep. I never told her that I'd answered the phone or what I'd heard."

She poked around the toppings she had pulled off her pizza and ate a couple of bites of the crust and cheese left behind. She glanced up at Zachary, then away again.

"I felt so guilty when Mom died, like it was my fault. Like I should have been able to do something to prevent it. I didn't have any idea that it had been anything but a car accident, but... Mom and I had been having fights. When I look back at them now, they weren't really anything. Just a kid who wanted more freedom. You know how teenagers are, thinking they're ready to be adults. And mothers and daughters... they fight a lot."

Zachary nodded. He knew his mother had carried on screaming matches with Joss and Heather. He'd heard that teenage daughters were a great trial for their mothers.

"We argued before her accident. I don't even remember what it was about. Probably a shirt that I wanted to wear to school that she didn't think was appropriate. Something little and inconsequential but, for me, it was the end of the world; I was really mad. I can't believe that the last things I said to her were angry words." Marissa wiped at the corners of her eyes. "I imagined she'd been in the accident because she was angry and not paying attention to her driving. I felt like it was my fault. And then I had to take care of the family. Look after the boys and the house. Get dinner on the table. It was really hard work."

"I imagine it was," Zachary agreed. A fifteen-year-old girl trying to take on all her mother's duties to make up for the fight they'd had before her death. To be an adult taking care of everyone while she was still attending high school. "Did you tell the police about the phone calls?"

Marissa frowned, looking at him. "No... what difference would it have made to them?" She shook her head. "It wasn't anything to do with her death. At least, I never connected it to what happened to her. I thought she had been in a *car accident.*"

"Right." Maybe if she had known that her mother had been shot, she would have thought to mention it. But then again, since the police said it was an accident from the start, maybe she still wouldn't have.

Would the police have done anything differently if they had known that Edie was getting threatening phone calls? Would they have dug a little deeper to determine whether it was connected or just a coincidence?

"What do you know about your mother's death now?"

"I don't know. Not a lot, I guess. It didn't make any difference whether it was a car accident or a shooting accident. What was the difference? Either way, she was out on a quiet country road, where it was isolated, and no one knew what happened to her until it was too late. Just a freak. You don't think those phone calls were related, do you? I know Dad wants to know if she was targeted specifically, but I can't see it. Wouldn't we have known at the time? The police would have known and not have said that it was an accident."

"The police can be wrong. But so could your dad. I'll poke around a bit and see whether I can find anything out. I can't say how it is going to turn out."

"Are you saying that it could have been murder? We would have *known* if it was murder."

10

"I haven't talked to the police yet. I don't know any of the circumstances or evidence they have, or what questions were asked at the time. This is very early on in the investigation. But I wanted some background about your mom's home life and what you kids could remember. It's important to talk to witnesses as early as possible, and…"

"And we've already waited ten years. The police never asked us anything. But why would they? She wasn't killed at home and we didn't know anything about it."

"It wasn't classified as murder, and I'm sure they didn't want to make things worse for you guys. You were already grieving. And most people wouldn't think that kids could have anything to contribute, even if there were suspicions at the time. What could you guys possibly know?"

"But you don't think that way. You think there was something to it. And that we might know something."

"I'm starting fresh. Looking into all possibilities. A new perspective can sometimes produce new theories and leads."

He didn't say that he was unbiased. He knew that his investigative bias was toward murder. That was where his client had pointed him, and he would be looking for evidence to support that theory.

But whether he would find anything… that was another question. It might be that Edie Dwayne's death had been exactly what the police had classified it as. An accident. Someone firing off shots without realizing that there was someone nearby who could be hurt.

"What are your brothers doing now? Your dad said that Jeff is starting college?"

"Yeah. My baby brother. Hard to believe. But he's grown up and ready to leave the nest. At least for a while, to go to school."

"You think he'll go back?"

"I don't know. He might. I think it would be good for Dad to have someone close by. And I don't know if Jeff is ready to be on his own yet."

"At his age, you were taking care of two teenagers."

"Not by myself. And Dad made me go away to school. I wasn't ready for it. I told him I wanted to stay home and would look after Jeff until he was old enough… but he said no, I needed to pursue my education. Jeff was twelve when I was eighteen. I didn't think he was old enough to look out for himself, but Dad said that was his job and he and Terry would look after Jeff."

She gave a little laugh.

"If he thought Terry was going to step up to the plate and stop playing games long enough to look after Jeff's needs…"

"Playing games?"

"Gaming. On the computer. That's all he does. Since before Mom died. They made a mistake giving him his first computer!"

The way she said it made Zachary laugh.

"So what does he do? He's not living in the basement, so I assume he is making a living somehow?"

"Computers," Marissa said, rolling her eyes. "He works at one of those tech support computer repair companies. People bring in their computers with problems and he fixes them up. And then goes home and plays. It's all computers all the time."

"And what is Jeff into? Is he pursuing a degree or just starting with general studies?"

"Biology. It is some vet tech program, I'm not sure of all the details. And I don't know whether he'll go on to take a full veterinary diploma, or whatever it is called. It's too early to know for sure. But he wants to do something with animals. He's always been a big animal lover."

"Did you guys have pets?"

"Rosie. A dog. We lost her a year or two ago. And she was always Jeff's dog from the time he was little. She was supposed to be everyone's, not just Jeff's. But she was sleeping on Jeff's bed since he was smaller than she was."

"What kind of dog?"

"Mixed breed." She rubbed the bridge of her nose. "A lot of pit bull features. But she was never aggressive. She was the sweetest, gentlest thing."

"I've heard they're very loyal. Get attached to their people."

"Their pack," Marissa agreed. "She loved and protected all of us. But Jeff most of all. He was her boy. I think she thought he was her puppy; he'd been with her since he was a toddler."

Zachary had never had a pet growing up. It sounded nice. Always having someone warm beside him in the bed. Someone to look out for him, protect him, keep him company. Rosie had probably washed a lot of tears from her boy's face after his mother had died.

"Well, I hope to talk to both boys soon. Oliver said he would talk to them and give them a heads-up so they aren't surprised. I'd appreciate it if you don't talk to them about anything that happened back then until I've had a chance to. We want to avoid tainting their memories."

"After this long?"

"After this long, it would be very easy to alter any memories they have of that time. A few words is all it would take."

Marissa's lips pressed together in disapproval, but she nodded. "Of course. I'll wait until you've talked to them."

"There may be things that the three of you remember after talking to each other, reminding each other of little things. It would be helpful for me to hear about those, too, if anything comes up."

Their collective memories might be true or might be a concocted family legend. But he would examine them anyway, teasing out any threads of truth that he could.

11

It was too late to continue the investigation any further. Zachary would have liked to have gone on to Middleton, the Dwayne family's hometown, to talk with the police department or Sheriff's Office there about the case, but they wouldn't be taking any public inquiries that late in the day, so he would have to wait. Likewise, he didn't have confirmation yet that Oliver had talked to the two boys, so he couldn't approach them. He would have to go home and do what he could there. Look for any articles from ten years earlier that might add some flesh to the bare bones he had been given by Oliver. Set up the new project on his computer, which he should have done as soon as Oliver retained him. He tried to do things in order and to do them the same way every time to help keep himself on track.

He considered what he knew so far and what Marissa had added to the investigation during the drive home. He really felt for her and her younger brothers. He knew what it was like to lose a parent or a family. It was hard to understand her feeling of guilt over her mother's death. Zachary still felt immense guilt over his family breakup, even though various members had told him that it wasn't really his fault. But he was the one who had lit the fire that had burned down the house and put everyone in danger. He had been the last straw that broke the camel's back. It *had* been his fault. He couldn't see how Marissa could blame herself for her mother's death.

But then, he was no therapist. Dr. Boyle might be able to understand and explain it to him. But whether Marissa felt guilty or not, she had not done anything wrong and had not been the cause of her mother's death.

Who was? Was it a premeditated, targeted killing made to look like an accident? Or was it just one of those things, a lightning strike of fate?

Neither father nor daughter had given him any explanation of why Edie had been on that lonely country road the day she died. Had she been running errands? Going to a music lesson? Going somewhere to think? To meet someone who didn't want to be seen with her in town? He would need to find that out in order to build a picture of what had happened out there ten years before.

Back in Roxboro, he slowed to the speed limit in town and navigated back home. He had a warm feeling when he thought of it as home. For a while, it had been "Kenzie's house" in his mind. The fact that he was staying there was a footnote, and he wasn't sure how long it would last. But now, he felt like it was his as well. He didn't think of the apartment Tyrrell now lived in when he thought of going home. He didn't accidentally go back to the apartment if his mind were on autopilot. Kenzie had made room for him in her life and he was immensely grateful for her.

He parked in front of the house, locked the doors after getting out, and armed the security system. He hit the door lock button again and looked at the locks to ensure they were sitting in the lowered position. The light for the security system was on. He looked up and down the street for anyone unfamiliar. Anyone out wandering after dark. Anyone sitting in their car. Any delivery trucks.

Finally, he walked up the sidewalk, checking for any packages on the front step or anything that might seem out of place. The security camera was on and didn't appear to be tampered with.

There were no longer any bushes right up against the house, nowhere anyone could hide and ambush him.

Satisfied, he unlocked the front door and punched in his security code to prevent the alarm from going off.

Kenzie peeked around the corner to the front entryway and saw him. She blew out her breath in a sigh of relief. Her eyes were wide and round.

"I thought you would call to tell me you were on your way home. I didn't know who was at the door."

"Oh, sorry." Zachary's mind reviewed recent conversations. Had he said that he would call her when he was on his way back? Had she asked him to let her know when he was traveling in the evening? When he was out of town? He couldn't recall anything in their recent conversations that would have suggested he had committed to keeping her better apprised of his travels. "I... didn't think."

"You could have let me know you were on your way," she pointed out. "At least I would have known to expect you."

"Yeah. I'm sorry. I meant to."

Kenzie looked toward the door and the burglar alarm panel. "Did you lock it? Rearm the door?"

"Yeah. Just like usual."

"You didn't see anything out there?"

He was the one who was usually paranoid. She really shouldn't have to ask whether he had double-checked for any suspicious persons around the neighborhood.

"Everything looks fine," he assured her.

"Are you sure?" They walked into the living room together and both looked out the big window into the night. Kenzie looked up and down the street as far as she could see. "There wasn't anyone hanging around?"

"No." He shifted and glanced sideways at her without turning his head. "Is there something in particular you are worried about?"

Kenzie scowled. "I just want to feel safe in my own home. Is there anything wrong with that?"

"No. Of course not."

"You know that your cases have attracted negative attention in the past. You haven't even healed from the package bomb you exploded in the kitchen."

Zachary's natural reaction to the accusation was anger. Did she think that he had *wanted* to explode a bomb? That he had done it intentionally? Did she think he wanted to get hurt or wanted the attention somehow? He hadn't had any idea that the package was not a legitimate delivery. He bit his lip, fighting with himself not to explode at her.

"There are no packages out there today. No delivery trucks. I checked. Did something happen today? Did you get a threat?'"

"No."

Zachary swallowed and tried to stay calm and relaxed about her worries. Drilling her wouldn't do any good, especially if she didn't know why she was so anxious.

She was just jumpy because she hadn't expected him to be home yet. He hadn't told her that he was on his way. Next time, he would.

But he thought about the anonymous calls made to Edie, and now to Oliver, the survivor. What if Kenzie had been receiving phone call threats and hadn't told him about it? He could see her deciding that such a thing would make him too anxious and keeping it to herself, letting it fester and grow, bubbling just beneath the surface.

"Are you sure you didn't get any phone calls?" he asked.

"No, I didn't get any phone calls," she snapped. "Why? Have you been getting calls? Is there something you haven't told me?"

"No. Just this case that I am on. The wife was getting threatening phone calls. I know that's not you. It just popped into my mind."

"Are you getting calls? Do they know you're on the case? Do they know where you live?"

"No. No, I promise I haven't gotten any calls. Haven't been threatened or followed. I just want to make sure that you're safe. That you haven't had any trouble."

"No." She licked her lips and looked around. "No, I haven't been threatened."

She looked so vulnerable and scared. Zachary reached out to her tentatively and, while she didn't move toward him, she didn't object to his touch or pull away. Zachary stepped closer and gave her a hug.

"You're safe," he assured her. "We're both safe."

"You say that, but you don't know. You can't know. There is no way to know all the dangers. You don't know who might have looked one of us up."

"Did you have supper?" Zachary tried to steer Kenzie toward the kitchen. "We should have some ice cream."

"I don't need ice cream. I need a glass of wine."

He nodded. "If that's what you want. There's no harm in one glass to calm your nerves." He winked at her. "Even a glass of wine *and* a bowl of ice cream."

"Maybe."

They both walked into the kitchen. Bright and clean with freshly painted walls and a new hanging light over the table. The table itself had been sanded down and refinished. Zachary checked the fridge to ensure that Kenzie hadn't opened a bottle of wine herself, then got one out of the cupboard and set to unwrapping the foil and removing the cork. Kenzie sat down and watched him pour her a glass.

"You're not going to have one?"

She knew that he rarely indulged. Sometimes on a quiet date night, they would each have a bit. It made for a pleasant evening.

But he wouldn't have one if he might have to take an anxiety pill or his sleep aid. They were contraindicated, and he wouldn't have even a little bit, assuming it would be out of his system and not have any effect on him by the time he took his pills.

And tonight, Kenzie's questions and behavior were winding him up. Rather than reassuring her that there was nothing to be worried about, he was beginning to have doubts of his own, worrying about shadows and movements caught out of the corner of his eye.

"So you *are* worried," Kenzie accused.

"I'm getting there," Zachary admitted, trying to keep his voice flat and non-accusatory. "But I wasn't before I got here."

"So it's my fault?"

He handed her the glass of wine and turned to the cupboard to get a couple of bowls for the ice cream. He didn't answer her question.

Kenzie sipped the wine.

Zachary didn't ask her what kind of ice cream she wanted. He didn't want to ask her anything that would make her snap back at him or increase her irritability. What had happened to make her so anxious about his absence or the possibility of intruders or a bomb? He supposed it was only natural after what they had been through recently. He had been the recipient of the package bomb, but that didn't mean it had been any less traumatic for her, racing home at the alert from the security company to find him screaming and covered in blood, stuck in a flashback to the fire.

Or maybe something else had set her off. Campbell had reminded Zachary that the anniversary of Kenzie's abduction was approaching, Some of the tension fell away as he realized that was probably the issue. She had been kidnapped right outside the house. Zachary had just driven up to the house unexpectedly while she had been alone. She might have thought that they were coming for her again. Even if it wasn't a conscious thought, her brain still knew what had happened and might have thrown her into panic mode.

He put a bowl of ice cream with a spoon in it in front of Kenzie, and sat down with one himself.

"How was work today?" he asked, electing not to apologize again for entering the house unexpectedly or not warning her that he was on his way home. Best to change the subject and not focus on it any more than they had to.

"Uh... long day," Kenzie said, running her fingers through her spiraling curls. She had another sip of the wine. It seemed to be helping. Or maybe it was just that the adrenaline spike was wearing off. "I got your message that you would be late, so I didn't have to hurry home, and I might have put in too many hours. Should have quit at the regular time anyway."

"Ah, I was wondering. You seemed *a little stiff.*"

"No little stiffs today," she shot back. "Only big ones. And you'd better be careful with the bad jokes unless you want to join them."

"I thought you said things were usually dead before… the holidays."

"I am warning you…" She laughed.

"Okay, okay. No need to tell me twice." He held up his hands in surrender. "Or not three times, anyway."

Kenzie stretched her shoulders back, then leaned over her bowl of ice cream and took a bite.

"Can't beat chocolate ice cream," she approved.

"That's not chocolate, that's double chocolate delight with hot fudge sauce."

She nodded her approval, not taking the bait. She had another bite, letting it melt in her mouth before swallowing, and looked at Zachary.

"So, how did your investigation go? Was it successful?"

"Well, too early to tell, but it was a good start."

"This is a new case?"

Zachary told her a bit about it without revealing any names or places. While he knew Kenzie would never leak anything to anyone about one of his cases, he tried to keep the client's wishes in mind. They wouldn't want him telling everybody about it.

"That sounds very tragic," Kenzie commented. "Those poor kids. And the husband, suddenly losing his partner and having to take over as primary caregiver. No one thought anything of it? That it might have been targeted?"

"Apparently not. What would you have ruled? Woman is killed in an isolated place apparently by a stray bullet."

"I'd have to hear more about what led them to that conclusion. Bullet trajectories are going to be pretty important. Where exactly did the bullet or bullets come from? How far away? Were any casings found? Any evidence of hunters or targets? Was the car stopped at the time? Did it come from the side? The front? The back? You have to build the scene, get a picture of what happened. I assume they did that and satisfied themselves that it had been accidental. But I don't have any of that data, so I couldn't hazard a guess."

Zachary pulled out his notepad and made a few quick notes for himself. "Hopefully, I'll talk to someone involved in the initial police investigation tomorrow."

"That quickly?"

"Well… I hope so. I'll be asking, anyway. But it will depend on who investigated it and if they are still with the department."

"Right. At least your chances are good. Around here, law enforcement officers tend to stay with the department for a long time. Often their entire law enforcement career. It makes it more likely that you'll be able to find someone who remembers the details of the case and you won't have to just rely on a written file."

They had a relaxed conversation until they finished their ice cream and put the bowls in the dishwasher. They turned toward the living room to sit down and put something on TV to veg out a bit before bed. Kenzie looked out the big window at the neighborhood cloaked in darkness and sighed.

"I'm sorry for jumping all over you," she said. "You didn't do anything wrong. I was just startled to hear someone at the door. You're allowed to come home and let yourself in."

"I didn't realize it would scare you, or I would have called. I didn't think about it."

"You've never had to before, so why would you have to start now? It's nothing, I was just surprised."

"All good now?"

"Sure. I'm fine."

"Get you anything else? Another drink? A massage?"

"I could go for the massage at bedtime. Until then…" Kenzie moved her head back and forth and massaged her neck. "I'm just going to relax and pretend I don't have any work tomorrow."

"You could probably sleep in and go in late since you worked so late today."

"Yeah. Maybe."

But he knew it was highly unlikely. She would sleep in if she were really exhausted. Maybe if she had to get up in the middle of the night for a call-out. But it was unusual under normal circumstances. She kept to a pretty regular schedule the rest of the time. Which was good for Zachary, because he liked the routine and predictability.

They would watch TV until Kenzie started to get tired. Then she would begin her bedtime routine, slipping into some comfortable warm jammies and putting moisturizer on her face and feet. Cuddles, quiet talk, and maybe massages before bed, and then she would be asleep.

Just like magic.

And she wouldn't wake up until her alarm sounded or her phone rang.

Zachary might take a couple more hours to get to sleep. Or he might fall asleep initially, but then wake up after a few short hours. Or a combination of both. By the time Kenzie got up in the morning, he would probably be at his computer hard at work.

12

The Middleton law enforcement needs were covered by the Sheriff's Office, consisting of the sheriff and a handful of deputies, along with a civilian handling the phones and front desk.

Zachary knew he would have to be careful how he approached them. If he did or said the wrong thing and made them think he was critical of them or how they had conducted the Dwayne investigation, they would close ranks and refuse to tell him anything. He would have to be very professional and make friends quickly.

He considered having one of his contacts at the Roxboro police department contact them ahead of time to warm them up for Zachary's inquiry, but decided that might be interpreted as special treatment and a PI who thought he had the way paved for him and expected to get everything he wanted.

He didn't want them to see him as an intruder sweeping in to set things right and correct all their mistakes from ten years before.

Zachary entered the small reception area of the Sheriff's Office. It was warm and inviting, with twinkle lights and a bit of greenery decorating the walls. He looked away from the evergreen boughs and tried to ignore them, focusing on the woman at the reception desk, who appeared to be in her seventies or eighties.

He stood waiting politely for her to finish what she was doing on the computer and look at him. It was an extended length of time, during which he was careful not to move, sigh, or do anything else to show his frustration with having to wait. Chances were, it would be a few hours before he was able to talk to anyone about the case. That was why he had come as soon as he had finished breakfast and dropped Kenzie off at work.

While Kenzie had her own car, it was a sporty little convertible that was difficult to keep warm during the winter and didn't have the best grip on the road. So they tried to share Zachary's car during the winter, using a cab, bus, or ride-share when they both needed transportation at the same time.

"Can I help you?" the receptionist asked, startling Zachary out of his reverie.

He tried not to show his surprise and gave the woman a warm smile.

"Hi, my name is Zachary Goldman. I was hoping to talk to someone about a case from a few years ago…"

He didn't tell her right away that it was ten years ago. Let her think it was more recent so that she didn't immediately say it was too long ago and they didn't have any records stored there that he could look at. Small steps, getting her cooperation a bit at a time, and she would work harder to help him when all the details were revealed.

"What kind of a case?" she demanded. "And what is your interest in this investigation?"

"A woman died in an accidental shooting," he explained. "Her husband asked me to take a look at the old files and maybe talk to someone about it… just to convince himself that everything had been done that could have been."

"Are you a reporter?" she asked suspiciously.

"No, just a family friend. It's the anniversary of the accident, and it has been on his mind…"

"A few years ago, you said."

"Yes."

She fixed him with a stare. "Well, which is it? The anniversary or a few years?"

"Well, I didn't mean it was the first anniversary."

"I don't recall a woman being killed in an accidental shooting in the past few years."

"Ah. Do you remember a woman named Edie Dwayne?"

"Certainly I remember Edie." She pursed her lips. "That was ten years ago, if it was a day."

Zachary nodded. "That sounds about right," he agreed, as if he weren't exactly sure of the date.

"You're looking into Edie's death?" She shook her head. "Why would you be interested in that? You say you are friends with Oliver?"

Zachary nodded. He was very good friends with Oliver now, a trusted friend tasked with finding out what he could about Edie's death.

"Oliver knows it was an accident. Why are you really here?"

"Oliver is looking for a few answers. I realize it has been a long time, but he has been focused on raising his children. And now… he would like to revisit it, just to reassure himself about the circumstances of her death…"

"He already knows the circumstances. She was hit by a stray bullet. It was an accident."

She said it with such certainty that Zachary had to ask. "Did you ever find the person who fired the shot?"

"No one ever came forward. But that wasn't unexpected. You think someone would come forward and offer himself up as the person who had been careless enough to kill an innocent woman? If he was even aware that he had done such a thing."

"I'm glad you're so familiar with the case. Do you remember who the investigating officer was? Maybe you could tell me where I would find him."

"Sheriff Taylor was the lead investigator," she told him promptly. "But he has retired. He isn't here anymore."

"Is he still in town? Or in the state? I'm willing to go to him. I don't intend to inconvenience anyone."

"You might be able to catch him. He keeps himself busy with fishing and visiting his grandkids."

Zachary raised his brows. "He fishes during the winter?"

"Vermont has plenty of ice fishing. And his kids are scattered around the country. He isn't always in town."

"I see. You don't know whether he is in town right now, do you?"

"What makes you think he would want to talk to you about it?"

"I assumed… that he would want to put Mr. Dwayne's mind at ease about the accident that killed his wife. I know it was a long time ago now, but in the broader scope of things… it isn't really that long at all. You hear about fifty-year-old cold cases being solved these days. It's amazing what can be done with the new technologies…"

"There wasn't anything like that in the Edie Dwayne case. There isn't any DNA analysis to be done. It was a bullet. A stray bullet. And no, there was no match for it in the forensics database, and hasn't been since. Whatever gun was used, it hasn't been used in any violent crime since then, or we would know it. There isn't any other evidence. Sheriff Taylor might have had some ideas of who the shooter could have been, but there was no direct evidence."

"You're very conversant in the details of the case. I'm really grateful to you. Do you have a number for Sheriff Taylor, or should I look it up in a directory…?"

"I think I know my own son's phone number."

Zachary's eyes dropped to the nameplate on the desk, surprised that he had missed such an obvious connection. But the nameplate didn't say Taylor, but Humphries.

"My maiden name," the woman told him. "A woman doesn't have to take her husband's name these days. Back when we were married, I couldn't even get a credit card without his permission. There was no question of whether I would take his name or not. But I'm an independent woman now. I can go by whatever name I like."

"Yes, ma'am," Zachary agreed. "Do you think I could get your son's number?"

13

Despite what his mother had said, Sheriff Taylor was at home and not out fishing or visiting grandchildren when Zachary gave him a call. Zachary wasn't sure how he would take a call from a "friend" of Oliver Dwayne's who was looking into Edie's death ten years later, but Taylor was friendly and invited him over to talk.

Zachary followed Mrs. Humphries' directions to the RV the retired sheriff lived in. It was well-maintained and on its own property, but was still just a small home on wheels. He supposed Taylor must use it when visiting his children out of town and around the country. Instead of packing his suitcases and having to rent a hotel room or impose upon his children's hospitality, he just drove his whole house out and could live independently while he stayed for however long he wanted to. There was a certain attraction to such a nomadic lifestyle. Zachary was lucky to have found him at home. Or to have found his home at home.

The camper door opened and Taylor stood in the doorway looking out at Zachary as he climbed out of the car. Zachary tried to shorten his routine of locking the car and arming the security system. Out on this rural property with no neighbors, who was going to happen by and do anything to interfere with it?

"Having trouble there?" Taylor asked, nodding toward Zachary's car. "Need to have that looked at?"

"Uh, no, it's okay. I think everything is fine now. It's just a little finicky," he lied.

"Well, I know all about finicky vehicles. Don't I, Gloria?" Taylor patted the wall of the camper.

Zachary smiled. "This is very cool," he said, as he climbed the steps into the RV and looked around. Everything was clean and neat. Shipshape, if it had been a boat rather than a camper. "You travel in style."

"It comes in handy," Taylor agreed. He extended a rough, calloused hand. "Ian Taylor."

"Zachary Goldman. Please call me Zachary."

"If you'll call me Ian."

Taylor motioned for Zachary to sit down. The retired sheriff was slightly rotund, with short white hair and ruddy cheeks. There were a couple of mounted fish on the walls, testifying to the fishing hobby his mother had mentioned. Zachary was glad that he wasn't out ice fishing now, but had been available for Zachary to talk to him.

"So, explain to me again why you are here," Taylor invited. "You said you are a friend of Oliver Dwayne's?"

Zachary nodded and didn't expand on their relationship. "I realize that the death of Edie Dwayne was ten years ago, and it may seem strange for me to be asking questions about it now. But when it happened, Oliver wasn't really in any position to ask questions about the investigation. He had three young children to take care of, and that took his time and attention. He didn't have a lot of time to spend mourning for Edie or asking questions that would make sense of her death."

Taylor nodded understandingly. He got up from the easy chair he had only just sat down in and moved into the kitchen area, where he poured a couple of mugs of the coffee that was filling the air with its rich, enticing aroma. He handed one to Zachary without asking if he wanted it or how he took it and sat back down.

"Now that the kids are gone and even Jeff has gone off to college," Zachary went on, "he has started to wonder about some of the details and exactly what happened ten years ago."

"He didn't ask me anything at the time. Has never come by here to ask me anything about it, and he knows that I've been off the job for a couple of years now."

Zachary weighed whether to mention the anonymous phone calls, and elected not to. Not yet. "It wasn't until now that he felt like he should be looking into it further," he said slowly. "And even so, he preferred a third party rather than doing it himself. He just wants some peace. To know exactly what happened all those years ago."

"I told him everything there was to tell at the time. It wasn't exactly a complicated case. Tragic, yes, but there weren't really any unanswered questions."

"You caught the culprit?"

A shadow passed over Taylor's face. "Well, no. We didn't find out exactly who it was that fired the fatal shot. But it was obvious what had happened."

Zachary nodded. "Well, if you wouldn't mind just running through the scenario with me, I would appreciate it. I know what Oliver told me, but his recollection after ten years, when he was all caught up with grief and his children, might be different from yours. There may be important things that he has forgotten or didn't think to tell me."

"You're not from around here, are you?"

"Not in town," Zachary agreed. "I'm over in Roxboro. Vermont born and bred."

He wanted Taylor to know that he wasn't an outsider. He wasn't someone coming in from New York or LA or some other culture where they didn't understand how things worked in rural Vermont. Zachary was a Vermonter. Not some detective from halfway across the country.

"Roxboro," Taylor gave a nod. "Nice little town."

"It is," Zachary agreed. "I've been very happy there."

"You're a cop?"

"No. Private citizen. Just... someone who is interested in helping Oliver to understand what happened to his beautiful wife ten years ago."

"She *was* beautiful. A lovely young lady, inside and out. It was very sad, what happened to her."

Zachary nodded. He waited, leaning forward with his elbows on his knees. He drank a few swallows of hot coffee, waiting for Taylor to tell him more about it.

"It was on a country road not far from here," Taylor said. "A few farms over. Mrs. Dwayne had pulled over. Don't know if she was having car trouble or needed to answer the phone, maybe wanted to take a picture of the scenery. She just happened to be in the wrong place at the wrong time. Someone who was out shooting in the woods nearby missed his mark, and the stray bullet killed Edie. She never knew what had happened. Didn't suffer. She was killed instantly."

"Where did the shot hit her?"

"In the head. Bullet to the brain. Not much hope in surviving that. Especially when she wasn't found for hours afterward."

"Who found her? One of the hunters who was shooting in that area?"

"Woman coming home from shopping at the market. Quite the shock for her. Not something you expect to come across like that."

"She pulled over, thinking Mrs. Dwayne was having car trouble?"

"Something like that. Wasn't normal to have someone sitting on the side of the road in the evening like that. Pretty quiet place. Isolated. People like their privacy around here."

"I can see why." Zachary gazed at the snowy trees framed in Taylor's living room window. "It's beautiful out here."

"That it is," Taylor agreed.

"So this woman coming back from her shopping found Mrs. Dwayne in her car. Looked inside, saw that she had been shot, and called the Sheriff's Office."

"Yep. That's about it. I went out and took a look. Out there on a lonely road like that... it was obvious what had happened. I'd warned kids before. Don't go target shooting out near public roads. Gun safety. All of that."

"Kids that lived near there?"

"Yeah, I'd seen kids out there before. Been called by folks who didn't like hearing all the gunfire when they were out practicing. Folks worried about possible accidents. Sometimes when kids are not supervised, things happen. They don't have the same experience as grown men and women. The same judgment."

"No," Zachary agreed, nodding. "Do you have any recollection of which kids you had warned before? Who might have lived nearby?"

"Now, I don't want to get any of these kids in trouble," Taylor said. "What happened was a tragic mistake. It wouldn't do to punish someone unnecessarily for something that was a youthful mistake."

"You don't think they should be held responsible for what they did?"

"These are good kids. Grown adults, now. Haven't been in trouble. Why would I want to ruin their lives? If they know what they did, they have to live with the knowledge that they killed a woman with their careless shooting. And you can bet that they never did anything like that again. Kids being bored and doing some target practice… there's nothing criminal about that. There's no intent. No malice."

Zachary could see his point. Such a mistake could follow a person for the rest of his life. The knowledge that he had killed someone by mistake. Having it on their record, preventing them from being able to get a job in their chosen profession. Having it in the news so it showed up with any search of their name. A scarlet letter that could not be wiped out or ignored.

But that didn't mean that he agreed with Taylor's decision not to chase down every lead to find out exactly which kid or group of kids had been out there shooting that day. Didn't Edie Dwayne deserve justice? Didn't Oliver deserve to know who was responsible for his young wife's death out there on that isolated road?

"So you won't say anything about who you think might have been involved in the shooting, even though it was accidental."

"No. Let them live their lives. They've all gone on. Oliver and his kids have gone on. There isn't any point resurrecting the whole thing."

"What if it wasn't kids target shooting?"

"Maybe a hunter who missed his quarry. That happens sometimes. You tell people not to shoot near public roads or populated areas, but mistakes are made. People aren't always as careful as they should be, and tragedies happen."

"What if it was intentional?"

Taylor blinked at him. "Intentional? What are you talking about? It was determined to be an accident."

"But what if a mistake was made?" Zachary was careful not to say Taylor himself had made a mistake. He wanted to keep his words neutral and non-accusatory. Passive language, not active. "What if a piece of evidence was misinterpreted or something was missed? What if you did not have all the facts?"

"Well, I'm the first to say I'm not perfect. I've made my share of mistakes in the past. But on this case? It was pretty straightforward." He crossed an ankle over the opposite knee, a deliberately relaxed posture. "We're talking about a mom here. A homemaker. There wasn't anyone with a motive to kill her. Not even her husband. They always say the spouse is the first suspect. But Oliver wasn't stepping out seeing someone else. He was devoted to her. There were no drugs. Neither of them were drinkers or had any criminal record." He shrugged. "What could it be besides an accident?"

"A killer who picked a random victim?" Zachary suggested.

"Out on that road? In the middle of nowhere? I don't know why she was sitting out there, but what random murderer would have seen her there? There isn't any traffic through there. Just people going to their own farms. And if we had some sick serial killer around town, then she wouldn't have been the only victim."

"What if someone targeted her?"

"Who? I told you, no one had any reason to want to kill her."

Zachary weighed whether to tell Taylor the story or not. He seemed like a good guy, open to discussing the case. It might be Zachary's only chance to talk to one of the law enforcement officers involved in the case.

He took a long sip of coffee and looked out the window. Taylor was a family man—someone who cared about spending time with his grandchildren. He had apparently hired his mother to work for the Sheriff's Office when he'd been there. He knew Oliver Dwayne personally and had known Edie. If there was anyone who was likely to help him sort out the details of the case, it was Taylor.

"Oliver recently started to get anonymous phone calls about the shooting," he revealed in a low, confidential tone, "Someone who says that it was not a random or accidental shooting."

Taylor shook his head immediately. "Crank caller. Doesn't prove anything."

"No, it doesn't prove anything," Zachary agreed. "That's why Oliver wanted me to look into it. To see if any detail or piece of evidence was overlooked. If there was something going on in his wife's life that he wasn't aware of at the time."

"There was very little evidence. And I certainly wasn't aware of anything suspicious going on in her life. What's he saying now? That she was seeing someone? That he didn't tell me about it at the time?"

"No. But she was getting phone calls, something she didn't want to talk to him about. He said that she was jumpy. I talked to the daughter, and she said that once she answered the phone, and the caller was very threatening."

Taylor stared out the window, thinking about that. He scratched his whiskery chin, the sandpapery sound making Zachary grimace.

"No one said anything to me at the time."

"They were probably too shocked by her sudden death. Marissa didn't connect the phone calls in any way to her mother's death, and she had kept them from Oliver. Why would Marissa say anything, if she believed it was an accident? There was no reason for her to bring it up. Unless you asked her."

"No, of course I didn't. I didn't know there were any phone calls."

"You just saw a woman killed by accident on a lonely country road."

He nodded. "Exactly. Why would I think it was anything else?"

"Can we look at the evidence again? Do you have any access to your old notes or files? Just to see if there is anything that could possibly bear out the possibility of a targeted hit."

14

"I have old notebooks," Taylor said. He shifted, his eyes suddenly alive with interest. Up until then, he'd been happy to just confirm the circumstances of Edie Dwayne's death. But now his gaze sharpened. He was more alert and alive. "It might take me a little while to find the right one."

"Are they here?" Zachary asked, wondering if they might be stored at the Sheriff's Office or somewhere else. Storage space was limited in an RV.

"In a shed. Sealed boxes. Moisture proof. Rodent proof." He glanced toward the shed as if he could see through the walls and confirm everything was still in order. "It won't take me too long." He started levering himself to his feet, and paused halfway up. "Do you want to go deal with something else and then come back here? Your time is probably at a premium..."

Zachary shook his head. "I don't mind waiting."

If Zachary left, then there was the chance that the ex-sheriff would change his mind by the time he returned. Having a chance to think about it, Taylor might decide that he wasn't that comfortable revealing details of the investigation to Zachary and turn him away again.

"You don't mind waiting?" Taylor repeated. "You must have other people you want to talk to."

"Who else would I talk to?" Zachary countered. "You're the one who investigated the shooting. I've already talked to Oliver and his daughter. And the boys are not in town."

"I don't know. Maybe some of her old friends or coworkers. Or maybe you want to talk to the other cops here at the time."

"Are there others you think would be willing to talk to me?"

Taylor thought about it for a moment and then laughed. "No, probably not."

"I'm happy to wait. I can arrange to speak to friends later. Or to other cops... probably never. I'd rather stay where I am having some success."

"Fair enough," Taylor agreed with a shrug. "Turn on the TV. Have a nap. Play on your phone. I'll be as quick as I can, but it will take a while to dig everything out and sort through it."

Zachary nodded his agreement. "I'll be fine. Don't worry about me."

Taylor grabbed a hat, coat, and gloves and headed outside. A cold blast of air blew in, and then the door closed again, leaving Zachary alone.

He looked slowly around the RV, taking everything in. He had only given the place a cursory glance before, but now he gave it his undivided attention. He would not snoop around Taylor's private areas, but anything out in the open was fair game.

Taylor's fishing trophies. A plaque on the wall that said, "I'd rather be fishing." A row of old Reader's Digest Condensed books on one bookshelf. There were pictures of his children and grand-children. Happy grandpa and the grandchildren holding his hands, sitting on his knee, or in various other poses. Zachary did not see a wife. She must have passed away some years before. The RV was home to one. Taylor did not need a lot of space.

There were some collectible shot glasses, but no alcohol in evidence. A calendar hung on the wall had appointments written into the small squares. Zachary got up and walked over to look at the notations.

He honored his commitment to himself and didn't go into the bedroom or bathroom of the RV. He stayed in the living room and kitchen areas and did not dig through the drawers looking for personal papers and secrets. Those things would not help him find out who had killed Oliver's wife.

When Taylor returned to the RV with a small stack of notebooks, Zachary had returned to his seat with a fresh cup of coffee.

Taylor stomped snow off his boots and kicked them onto a mud mat. He shed the other winter clothing and brandished the notebooks. "Here they are. Everything in the months after Edie Dwayne's death, just to make sure that I didn't miss anything. But it was all cleared up pretty quickly." He looked at Zachary. "That's not because I was negligent. Just because it was an open-and-shut case."

Zachary nodded.

Taylor sat in his easy chair and started leafing through the notebooks.

"I was out there warning the kids not to be shooting near the public road two weeks earlier," he reported to Zachary. "Told them to tone down the shooting a bit if they could. It was bothering the neighbors."

"Which kids were involved?" Zachary asked, hoping that Taylor would give him something this time. But he still was not forthcoming with names.

"They were good kids," he told Zachary. "Not even that wild. They were just looking for something to do. Entertaining themselves like country kids do. Everyone out here shoots."

"But not everyone shoots innocent people."

Taylor sighed. "You're right, of course. But I don't want to ruin those kids' lives." He deliberately turned the page in his notebook and read on. Zachary wished that he could see what Taylor was seeing, could read all the notes he had scribbled down from the weeks and days before the shooting. Who knew what else might be connected?

But Taylor said nothing else as he leafed through the pages until he arrived at the page describing the call out to Edie Dwayne's shooting.

"Here it is. Call about a dead body discovered on Riverside Road. Caller didn't give very many details. I thought I would get out there and find some hiker who had been in a hit-and-run. Or maybe who'd had a heart attack. We don't have a lot of violence out here, you know. Mostly just domestic calls. Other than that, we get disturbin' the peace, drunk in public, theft of property, maybe graffiti. We don't have gangs. Don't have any drug trade to speak of. Marijuana growers and moonshiners, maybe, but no meth labs. No gangs selling cocaine or heroin. You gotta go to the city for that."

Zachary nodded. He had his own notepad out and wrote down any salient details as Taylor read them.

"So I get out there and find Edie Dwayne sitting in her car, dead and cold." He shook his head. "Not what I was expecting. Poor woman. Looked like she had just pulled over to look at her phone or map—Who uses maps anymore? —Put an address into her phone GPS or pick up an email or something. And there she is… shot came in through the side window. Penetrated her skull. Dead instantly, not much blood. She looks like she's just sitting there waiting for someone. Death himself, I suppose."

Zachary nodded and scratched out a few words in his notepad.

"Window was open or closed?"

Taylor frowned, looking at his notes. Zachary would have expected him to be able to answer that without looking it up. Wouldn't he remember whether there was broken glass or not?

"Window was open," Taylor said. "I think."

"There wasn't any broken glass?"

"No. Don't think so." He looked down at his notes. "Not that I recall."

"And what can you tell me about the weapon?"

"Twenty-two. Lots of .22 rifles in this county. Would be hard to find a farmhouse that didn't have at least one."

"Your mother—Mrs. Humphries—said that the ballistics didn't match any known weapon or any other crime before or since."

Taylor nodded his agreement. "You see? If this had been a

targeted shooting, if it was committed by someone who actually went out there to kill Mrs. Dwayne, then it would likely have matched some other crime. Another hit. Drug runners. Something like that. The fact that it has never matched any other crime just bears out my belief that it was an accidental shooting, and that gun was never fired in the commission of any other crime."

Zachary nodded. He wrote down a couple of points in his notepad. "Okay. Right. Continuing with your notes," he indicated Taylor's notepad, "Who else was on the scene? Was anyone questioned? Any witnesses come forward?"

"A couple of deputies came out to the scene. Youngsters still wet behind the ears. I walked them through everything, showed them how to process the scene, preserve the evidence, and so on. They're not with the county anymore. Gone on to bigger and better things." He lifted his chin and puffed out his chest a little. "I trained them well. They were good cops."

Zachary was disappointed that the deputies were not around to testify about what they had seen and done that day. But he hadn't expected to get a lot of help from law enforcement anyway, he was happy with the fact that Taylor was cooperative.

15

"As far as witnesses, there were none. The woman who happened on the body was the only one. We canvassed all the nearby farms, and no one recalled seeing Edie on the road. There had been the sound of gunfire earlier, but everyone assumed it was just more target practice, and no one had paid close enough attention to pin down the time."

"Did the kids who had been shooting that day come forward?"

"No. We called for witnesses. Asked for anyone who'd been out shooting that day to come forward, but folks didn't really believe that we only wanted information and that no one who came forward would be in trouble." He shrugged. "Word spreads pretty quickly in a place like this. They knew that we believed it was a stray bullet that hit her, and no one wanted to be accused of being the ones who were out shooting that day."

Of course not. And if they were kids, they had probably been scared to death.

"Did you talk to the kids that you had previously warned away from the area?"

"Sure. Would have been negligent not to. But it wasn't any of them." He tapped the side of his nose. "They were all doing other things that day, and they all alibied each other. They said they had taken my warning to heart and had not been back there since I warned them off. Since there were no witnesses and they alibied each other, I didn't have anything on them. It could have been some other hunter or loner out practicing. Like I said, every household around here has guns."

"No one ever came forward to say that they were out that way, or that they had seen anyone close to the scene? No one saw any strangers, no kids, not Mrs. Dwayne herself."

"Nope. If she'd had a gun in her hand, I would have made it suicide. But she didn't, and the shot was obviously not a contact wound."

"How far did it come from?"

"Hard to say."

Zachary waited for more details, but Taylor didn't provide them. Zachary raised his brows. "Not point blank," he prompted. "So, are we talking ten feet? Thirty? A hundred yards?"

Taylor studied his notes, turning pages back and forth as he thought about it. "The tree cover was maybe a hundred feet away. Assuming that the person who fired the shot could not see Edie sitting in her car, it had to have been from over one hundred feet."

Zachary grimaced and tried to put his objection into words. "You're giving me a range based on your assumption that it was an accidental shooting. But what did the gunshot wound tell you? How far away was the shooter based on how fast the bullet was moving when it hit Mrs. Dwayne?"

"You make it sound like that could be calculated to the inch. There are too many variables to make an accurate determination."

"I don't need anything to the inch. Just how far away the gun was based on the bullet's path and penetrating power."

"That would be in the police file, not in my notes, if a calculation was done. We don't have the budget to call in ballistics experts on cases like this. It was clearly an accident. A stray bullet from someone who couldn't see her sitting there. There was no other sign of violence. No other crime committed. She still had her wallet and jewelry. She was a housewife and mother. Just a tragic accident."

"You didn't have any ballistics done."

"We had the bullet processed and put into the system. We did not hire an expert to tell us how far the bullet had traveled. It wasn't in the budget and we didn't need to. We knew where she was shot from."

"Do you have any diagrams that you made at the scene? Any pictures you took? Or could you draw me a picture of the scene? Just showing where everything was?"

"Well…" Taylor pondered this. "I suppose I could do that for you. As far as what is in my book…" He hesitated, then stood up and handed Zachary his notebook, open to one page. "You can look at that page and the next one. You don't have my permission to read anything else written in that book."

Zachary would take what he could get. He looked at the first page, a sketch of the body in the car and the location of the mortal wound.

"Can I take a picture of this with my phone?"

Taylor nodded slowly. "Suppose so. But you realize it is just a sketch It is not drawn to scale or accurate in any measurements. Just a rough sketch of what I saw when I arrived at the scene."

"Sure. I understand." Zachary took out his phone and snapped a picture of the small picture. "And the next page?"

Taylor nodded, which Zachary took as permission to flip to the next page and take a look at that one too. A birds-eye view of the car and the nearby trees and a dotted line from the trees to the car. Again, not to scale, of course. Zachary positioned his phone and took a picture of that one too, then handed the notebook back without attempting to look at any of the other notes. He needed to show Taylor that he was trustworthy and would follow the rules that were set out. A PI didn't make friends breaking the rules.

"I'll draw you a bigger picture," Taylor said, rifling through a drawer in the kitchen to find a piece of paper and pen. He pulled a book from the bookshelf to put behind it and carefully drew the scene for Zachary. Zachary left his seat to watch over his shoulder.

"This here is Riverside Road. That's where she was stopped. It's by the McIlvoy property." He drew in several other crossroads and driveways or unpaved tracks, detailing each one. "Car was parked here, on Riverside. There isn't really a shoulder, but it was pulled to the side, passenger side wheels off the pavement, in the dirt. Leaving enough space for a car to pass her. Here are the trees in the direction the shot came from. Like I said, about a hundred feet. The kids' targets were set up deeper into that wooded area, maybe another two hundred feet. They're shooting into the targets and don't realize that a misfired bullet could go thousands of feet and still do damage when it strikes. They figured they're off in the trees, they're safe. That's why I had a talk with them, told them they couldn't fire toward the public road, even if they couldn't see it."

Zachary nodded, studying the picture. "This is great. Thank you. It will be very helpful."

"I don't know how much it will help you. I've been going over everything in my mind, and I can't find anything that would suggest it was a targeted killing. It really was just a random, tragic accident. I can't think of anything that would suggest otherwise. How sure are you that this anonymous caller actually knows anything?"

"At this point, not at all. It could all just be someone trying to get Oliver's attention. How often do you get people reporting 'facts' on tip lines that are totally made up?"

"All the time. People like to think they're important. Or that they deserve more attention. Some of them believe the stuff they make up. Some people seem to be truly unable to tell fact from fiction."

Zachary nodded. "I don't have anything that says this caller actually knows anything about the case. This may just be a pointless exercise. But the fact is, Edie *was* getting upsetting anonymous calls before her death. Is it a coincidence that she was getting threatening phone calls and then was killed? Or that Oliver started getting calls on the tenth anniversary of her death? Is it the same person? I have no idea. Maybe it is just a weird coincidence. But it upset Oliver enough for him to hi—to ask me to look into it."

"Well, you're a good friend. I'm not sure how many people would take something like this on."

Zachary nodded, smiling. "Now can I drive out here, to this

location, without trespassing on someone's private property and getting myself shot?"

Taylor chuckled. "Yes, you can. Here, give me your phone, and I'll drop a pin for you."

Zachary opened his maps app and handed it to Taylor, who swiped and zoomed until he found the right spot and saved the destination location for him. He scrolled some more, checking the route the app had laid out, then nodded and handed it back to Zachary. "That should take you there without having to cross any private property or washed-out bridges."

"Much appreciated," Zachary laughed. "I prefer not to get shot or drive into any rivers."

"Some people are funny that way," Taylor said with a smile.

"I really appreciate you taking the time to talk to me about all of this. Do you mind if I call if I have other questions? Any follow-up?"

"Sure. I can't promise to always be available. I turn off my phone when I'm fishing or need some quiet time to think."

"Understood. I know how to use voicemail."

"A lost art. My kids don't seem to know how to leave a message. They just expect me to call if I see their names on my missed calls list."

Zachary had noticed this tendency in the younger generations, and had sometimes been guilty of it himself. But he would be sure not to do that to Taylor.

"Is there any chance I could get access to any of the reports or crime scene photos in the police file?"

Taylor shrugged. "Not my department anymore. You can put in a public information request. It's a closed file, so you might be able to get some of the documents. But they might also take months to get back to you."

"I'll give it a try. Might get lucky."

"Might. The admin over there is something of a dragon, but she does have a sweet tooth," Taylor said with a grin. "A low-level bribe might give her the energy to pull out old archives to find what you need."

"She gave up your phone number easily enough."

"She thinks if she keeps me busy, I'll stay out of trouble."

Zachary chuckled. "And do you?"

"Do I look like a troublemaker?"

"Your mother is more likely to know than me."

16

Since Taylor had thoughtfully entered the coordinates of Edie Dwayne's death into Zachary's phone GPS, he decided he'd better visit that next, in case the phone decided to wipe the information if he went to other places first. Technology was great, but it didn't always work as it was supposed to without glitching. Besides, it gave him additional highway driving time to review the new information he had received.

Working on a cold case without any solid evidence was not easy. It felt like trying to grasp water. But he had worked on a couple of cold cases that were even older and had been able to come up with answers. He hoped that if he were persistent, he would be able to give Oliver the answers he needed. He didn't think it mattered whether he proved or disproved Taylor's theory, as long as he did a thorough investigation. Oliver would feel better when Zachary gave his final report, even if it was to say that the original theory of the crime still held.

The GPS eventually led him to Riverside Road, a tertiary road that was paved, but otherwise seemed unused. He was lucky that not too much snow had piled up yet, because it didn't appear to be a road that the county cleared in the winter. They too probably had budget constraints. It seemed everyone was working on tighter budgets the last year or two.

Zachary got out of his car and looked around. The shooting had been in the summer, so he was hampered by the fact that it was now winter and the road and the surrounding landscape did not look the same as they had at the time. He tried to imagine it as it would have been then. A dry, dusty road. Yellowing grass and weeds alongside the road. Thick foliage on the now-bare trees.

The trees were farther away from the road than he had pictured when Taylor had described the scene. The wooded area was not as dense. He walked from the road to the edge of the trees. It looked like just a little stand of trees at first but, when he got closer, he saw that they went quite deep, getting denser the farther he got. It didn't take long before he felt swallowed up by the trees. He felt isolated, completely removed from civilization. He could understand why the kids thought that there was no danger target shooting there. It didn't feel like there could be anyone for miles around. It didn't feel like a bullet could find a straight path through the trees to the road way off in the distance, no longer visible. Taylor had warned them, had tried to explain to them that it was dangerous to shoot toward the public road even if they thought it seemed impossible that a stray bullet could make it that far. Zachary looked around for any sign of the targets the kids had shot at, for bullets in the trees or lying on the ground. But the ground was covered with snow, and any bullets would have disappeared into the dirt and underbrush in the long time since Edie Dwayne had been shot. It had been ten years, and the targets had been cleaned up or lost.

He looked around some more, not sure what he expected to find. There was no smoking gun after ten years. No way to identify the kids who had been out here when Sheriff Taylor had confronted them about the dangers of shooting near a public road. No way of knowing if those same kids had been out there the day that Edie Dwayne had been killed.

If Edie had been killed by accident, then there was no need to pursue the phone calls she had gotten. They were just from some run-of-the-mill crank caller. Maybe an ex-boyfriend or someone she worked with who felt like she had overstepped her bounds on something. Maybe someone who just dialed random people in the phone book and had been pleased with the reaction he had gotten from her, so he kept calling to get the attention he craved. The phone calls and the shooting might have had nothing to do with each other. The phone calls before her death and the phone calls that Oliver had started to receive after the tenth anniversary might have nothing to do with each other. Though Zachary had a hard time seeing how they could be coincidental.

But why call Edie to threaten her before her death, and then call her husband to tell him that the shooting had been intentional? If the person who had threatened her had shot her, why would he then turn around and tell Oliver about it? Just for the attention? It didn't feel right to Zachary. He couldn't make the motives align.

Eventually, his toes were getting cold and it was time to move on. He pulled out his camera to take a few pictures. The snowy wilderness was stunning, even if he hadn't found anything that would be helpful to the investigation. He spent five minutes capturing his surroundings on film—or on the camera's digital memory—and then started back toward his car.

"Who the hell are you?"

Zachary raised his hands to his shoulders before turning around slowly. He heard the threat in the deep male voice and, as he turned, he saw that he had correctly assessed the situation and the man standing there was holding a gun on him.

A twenty-two? Even if it was, Taylor had said that practically everyone in the county-owned one. It meant nothing.

"Sorry," Zachary said. "I wasn't aware that I was trespassing. I was just having a look around."

"And taking pictures," the man pointed out. He was tall and wide, a big man, bulked out even more by his winter coat. A bushy beard bristled around his face, making him look like a wild mountain man.

The gun was held casually, pointed in Zachary's direction. He wasn't holding it to his shoulder and sighting Zachary down the barrel. But he looked like he knew exactly what to do with a gun. Zachary had no doubt that he could either pull the trigger from the position he was in, or bring it up to brace against his shoulder in a split second.

"Yes, sir," Zachary agreed. "The trees are beautiful this time of year. I took a few shots."

"What are you doing here? I've never seen you before. You're not from these parts."

"No. I live in Roxboro. I'm a friend of Oliver Dwayne's." Zachary still wasn't ready to reveal to anyone in the area that he was a private investigator. The police often cooperated more readily with a "friend" than a PI, and if he told one person he was a private investigator, it wouldn't be long before everyone in the county knew it.

"Oliver Dwayne." The man lowered his gun so that it was pointing at the ground. "Why would you be out here?"

But he looked toward the road to where Zachary was parked, even though it was not visible through the trees. To the spot where he knew Edie Dwayne had been killed. So he knew why Zachary was there—or had an idea.

"I know this is where his wife was killed," Zachary said. "I wanted to have a look around."

"Why?"

"I can't tell you any of the details. It's Oliver's business if he wants to share it with you. I didn't mean to trespass, though, if this is your land. The sheriff said that the shot came from this direction, so I just wanted to be able to see it for myself. Get a feel for it."

"The shot didn't come from over here."

"Oh?"

"Weren't nobody on my land that day. I told those kids to move on, and they did. Whatever happened out here, it wasn't kids."

"It wasn't?" Zachary echoed. He looked around again. "Then who was it? Who was here that day?"

"Don't know. Never saw anyone on the property."

"Would you have? If someone was out here meeting with Edie, would you have seen them?"

"Not likely. I was watching for those kids, but they were easy to see. Noisy and rambunctious. High-spirited."

"Did Sheriff Taylor ask you whether you had seen them that day? When he canvassed the area?"

"Nobody asked me if I had seen them. They asked whether I had seen anyone around with a gun, or if I had been down to the road and seen Mrs. Dwayne or her car any time that day. I hadn't. Hadn't been over that direction."

"Did you hear any shots?"

"That day? Not that I can recall. But it ain't unusual to hear shots around here. Hunting, target-shooting, bored kids. Not unusual at all. I couldn't tell you from one day to the next when I heard shots or what direction they came from. It's like you city folk. You get concerned every time you hear sirens? Remember whether it was yesterday or the day before that a cop car went down your street?"

Zachary thought about it. The man had a good point. Some things just blended into the background of the day and he couldn't have sworn to what days he had heard sirens. He shook his head slowly. "I couldn't tell you."

"Same thing out here. I heard shots when I was out and about. Was that yesterday or today? Or even the day before? If I heard that Edie Dwayne was shot, I might say, 'Oh, I heard shots—did I hear the shot that killed her?' And I might convince myself that it was today, and it was at the time they said she was killed. But I might not even be remembering the right day. It might have been yesterday. But people convince themselves that they know more than they do. That they know something important."

"So you don't think anyone heard the shot when Edie was killed?"

"Don't rightly know. I know I didn't. I know those kids were not out here target shooting that day. But who did it and who heard it or didn't hear it, I don't know that."

Zachary nodded slowly. He lowered his hands. "Well, that's

very helpful. I appreciate hearing your thoughts on it. Ten years ago... I didn't expect to be able to get any eyewitness testimony."

"And you still haven't," the man said sternly. "I didn't hear or see anything. Whatever happened on that road... I can't help you."

17

Terry, Oliver's middle child, was in Essex Junction, so Zachary was on the highway once more, relaxing and reviewing what he had learned in his inquiries so far. After visiting with Terry, he was probably done for the day. It took a lot of energy to talk to people and he found himself running out of energy and patience. The highway time would help to recharge his batteries, but they could only be recharged so many times in one day, and then he would crash. He wanted to still have the time and energy to have dinner with Kenzie and visit with her afterward.

As much as he wanted to find the answers for Oliver and his kids, he couldn't spread himself too thin, risking his own health and not leaving him with enough energy to support Kenzie. And she needed him, particularly as she approached the first anniversary of her abduction.

Zachary had heard Essex Junction was a technology hub. Terry was into computers, so Zachary supposed that was why he had ended up there instead of back in Middleton or in Burlington with Marissa. It had been challenging to pin Terry down. At first, he said he didn't have any time, but when Zachary pressed him, saying he could meet whenever it was convenient, even if it was only for a few minutes, Terry had conceded that he simply didn't want to meet with Zachary. It was something that his father wanted, but Terry wasn't invested in trying to find out what had happened to his mother and why. He accepted that it had been an accident and went on to live his life.

He had finally agreed to meet with Zachary for just a few minutes. He didn't think Zachary would agree to drive all that way only to meet for a few minutes, but he had misjudged Zachary's zealotry. When he was on a case, it was all-consuming. He would do whatever it took to find the answers. Sitting surveillance for three long nights, all night long? Done. Scrubbing forty hours of video surveillance? Just ask. Driving all the way to Essex Junction for a five-minute conversation? He was there.

His phone GPS directed him to the internet cafe. He hadn't even known that there were still internet cafes. It seemed like they would have gone the way of the dinosaurs, with everyone having internet in their homes and even in their pockets.

It wasn't one of the dark and grubby places he had gone in the early years when he'd had to do research but couldn't yet afford his own computer or a monthly internet bill. Instead, it was a bright, airy space with peaked skylights. There were tables for groups to gather at, big screens for virtual meetings or presentations, and single-person desks in semi-private cubicles where users could hunker down. Zachary scanned faces, looking for someone who was looking for him.

"Help you?" asked a gum-chewing young woman near the front of the store, like a hostess for a restaurant.

"I'm meeting someone here. Are there bookings? I'm looking for Terry Dwayne."

She tapped her ear. "Terry, you waiting for someone?"

She listened to the reply and nodded to Zachary. "This way."

He followed her through a maze of shiny white tables. A young man of similar age with large plugs stretching out his earlobes looked Zachary over. He nodded. "Goldman?"

"That's me. Zachary."

"Goldman would be a good screen name," Terry told him. "Maybe with something else meaningful. Gold Man Seeker or something like that." His eyes wandered over the people working or playing throughout the internet cafe, looking for anyone who was having problems.

"Is there somewhere less distracting that we could meet?" Zachary suggested.

"This? This is nothing. You should see it when it's really shaking," Terry said with a laugh.

Zachary could only imagine how overwhelming that would be.

"Break room three is not in use," the woman told Terry, consulting a tablet that seemed to be fused to her hand. "You want it?"

"Sure. This way," Terry told Zachary and started walking away without checking whether Zachary was with him.

The woman tapped and scribbled on the tablet and nodded to him. "You'd better keep up. He'll be gone."

Zachary hurried after Terry. After winding their way through another portion of the room, Terry ushered him into a meeting room stocked with a coffee machine, snack vending machine, and a big screen on the wall. Terry pulled out a drawer under the table that revealed a keyboard and started typing away. Watching the information displayed on the big screen, he apparently checked for some kind of system problem. In a couple of minutes, he turned his face toward Zachary, though his eyes were still on the screen.

"So, what was it you wanted to talk to me about? It was something to do with my mom? I haven't thought about her in years. I mean, I think about *her*, but not about the accident, about how she died. We never talk about that."

"What do you remember about her accident?"

"I wasn't there when it happened, so I don't remember anything about it." He glanced at Zachary momentarily before looking back at the screen again.

"I know that none of you were there when it happened. She was by herself. Do you remember what you were told?"

"That it was an accident. The sheriff came by and talked to my dad about it. I didn't really hear anything about it. We were all upset. Crying, didn't know what to do with ourselves. That's how it is when you lose someone like that," he said philosophically. "You just try to get through it together."

Zachary nodded. "It must have been very difficult." He paused, waiting for anything else from Terry. "I lost my parents at a young age."

He didn't say they were dead, but definitely left Terry with that idea. He wanted to see how he would react emotionally. But Terry gave nothing away.

"That would be hard. At least for me, it was only my mom. That was hard enough."

"Do you remember anything that was going on around that time? If your mom was having any problems with anyone? Personal life? Work?"

"No, nothing I knew about."

"Marissa remembers there being some phone calls. I wonder if you knew anything about them."

"Phone calls?" Terry's fingers stopped tapping and rested. "I don't know. What kind of phone calls?"

"Calls that upset her."

Terry considered this, pulling his eyes away from the big screen to frown at Zachary.

"Calls that upset her. You mean like obscene phone calls or hang-ups?"

"Do you remember anything like that?"

He shook his head. "No… we weren't allowed to answer the house phone," he said, which seemed like a non sequitur. "So I didn't, but sometimes it would ring when no one else was home, and I wondered who it was. Who would even call on a landline? It must have been an old person, right? Someone who didn't have a cell phone."

"Sometimes people have both. A landline and a cell phone."

"Old people," Terry repeated. "Like I said."

Zachary shrugged and didn't argue it. Chances were that someone who had grown up with a cell phone in his hand would see no point in a landline.

"You're right. It was probably someone older than you," he agreed.

Terry nodded. "But I don't know what it was all about. I didn't ask." His eyes skated around the room, taking everything in, processing it, and moving on. His restless energy reminded Zachary of Blair Bieberstein, a brilliant analyst he had worked with on a previous case. Constantly on the move, thinking about a hundred different things at once, his brain overflowing with ideas and half-finished conversations. "I don't know what it was all about," Terry went on. "I guess Dad must know something about them. You're asking the wrong guy because I really don't."

"She never said anything to you about the calls?"

"No. Just to ignore them. Not to answer the phone. And I already knew that, so…" He shrugged. "I just ignored them and kept gaming with my friends. Put headphones on and didn't worry about it. It was her own business."

"Did you think she was having an affair? Or that they were from someone at work?"

"Having an affair with someone at work?" Terry stared at the long lines of text on the screen. He flicked the arrows to move through the text, frowning. "No, I don't think so. She liked to work, but that was just… she didn't like being home all the time. She liked being a mom, and it wasn't anything against us, but she needed something more. She needed outside contact, needed to be doing something worthwhile."

That sounded like a verbatim account of what she had once told him. She loved working at home, but she wanted to work outside the home as well. Who didn't? Zachary enjoyed working from his computer at home—and he didn't have any children to look after—but he would go stir crazy if he never got outside the house to investigate or make face-to-face contact with friends or loved ones who didn't live in the same house as he did.

"That makes sense to me."

"It wasn't because she liked anyone at work more than us."

"Does that mean you do or don't think she might have been having an affair with someone at work?"

Even though he was marshaling arguments against it, that didn't mean Terry believed the words he was repeating. He might have just heard those arguments repeated so often that he was programmed to regurgitate them.

Terry considered the question. Zachary waited, watching Terry. Although he didn't appear to be paying much attention to the argument and seemed instead to be consumed by whatever code he was working on, Zachary had a feeling that was just the way he processed things. One part of his brain worked on one problem, opening another pathway to cogitate over another.

"I don't think so," Terry said finally. "She probably could have if she wanted to, but she was in love with Dad. They were close, even if he had to work late. I think he would be more likely to have an affair than she was. But I don't think either of them were."

"What do you think the phone calls were about?"

"Maybe something to do with work. Not an affair, but… a problem. Or something she was supposed to do… I don't know."

"Did she say anything to make you think it was about work?"

"No… I don't think so. I just figured that was what it was about."

He might have absorbed something subconsciously that he didn't even realize. Zachary wrote a note in his notepad.

Terry's eyes slid over to him, catching him using this non-technological method to capture his thoughts.

"You should make a note on your phone," he said. "It would be more efficient. It would be digitized and backed up. You would be able to read it." This last comment clearly aimed at the fact that Zachary's handwriting was nearly unreadable. Even Zachary sometimes couldn't make out his own notes.

"Maybe so," Zachary agreed. "Writing is quite difficult for me due to learning disabilities. But I have found that phone capture has its own problems. My brain doesn't necessarily work that way."

"What about dictating? You could use voice recognition. It's built into your phone."

"If it actually recognizes what you tell it. And when I'm making notes of a meeting like this, it isn't particularly helpful to verbalize observations in front of the person I am interviewing. Or to echo back everything they say."

"Meeting transcription software," Terry told him. "You turn on the recorder at the beginning of the meeting, and it transcribes in real time what you each say and make notes that you might find helpful later."

"But the software wouldn't make the notes that I would. It wouldn't figure out the connections I do or write down the questions I need to ask or the points I need to follow up on."

"You could add your own notes…"

Zachary held up his notepad to point out that they had gone a full circle. One way or another, he needed to be able to make his own notes of the meeting, and the way he found easiest to do that was to write them in his notepad.

Terry shrugged and rolled his eyes. Zachary could almost hear him commenting on "old people" who were set in their ways.

Like the young people weren't set in theirs.

"When I talked to Marissa, she said that she hadn't realized for several years that your mother was not killed in a car accident," Zachary told Terry.

Terry frowned at this. "She was," he argued.

"She actually wasn't. The sheriff might have said 'an accident' and you both interpreted that to mean a traffic accident, but that's not what happened."

"She had an accident in her car," Terry said firmly.

"No. She was shot. The sheriff believed that it was an accident, just a stray bullet from someone who was shooting targets close by. He thinks it was an accident but not a car accident. She was shot."

"She wasn't," Terry said stubbornly.

Zachary pulled out his phone and showed Terry the pictures he had taken of the diagrams Taylor had drawn. Where the bullet had hit Edie and where Taylor believed it had been shot from.

Terry shook his head. "That's crazy. That's not what happened."

"You guys never talked about it in the family?"

"No. We avoided talking about it at all." Terry rolled his eyes again. "Jeffy, you know. The *baby* of the family. Any time anyone talked about Mom, he would start crying. If we wanted to avoid all the tears and drama... well, we just had to go on as if nothing had happened. I mean, we didn't have a mom anymore, so it wasn't like *normal*. We all knew what had happened. But we couldn't talk about it."

"You didn't try family therapy?"

Terry shook his head. "Dad said that would just mean talking about it, and we already knew that talking about it made Jeff worse. If we went to therapy, he would just spend the entire time crying, and none of us could stand that. In every other way... everything was okay, so we just avoided the subject. If we talked about Mom, it was after Jeff had gone to bed or if he was out of the room. Out of the house was better, because he could sneak back into a room and start blubbering as soon as he even thought someone was talking about Mom or saying something behind his back. I don't blame him for being sensitive. I mean, it hurt me to talk about her, too. And he was the baby. He was only nine when Mom died. That's pretty young."

"I was ten when I lost mine."

"Yeah, and I'll bet you cried over it plenty."

Zachary nodded. He had soaked his pillow many nights. He learned quickly not to cry in front of anyone else. But if he were in his room at night and no one could see or hear him, he could let go for a few minutes. "I did," he agreed. "And you probably cried when you were alone and Jeff wasn't there to see it, too."

Terry's eyes went back to the screen. "I learned not to think about it. Tears wouldn't change anything. The only thing they did was give me a headache. So I wouldn't think about her. I would think about my game or a new project, my homework, anything else, and not think about where she was and the fact that she was never going to come back again." His voice was flat and toneless. Talking about what he did without talking about how he felt or about what had happened to his mother.

Zachary tried to think of what else he needed to ask Terry. It was difficult when he wouldn't even talk about his mother or how she had died. When he didn't even believe that it was a gunshot rather than a car accident. He had told Zachary what he could about the phone calls, which was really nothing. Just an instinct that it might have been something to do with work. At least that was one direction Zachary could pursue. He would have to find out who else had worked at the campaign office and who was still around for him to interview. Maybe he would be able to find something out from that direction.

"Is there something wrong with him?" Terry asked.

Zachary looked at him. "What?"

"Do you think there is something wrong with him—my dad? Do you think he has dementia or something? Bringing all this stuff up from the past, saying that Mom was shot, that he's getting phone calls like she got before she died? Do you think he has dementia? Or that he knows he's going to die and wants to get all of this cleared up first?" Terry shook his head. "It's not going to make any of us feel better. I don't know why he has to go disrupting everything. Everything was going fine before."

"No... as far as I can tell, there isn't anything wrong with him. He's just alone for the first time, grieving your mom like he wasn't able to when he had you kids to look after. And with these phone calls... yes, he is worried about why he is getting them and about whether there is any truth to the suggestion that your mom was targeted, rather than it just being an accidental shooting."

"It was just an accident." Terry pressed his lips together. "The sheriff said right from the start that it was just a tragic, senseless accident. He said everyone loved Mom and no one had wanted this to happen to her. Everyone else should just quit stirring it up."

18

Zachary timed his return to Roxboro perfectly, allowing him to pick Kenzie up from work rather than her having to call a cab or ride-share. Picking her up from work meant that she needed to finish what she was doing and put it aside rather than staying late and not getting home for a couple more hours. Dr. Cook knew that Kenzie put a lot of hours in at the office, so it wasn't a big deal if she left a couple of hours earlier than usual. Kenzie settled into her seat, put on her seatbelt, and sighed.

"This is nice. We have the whole evening."

"A nice relaxing evening," Zachary agreed. "No more work."

He was telling himself as much as he was telling her. He was inclined to sit down at his computer, process his notes, check his email, and make a plan for the next day. But it was time to put work aside and spend time with Kenzie now, just like she was doing.

She gave him a sideways look that said she knew he was more likely to continue doing work instead of relaxing. Zachary shrugged with one shoulder, grinning.

"Does that mean we can't talk about work?" Kenzie asked.

"Of course not. I love hearing all the gory details of your work."

Kenzie chuckled. There weren't a lot of jobs that did actually involve gory details, but hers was one of them. "Well, I didn't have anything too exciting today. But you have been out all day, you must have learned a lot."

"Not as much as I would have liked," Zachary admitted. "But... it is a ten-year-old case. Any details I can dig up count as progress."

"You've been all over Vermont."

"Well, only northern Vermont, really. But I did put on a good number of miles." Zachary patted the dashboard of his car affectionately. It was a real workhorse. Put in a lot of hours without causing him any trouble.

"So, who did you talk to?"

Zachary started outlining his interviews for the day, working his way backward through the day, starting with the most recent interview and working his way back to talking to the retired sheriff, Taylor.

"He sounds like a nice guy," Kenzie commented, as the conversation continued in the kitchen as they worked together on supper. "Not your typical crusty old soldier who doesn't want anything to do with a PI."

"Well, I didn't introduce myself as a private investigator but, yes, he was quite happy to help a civilian. Went out to the shed to dig out his old notebooks to refresh his memory on all the details of the case. But he's pretty determined that it was an accident and could not have been anything else."

"Maybe it was."

"Maybe," Zachary admitted. "I don't have anything yet that points me toward it being murder. Other than the calls she was getting before she died. I haven't talked to all the kids yet, but the older two do remember there being phone calls, and the daughter got an earful when she answered the phone one day. Some pretty nasty threats."

"So the mother *was* getting threats."

"Yes. She definitely was."

"What did the ex-sheriff have to say about that?"

"I didn't push it hard. I'm more interested in getting anything he might have than in pushing my own agenda. If I insist it was murder, he'll just resist and I won't get anything."

"Sounds like the approach has worked so far."

"Yeah." Zachary laid plates on the table. "I do have some concerns, though."

"Of what? A cover-up?"

"Not a cover-up, exactly, But maybe it wasn't investigated quite as thoroughly as it could have been."

"All police investigations have to take costs into account, weighing them against the likely benefit. You only screen for a few drugs, for example, based on the symptoms and observations of witnesses. You don't screen for everything on the planet. And if someone dies under a doctor's care, and they believe they know the cause of death, there is no need for the medical examiner's office to get involved and no need for an autopsy. Unless the doctor thinks there is a reason."

Zachary considered Sheriff Taylor's investigation against this cost-benefit analysis. He believed that it was an accident. He'd seen kids doing target practice in the area. The victim was not someone who was likely to be the victim of a targeted attack. There were no witnesses, no evidence that pointed to murder. So why would he put a lot of time into conducting interviews with everyone who knew Edie Dwayne or getting experts in to analyze the bullet, its trajectory, and anything else they might have questions about?

"That all makes sense," he agreed. "But I'm worried about whether he was the best judge of whether it was an accident and if they needed to conduct a more thorough investigation."

"It sounds like he was pretty experienced. Why wouldn't he be a good judge?"

Zachary sighed. He thought about what he could or should say. Kenzie glanced back at him, but didn't push it, letting him think about it some more.

When they sat down to eat, Zachary outlined the portion of his investigation he had skipped over until then.

"When I was in his RV and he was outside looking for the notebooks, I couldn't help but look around a bit…"

"Get a little bit of snooping in," Kenzie said disapprovingly. "He didn't exactly give you permission to invade his privacy."

"And I didn't," Zachary protested. "I stayed in the living room and kitchen area. I didn't go through any drawers or cupboards. I only looked at what was in plain sight. Just like a cop."

"Plain sight?"

"Really," he assured her. "I didn't do so much as take a book down from a shelf."

"Okay. And what was it about this little look around that concerned you?"

"He had his calendar on the wall."

"Uh-huh…?"

"With all of his appointments on it."

"And you read through his private schedule."

"It wasn't private, it was posted on the wall for anyone to see."

"I don't know… if you're doing things like getting his doctor's name or details about private health matters…"

"No. No special medical tests. No names of therapists or medical professionals."

"But there was something."

Zachary ate a few bites of the salad, giving it his full attention as if he were greatly enjoying it, which, of course, he was not. He was never going to be a salad person.

"He had a meeting at the local church a couple of times a week."

Kenzie raised her brows. "Meetings at the church. Okay. Doesn't sound like anything concerning to me. What kind of meetings?"

"It didn't say on the calendar. So, I stopped at the church before I left town. Looked at the bulletin board and talked to a caretaker who was there. The priest wasn't around. I don't think they actually live at the church like they do on TV."

"Not always," Kenzie agreed, with what Zachary thought was a suppressed laugh. "And what did you find out? Is he doing youth outreach or something dreadful like that?"

"No. AA."

19

K enzie sat back in her seat. "Oh."

Zachary nodded and continued to eat, working his way through the unpalatable salad and giving her a chance to think about that.

"Did you talk to him about it?" Kenzie asked eventually.

"No, I haven't talked to him since I went to the church."

"And I don't suppose the janitor or anyone else there knew or would tell you his history. Whether he was sober ten years ago."

"I didn't ask. But the possibility has to be taken into consideration. There was no wife in the family pictures. Not for a long time. Pictures of him with his kids and grandkids. No pictures of his wife. She is in some of the early pictures when the kids were younger, but nothing in, say, the last ten years."

"Did she die or is he divorced?"

"I assume that if she had died ten years ago when Edie Dwayne did, he would have made a connection while we were talking. 'It was that same year that my wife died,' or 'I knew exactly how he felt,' or something like that. If she's died, he would have been very empathetic toward Oliver and his family."

"Wasn't he?"

"He was sympathetic," Zachary told her. "He felt sorry for him and the kids. He gave him space and didn't ask him a lot of questions. But he wasn't empathetic. He didn't know how Oliver was feeling. Didn't agonize over the children's loss. Nothing about taking him food or flowers or talking about how the community would take care of him." Zachary cut a piece of chicken. "I could be wrong. People don't always behave the way you would expect them to. Maybe if his wife had just died, that was all the more reason to withdraw from the Dwayne family emotionally, to tell them it was an accident, and not to investigate it thoroughly."

"The drinking is worrisome," Kenzie admitted. "It doesn't mean that he was negligent in the investigation, but it opens up the possibility."

Zachary nodded his agreement. Up until then, he hadn't been too worried. Taylor seemed like a competent cop. He remembered the investigation and details about it. It seemed like he knew what he was talking about. He resisted any suggestion that it had not been an accidental shooting, but what law enforcement officer would not stand up for his own theory of the crime? He had a gut feeling about it. He had experience. He trusted his feelings. If he had waffled about it, let Zachary push him around, and changed his opinion about what had happened, Zachary would have been much more worried.

"Do you have copies of his notes?" Kenzie asked. She didn't sound too hopeful about it.

"No. I did take pictures of two of his crime scene sketches, and he drew a larger scene view for me." Zachary brought them up on his phone and passed it across the table to Kenzie.

She hesitated for a moment, then picked up the phone and looked at the diagram. Zachary watched her pinch and zoom and manipulate the photo. He didn't know what she was looking for, but was patient and worked his way through the chicken and salad while she looked at them.

"You could have a graphologist look at the diagrams," Kenzie said, "But I don't see anything in his lines that indicates he was impaired when he drew them. His lines are confident, not shaky. Everything is oriented to the square, not splayed out every direction. Comparing what he drew then to what he drew today, there is not much variation in the lines or the content."

Zachary let out his breath. Kenzie passed his phone back to him. Zachary did as she had, zooming in on the lines and looking for shakiness or sloppiness. But she was right. His lines didn't wander or shake, and the diagrams all hung together well.

"It's always possible that he drew the pictures later, when he was sober, and that he was drunk when he arrived at the scene. But just taking this at face value, it looks good. It's very professional. I've seen a lot of scene-of-crime sketches, and this contains everything that a medical examiner or court would want to see. All the pertinent information is clearly laid out. I don't suppose you have any crime scene photos."

"No, not yet. I will request them under a Public Records request, but I'm not sure yet whether I'll be able to get anything. Or whether I'll get it in a timely manner or without everything being redacted."

"You should be able to. It is a closed case. If the police thought that it was an accidental shooting, then there is no danger to the public. There may be some stuff that they redacted because of privacy concerns for the individuals who were questioned. But other than that... I can't see how a request for an accident investigation file could be denied."

Zachary nodded. He had dealt with a number of requests under the Public Records Act before. Sometimes it was remarkably easy and he got exactly what he needed in a timely manner. Other times, it was like pulling teeth and going back and forth with the agency involved would take months, even years, to get what he wanted. And then it might be so heavily redacted that he couldn't get the details he was looking for. Maybe he would have Heather put together the request. She was better with wording administrative stuff than he was, and he thought agencies like the police department were more likely to provide a woman with the information she requested than a man, especially a PI. Even if they were required to do so by law, it would always be more difficult than it should be.

"You took some pictures?" Kenzie asked.

Zachary nodded. He retrieved his camera from his pocket and turned it on. He rewound to pictures he had taken in the woods. And of the road when he had returned to his car.

"Keep in mind that it happened in the summer and, of course, it is winter now, so everything is covered with snow and the trees are bare. They would block more of the view if they were out in leaf."

Kenzie nodded her agreement. He probably didn't need to tell her that. She had eyes and she was bright. She'd looked at a lot of crime scenes. She was used to this kind of analysis.

"Those woods are pretty thick," Kenzie observed, paging through the pictures. "I wasn't expecting them to be so dense."

"Yeah. You can see why kids target shooting here wouldn't think there was any danger firing toward the public road. There are so many tree trunks in the way; you wouldn't think a bullet would be able to make it all the way there unimpeded."

"You're right," Kenzie agreed. "I guess as a rural law enforcement officer, he would have a pretty good idea of what was possible. But I'd be hard-pressed to find a straight line from here to the road."

"Yeah, I was thinking the same thing."

20

J eff was living closer to Zachary than the other Dwayne children, going to school in Randolph Center. When Zachary called him to discuss the possibility of coming to talk to him, Jeff betrayed no surprise or resistance. He seemed to welcome the chance to meet with Zachary about the accident.

Zachary usually met with clients or witnesses for the first time in public places like restaurants, coffee shops, or their workplace. Jeff, however, invited him to his dorm room, and Zachary accepted. Zachary found his way to the correct building, and Jeff was waiting for him in the lobby and took him up to his room.

It was small, as Zachary had expected. He had never gone to college or lived in a dorm himself. He had taken night classes here and there where he needed to upgrade his skills or learn new investigation techniques, but that was different from being a full-time student.

Zachary could not see much of Oliver in his son's features. The boy had short, sandy hair and hadn't yet outgrown gawky adolescence.

There were a couple of beds and several computers, tablets, and speaker systems. One of the beds was neatly made and the other a mess of blankets. Jeff offered Zachary a wobbly chair and sat on the neat bed.

"This is nice," Zachary commented. "How are you enjoying the program?"

"It's good. I'm excited about being able to be certified and get a job in veterinary medicine. I've always loved animals and wanted to work with them."

"I hear you had a dog when you were younger."

"Rosie. She was the best. I really miss her. You know in the Peter Pan movie, how that Nana dog takes care of the kids? That's kind of how I thought of Rosie. As far as she was concerned, I was one of her pups. She protected me, kept me company, looked after me. I don't think she could have done anything more for me if she had been a human nanny."

"That's cool. You must have been sorry to lose her."

Jeff's eyes welled with tears. "I was," he agreed. "I wish animals could live forever. And people, of course."

"The world would get overpopulated pretty quickly."

"I know that. Maybe just the people and animals I love could live forever." He gave a little smile. "It's a fantasy. I know there are all kinds of logical problems and consequences involved."

Zachary nodded. He understood the desire. He had lost his family and mourned them greatly, even though it had not been an ideal family, or even a very functional one. He had been abused and neglected, but he had still wanted to go back home, to go back to the family that he longed for. He had wanted everything to stay the same, to stay with the people he loved. That fantasy had taken years to fade. Maybe it was still there, lodged in a dark corner of his mind.

"Moving on is hard," he told Jeff.

"Yeah. You're right about that."

"So, you know I'm here to talk to you about your mom."

"Yeah. It's kind of funny, Dad deciding to look at it now, so many years later. I thought everyone just wanted to put it behind them." He grimaced. "I thought I was the only one still hanging on to it."

"Did he tell you why he was looking into it now?"

Jeff cocked his head slightly. "No, he didn't say... but I guess, now that I'm out of the house, he's been thinking about it again. All by himself... must have long nights."

Zachary wondered how much of it was just that. Oliver had a lot of time to think now. He had occupied his life with raising his children without their mother but, now that he was by himself, he must be lonely. And he was still in the house he had bought with his wife. Still in the bed they had shared together. The phone calls might just be a coincidence. Or they could even be a complete fabrication. He might have known about the calls that Edie had been getting before she died and resurrected them for his own purposes. That would account for why he was getting calls now, when surely the killer—if there was one—would not want the case reopened.

Oliver said that the police had not bothered to trace the calls, so there was no proof that the calls even existed. In fact, Zachary had not even talked to the current sheriff to find out whether Oliver had reported the phone calls. He could have just made that up too.

If Oliver wanted to fabricate calls, hoping that the police would reopen the case, that wouldn't have been hard. He didn't need long calls. Just evidence that the calls had been made, and that they had been made from somewhere untraceable like a public phone or a burner located several miles from his house. With an answering machine on his home line, it would be easy to call from somewhere else and then offer evidence that the call had connected and had lasted ten to thirty seconds.

Zachary shook off these thoughts. Whether the phone calls were real or not was academic. He was still on the case and looking for any clues that Edie Dwayne's death had not been accidental.

"There's more to it than that," he told Jeff. "Your father said he's been getting anonymous calls telling him that your mother's death was not accidental. The police were not interested in looking into it, so he asked me if I would see what I could find."

"Calls like Mom got?" Jeff asked, eyes widening.

"What do you know about your mom getting calls?"

"Well, she was." He blinked and looked at Zachary. "Didn't you know about that?"

"I did. But Terry doesn't seem to know anything about it, and Marissa couldn't tell me anything about them, other than that they were upsetting to her." He didn't tell Jeff that Marissa had once answered one of the calls. He wanted to know what Jeff knew independently of anyone else. He didn't want to feed him memories.

"Well... yeah, I know she was getting them. I probably wasn't supposed to know, but how do you hide something like that from a kid? I was right there. The phone rang, I heard it. Mom either ignored it, or when she answered it, she got all pale and quiet. She didn't have a conversation. She might ask a question or yell at him for calling her, but... they didn't ever talk to each other."

"What did she tell you about them when you asked her?"

"Why do you think I asked her about them?"

Zachary smiled. "I can't imagine that you would see her getting upset over these calls and *not* ask her about them."

Jeff nodded and shrugged. "Of course I did," he agreed. "But I was only a little kid. I was just nine when she died. She didn't think it was something she should be talking to me about. Telling your kid about obscene or threatening calls... who would think that was a good idea?"

"So what did she say?"

"She just brushed it off. Said it was nothing for me to worry about. She would take care of it. Everything would be fine. But I knew she was lying."

"What did you think it was all about?"

Terry had thought that it was something to do with work. Zachary wondered whether Jeff had thought the same thing.

"I don't know. I thought... it was someone who wanted to hurt her. I didn't know if they wanted to hurt her physically, or just verbally, but someone wanted to hurt her. Maybe to scare her."

"Why would they want to hurt or scare her?"

"I don't know."

21

*Z*achary considered. "You never saw her with anyone you thought wanted to scare or hurt her?"

"No. I don't think so."

"Did you see her with a stranger? Someone you didn't know?"

"She knew a lot of people that I didn't know…"

"Did any of them make you uncomfortable? Make you think you didn't want her to be with him?"

Jeff sat quietly, touching his curled forefinger to his chin and pondering the question. He shook his head. "I don't know," he said again. "I can't separate my feelings about her working at the campaign office… I don't know if maybe I was jealous about her going out to work instead of not staying home to look after me anymore, even if she was only out while I was at school. And she did computer stuff at home sometimes. I didn't like that. I thought she should be paying attention to me, not office work, when I was home."

Jeff rolled his eyes a little over how entitled it sounded. He had everything a boy could want, and he had resented the time that his mother had spent on her computer because he was home and should be the center of her world.

Zachary smiled reassuringly. "We're all immature and self-centered as kids. That's expected. Terry and Marissa might not have been as needy as you because they were older and starting to separate from her psychologically. Teenagers are supposed to become more independent. You weren't a teenager yet; you were only nine."

"I guess."

"So you didn't like her working at the campaign office?"

"No, not really. I mean, it was fun when I got to go with her and to pretend to be an office worker. But on the whole, no, I didn't think she should be working there."

"Who do you remember from the office? Did you know very many of her coworkers?"

"Well, there was Mrs. Neufeld. The senator guy's wife. She was kind of in charge. And there were moms of some of the other kids I went to school with. Uh... Georgina Smith. Georgie. And Ruby Brown. What was Bob James's mom's name? Summer, I think. Summer James. And then some old ladies. Like the bingo ladies. But I don't remember their names."

"Any men?"

"I guess. But Mom and Dad were always just talking about the campaign ladies like they were the only ones there. I guess there were... a lawyer and an accountant. Some kind of campaign manager. But they had *real* jobs, not like the women. The women were there to make flyers, stuff envelopes, you know. There were hundreds of letters to send out, someone had to coordinate all of that and get them out the door. The lawyer and accountant aren't going to do that kind of thing. They need the campaign ladies for that work."

"Sure," Zachary agreed, nodding. "So, I'm just going to write this down. Wait a moment..."

He tried to capture the details of the people who worked at the campaign office and what they had done without taking too much time. Jeff watched him and, as he struggled to get the words down, Zachary felt heat rising in his neck, nervous and embarrassed over his handwriting being examined and critiqued.

"You have dysgraphia," Jeff commented.

Zachary looked up at him, surprised. "Yes." He hesitated. "Do you?"

It was so unusual for anyone to recognize and know the name for this disability.

"Not me, but one of my friends does," Jeff said. "It was really hard for him in school."

He looked away from Zachary, looking out the window at the campus. His friend had probably explained to him how hard it was to have someone watching him as he struggled to get the letters and words down on paper. Zachary could relax and take his time writing his notes. Jeff understood and would wait.

"So how did you feel about the men at the campaign office?" Zachary asked, proceeding with the interview once he was finished. "You felt like they were the professionals. Anything else?"

"I don't know... I didn't really like any of them. Mr. Baxter, he was the accountant, he would give me candy sometimes. I was always a little suspicious about him. You know at school we were taught stranger danger and not to take candy from people we didn't know. Mom said it was okay, but I was always afraid he was a pedophile. He was probably just a nice guy. But I didn't like him giving me things or talking to me."

So far, Jeff had good instincts. Zachary wasn't inclined to believe that he had been overreacting. In the current climate, any adult who tried to give kids candy had to be viewed with suspicion.

"What did your mom think of him?"

"I don't know. I think she liked him okay. Like I said, she told me it was okay to accept candy from him. But I just didn't feel right about it. She didn't seem to think he was creepy. Then there was the lawyer. He was... I think he thought he was better than anyone else. Maybe even better than Senator Neufeld. Except he wasn't a senator yet. He was still just Mr. Neufeld. The lawyer... I can't remember his name for sure. He was a jerk. Didn't like me to be around there, even if I was helping with envelopes or entertaining myself while Mom was working."

"Why did she take you in to the office? I thought she only worked while you were at school."

"But sometimes we had days off from school, and the elementary school kids didn't get them on the same days as the older kids. So I would get a day off, and the other kids would still be in school. If she didn't want to take the time off, she had to either get a babysitter or take me with her. I preferred going with her."

"You wouldn't rather have been at home with your toys and TV?"

"No. If she was at work, I preferred to be near her. I liked playing office and helping out with the things I could. Mom would usually only go in for a few hours, and we would go out for lunch together, just me and her like we were on a date. I loved it." Jeff shrugged his shoulders, smiling and wiping a tear from the corner of his eye. "I guess I was a mama's boy. We were really close. I liked spending time together. Going to the office and out to lunch together... I felt like a grown-up. Like we were friends instead of mother and son."

Zachary had to admit it sounded like a nice time. Even though he wasn't sure if he would ever have enjoyed stuffing envelopes, he could see the draw of Jeff being away from school hanging out with his mom.

"I'm sorry if this is painful..." Zachary hated to smash the pleasant memories with questions about Edie's death. Still, he was there to help Oliver and the children get justice for Edie Dwayne, even if no one else had been willing to look at the case objectively. "Can you tell me what you remember about your mother's death? Any of the events leading up to it, and when you first heard something had happened?"

Jeff puffed out his cheeks and blew his breath out in a stream. "Yeah. I guess I knew that question was coming. I knew about the phone calls, but Mom said that was nothing to worry about, so I didn't think much about it. I trusted that she would take care of it and it would all work out okay. But one day... she wasn't there when I got home from school. I was upset about it, but I was trying to be good and not be jealous about her job since she enjoyed it so much. I didn't want to rat her out to Dad and have them get into an argument over it. If he knew she wasn't home, he would have had to rush home from his work to look after me and then he would be upset with Mom. I didn't want to cause her any trouble."

"Did they argue a lot? Did Oliver not like her working?"

"I don't think he minded her working. He just didn't think it was necessary. And he did think it was important for her to be there when we were not at school. They didn't argue much, but I'd heard them talk about it before."

"So you just stayed home alone and didn't call him to ask why she wasn't home yet."

"Yeah. And Marissa and Terry got home. Terry just saw it as an opportunity to play on his computer instead of doing his homework. Marissa asked me where Mom was and why I hadn't called Dad. She made us supper. Macaroni and cheese. We thought Mom would come home any time, and she would be grateful that we had just taken care of ourselves and not made a big fuss about it. But she didn't get home. It was getting dark before Dad came home."

"How did he react to coming home and finding her missing?"

"Not happy. He tried calling her on her cell, but she wasn't answering. We had already tried that. He told Marissa to look after me and drove to the campaign office. But it was closed. There was no one there. So he went over to the Sheriff's Office and talked to them. They said he should wait, because adults who went missing like that usually came back within forty-eight hours. People were allowed to leave if they wanted to. But Dad said he was filing a report because he knew something must have happened to her."

"Good for him."

Jeff nodded. "Not that it made any difference. The sheriff got the call about her being found out there on Riverside Road. He came to our house. Told us that there had been a terrible accident." Jeff swallowed. Tears brimmed up and slid down his face. He cleared his throat. "*A terrible accident.*"

22

Zachary nodded sympathetically and gave Jeff a few seconds to recover before asking, "How did he seem?"

"How did he seem? Dad?"

"Sheriff Taylor."

Jeff frowned. "What do you mean?"

"What were your impressions of him? Do you think he was competent to make a decision about it being an accident?"

"Was he competent? He was the sheriff. Why wouldn't he be? He was the sheriff for years. I don't know how many times he was reelected. Everyone knew he was the man for the job, until he decided to retire."

"When was that?"

Jeff frowned, thinking about it. "I don't know. Maybe a couple of years after Mom died. I think it was about that."

"And you never saw or heard or *felt* anything about him not being able to do the job?"

"No." Jeff shook his head. "And it isn't like he retired because of dementia or something like that. He's still around, living on his own, driving that RV around the country. What do you mean 'not competent'?"

"It was just a question."

"No, it wasn't. You don't go around asking whether a guy like Sheriff Taylor is competent. Not without a good reason."

"Okay," Zachary conceded, "but I can't really say anything about it. That could be slander. I don't have any evidence that he was not competent. I just wanted to get your read on it. You seem like you have good intuition."

"You ask whether he is competent and then won't say anything about it. You don't think that is slander in itself?"

"Please don't repeat it to anyone. I don't want to wreck anyone's reputation. I am just trying to find out the truth about your mother."

"Is there any reason to think it was not just an accident like they originally said? I didn't think there was any doubt."

"It wasn't questioned at the time, but I'm not sure it was fully investigated, either. I think that some avenues of investigation might have been... overlooked because the sheriff already thought he knew what had happened. He didn't really consider that it could have been anything but an accident."

"And you think it could have been something else? Really? What, exactly?"

"I don't have enough information to form a hypothesis yet. I'm just in the information-gathering phase. I am trying to keep an open mind. So it was the sheriff who told all of you that it had been an accident? He didn't tell your dad, and then your dad told you?"

"No. The sheriff told all of us at the same time. And we cried and hugged... I don't remember much beyond that. A lot of crying. Marissa held me. Dad held me. People started coming to the house, bringing casseroles, offering to help with arrangements. Mrs. Gertrude, Marissa's piano teacher, she held me for a long time. She was... all fat and soft, and I just curled up against her and cried into her half the night. I don't know when I finally got to sleep. I was only nine, so it probably wasn't any later than ten o'clock, but it felt like... crossing into a different time continuum. Everything was different. I had somehow passed through... something."

Zachary understood the feeling of passing through some kind of mile marker in his life. His life would forever be divided between before and after the fire. And to a lesser extent, after foster care, before and after Bridget, and now, before Kenzie. He prayed there would never be an after.

"Was there any discussion about the accident?" Zachary asked. "Marissa and Terry said that they didn't know at the time that it had been a shooting accident rather than a car accident. Did your father tell you that it was a car accident? Or did Sheriff Taylor imply that?"

"Yeah, they all talked like it was a car accident. I heard the people who came to visit speculating on what had happened, whether she had fallen asleep at the wheel, something was wrong with the brakes, and so on. I think Leon, the guy who ran the town's only garage, was probably kept busy for months with everyone getting their cars checked out. Making sure that they wouldn't have an accident like Edie Dwayne's. But I know."

"You knew it wasn't a car accident?"

"Yeah. I think, right from the first few days. I... listened to conversations I wasn't supposed to hear. I was just a skinny kid, quiet, and I wanted to be around my dad all the time. I had a horrible feeling that I would lose him too, and then I would be an orphan. So I stuck to him like glue. I couldn't go with him to work, but the rest of the time, I was always as close to him as I could be, and I heard him talking to the sheriff and other people who knew what really happened. So I knew right from the start that it wasn't a car accident; it was a shooting accident. But I also knew that I wasn't supposed to know or wasn't supposed to talk about it. Whenever one of the others would start talking about it, Dad would shush them."

Oliver had instituted a policy of silence. No one was supposed to talk about it. He didn't want any of the kids to know that it was a shooting. Maybe didn't want anyone in town to know that. He didn't want Marissa and Terry to discuss it in front of Jeff. They had all obeyed, learning to suppress it and go on with their lives without dealing with it.

Had they all mourned her, grieving in isolation? Or had they stuffed all those feelings down, unable to deal with them? Until it all came bubbling up again later in life. Maybe when they had kids of their own. Perhaps they would find themselves unable to deal with intimate relationships or to parent their own children until they went back and dealt with those feelings.

Zachary flipped open his notebook for a moment to review the questions he had noted that he wanted to ask, some for Jeff and some to be answered by other people or investigated through some other means.

"So… you think they're back?" Jeff asked.

"Who is back?"

"Whoever shot my mom. You think that he's back, and is calling Dad. Is Dad in danger?"

"I don't think he's in any danger. He hasn't received any threats. And I don't know if it is the same person as was making phone calls to your mom."

"But the person who shot her… where do you think they are? You think they went away and now they're back? Or you think they never left? And you think it was on purpose, not an accident like Sheriff Taylor said."

"I don't know. I can't answer that. I can't answer any of those questions. Your guess is as good as mine." Zachary waited a few seconds. "Do you think you know who it is? Do you have an instinct about it? Someone she didn't like? Someone like Mr. Baxter, who made you feel uncomfortable? Someone who hung around your house or your mom's campaign office?"

Jeff took a long time to answer, and Zachary thought he was going to come up with a name or maybe even two. People that he'd never felt right about. That his mother hadn't trusted or told him to stay away from. A dark shadow that he had seen around the property one too many times.

But in the end, Jeff shook his head. "I'll call you if I think of someone," he promised.

Zachary didn't like it. "If you thought of someone, you should let me know who it was now rather than later. It's important information. I know it's been ten years and nothing has happened, but sometimes when you investigate a cold case, it makes people anxious, and they might think about doing something else violent, even though they have been quiet for years."

Jeff shook his head and didn't offer anything. Zachary took out a business card and snapped it down on the desk beside him.

"Don't wait. If you think of someone, let me know right away."

"Sure," Jeff agreed. "Of course."

23

While Zachary could request information from the Sheriff's Office over the internet, he decided it would be worth his while to go back in person and take an offering of chocolate with him for Taylor's mother, as he had suggested. It paid to know how to grease the wheels of justice sometimes.

It meant more driving, but that wasn't a deterrent for Zachary. He thought about Jeff as he drove back to Middleton. From talking to the older kids, he had expected to find a sheltered, fragile boy who couldn't talk about his mother and had been kept in the dark about the circumstances of her death. Instead, Jeff had known more than the other two combined. It was an interesting dynamic.

Maybe Mrs. Humphries could also give him contact information for the other campaign ladies, the senator, and anyone else who had worked at the office with Edie. If someone had a grudge against her, he felt like he would find the answers there.

He wondered about Mr. Baxter. Could he have ended up in a disagreement with Edie Dwayne? Jeff said his mother had been fine with Mr. Baxter giving Jeff treats. Had he at some point crossed the line and Edie had realized that he was a danger after all? That he was grooming Jeff? It was a terrible thing for a parent to realize, but it sounded like Jeff had been wary of any attention from Baxter and would not have been easily taken in by him. A predator would move on to a child who was easier to influence.

It didn't make any sense for a pedophile grooming a young boy to be calling his mother, making threats, or calling her names. Why would someone who wanted to be seen as a nice guy and trying not to set off any alarm bells do something like that? He would not want Edie to be anxious or worried about her son.

Unless it had been a distraction. Something to pull her attention away from what was happening under her own nose. Was that what it had been? Just a distraction while Mr. Baxter tried to get closer to Jeff without her knowing it? But Jeff had not been responsive to his advances and had not said that Mr. Baxter had made any moves to get closer after Edie's death.

Even if he had been desperate to get closer to Jeff, killing Edie wouldn't make any sense. He would be removing his access to the boy. Jeff would stop coming to the campaign office. There would be no more opportunities to groom him.

No, Zachary couldn't make Edie's death or the threatening calls square with Mr. Baxter, the potential pedophile.

Maybe Mr. Baxter was only clueless, a man with a sweet tooth who was happy to share with those around him, and had no designs whatsoever on a young boy who came to help out at the office.

"You again," Mrs. Humphries said when she saw Zachary at the counter. "I thought we got rid of you the other day."

"Like a bad penny," Zachary offered. "I just keep coming back."

"You talked to Sheriff Taylor already. He didn't give you everything you wanted in the Edie Dwayne case? Such a tragic thing, you know, leaving those poor children motherless. What a senseless thing to happen."

Zachary nodded. "It really was," he agreed. "Tragic and senseless."

She eyed him as if thinking he might be making fun of her, but Zachary wasn't teasing or mocking her. He fully agreed with what she said. And so far, there was nothing to indicate that there was any motive behind Edie Dwayne's death. It had just been an accident, as Sheriff Taylor had initially thought.

"Then what are you doing here?" Mrs. Humphries demanded.

"I am still doing whatever I can to get answers. Even if the answer is just that it was senseless and random. And I wanted to thank you for your help in pointing me in the direction of Sheriff Taylor." Zachary put the box of chocolates on the counter. "That was very helpful."

"I don't know how it could help you when all he can tell you is what was already on the record." She eyed the box. "What's this?"

"Just... a little something to show my appreciation."

"You aren't going to try to tell me that the only reason you came all the way back to Middleton was to give me a box of chocolates to say thank you."

"Well, I was hoping to get some other information as well. But I did want to thank you."

He pushed the box of chocolates closer to her. Mrs. Humphries touched the box with her fingertip, uncertain.

"Are you trying to bribe me?"

Zachary raised his brows. "I just wanted to thank you for your help. I was raised to show gratitude when someone helps me out."

That part was completely untrue—unless he counted the foster parents and other authorities who had insisted that he say thank you for everything they did for him, even if they were paid to do it. But he knew Mrs. Humphries's type. She had raised her son right, and she liked to believe that the rest of the world operated with a certain kind of order, a certain kind of gentility, even if there was very little of it left.

She turned a little pink and eventually took the box and cut the seals with the blade of a sharp pair of scissors. She opened the box, selected a chocolate, and offered the box to Zachary.

Since he was giving them to her, he thought that the proper thing to do was probably to turn the offer down and say that they were for her, or he wasn't hungry, or something else that would be considered polite.

But he had a taste for sweets himself, and the chocolates looked particularly appetizing. He selected one, smiling and nodding his thanks.

"What other information could you possibly want on the Edie Dwayne file?" Mrs. Humphries asked. "I'm sure my son told you everything you needed to know."

"He was very helpful. I really appreciated him taking the time. He could have just turned me away at the door."

"He's a good boy. I tried to raise him right."

"I knew you did. And I think you can be proud of yourself for how he turned out."

Mrs. Humphries nodded. But Zachary still hadn't answered her question.

"I would like to file a request for public records on the Edie Dwayne case. I want to see everything I can about the investigation, get copies of any pictures that were taken and the medical examiner's report…"

"There's a form for that, which I'm sure you know. And it is available online. You didn't have to come all the way out here to request it."

"I know," Zachary admitted. "But It's just not the same as asking for it face-to-face."

"Especially with a box of chocolates."

Zachary chuckled. "I didn't see how it could hurt."

"Did my son tell you to do that?"

Zachary pursed his lips, thinking about his answer. "Well… not in so many words."

"That boy thinks he knows everything. I would have processed your request anyway; it isn't because of the chocolates."'

"Well, of course," Zachary agreed. "You know your job."

She opened a file drawer and paged through it to find the proper form.

"Do you think it strange that I'm still working here, and my son is retired?"

"Not really," Zachary said, taking the form from her and putting it on the counter in front of him. She handed him a pen to fill it out. "Different people have different needs. Sheriff Taylor enjoys going out fishing. You don't feel like sitting at home in an empty house. You want to feel useful."

"I do," she agreed. "I'm not one of those old ladies to sit around the nursing home watching daytime soaps and complaining about their bunions."

Zachary chuckled. "No, I can't see you being happy with that."

She watched him carefully filling in the squares on the form. For this job, Zachary had to go painstakingly slow so that she would be able to read his request. Even though she already knew what he wanted.

"How has Sheriff Taylor been enjoying his retirement?" Zachary asked. "It's nice to see that he's still in contact with his kids after… what happened with his wife."

Mrs. Humphries sighed, looking at the chocolate box and selecting another candy. "It was too bad things couldn't have turned out better. But I could have told you the day they got married that things were unlikely to turn out well."

24

Z achary looked politely inquisitive. Nothing too intrusive. If she didn't want to tell him more about it, he hadn't even asked. But he had given the impression that Taylor had talked to him about the marriage and what had happened between him and his wife. He knew just from those few words from Mrs. Humphries that Taylor's wife hadn't died, but the marriage had fallen apart for one reason or another. Not that it made any difference to the real question in Zachary's mind, and that was whether the breakup of his marriage had driven Taylor to drink. Or whether drink had broken up his marriage.

Whether he had been drunk the day that Edie Dwayne had been shot and he had gone out to Riverside Road to see what had happened.

"The two of them were not compatible," Mrs. Humphries went on. "It was obvious that she was not a small-town girl. She was never going to be happy living in a place like this. With a law enforcement officer for a husband." She snorted. "She wasn't the type to appreciate the hard work that he did."

"You think it was because she was a city girl?"

"Not just that. All kinds of things drive two people apart in a marriage. If you're not doing everything you can to keep it together

—both of you, not just one person—those things keep multiplying until there's nothing else left."

It was a pretty good description of what happened in Zachary's marriage to Bridget. She had never been interested in working together to make the marriage work. She wanted Zachary to change to suit her. He had done his best. He had tried to do everything she demanded of him. But desire could never overcome his ADHD, his traumatic past, his rough upbringing. He couldn't control his impulsivity, lost track of time, forgot which fork to use. Zachary had wanted children, Bridget hadn't. He had been willing to try couple's therapy, but she had never shown the slightest interest in changing anything for him, had never admitted that her attitude could have been a problem.

"And they broke up… just before Edie Dwayne's death," Zachary suggested, trying to make it sound like a fact that he knew rather than something he was just guessing at.

Mrs. Humphries nodded. "She broke his heart. Left him and took the kids with her. She said she was never going to let him see them again. Of course, she couldn't control that like she thought she could. The courts are not too happy when a parent tries to deny visitation. And the kids were already almost adults; she couldn't control whether they went to see him."

"But it still hurt, her trying to keep them from him."

"Of course," she nodded wisely. "It was like she was trying to take the legs out from under him. Trying to prove that he wasn't really a man, wasn't a good father. It was much worse than it sounds. It felt like the end of the world to him. He was hurt. Badly hurt."

Zachary sighed and shook his head, looking up from the form he was filling out for a moment. "That can really affect a man. That was when… things went off the rails for him?"

Mrs. Humphries frowned. "Well, what would you know about that?"

Zachary met her eyes, keeping his gaze steady, not allowing a flicker that would let her see he was still just guessing, filling in the cracks with what he thought was the next logical step. "I know that he goes to the church two nights every week."

And how would he know that unless her son had already confided in Zachary about how bad things had gotten? And how he had managed to pull himself back up out of that dark place again?

"I hate that woman for what she did to him," Mrs. Humphries said matter-of-factly. "I know very well that it's unchristian and I shouldn't hate anyone. Leave judgment to the Lord. But what she did to him was unforgivable." She took another chocolate. "But he should have known better than to crawl into the bottle. Hadn't he seen what drinking leads people to every day on the job? Drinking to numb the pain doesn't make anything better. As much as you want to escape it, alcohol is never the solution. One drink to escape leads to another, and another, and pretty soon you're not just having a nightcap, you're emptying a bottle every night, maybe more, and maybe a few during the day too."

So Taylor had probably drunk on the job, not just when he was off duty. Zachary nodded. He worked on filling out the form and didn't look at her. "Things got pretty bad?"

"For a while there, yes. But he had good people working with him who approached him and told him he had to do something. That he couldn't keep acting as the sheriff if he was impaired. And he listened to them. He picked himself up and he started going to meetings. And those people are very good, you know. They know how to help."

"I've heard good things about AA."

Zachary's brother Tyrrell had been through a number of rehab programs. If Taylor had been able to get himself straightened out just by going to AA meetings, he was doing well. It would probably have been difficult for him to continue as the sheriff if he'd had to check into a rehab program for a few months. There would be talk. He wouldn't be reelected. He would be lucky not to be asked to step down before the election.

"And no setbacks? He's been okay since then?"

"There are always setbacks," Mrs. Humphries told him. "Part of growth is failure. You fall, you get back up and you move forward.

But it has been a long time. More than five years since his last slip. He had a bad year, maybe two, after Meghan left."

"And that was right around the time Edie Dwayne was killed."

"The time of her *accident*," Mrs. Humphries emphasized. "There was never any question that it was anything but an accident."

"There wasn't... but should there have been? Is it possible Sheriff Taylor missed something because he was impaired? Something that his deputies didn't catch?"

"Are you suggesting that he was not competent to serve?"

"I wouldn't be the one to judge that. I'm not making any overall judgment at all. I just wonder whether it's possible he missed one thing on this one case."

"Anyone could miss one thing on one case," she pointed out. "Whether or not they are impaired."

Zachary nodded. "Exactly. It could happen to anyone. And it's more likely to happen if he'd had too much to drink. Or if he was tired because he'd been walking the floor the night before with the jitters. Or was thinking about his wife and kids when his mind should have been on his work. We're not machines. I'm just playing the odds. What are the chances that he missed something?"

He shrugged and spread out his hands.

Mrs. Humphries looked at the form he was filling out. "And if you find that he missed something or made a mistake, will you be smearing his name all over the papers?"

"No. Anybody could make a mistake. My only concern is finding out for Oliver what happened and finding the culprit if it was intentional instead of accidental. I don't know anything about these meetings that he may or may not be going to in the evening." Zachary made a key-locking motion at his lips. "It doesn't have any bearing on whether someone intentionally targeted Mrs. Dwayne. That is all I am concerned about."

She stared at him for a long time. Zachary tried to keep his gaze steady and non-confrontational. To reassure her that he wasn't going to take the information she was required to give him and then crucify her son in the eyes of the public.

"I don't want to hurt anyone," he assured her. "I want to get justice for Edie Dwayne and for anyone else who might be victimized by the same man."

"Edie was a nice girl. Younger than my son. I always liked her. She was always kind to everyone. Not the sort of person who was only nice to your face and then stabbed you in the back. She was someone you could trust to do the right thing."

Even if doing the right thing meant putting herself in danger? Had this nice girl, this do-gooder, gone too far?

25

Mrs. Humphries had directed Zachary to a business a few stores down Main Street from the Sheriff's Office. One of the women who worked at the bakery was Georgina Smith, or Georgie, as Jeff had remembered. She wasn't the owner, but Mrs. Humphries had guessed that she would be at work in the afternoon, and she had been right.

Zachary walked into the warm, yeasty smell of the bakery, enveloped by warmth and visions of freshly baked bread and buns. The walls of the bakery were painted a pale yellow. Zachary had apparently arrived at a slow period. There were no other customers being served ahead of him. The bells over the door jingled, announcing his arrival, and a woman came to the front of the store, wiping her sweaty forehead with the back of her wrist. Her hands were gloved, she wore an apron with the name of the bakery stenciled on it, and her hair was fastened back into a bun and covered by a paper hat. Her broad, red face shone. She gave Zachary a welcoming smile.

"Hello. I don't think I've seen you here before." Her eyes were curious. "Are you new in town?"

"Yes and no. I am new here, but I haven't moved into town. I'm just passing through."

"Oh, well, that's very nice. I hope you're hungry! What can I get for you? If you'll be on the road for a while, you might as well stock up here. No point in paying for gas station sandwiches." Her nose wrinkled at the thought of such a distasteful thing. "Not when you have all of this available."

Zachary couldn't remember the last time he had been in a bakery. He normally bought bread and other baking at the grocery store. Commercial, prepackaged stuff, not the beautiful loaves, buns, and desserts that were on display in the bakery. It made the uniform, presliced loaves of soft bread he liked best look anemic and paltry by comparison.

Kenzie was the same way. They didn't go from one specialty store to another, picking up what was best at each. They both liked one-stop shopping. But the smell and the mouthwatering sight of the baking might make him change this practice in the future.

Tonight, they were going to have fresh bakery bread.

"Oh, wow," he murmured, feasting his eyes on the plenty. "I don't even know where to start."

The woman's apron was embroidered with a name in cursive that might have been Georgie. He had an even harder time reading cursive than he did printing clearly on a form. Especially cursive letters like "G" that looked nothing like their printed counterparts. She smiled, pleased by his dilemma.

"Well, how far do you have to go and what are you planning to eat in the next few days?"

"To start with, all of this," Zachary teased, making a motion to take in all the baked goods. "After that, we'll see if I have any room for anything else."

She laughed. "Where are you from?" she asked. "You sound local."

"Yes, just over in Roxboro."

"Oh, you're a local boy, then. Not native to Middleton, maybe, but close enough. Are you back in Roxboro tonight or on the road?"

"Back in Roxboro."

"You don't need much then, just what you'd normally eat over the next few days. You don't want anything going stale or moldy."

"It would freeze, wouldn't it?"

She smiled. "Yes, most of the baked goods freeze well."

Zachary let his eyes roam over the pies, cookies, and cakes. He shouldn't eat too many sweets. He'd already had a chocolate, but that didn't count. He'd had to take it to be polite, and one single chocolate couldn't have that many calories in it. It was much healthier if he bought bakery desserts than, say, chocolate bars and Coke at the gas station. And if he bought some regular bread and buns, that would balance out the sugar.

"I had a friend who used to live here," he commented to Georgie, "But it's been a few years, and we fell out of touch. When I looked her up, I found out she was in an accident…"

"Oh, dear, I'm sorry to hear that. Who was it?"

"Edie Dwayne. I knew her from way back…"

"Edie. Oh, yes." Georgie wiped the back of her wrist across her forehead again. "Oh, that was so sad. So shocking and senseless. We were all just floored by it."

Zachary nodded. "I thought it was a car accident…"

Her eyes were bright and curious, but she didn't ask him what he had found out or correct him as to the cause of death. She waited to see whether he knew the story or not.

"They said it was a shooting," Zachary said in a lowered voice that was almost a whisper.

Georgie leaned toward him, resting her arms on top of the display case. "It's true," she said softly. "Not a lot of people knew that part. I think the family asked for it to be kept quiet. So it wouldn't upset the children, you know. But I worked with her. Me and some of the other moms who had kids the same age. We worked or volunteered with Senator Neufeld's campaign office." Her smile blossomed despite the fact she was trying to remain somber for the discussion. "And we got him elected! Edie didn't live to see it. She would have been pleased. She really believed in what he stood for."

Zachary smiled. "She was very family-centered," he said, hoping that would explain whatever political views she'd had. No politician would admit to platforms that were clearly anti-family.

"Yes. She was so close to Oliver and her children. They were very important to her."

"Are they all okay? They couldn't have been very old when she died."

"Jeff was still quite little, but the others were teens. They're all adults now. Jeff has gone off to college. He's a homebody. I think it was hard for him to leave Oliver alone. But they wanted him to get an education. Edie would have insisted."

"You must have known her pretty well."

"Well, yes, pretty well. We were friends at the campaign office, and the kids went to school together. I had one close to Jeff in age."

"Was it someone at work?"

She blinked at him and shook her head, confused. "What? Was what someone at work?"

"The person who shot her. Was she having trouble with someone at work?"

"Oh, no. No, nothing was wrong at work. It was just a freak thing. She was in her car close to somewhere they were target shooting or hunting… and it was just an accident. No one intended to shoot her."

"I thought maybe it was someone at work, but they didn't mean to."

"No. Everyone loved her. She was very kind and supportive. No one had any problems with her."

"I heard she didn't like a couple of the men who worked at the campaign office."

"Where did you hear that? No, she didn't have trouble with anyone at the office. One of the men?" She thought about who it might be. "Senator Neufeld was never there, you know. So it couldn't have been him. Other than that, it was mostly just us campaign ladies."

"I heard there was an accountant…"

"Yes… Ronnie Baxter. Oh, I forgot about him. But I don't

think he ever had any problems with Edie. I never heard her complain about him."

"And the lawyer?" Jeff hadn't been able to remember the lawyer's name, so Zachary assumed that he had little to do with anyone other than Senator Neufeld. If he'd had a lot of contact with the campaign ladies, Jeff would have been able to remember his name, just as he'd remembered Baxter's.

"The lawyer?" Georgie frowned, her brows drawing down into deep creases as she concentrated. "I don't remember. How do you know there was a lawyer? Did Edie tell you something about him? It's been a long time. Maybe he still has the same lawyer. But we never had anything to do with him. We just did the marketing. Stuffing envelopes, press releases, banners, phone lists. Getting Senator Neufeld's name out there and telling people to vote for him."

"You don't think that Edie had a disagreement with the lawyer over anything?"

Georgie shook her head. "I don't think so. I never heard anything. I don't even remember her talking to him. Only... maybe I did." she hesitated, trying to recall what had happened so many years before. "Maybe... maybe I remember them talking. But I don't remember her having a disagreement with him over anything. We all got along pretty well at the campaign office. It was a lot of fun. We felt like we were really doing something to contribute. That we were part of making change happen in the state."

She sighed and looked down at the baking on display in the case. "But that was a long time ago. It turns out that Senator Neufeld is... pretty much like any other government representative. Once he got into office, he toed the party line and said he couldn't make the changes he had promised. You know how it is."

"That's too bad. You thought he had a lot of promise?"

"I did. We all did. We thought he was going to revolutionize the way things were done in Vermont. Maybe across the country. But... like I said. Once he was in, all the promises evaporated."

"Edie wouldn't have been happy about that."

"No. But she didn't live to see it, poor girl. I wish she had, even if she would have been disappointed. I wish she wasn't gone."

"Yeah. Me too. She was a special lady."

"I wish she was the one who had been running for senate. She would have made a much better senator than Neufeld. She would not have abandoned her principles once she got into power. She would have stuck to her guns and insisted on change."

"Was she... vocal about making changes? Is it possible that she might have irritated anyone with her demands?"

"She was stuffing envelopes."

"She didn't argue with anyone? Say that she knew how to make it better? That she would run against Neufeld and do a better job than he did?"

Georgie shook her head. "She wasn't like that. She did say that she wished she could run... but she knew she was too busy and she couldn't even afford to campaign. It takes a lot of money, you know. You can raise donations, but how is a housewife going to raise donations? That world belongs to people like Senator Neufeld. Not to someone like Edie. Like me. Like you. They're a whole different social stratum. What he can do in a few phone calls would take us years to accomplish."

"She wished she could run?"

"Yeah. I guess she did. But we knew it wasn't feasible. Someone like us couldn't run. Couldn't get anywhere."

"Why did she think she would do better? Why would she run against him, if she could?"

"She just said... she would do things differently if she was running. She would run..." Georgie dredged up the conversation of years before, trying to recall the details. "She would run a clean campaign. She would do things differently. Be... ethical." Georgie drummed her fingers on the top of the display case. "I don't know exactly what that meant. As far as I know, Senator Neufeld's campaign was completely by the book."

"But Edie didn't think so?"

"I don't know why we're taking this trip down memory lane," Georgie said, straightening up. "I have a timer that is going to go off in the kitchen in about two minutes, and I'll need to take care of it. If you could pick out what you would like, I'll ring it up for you."

Zachary knew that he had pushed Georgie as far as she would go. If he pushed any harder, she would just dig in her heels, maybe take back everything she had said to him.

He selected some tarts and a black forest cake with all kinds of cream, cherries, and chocolate shavings piled on top. Some dinner buns and a rustic loaf of bread.

"Is that garlic bread?" he asked. Garlic bread was one of his favorite treats. He would live on garlic bread if he could.

"It's just a regular loaf of white bread," Georgie said. "If you want to make it into garlic bread, you slice it open, pile on the butter and garlic, and toast it in the oven for a few minutes. Best thing you ever tasted."

"Uh-huh!" Zachary agreed fervently.

Georgie laughed. Without his having to ask for it, she slid it into a foil sleeve and added it to his order. They were able to complete the sale before the timer started ringing in the kitchen. Zachary thanked her for everything and was on his way.

26

Zachary had not counted on being able to talk to Senator Neufeld or his wife. He figured it would take a miracle. He would need to know someone who would make a call on his behalf or come up with a fiction that would make Neufeld think that he had something urgent and important to talk to him about.

But he didn't have either of those things, so he tried a different approach. When he called the number listed beside Senator Neufeld's name on his campaign website, he expected it to go to voicemail, or maybe not even be an active number anymore. But it was answered by a pleasant-sounding woman.

"Senator Neufeld's office."

"Oh, hello. My name is Zachary Goldman, and..." He thought quickly, trying to come up with something that might get him the senator's ear, or at least the ear of his aide or this receptionist. Someone who wouldn't just dump him in a pile with all the other kooks who called to talk to the senator without a good political reason. "I am trying to put together a memorial tribute for a woman who worked for the senator's campaign ten years ago. I don't know if he will remember one of the women who worked on his campaign who was killed in a tragic accident. We just passed the tenth anniversary of her death, and I wanted to do something for her husband and children. I know sometimes politicians will sign special letters of commendation or recognition..."

"Yes, of course. Do you have the details you would like to have included in this letter?"

"Well, I wondered whether he remembered her. If he does, he might have something specific that he wants to include in it..."

"Okay. We don't usually do things that way, but if this was a personal acquaintance..."

"He didn't go to the campaign office very often, but she worked for him tirelessly. It would mean a lot to her family and friends if it was a personal message. Of course, if he doesn't remember her, it could just be a stock letter, but..."

"Well, why don't I take down the information, and I can present it to the senator and get back to you? I don't know how long it will take. He is very busy, but he tries to answer all queries personally."

"It is for a woman named Edie Dwayne. She was shot and killed while she was working on his campaign."

"Oh, how terrible. He never mentioned it to me."

"I don't know how closely they would have worked together or how much he would have been told about her death. I imagine he was very busy at the time. But his accountant, Mr. Baxter, knew her very well, and his lawyer..."

"Brent Cousins."

"Yes, Mr. Cousins would probably remember her as well."

"And where can I reach you when I have an answer, Mr. Goldman?"

"Is there any way I could meet with the senator? Talk to him about this face-to-face?"

"He is a busy man."

"I am only in Middleton for the day. I know that's probably impossible, but I was hoping to contact as many people as possible while I am here, and then I don't have to go back and forth..."

"He *is* in town today. I have... a fifteen-minute opening at four o'clock today. What time are you leaving?"

"I can make that. I would really appreciate being able to talk to him. I didn't think there was any hope..."

"You will have to present your case very quickly, and you won't have a long time to discuss it. You understand that he will have another meeting at four-fifteen that he will need to take."

"Yes, I understand. Thank you." Zachary looked at the website information and read out the office address. "Is that right?"

"Yes, that's correct. I will see you later this afternoon, then."

Zachary wasn't able to make contact with any of the other campaign ladies that he wanted to, wasting his time making calls to their cell phones or old farm landlines while they worked, volunteered at their kids' schools, or did other things. They were not just lazing around at home, letting the world pass them by. These were the kind of women who volunteered for campaigns that they thought would change the world, or at least Vermont. They had things to do.

He made his way to the senator's office some time before the four o'clock appointment. If the senator were free earlier than that, he wanted to be on hand. He didn't want to rush in at the last moment, hoping to get the fifteen minutes promised. A blond woman greeted him at the reception desk. She was perhaps in her mid to late thirties, though he wouldn't want to be put on the spot. She could have been another ten years older. Or perhaps with some plastic surgery, even in her fifties. The name placard on her desk said Cathy Neufeld. After looking around the reception area at various publicity photos, he was pretty sure she was Neufeld's wife, not his daughter. If so, she was more likely to be in her fifties than her thirties.

"Are you..." He felt his face flush red and hot and wished he wasn't so prone to blushing when talking to a beautiful woman. "You're too young to be the senator's wife, aren't you?"

She laughed pleasantly. "I hear that a lot," she told him. "But actually, yes, I am his wife."

He had been told that she had worked on his campaign and that she had been in charge of the campaign ladies rather than Neufeld himself. So he was surprised that when he had talked to her on the phone she hadn't said anything about recognizing Edie's name or recalling what had happened to her. Had she been so involved with her job that she had forgotten all that had happened? Or was she pretending ignorance?

"I really appreciate you finding a little time for me to meet with your husband today. I really didn't expect to be able to see him in person."

"Well, if you don't ask, you don't get it, do you?" Cathy Neufeld said. "You just jumped in and asked for what you wanted, and it paid off. You had initiative."

He nodded, feeling even more embarrassed by her words. He hadn't done anything special. He imagined Bridget would have been horrified to find out how he had bumbled his way in here. She had always told him not to make a fool of himself or to overstep his bounds when talking to someone with power like the senator.

27

The door to the inner office opened, and the senator himself stood there. Expensive suit, graying at the temples, a beautiful person who had the time and money for expensive manicures and a shiny gold watch on his wrist that probably cost half of what Zachary made in a year.

"Is this my next appointment, Cath?"

"Yes, this is Zachary Goldman. He is a friend of a woman who worked for you during your campaign. I told you about that. He is looking for a memorial tribute on the tenth anniversary of her death. If you can remember her personally, that would be great. If not, we have some stock language we can use, and we can tweak it." Cathy Neufeld looked at Zachary to make sure this was acceptable.

"Right," Zachary agreed. "I didn't know whether you would remember her personally."

"Okay," the senator motioned Zachary into his inner sanctum. "Come on in, let's have a sit-down."

There were a couple of armchairs in front of a big, heavy, dark desk. Zachary took one of them and found they were not nearly as comfortable as they looked. He suspected that was intentional. The senator could look like he was offering comfort and warmth, but he made his guests too uncomfortable to stay long. Keep people moving out and on their way. The senator settled into his large swivel chair, which Zachary assumed was much more comfortable, perhaps built specifically to his measurements.

"So…" Neufeld leaned forward on his desk to show interest in Zachary. "Who is it that you are here about? Someone who worked on my campaign?"

"Edie Dwayne." Zachary watched the senator's eyes for recognition and any emotion.

There was no response. Maybe he had already been told who it was about, so there was no surprise or other unguarded response.

"Edie Dwayne," Neufeld repeated. "The name is vaguely familiar. I'm sorry, there were a lot of women working on my campaign and I don't remember all the names or faces."

Zachary had a picture of her on his phone, which he slid across the desk to the senator. He looked at it, again without a flicker of recognition.

"An attractive young woman," he observed. "As I say… vaguely familiar, but I'm afraid I meet an awful lot of people. Did I know her personally?"

"No one has said you were close to her; it's just that she worked on the campaign. She would have had more to do with the other women on the campaign, maybe your accountant and lawyer."

He nodded. "Okay. And this recognition you wanted issued to her…?"

"Well, it would be a memorial tribute. For her husband and children."

"She died?"

"Yes." Zachary paused, analyzing the senator's body language, looking for any tells. He should have known Edie's name and how she died. Edie had been one of his campaign ladies and had been killed unexpectedly by an unknown gunman. Things like that were not just background noise. They made an impression on people. She was not just one person in a sea of faces. She was the woman who was killed out on Riverside Road. Shot and killed in the middle of his senatorial campaign.

"She was shot, actually," he told Neufeld.

"Oh, dear." Neufeld looked unmoved. No shock or dismay. "How terrible. What happened to her?"

"It was thought to be an accident at the time. Maybe some kids out target shooting or a hunter. But further investigation has suggested there might be more to it."

He was deliberately overstating, hoping to see a real reaction, some emotion or concern. But he had been told that Neufeld hadn't spent much time at the campaign office so, while he might mouth the words saying he was sorry for what had happened to Edie Dwayne and her family, the emotion did not reach his eyes. He was just hoping to get Zachary out of there before his next appointment showed up.

"What do you think happened to her? Was it suicide? Murder? We don't see a lot of that kind of thing in this county."

There was probably a lot more than Neufeld was aware of. He might see statistics, but they didn't reflect the personal stories of the people who had been shot or killed.

"We have received information from an informant saying that it was a deliberate, targeted shooting."

"Really? You never expect to see something like that in a small town like this. How terrible."

Zachary nodded. "It really was very tragic. Three children still at home."

"Ah," he nodded gravely. "That is a tragedy."

He moved a thick silver pen from the side of his desk to the middle, signaling that it was time to get on with the task.

"So you were hoping for a letter to her husband and children, expressing my sympathy for the loss of wife and mother…"

"Yes. You don't remember her? No impressions, recollections of anything that she might have contributed to your campaign."

"Contributed? Contributions are tracked in a database…"

"I don't mean donations. I mean practically, what she did for you. How she helped to get you elected. You wouldn't have made it without the employees and volunteers who helped with your campaign…"

"I can include something to that effect."

"But you don't remember her as an individual."

"I'm afraid not."

"You must have heard the news when she was killed. It would have been in the local news, talked about in your office. It isn't every day one of your employees is shot."

"I remember something about the accident," he said vaguely. "But it seems to me that there wasn't a lot of concern over it. I don't mean that no one was concerned for the family, of course. Just that… it wasn't like there was worry about a sniper or serial killer out there. It was just an accident, like happens out there. There are hunting accidents, people cleaning their guns, doing target shooting. It happens. In the big city, guns mean gangs and violence, but out in the country… guns are a tool, a part of country life. There are accidents, and they are tragic, but it is not something that I would have spent a lot of time thinking about."

Zachary nodded slowly. All that made sense, but he still didn't think the senator was being completely open. Even an accident would have been memorable. But he preferred pretending it had not meant anything to him, hadn't made any impact on him.

"I wonder if I could talk to anyone else from your office who might have worked with Edie and remember her more clearly," Zachary suggested. "Maybe the accountant or lawyer who worked with your campaign office."

"I don't see what that has to do with a tribute letter. You want something from me, the elected official. What does it matter what my lawyer or accountant remember about it?"

"They might remind you of a specific incident…"

Zachary knew it was a feeble attempt. As the senator said, who cared what his accountant or lawyer remembered? A letter to the family wouldn't include any funny little anecdotes about Edie working at the campaign office. It would just use some stock phrases. *A hard worker. Devoted to the campaign. A ray of sunshine.*

"No, sorry," Neufeld brushed him off. "I doubt if they will remember anything about her."

"They are the ones who would have worked directly with her. I understand that she was friends with your accountant. Maybe I should contact him directly for a comment."

"I suppose so."

"Could I get contact information from you for Mr. Baxter?"

"I'm afraid I haven't seen or talked to Ronnie Baxter in years."

"Would your wife have his information?"

He raised his brows. "Why would she have it?"

"I understand she worked closely with the campaign. Maybe she kept in contact with him or knows where he went after the election."

He frowned momentarily as if confused, then shook his head. "No, I don't expect she would know anything. As I recall it... he retired to the family home in Scotland."

Zachary was surprised. He had been picturing the possibly predatory Mr. Baxter as a fairly young man. In his thirties, maybe. Not as a sixty-year-old. But that might explain why Edie Dwayne had not been concerned about his offering her son candy. An older man with breath mints in his pocket. Not a virile, hormone-driven man in his prime.

But there were plenty of grandpas and other older men who used their age as a cloak for predatory activities. Even into their seventies and eighties, harmless older men were not always harmless old men. With modern medicine, people were healthy and active much later in life. Not drooling, senile, white-haired men slumped in rockers. Men who hiked and biked daily, who took on second or third wives or mistresses, and who continued to prey on children long past what would have been their expiry dates in decades gone by.

Zachary realized the senator was watching him, waiting for a response.

"Oh, I didn't realize he was that old," Zachary told him. "I didn't realize that he was retirement age."

"What is 'retirement age' in this world? Tech mavens retire at thirty. People like me are still going strong in their eighties. Our lives are not as cleanly divided into seasons of life as they once were."

"No, I guess not. How old was he? Is he?"

The senator waved this question away without answering it. "I think that as far as a tribute letter goes, we will stick to stock language. If you give my wife the address that it is to be sent to, she will prepare something. I'll sign it and we'll get it out to them. I assume that would be satisfactory?"

"Uh, yes. Of course. I would like to make contact with some of the other people she worked with."

"That's up to you. I'm afraid I am not in touch with Ronnie anymore and don't know of anyone who is. He's entered another phase of his life—landowner in Scotland rather than American accountant. I imagine there are people in town who are still in contact with him, but I don't have any suggestions."

"And what about your lawyer? Brent Cousins?"

"What about him?"

"Do you have his contact information? Maybe he would remember something about Edie Dwayne."

"Maybe he would… I'm sure you can find him in the directory."

Zachary didn't ask what directory. Of course it would not take him long to track down the phone number, email address, and postal address for a lawyer practicing in Vermont. The name was all he needed.

"Is he not working for you anymore either?"

"He is, but I'm not wasting billable hours having him draft a congratulatory letter to this woman." He seemed to have forgotten for the moment that they were not talking about a congratulatory letter, but a tribute for a woman who had died. "If you want to contact him personally, go right ahead."

"Of course." Zachary rose to his feet. "I've taken up enough of your time. I really appreciate it. You've been more than accommodating."

He could see the relief in the senator's eyes that he was going to leave on his own without any cajoling. There hadn't even been a tap at the door to indicate that his next appointment had arrived. He would have a few minutes to breathe and maybe take a bathroom or coffee break before meeting with the next person on his busy schedule.

And how much of the relief was due to not having to discuss Edie Dwayne any further?

Zachary extended his hand across the big desk, and the senator rose, smoothed his bespoke suit, and shook Zachary's hand briskly and firmly. "Thank you for coming. It was good to hear from one of my constituents."

28

Zachary gave Cathy Neufeld the information she would need to pull together the appropriate tribute letter for Edie Dwayne. He had to follow through or they would wonder just what the heck he had been there for if it wasn't really to get the requested letter.

Neufeld's next appointment arrived while Zachary and Cathy Neufeld were talking. She nodded at the dark-haired man in a well-fit three-piece suit.

"He's ready for you."

The man nodded back and entered Neufeld's office.

After giving her the information she would need, he returned to his car.

In the car, Zachary called Heather to give her a few more assignments.

"Hey, Zachy," Heather greeted. "How is the new file going?"

"I'm not sure I'm getting any traction on it. But I'm still working on it. How is your workload?"

"I can take more on."

"Okay. I am looking to speak to Ronnie Baxter and Brent Cousins. Ronnie Baxter was an accountant and apparently retired and moved to Scotland sometime in the last ten years. Cousins is a lawyer, so he should be easy to track down. Both of them worked for Senator Neufeld during his election campaign. He may or may not still have contact with them. I would be interested in any connections you can find between them."

"Senator Neufeld?"

"Yeah. Our victim, Edie Dwayne, worked for him. Or for his election campaign. He professes not to remember her, but I think that's a load of crap. I think he just doesn't want to get involved."

"Well, that's understandable. I'm sure he has plenty of work to do without getting himself involved in a ten-year-old accidental death."

"The thing is, I didn't ask him to. I just asked him to write a tribute letter to Edie Dwayne, since he knew her through the election campaign. But he denies ever knowing her."

"Oh... well, that does seem a little bit odd. But he probably didn't have much to do with the election campaign employees and volunteers. He would have had a lot of other stuff to do."

"Yes, but he doesn't even remember her? Don't you think you would remember if someone you worked with died? Or even someone at Grant's office?"

"Yeah... you're right about that. If Grant came home and told me that someone at his office had died—even if it was just an accident—it would be a big deal. I'd want to know all the details. Talk about it with my friends."

"And you wouldn't forget it next week. Or in a few years, when someone says, 'Oh, do you remember that woman who was killed at Grant's office,' you wouldn't say that you didn't remember it."

"Do you want me to do background on the senator?"

Zachary considered that. He was sure there would be plenty of information online with his official biography and social media channels on it, but there could be a lot of information that was suppressed or kept quiet. Joe Blow voter and the spoon-fed media would never find out about it, but a good detective could dig up a lot that an elected official would prefer to keep quiet.

"Yeah. Why don't you do some background on him for me?

Medium depth. I don't need to get deep into his financials or acquaintances, but more than is in the official biographies."

"All right," Heather agreed cheerfully. "I will track down these two guys and find out what Senator Neufeld has been doing that he would rather the rest of the world not know about."

After talking to Heather, Zachary headed to Oliver's acreage. He had the geo-coordinates, which he plugged into the maps app on his phone. He hadn't arranged for the visit ahead of time, but he figured it was time to give Oliver an interim report. And he wanted to see where Edie Dwayne had lived. She hadn't been there for ten years, but Zachary still wanted to get a feeling for where and how she had lived before her death. The more he could get into her head, the better chance he had of finding out what had happened to her on the isolated road.

He still didn't know why she had been out there. Had she been planning to meet someone? Taking a shortcut? Running an errand? What reason did she have to be sitting out there where it was so isolated when she was shot? Oliver had not suggested any reason for Edie to be out there. But he hadn't said it was unusual either, so maybe she had a legitimate reason that he hadn't bothered to mention.

The house was about half an hour out of town. Far enough to feel like it was secluded, but still close enough to get to the schools, Edie's and Oliver's work, the grocery store and bakery, and whatever other amenities they needed without having to drive for hours.

Oliver's car was parked beside the house, not in the garage. Zachary stopped and listened before getting out of the car. He didn't want to run into a guard dog unexpectedly. They'd previously had a pit bull and might have a new one.

But apparently, Rosie had not been replaced, and there was no guard dog in place. No other obvious security measures. Zachary looked around, pondering that. Oliver had been getting odd phone calls and had not bothered to beef up security? If he thought that it was possible that his wife had been murdered, then why hadn't he taken the steps necessary to protect himself and his home better?

Zachary climbed out of the car and took a step away, intending to go straight to the door. There was no one out here to break into his car or to plant a bomb or mess with any of its electrical systems. But he couldn't make himself leave it unlocked and go up to the doorway of the house.

He locked the car, pressing the button several times to arm the security system. The locks depressed as they were supposed to, and the light came on to indicate that the proximity and tampering sensors were armed. He could rest easy that it was well-protected, even out in the middle of nowhere where no one could touch it.

But he didn't feel happy about it. He pressed the button on his key fob a couple more times. He wanted to try the handle of the door, but knew that would set off the alarm. Not the impression of competence he wanted to give his client.

The door to the house opened and Oliver stood on the threshold.

"Zachary?"

Zachary was able to break away from the car. He strode up the gravel walkway, mostly cleared of snow, and approached the door.

"Hi, I was in the area and thought I would stop by," he told his client with a smile.

"You were in the area."

"I have been making some inquiries. If you're not too busy, it might be a good time to stop by and let you know what I have found so far."

"Yes, of course. That's just fine."

He pushed the door open wide for Zachary to enter.

The house was rustic but well-lived-in. The furniture was twenty years old and had not been updated since Edie's death. Pictures on the walls and fireplace mantle showed the family's maturation over the past twenty-some years since Oliver and Edie had gotten married: young children with both parents, older children with just Oliver. The pictures of Edie had not been cleared away or lodged in a photo album but remained on display.

Zachary saw a picture of Jeff with a square-faced dog that must have been Rosie. A happy boy, despite all that had happened to him. He had been lucky enough to be able to stay with his father and siblings, and they had helped to cushion the fall. Not like Zachary, cast out and on his own, trying to deal with burns and PTSD, new families, bullies, no friends, learning disabilities, meds and their side effects, and the various abuses that went on in the foster families and institutions that he churned through. Jeff had still had a loving, caring family.

29

He forgot all about the car, the security or insecurity of their isolation, and even the Christmas decorations on display inside the house when he saw the roaring fire in the fireplace.

He had been able to push through his anxiety over fire. At least, he was no longer thrown into a tailspin of controlled flashbacks to the fire that had burned down his boyhood home. But that didn't mean he was comfortable sitting in a room with a fire burning or didn't worry that an ember could fly out and set the house on fire...

He forced himself to keep his breathing even, counting out each breath. He sat on the couch that Oliver indicated, shifting some pillows and a throw blanket to make himself comfortable. The large living room window was behind him, and was a bit drafty. The fireplace was in front of him, which he found too warm. Too warm and too cold at the same time, depending which way he turned his body.

"You get used to it," Oliver said with a smile, "feel free to rearrange the pillows and put the blanket over your shoulders."

Zachary tried draping the woven blanket over his shoulders to block the draft from the window, without wrapping it around his arms or legs, which were warm from the fire. It was reasonably comfortable.

"Cold in the winter and hot in the summer," Oliver said philosophically. "But it's home. I wouldn't want to be anywhere else."

"It's nice. Very homey. I can see why you're happy here."

But it did feel empty. There should have been sounds from the kids playing on computers, talking on phones, playing with the dog, and making themselves snacks. Instead, it was silent other than Zachary's and Oliver's movements and voices; truly an empty nest.

"So you have something to report?" Oliver asked.

"Well… I'm not sure. I've been asking questions, looking around, getting up to speed. I've talked to the old sheriff who investigated, requested whatever public records I can get, talked to a couple of the people Edie worked with and the landowner out there. I even spoke to the senator and his wife today."

Oliver's eyes widened slightly in surprise. "Well, I didn't expect you to do all that."

"I'm not done. There are still a few directions to be investigated."

Oliver nodded. "And have you found anything out? Anything that answers the question… one way or the other?"

"Not yet. I don't have anything to disprove that it was an accident. But there is reason to believe that it might not have been investigated as fully as it might have been."

"The sheriff said it was open and shut. That there wasn't anything else to do."

Zachary nodded. "That's what he believed."

"He's a good sheriff. Experienced. He knows his stuff."

"Yes. But he might have overlooked some things."

"Huh. Okay. But you don't think the anonymous caller was right, do you? That it was targeted, that someone actually wanted to kill my Edie?"

"I don't know yet."

"What do you know?"

"Nothing for sure. I wonder if you could tell me about some of the people that Edie worked with."

"I'll do my best. The other campaign ladies?"

"Did you know the accountant? Ronnie Baxter?"

"Not personally. I remember him. He must have gone away shortly after Edie died. I'm not sure what ever happened to him."

"I'm told he retired to Scotland."

Oliver frowned. "He must have come into some money."

"Oh? You don't think that he was old enough or financially stable enough to retire?"

"I don't think so. He was... well, he was younger than me. For him to retire in the last ten years... like I say, he must have come into some money. I never got the feeling that he had any money to speak of. You can't always tell, of course—some people squirrel it away and you would never know that they have anything—but I didn't think... he wasn't a high-powered corporate accountant, you know. He did bookkeeping and such for smaller companies. I doubt if he was having problems making it from paycheck to paycheck, but if he had more than six months' salary in the bank, I would be surprised."

Not the kind of guy who was likely ready to retire. It would be interesting to see what Heather was able to find on him. Maybe there had been an inheritance in Scotland. A grandparent who passed on the family home to him, so he no longer had to pay a mortgage. Or who offered him a job in the family firm. Maybe an opportunity had come up for him there, rather than retirement.

"How about the lawyer? Did you know him?"

"Brent Cousins? Only by name. I never had anything to do with him personally. I don't think Edie did either. He might have been at the campaign office occasionally to meet with Senator Neufeld, but I doubt he was there very often and wouldn't have had anything to do with the campaign ladies stuffing envelopes."

"You can't think of any reason he would have gotten cross-threaded with your wife?"

"No. Why? Did someone say that something happened between them? I just can't see it."

"No, I'm just trying to learn the dynamics at the office."

Zachary didn't bother to say that he didn't think any of the campaign ladies had anything to do with Edie getting shot on Riverside Road. What would they argue over? Being too slow folding flyers? Taking some prime job away from one of the others? So far no one had suggested that there were any jealousies or competition among the campaign ladies. They knew each other from their kids' school, were devoted to the campaign, and many of them were volunteers rather than employees, so it wasn't about getting a better position or being paid more.

"Edie didn't have a beef with anyone in town," Oliver declared. "This whole thing sounded ridiculous from the start. I just don't see how anyone could have had anything against her. Someone is just having fun with me, trying to get me upset or seeing if I'll fall for these ridiculous suggestions… I should have just ignored them."

Zachary adjusted the blanket around his shoulders and tucked it in around the back of his collar. "You had enough doubt to hire me," he said. "People don't generally hire me if they only have a passing doubt or question. They hire me when there is a significant reason to investigate. You had enough questions to bring me in. And I'm not finished. There are still avenues to explore."

Oliver grimaced and stared out the window behind Zachary.

"She was getting calls before she died," Zachary told him. "That is suspicious in itself."

Oliver frowned. "They couldn't have been that bad, or she would have told me. Maybe just… wrong numbers. A nuisance. Our line crossed with someone else's. Misdials. Someone's grandma with dementia or kid pressing a speed dial number."

Zachary leaned forward on his knees. "They were not just innocent misdials. The kids noticed that they upset her. You noticed she was upset and on edge and didn't want to answer the phone in front of you. And… Marissa answered once."

He paled. "Marissa. She never told me that. What was it? She never said anything to me about it."

"The caller probably thought it was Edie; Marissa said that she and Edie sounded the same on the phone."

"They did. They would fool me. I wouldn't know which of them I was talking to."

"The caller was angry, threatening, calling her names. Told her not to get in his way, or he would come after her or the kids."

Oliver was pale as a ghost. "He would come after her?"

"And no one would ever figure it out."

"And... we didn't."

Zachary didn't say anything, just letting Oliver think about that. He had come to Zachary about why he had started to get anonymous calls now, ten years after the fact, and what they meant. Zachary hadn't reached the answer yet, but he had made a few discoveries.

"Who would do that?" Oliver asked softly. "Edie never caused anyone any trouble. Who could think that? Who would make that kind of threat?"

"I don't know. Can you think of anyone in Edie's life or in yours who might have done something violent if she didn't listen to him?"

"No." Oliver rubbed his forehead. "We never had any trouble with anyone. Even just small domestic problems. No arguments over property lines with the neighbors. Or water rights. Nothing like that. Everything was always worked out amicably."

"And she didn't have any arguments with anyone at the campaign office."

He pressed his lips together. "I don't really know. It was *her* thing. We didn't really talk about it. I was okay with her doing it, but I would have preferred her to be at home. She knew that, so she didn't really bring any of it home with her. I suppose if she had any arguments or problems with anyone, she figured I would just suggest she stay home. That she didn't need to be there, didn't need to put up with any problems."

He frowned, not happy to think that he might have blocked her from saying anything because of his attitude toward her working.

It would be like Kenzie telling Zachary that he didn't need to work. The house was hers, she had lived there before he had moved in with her. She was already paying all the bills, and there wasn't really any incremental cost of his moving in, other than the groceries that he consumed. She could have supported them both if Zachary were unable to work. But he had always been proud of his ability to support himself and, if Kenzie had told him that she thought his work was too stressful, especially at this time of year, and he should give it up and just let her handle the bills, he would have strongly objected. There were times he was unable to work, but he had continued to support himself, even when the medical bills had piled up and he'd had to set up payment plans to cover them.

"You were trying to be supportive," he told Oliver. "You weren't trying to hurt her or to say that she didn't have the ability to work outside the home."

Oliver nodded his agreement. He was quiet for a long time, and Zachary let him think.

"I have some boxes," Oliver said eventually, his voice far away. "Some personal things. I never had the mental energy to go through them. I had to stay focused on the kids and moving things forward. I never had the courage to go through them."

"Edie's personal things? What kind of things?" Zachary leaned toward him eagerly.

"I don't know. Paperwork. I never went through her files, I just started my own. Picked up after her death. It might not be anything. Bills and household stuff. I didn't want... I honestly didn't have the ability to read through journals or anything personal. It just hurt too much, and I didn't want to read about her hopes and dreams for the family and her future when it had all been cut short."

"Do you want me to look through them?"

Oliver held his palms over his eyes, elbows resting on his knees. Sweat glistened on his forehead from the heat of the fire in the fireplace, or maybe the stress of his decision.

"Yes," he said finally. "It would be best if... you took them out of here, and looked through them. I have no idea what you're going to find."

"I can do that," Zachary assured him. "I'll just look through to see if there are any journals or logs about her work or the phone calls, if she recorded her concerns at all. We don't know what it might have been about. I don't know whether she knew or whether it was a mystery to her as well. Do you?"

"Yeah, I don't know," Oliver agreed. "She didn't talk to me about the phone calls. She might have known who they were from... or not. What did the sheriff say? Did she ever go to the police? File a complaint about them?"

"No, he wasn't aware of any trouble she was having."

Oliver let out his breath slowly. "I feel like it's my fault she didn't tell anyone about the calls and whatever threats were made... If I had been more open to hearing about problems at work without suggesting that the solution was for her to come home..."

"Did you ever tell her that?"

"Well..." Oliver's brow wrinkled. "No, I never told her that. But she must have been afraid that I would. That must be why she never discussed any issues she was having at the campaign office with me. Because she thought I wouldn't listen, that I would just try to solve it by making her stay at home."

"You don't know that's what she thought."

"No, I guess not. And if that's what you find in her papers..."

Zachary would not tell him if he found anything where Edie complained about not being able to go to her husband with any problems she was having. What would that solve? Who would that help? It would just make Oliver feel worse.

"I don't know what she thought," Zachary said slowly, "but I *don't* think she ever thought she was in any danger. If she'd thought that, she would have gone to the police. She wouldn't have been sitting alone on an isolated road. Even if she was worried about what you would think, if she thought there was a real danger rather than this guy just being a nuisance... don't you think she would go to the police with that?"

Oliver nodded silently.

"If she thought this guy was dangerous then, not only would she be in danger, but also her children and you. Marissa said that he threatened to come after the children in the call that she picked up. If she had thought that there was a real danger from this guy, she would have done whatever it took to protect her children. She wouldn't have been worrying about whether you thought she was being soft or not."

Oliver raised his head and looked at Zachary, his eyes squinted slightly. "Yes, you're right," he said in a stronger voice. "If she had thought that her children were in danger, she would have done something about it. She would never have left them at risk."

30

Zachary carried three dusty boxes to the car and arranged them in the trunk. The air outside was brisk and refreshing; he was glad to get out into it and feel like he could breathe again. Inside the house, despite the draft from the window it had been too warm and airless. He knew this was magnified by his anxiety over the fire burning in the fireplace, but thought it would have been uncomfortably warm for most people. But maybe Oliver was one of those people who was always too cold, and he didn't notice the stifling quality of the room.

Oliver stood at the door now, watching Zachary load the boxes of his wife's personal belongings into the car, looking as though he might change his mind at any moment and call Zachary back. It had to be difficult for him to part with these last mementos of his wife, even if he had not been able to look at them for the ten years they had languished in his storage room.

While they were not the sealed plastic archival boxes like Taylor had used to store his notebooks in his shed, they did not appear to have been disturbed by vermin. Zachary had not opened them while at the house, not wanting to look at them in front of Oliver.

"I'll let you know if I find anything," he promised Oliver. "And I will get them back to you as soon as possible."

"Keep them however long you need," Oliver told him. But Zachary caught the undertone that told him not to keep them for any longer than necessary. Oliver would be thinking about them the whole time they were gone, worrying about what was happening to his wife's personal effects.

Zachary waved at Oliver, disarmed the car's security alarm, and climbed into the driver's seat. The sun was lowering in the sky and, as Zachary put the car into gear to back out and pull back onto the road leaving Oliver's house, lines of Christmas lights turned on outside the house, either on a timer or light detector or switched on by Oliver as he went back into the house.

Zachary was back on the highway and half an hour from the Dwayne home when his phone lit up with messages and chirped alerts at him. It had obviously just gotten a cell signal after being out of service. He glanced at the phone in the dashboard mount and saw several messages or missed calls from Kenzie. With his Bluetooth earphones in, Zachary gave the phone instructions to call Kenzie back. Cars stretched out in front of him and behind him on the highway like another string of Christmas lights.

"Zachary!" Kenzie's voice was anxious, distressed over something. "Where have you been? I've been trying and trying to get ahold of you."

"Just out of service for a little while. You get out into the sticks here, and service is patchy. I guess that's why he still has a landline. What's wrong?"

"I couldn't get you. You weren't showing up anywhere on my maps app. I was scared that..." She didn't finish the sentence.

Zachary rubbed his head, trying to ignore the headache and rising anxiety he felt over hearing her worry. What had happened? Had something happened to one of her parents, and she hadn't been able to get Zachary on the phone? Or was it her anxiety over the approaching anniversary of her kidnapping? He had hoped she would talk to Dr. B and be able to feel better about the holiday. But who was he to talk about the anniversaries of traumatic events? When was the last time he'd been able to get through the holiday season without hospitalization or a close call?

"Zachary! Are you there?"

"I'm here," he confirmed. "Can't you hear me? Do you want me to try calling you back?"

"You didn't leave me a note or anything."

"Sorry. I didn't think about being out of service. And I'll be back in a couple of hours." He looked at the time on the phone. It was too early for her to be back from the medical examiner's office. "Is everything okay? Are you still at work?"

"No, I'm home, and I was expecting you to be here."

The time on Zachary's phone must be wrong. Maybe being out of service had messed with the time syncing or somehow put him into the wrong time zone as it searched for a satellite.

"Sorry, I'll be back in a couple of hours. Is everything okay? You sound... really stressed."

"I am!" Her voice broke. "I thought something had happened to you. I thought..." She cut herself off and, for a few seconds, all he could hear was her breathing and sobbing quietly, trying to get her emotions back under control. The stress of the anniversary must really be bothering her.

"Do you want to talk about it?" Zachary suggested softly, trying to keep his voice as even and reassuring as possible. "I'll stay on the phone with you."

"Tyrrell came by with a present," Kenzie told him.

Zachary frowned, trying to figure it out. He had left a gift with Tyrrell several months back, with instructions that it was to be delivered to Kenzie. He wanted to make sure that she got it, whether or not he was around and able to give it to her. But Tyrrell wasn't supposed to deliver it to her so early.

"But it's... he wasn't supposed to bring that by until..."

"Zachary, don't you even know what day it is?" Kenzie demanded, her voice cutting.

"I... no..." He tried to calculate it, but it had been a few days since he'd paid much attention to the date. He had been too focused on the investigation into what had happened to Edie Dwayne. He counted off the days and squinted at his phone between switching lanes.

P.D. WORKMAN

"It's the twenty-fourth," Kenzie pointed out. "Christmas Eve."

Zachary blinked and again tried to calculate the date to see if she was right. He knew she wasn't wrong, but he honestly hadn't realized that he was so close to his own crisis point. That black abyss always loomed so big and all-encompassing in front of him that he could never miss it. Yet he hadn't realized he had already reached the date. The med cocktail he was on was definitely doing its thing.

"Today?" he asked, not sure if he believed it.

"Today," Kenzie confirmed irritably. "You weren't here. I couldn't reach you or find your location. And then Tyrrell comes by with this present!" There were tears in her voice. "He said you'd arranged with him to deliver it today. I thought... I was worried that you might have done something to harm yourself. I've been frantic!"

"No, no," Zachary assured her. "I was just out of service, checking in with my client. Nothing happened. I didn't even realize... I guess I lost track of the date," he said lamely.

And, of course, Kenzie hadn't pointed out what day it was to him, not wanting to throw him deeper into depression. She didn't want to push him right to the edge of the cliff.

She snorted. "You lost track?"

"Sorry."

"You're unbelievable. Right when I think I have you figured out."

He was still sorting things out, trying to get everything to fit into place. "So you got home from work early. You just worked in the morning."

"Yes. We only work half a day on Christmas Eve unless there is something really urgent. I figured you would need me. But you weren't here. You weren't reachable. I was calling the hospital... I thought you might have checked yourself in without letting me know... Calling the police to see whether they knew anything, whether..."

She didn't say "whether they had found a body" or "whether

162

there was a suicide call," but they both knew that was what she was talking about.

"I'm really sorry," Zachary told her again, heart squeezed with pain over what she had been going through that afternoon, while he hadn't even known there was a problem. "I'll get home as quickly as possible, and we'll… have a good evening together."

She sniffled and snorted, trying to keep her emotions under control.

"You're okay? When was the last time you had a good Christmas Eve?" She laughed feebly.

He tried to remember. It had been a few years since he had been with Bridget, and his Christmas Eves with her had been volatile despite his visions of how they would be romantic and happy, and maybe there would be baby's first Christmas a year or two into the marriage. Even though Bridget had never wanted children with him. Now she had babies with Gordon, twins enjoying their first birthday as well as their second Christmas.

And before Bridget? During the long, empty years between aging out of foster care and meeting Bridget? He'd mostly ignored the holidays, trying to avoid the Christmas reminders and keep to himself.

"I don't know. Never," he admitted. "But this could be the first."

He heard her blow her nose some distance away from her phone. Doing her best to get herself back together and under control.

"What do you want to do?" she asked. "Order in?"

They hadn't made any Christmas Eve plans, knowing that Zachary could end up hospitalized and, whatever happened, would not likely be in a celebrating mood. A frozen dinner or pasta didn't seem appropriate.

"Hey, I stopped at the bakery," he told her. "Got some really nice bread. And pie. And a cake."

"You what?"

"The woman at the bakery told me how to make garlic bread out of it."

"Garlic bread and pie? That's your idea for a Christmas Eve dinner?"

"Well... yes. Or cake."

"Sounds good," Kenzie said, her laugh muffled.

"I really am sorry for scaring you. I didn't mean to. I would have told you where I was if I'd realized what day it was and that I would be out of service. I just didn't think, and you know how I lose track of time sometimes."

"I'm very glad you're okay."

"I really am. And you know what? I actually sat in a room with a fireplace in it today."

"With a fireplace?"

"With a fire in it."

"Really?" Another sniffle from Kenzie. "Boy, that's really good, Zachary. You wouldn't have been able to do that a couple of years ago."

"I wasn't even sure I could do it today. It's one thing to be able to deal with lit candles. But a fire like that..." He puffed his chest out in pride. It might be nothing to the average person, but Kenzie knew what a big deal it was for him.

Maybe he was over the hump. Maybe after decades of fighting with his past, he was finally pushing past the summit and had reached the other side. Maybe he could be a normal person and enjoy Christmas and the celebrations surrounding it.

"That's really good," Kenzie repeated. "You should be proud of yourself." She choked up a bit again. "And here I am, falling apart..."

"You're doing fine," Zachary assured her. "Of course you were worried. That's perfectly understandable. And you're dealing... with your own stuff right now. I think you're doing a great job."

"My own stuff?" Kenzie's voice was tight. "What's that supposed to mean?"

"Well... I guess it's because of everything you went through last year. And you had to deal with it all without me because I was in the hospital."

He didn't say "kidnapping" or "abduction" or mention her father. But she had to know what he was talking about anyway.

"I'm not going through anything," Kenzie told him, a bit of a snap in her voice. "I'm just fine."

31

Zachary's foot was pretty heavy on the gas pedal on the way home. He kept an eye out for cops, but didn't think there would be too many on the highway looking to hand out speeding tickets on a chilly Christmas Eve. Let people get home to their families. Stay inside coffee shops and other locations where it was warm until they got called to something important.

He didn't like Kenzie being home alone, especially knowing how anxious and upset she was. He should have been paying more attention to the date and time. He had headed off on his own investigation without paying any attention to what her needs were. Here she was worried that he had done something to harm himself, and he hadn't given her one thought.

It was good, though, on the other hand, to realize that he had gotten to Christmas Eve without even knowing what day it was. In another day, the cyclical depression would start to lift. Knowing that the worst was behind him, he would begin the climb back into the light.

He was grateful for family and friends who knew how much the holiday decorations, music, parties, and other stuff bothered him. They were careful not to bring it up or surround him with the glitz and glitter of holiday preparations. With no one reminding him, he

166

had been able to stay in his own little bubble of ignorance and let most of the season pass him by without notice.

Zachary pulled up in front of the house. Some of the houses on the block had Christmas lights strung up outside and Christmas trees in the living room windows. A few yards were decorated to the hilt with a crazy number of campy holiday decorations. He normally shut them out of his mind. He left home and returned with tunnel vision, shutting out the visual clutter.

Now, he took a minute to look at it and remind himself that for most people, Christmas was a fun family time, that they enjoyed all the decorating, gift-giving, holiday feasts, and everything else. They had not grown up dreading the day and knowing that Christmas meant nothing more than depression, another institutional meal, and suppressing traumatic memories that threatened to bring him to his knees.

For other people, it was a happy time. A family time. And that was what Kenzie would be hoping for, even though she'd had to accommodate him by not decorating with anything more than a few twinkle lights on the wall, collectible magnets on the fridge, and a little line of brass bells in graduated sizes on one of the book-shelves. She knew a Christmas tree, greenery, candles, and paper decorations were out of the question. Nothing would drive Zachary to the hospital faster than repeated flashbacks to that fateful Christmas Eve when he was ten years old and burned the house down, nearly dispatching himself and his whole family with him.

He unloaded the baked goods and left the boxes of Edie's files in the trunk. He would take a couple of days off to do whatever Kenzie wanted to do and not look at anything case-related until she was ready to go back to the medical examiner's office.

They both knew there would be a glut of bodies after Christmas. They both understood why.

Zachary locked the car and double-checked the handles and locks before pressing the key fob again to arm the security system. He looked up the sidewalk at the house, glad to be home, glad that Kenzie was there waiting for him, no matter how irritated she was with him for being unreachable.

He pressed the fob button a couple more times and looked up and down the street. Everyone was home, of course. There wasn't anyone sitting out there in their cars watching him, waiting for him to arrive. There was a lone dog walker down the street, but Zachary recognized him as a neighbor, recognized the ancient schnauzer who was out ten times a day to relieve his failing bladder.

He picked up the bags of baked goods and walked up the sidewalk to the house. Kenzie opened the door to let him in. She didn't greet him with a hug and kiss, but grimly armed the security alarm after Zachary entered and ushered him into the kitchen.

Zachary put his bags on the table, and he and Kenzie unpacked them. Kenzie looked at the assortment of baked goods, bemused. She shook her head. "What exactly possessed you to go to the bakery? Did you hold the place up?"

Zachary laughed. "No. I had to talk to a witness, and she was working at a bakery, and… all of this stuff basically jumped off the shelves and into my bags…"

"Sure it did." Kenzie shook her head. "We'll have to freeze some of it. We won't be able to eat it all before it goes stale or moldy."

"But we'll make garlic bread tonight."

"We'll make garlic bread," Kenzie agreed. "I need butter, garlic, and a little parsley."

Zachary hunted down the ingredients, his mouth already watering. "And can we have the cake for dessert? If you want the pie or something else instead, we could, but…"

"Yes, we can have the cake for dessert. I don't want to freeze the cream. But I'm going to have to have a very small sliver, or you will be rolling me back to the medical examiner's office, I will be so fat."

"You wouldn't be," Zachary argued, but he didn't say anything else about weight or stress-eating. If he said too much, she would think that he *was* protesting too much and secretly thought that she *was* getting too fat. She had been very sensitive about her weight over the past year, though he could not see any indication that she had gained anything unless he were really looking for it.

They worked together to sort out the baked goods and get everything put away for later.

"We should have a vegetable, too," Kenzie pointed out. "Even if it is just tomato sauce on pasta."

He looked at her, resigned to eating whatever she said they had to eat.

"You don't have to look so forlorn," Kenzie laughed. And she didn't get out the pasta and tomato sauce.

"We could eat Alphaghetti," Zachary suggested, opening the cupboard to look at the shelf where cans of his childhood favorites were located. "That has tomatoes in it."

"We are *not* having Alphaghetti for Christmas Eve dinner."

"Do you want pizza? We have one in the freezer."

Kenzie considered, then shook her head. "I think I'm just going to stick to the garlic bread," she admitted. "I would just be forcing myself to overeat in the name of getting some extra vitamins."

"We'll eat vegetables later," Zachary agreed. "Tomorrow or the next day."

She would want to visit her parents. If they ate at her mother's home in Burlington or went out to a restaurant, they would have vegetables with their main courses. Potatoes, at the very least. Maybe even some other kind of vegetable, steamed for the ladies and grilled in butter for the men.

It didn't take long to heat up the bread enough for the garlic butter to melt down into the air bubbles and crevices, and they sat at the table, pulling pieces off and licking their fingers.

"What is Tyrrell doing tonight?" Zachary asked. "He didn't want to stay?" He was sure Kenzie would have offered, even if she didn't feel like company. She was always a good host and especially attentive to Zachary's little brother.

"He and Robbie had plans," Kenzie said with a shrug. "I didn't ask for details."

Tyrrell had recently been reunited with his childhood friend, and they did a lot of things together. Maybe Tyrrell would also have plans to visit some of the other siblings. He kept in touch with them more than Zachary did, and he could make plans for Christmas, unlike Zachary, who absolutely could not plan anything for

Christmas Eve or any time after that. The black wall of his memories formed a barrier he could not get past.

He had done well this year to organize a family dinner so close to the holidays and had not flaked out and left it to Kenzie, Heather, and Tyrrell to pull everything together.

"Do you want to call anyone tonight?" Kenzie asked. "Wish them a Merry Christmas?"

"Not tonight." Zachary was doing well, but not that well. Christmas Eve was a time of mourning rather than celebration. He couldn't bring himself to call family or friends and wish them the best the season had to offer. He just needed to spend time with Kenzie. To keep watch through the night to make sure that nothing happened.

"Okay," Kenzie agreed. "Do you mind if I take a break and make a few calls before the cake? Let the garlic bread settle a little?"

"Sure," Zachary agreed. He looked around for something to do. He didn't want to log in to his computer, because he had decided he was not doing any more work over the holiday. If he started, he would get sucked into it and potentially neglect Kenzie on the night when he should have been giving her the most attention. And he didn't want to turn on a Christmas movie on the TV. "I'll clean up. And then... maybe a movie from the action/thriller shelf..."

She laughed. "I hear *Die Hard* is a great Christmas movie."

That would suit Zachary just fine.

Kenzie retreated to the bedroom to make her calls. He didn't think anything of it at first, figuring she would want to talk to her parents, maybe a few friends. When he walked past the bedroom to wash up and shave, thinking Kenzie might appreciate snuggling with a non-sweaty, non-stubbly boyfriend, he caught a few unconnected sentences and realized she wasn't calling her family and friends to wish them a Merry Christmas. She was talking to Mr. Peterson to let him know that Zachary was home and safe tonight. He stopped with his hand on the door, listening to her goodbyes. She had probably made another call or two while he had been putting the plates and cutlery in the dishwasher. Maybe to Tyrrell to let him know that Zachary had returned unharmed. Maybe to

Heather, who might also be wondering why he hadn't called her back for the background checks.

Everyone else had been worrying about him while he'd been completely oblivious.

He tried to swallow the lump in his throat and went into the bathroom to finish getting cleaned up.

32

They had the rare treat of a couple of glasses of wine before bed. Zachary typically avoided alcohol since it was contraindicated by his anti-anxiety and sleep aid medications. But he already knew he would not be sleeping and figured the wine would do as much as his anxiety meds to keep him calm and relaxed with Kenzie as the evening wore on.

They cuddled on the couch watching movies until Kenzie could no longer keep her eyes open. Then he went with her to bed and watched her fall asleep. He stayed awake himself to make sure that nothing bad could happen.

He knew logically that the accident that had destroyed his world when he was ten would not repeat itself. Christmas Eve itself was not a harbinger of doom. But logic was not in control on the anniversary of the fire. Trauma was. And trauma demanded that he sit there on the bed, watching Kenzie sleep and waiting for the late winter sun to finally start creeping up over the horizon.

Eventually, the room started to brighten. He had made it through another Christmas Eve without the world ending. He was safe. Kenzie was safe. His family, spread out over Vermont, were all safe. He hadn't brought another disaster into their lives. He rubbed his gritty eyes and thought about getting up to make some coffee. Kenzie would probably wake up before too long. They could have a lazy Christmas morning unless she wanted to go somewhere. Her parents probably wouldn't have Christmas dinner until the evening, but if they decided on a noon meal, Zachary and Kenzie would have to head out mid-morning.

"Are you up already?" Kenzie murmured.

"Yeah."

"What time is it?"

He looked at the time on his phone. "Eight."

Kenzie groaned and rolled over. She looked at him and glanced swiftly around the room as if something might have changed while she was asleep. He tried to look reassuring. He smiled. "Do you want me to make breakfast?" he suggested. "I got some muffins at the bakery yesterday."

"Is there anything you *didn't* get at the bakery yesterday?"

"Everything looked and smelled so good."

"You must have been hungry. You're never supposed to shop for food when you are hungry."

"Maybe that was it."

"Muffins are good, but I don't think I'm ready to eat yet. Hey, you know, someone brought a present around for me yesterday." Kenzie pulled the covers down as she propped herself up. "We don't usually exchange Christmas presents."

She knew how difficult it was for him to observe anything to do with Christmas and that the closer they got to Christmas Eve, the harder it was for him to do anything. But Zachary had been determined that this year would be different. Rather than waiting until December, when he knew that he wouldn't be able to go to the highly decorated stores pumping out holiday music and wouldn't be able to think about celebrating with her, he had done his shopping in September. He told himself that it was just an early birthday present for her. He had refused to admit to himself that it had anything to do with Christmas. And then he had given it to Tyrrell and made him promise to make sure that Kenzie got it for Christmas even if Zachary were in the hospital. Then he had put it out of his mind and did not think about it again until Kenzie mentioned it.

"Oh yeah," he said. "I got you something."

Rather than getting upset with Zachary for getting something for her when she had gotten nothing for him, Kenzie bounced excitedly like a little kid. "I can't wait to see what it is. Can I open it now?"

"I don't know… maybe we should wait until later," he teased.

"I am not waiting until later! You're lucky I didn't open it yesterday before you even got home. I could have, you know."

Zachary laughed. "Yes, you could have," he agreed. He didn't tell her that she would have to wait until they saw her parents or come up with another reason for saying that she couldn't open it yet. He just waited while Kenzie hurried out of the room to retrieve the little package Tyrrell had left for her.

She returned a minute later and got back into bed, sliding her feet under the covers. She turned toward him so that the gift was cradled in her hands between them. She smiled at him, eyes shining. "This is so much better than last year."

"And the year before that," Zachary agreed, "and the year before that…"

She nodded her agreement. She tore the wrapping paper, silver and icy blue rather than red and green or gold—obviously Christmas colors—to reveal the small box. She would know from the brand name on the box that it was jewelry. She carefully lifted the top off the box and looked inside.

"Oh, it's a bracelet. It's pretty." She pulled it out and held it close to her eyes, examining the charms on the bracelet. She began to laugh. Zachary grinned as she looked at the tiny skeleton, gun, knife, and ruby heart.

"For the medical examiner who has everything," Zachary told her. "I was originally looking at scalpels and butcher aprons, but I was told they weren't very romantic."

"A skeleton bracelet is much more romantic," Kenzie agreed with a giggle. She held it out to Zachary, and he obligingly wrapped it around her wrist and fastened it for her. Kenzie turned her wrist this way and that, admiring it. "This is the best medical examiner gift ever."

"Not sure what I'm going to come up with next year," Zachary confided. "I found a really good source for fake blood, but I'm not sure what to do with it."

"Tie-dye?" Kenzie suggested.

Zachary chuckled. He rubbed his eyes. "I didn't know what you wanted to do this morning. Do you want to call your mom?"

"I will. Did you get any sleep last night?"

"No. I had to…"

"Keep watch?"

He nodded. She knew, by now, that it was impossible for him to sleep on Christmas Eve, no matter how sleep-deprived he was. Even when he was in the hospital and they tried to give him sleeping pills, he refused take them on Christmas Eve.

"Well, why don't you close your eyes and have a nap? I'm going to have a long, lazy shower. Then maybe coffee and call my mom."

"And a muffin."

"And a muffin," she agreed. "But having kept your vigil through the night, if you want to be able to drive at all today, you have to have a nap."

"That's not fair," Zachary objected.

"You think I'm going to let you drive when you haven't had any sleep? Not a chance. Do you know how many people I see on my table who thought being tired didn't count as being impaired? Nap." She gave his shoulder a little shove. "I'll talk to you later."

33

When Zachary awoke, something was wrong. He didn't know what it was, but he could feel it in the air. He'd slept heavily for a couple of hours. He knew instantly that it had been more than just a few minutes. He didn't usually sleep more than a few hours per night, so a two-hour nap was more than enough to keep him going until bedtime rolled around again, especially with the reassurance that Christmas Eve had passed and he could begin living again.

But something was wrong, and he wasn't sure what it was. He lay still for a few minutes, watching and listening, trying to analyze everything in his environment so that he could respond to it properly.

Kenzie was pacing. Back and forth across the house. Muttering to herself. Zachary sat up. He ran his fingers through his short, stubbly hair.

"Kenz?"

She walked into the bedroom and looked at him. "What's wrong?" she demanded.

Zachary shook his head. "Nothing. I'm fine. But it sounded like... I wondered if something was bothering you."

"I'm fine."

He waited, but she didn't provide him with anything more than that.

"Okay. Did you settle things with your mom? Did she want us to come over for dinner?"

"I don't know. Yes, she said that it would be fine if we came over. *If we wanted to come over?* What kind of an invitation is that? Is there something going on over there? Does she want me to come over or not come over?"

"She didn't say? Is she going to have dinner, or should we eat before we go over? Or take something for her?"

"She said we could come over for dinner if we wanted to. That it's up to us."

Zachary wasn't sure why Kenzie was so upset about the invitation. It sounded like Lisa was just being cautious, not wanting to pressure them into anything if they didn't feel like going over for a visit today.

"You want to go, don't you?"

"Well, yes, of course I want to go over. But I don't know if that's what she wants. Maybe she has someone else over and doesn't want company today."

"Who?"

"What?" she snapped.

"Who else would she have over? You mean someone other than your dad?"

Kenzie's parents had been divorced for many years, but Walter still visited Lisa when he was in Burlington, stayed at the mansion overnight and, of course, was invited over for Christmas dinner if he were available.

"She could have someone else over," Kenzie pointed out. "She's not exactly elderly. She could have a boyfriend. Or be making dinner for friends of the family. I don't know. How would I know? She doesn't ever tell me anything."

"But she said you could come over for dinner."

"Yes!" Her tone was biting.

"Do you want to call your dad? See if he is planning to be there? Maybe that will help you to decide."

She glared daggers at him. She left the room without bothering to answer this suggestion. But a minute later, he could hear her talking on the phone once more as she paced around the house.

Hopefully, her dad would be able to calm her down. She had been worried about him since the previous year. Walter had disappeared on Christmas Day and had not responded to her increasingly worried phone calls for days. He had not reappeared until Kenzie herself had been abducted. He had prevailed upon the kidnappers to release her, promising to do as he had initially agreed and get them the votes in the legislature needed to either approve or defeat a bill. Zachary didn't know the details; just that the Russians had been behind it.

Kenzie had not had anything else to do with the Russian oligarch who had been behind the kidnapping and other violence that had been rampant in the city the previous year. As far as Zachary knew, the man had faded into the background, and no further threats had been made or pressure applied, but maybe Kenzie had just chosen not to tell Zachary anything else. Maybe, the same way as Edie had kept quiet about the threatening phone calls, Kenzie had sheltered Zachary from any news of the Russians because she was worried about his mental stability. She had hidden it all from him the previous year, when he had been in hospital and she deemed him too mentally fragile to deal with it.

Zachary waited anxiously for her to get off the phone and tell him what was happening. Kenzie's voice initially got louder and shriller but, as she spoke with Walter, it gradually returned to normal. He heard her laugh once or twice. Not a full-out laugh like she found something really funny, but a social nicety, coming down from her high-anxiety roller-coaster and trying to act calm and good-humored for her father. Whatever he'd said, he'd been able to calm her down at least partway.

Eventually, Kenzie returned to the bedroom. Zachary tried to smile reassuringly, but his face felt twisted and he was sure it looked anything but natural.

"Okay," Kenzie said in an even tone. "We're going to Burlington for dinner."

"Sounds good," he agreed. "What time do we need to be there?"

"Not until late afternoon. We have the morning for ourselves. We should video chat with Lorne and Pat. I don't know who else you want to call, but they'll want to have a short visit with you, at least."

"With *us*, they'll want to see you too."

She didn't tell him she had already talked to them the previous night. She just shrugged. Lorne Peterson was Zachary's former foster father, so it followed that Zachary was the one he really wanted to see. Kenzie was a bonus.

"We should have breakfast first."

Kenzie raised her brows at Zachary. "And you should probably dress," she pointed out.

Zachary chuckled. "Well, I was planning to do that at some point."

Now that she seemed to have settled down and their itinerary was coming together, he pulled off the covers and grabbed himself some clothes.

34

The bakery muffins were good, Zachary had to admit. He wasn't big on muffins for breakfast. He remembered the dreadful muffins full of carrots or bran that had been imposed on him by various foster mothers over the years. Horrible things that he could barely wash down with a couple of glasses of milk. He sometimes wondered if their only purpose was to get him to drink the milk he refused the rest of the time.

But the ones from the bakery were more like dessert. Too sweet for Kenzie, who winced a little when she took a bite of one of the chocolate cranberry muffins and washed the mouthful down with a swallow of coffee.

"Good grief, but those are sweet. They must be pure sugar."

"They're pretty good," Zachary admitted.

"Pretty good if you want to give yourself diabetes. Your body is going to go into shock having to deal with all that sugar first thing in the morning."

Zachary was pretty sure that wasn't actually a thing. Of course, he had always been told that candy or desserts were not allowed first thing in the morning because he had to start the day off with a good breakfast full of vitamins, minerals, and fiber, but it couldn't hurt to mix things up one day and have something a little bit sweeter.

Or a lot sweeter. Zachary sipped his coffee to cut the cloying sweetness, grinning to himself at Kenzie's reaction.

He might have to eat her muffin, too.

Zachary wasn't sure what anyone's plans for the day were. He hadn't asked. Now, when he wanted to call them, he wasn't sure what time would be safe to do so. Would they be sleeping in? Visiting relatives? Children? It was all guesswork now, because he hadn't bothered to find out.

Mr. Peterson and Pat didn't have any kids or grandkids to worry about. Just Pat's mother and sister. And they probably wouldn't be visiting until later, arriving for one of Patrick's fantastic dinners. It was probably best to reach Lorne and Pat in the morning before the preparations got too involved.

Zachary figured that Tyrrell would see his kids later in the day after they'd had a chance to empty their stockings and open their presents with their mother. Kenzie had said something about Tyrrell and Robbie doing something together on Christmas Eve. They had probably been up late, so Tyrrell would be sleeping in. Zachary might try to reach him around noon, finding the space between Tyrrell waking up and going to get his kids for a Christmas visit.

And the rest of his siblings? Joss would be cranky no matter what time he called, so that didn't really matter. He doubted she had any big Christmas plans. She had a bunch of teenagers to look after, and who knew what kind of extra attention they would need from her. Christmas wasn't an easy time for teens away from home. Even those who had been through terrible abuse before ending up on the street, addicted and trafficked, might have fantasies about idyllic Christmas celebrations with their families. Christmas celebrations that would never happen and were bound to end in an emotional crash, resentments, and a craving for the numbing power of drugs.

Heather? Her kids were all adults, and there were no grandkids so, chances were, they would all sleep in. Christmas morning would just be her and Grant. Like with Zachary and Kenzie, gift-giving and breakfast did not take long, and then they were faced with what to do the rest of the day, or at least until the kids got up and they could have a long family chat online or get together for an in-person dinner.

Zachary tried a video call with Heather. Usually, they just had regular voice calls, but he wanted to see her face this time. It was supposed to be holiday wishes, not a business call. Something special. He was happy when Heather accepted the call, and he could see her face, appearing fresh and cheerful, not hollow-eyed and apprehensive, as he was afraid he was. The tiny thumbnail video of himself that he could see as he looked at Heather was not flattering.

He smiled at her. "Hi, Feathers."

"Zachy! Merry Christmas!" She gave him a wide grin. "It's so nice to see you home and happy for Christmas. How are you doing?"

"Good. We've had a nice day so far. How about you?"

"Sure. It's quiet around here Christmas morning, you know. No kids around today. They're doing their own thing. We'll see them next week if they deign to make some time for us."

"So it's just you and Grant. That's what I figured."

"But it's nice. It isn't just any old day. It's special."

He was glad that she could make it special for the two of them. The day apparently did not bring back dark memories of the fire, the separation of the family, and the desperate teenage years that had followed. She was able to leave that behind and just enjoy a special time with her husband.

"You and Kenzie doing okay?" Heather asked, looking a little concerned.

"Oh, yeah. We're good. We'll go up to Burlington tonight for dinner with her family. Just having a lazy day until then and calling everyone. Maybe we'll watch a movie later."

"A Christmas movie?"

"Well, you never know."

Zachary had never particularly liked Christmas movies. He'd

watched them in school or foster families as Christmas had approached, increasing his anxiety exponentially. The contrast between his memories of the fire and his loss and the happy families portrayed on the movie screen or TV made him feel like he lived in a completely different world from the rest of humanity, and he just wanted to escape. And when he watched movies on Christmas Day at Bonnie Brown, the institution where he had spent most of his Christmases at as a teenager, he and the other residents had rolled their eyes at each other, wondering if it was possible that anyone actually had Christmases like that. The endless Christmas classics with their happily-ever-after families. The angel appearances, miracles, and romances where the true spirit of Christmas was revealed and everyone ended up with someone they loved for Christmas. Children's Christmas wishes coming true when they got the present they wanted or the missing parent came home from the war for Christmas. It was all just too much to believe those kinds of lives actually existed.

Heather tried to fill the silence, changing the topic away from Christmas so Zachary didn't have to come up with anything positive to say about Christmas or Christmas movies.

"I got a good start on those backgrounds," she told him.

"Oh, we probably shouldn't talk business," Zachary told her. "That can wait a day or two. Grant won't like you talking work on the holiday."

"Oh, Grant is just fine with it. If he can watch sports on Christmas, I can talk business. It's only for a minute, anyway. It isn't like I'm spending all Christmas Day doing research for you and he resents it."

"Well…" Zachary glanced around for Kenzie to ensure she wasn't waiting for him to join her in some Christmas tradition. But she had disappeared into the bedroom, maybe making her own calls or deciding on her wardrobe for dinner with her parents. "A quick report, then," he said quietly. It wouldn't hurt him to do just a little work on Christmas Day, just to find out what Heather had discovered.

"The first one," Heather said, "Ronnie Baker."

"The accountant who went to Scotland."

"Yeah. Except, as far as I can tell, he didn't."

"He didn't go to Scotland?"

"He didn't go anywhere, as far as I can tell." Heather paused, waiting for Zachary's inquiry and, when he didn't ask the obvious question, went on anyway. "Everything stopped ten years ago. No credit information. No signatures on corporate tax filings. No residence information." She paused. "No social media postings."

"Nothing."

"Nothing," she confirmed.

That could only mean one of two things. Either Baker had gone dark, intentionally disappearing and changing his name and identity, or he was dead.

Forget the witness protection program. It was rarely used, and if Baker had been a witness in a big mob trial, Heather would have found records of it in her search.

Either he was dead, or he had covered his trail. Maybe he *was* a pedophile, and he had needed to change his identity and go underground to escape the wrath of a parent or a warrant for his arrest. It was a possibility. If he'd had a legal name change, Heather probably would have been able to find a record of it. If he had ever worked again using his social security number or filed taxes, Heather would have been able to find out. For Baxter to stay below the radar for that length of time, he would have had to work for cash under the table somewhere, using a new name and forged identity papers. Most people found that difficult to do without eventually giving themselves away.

So, dead?

He let that thought simmer for a while. Could Ronnie Baker be dead? If he were, then who had killed him? The parent of a child he had molested? Suicide? Or had he been killed in an "accident" like Edie Dwayne? He had disappeared around the same time as Edie had died. He doubted that was a coincidence. Had someone been trying to quiet witnesses? Had something been happening in Senator Neufeld's campaign office that had to be kept quiet?

"Zachary?"

He focused back in on the phone screen. "Yeah."

"Do you have anywhere else I should look? Do you want me to keep searching?"

"No. Let's leave that one where it is. What about Brent Cousins? Is he still around?"

"He is still a practicing lawyer. Big firm. Seven figures. Crappy credit rating."

"Does he still work for Senator Neufeld?"

"Yeah, it looks like it."

"Anything unusual or concerning in his background? I mean, he's a lawyer, so there could be anything but...?"

"I don't know. I haven't done a lot of backgrounds on lawyers, so maybe it is just me, but... a lot of the articles I can find online that mention him, he is 'no-commenting' about this or that scandal or political decision. I don't know what to think of him. The bios are all positive and recount some of the big cases he has worked on, but most are pretty old. I just get the feeling... they're not quite true. Just puffery."

"That could be. If you think that he's a scoundrel, he probably is."

She gave a little laugh. "You think I have good instincts about people?"

"I do," Zachary agreed, not making light of it. She stopped laughing, made an mmm-hmm noise, and went on.

"So I might still look for more on the lawyer because I think there is more there if I dig down deeply enough. And then there's the senator..."

Kenzie returned from the bedroom and walked into the kitchen. Zachary lowered his voice, not wanting her to know they had gotten onto the subject of work. He was just supposed to be wishing Heather a Merry Christmas.

"What did you find out about the senator?"

"Well, like you said, there is all this public stuff... They control what shows up in the media about him. But there's also... There are threads about him on some message boards and chat rooms. Maybe there are on all politicians. I mean, when you're in the public eye, people are bound to imagine that you're getting into all kinds of trouble even if you are not, right? People don't trust politicians, so they assume the worst motives, think they see things where there are not."

"Yeah, I would guess. Are there any recurring themes?"

"Oh, good question. I guess... there's a lot of stuff about there being a lot of money behind him. Not his own money, I mean. Not family riches. But money that he has raised, for campaigning or other purposes. I did a search, though, and the Secretary of State tracks donations to political campaigns, and they don't show anything suspicious."

"No violations at all?"

"No."

Zachary thought about that. He hadn't been that involved in any political campaigns, but he had worked with some politicians or people involved in fundraising. He had investigated a number of cases of insurance fraud and other financial issues, so he knew a little of how the world of high finance worked.

"Can you compare some of the other campaigns?" he suggested. "I know that in the past... I've worked with people who have accidentally over-contributed to a campaign. They didn't know the legal limit, or they accidentally contributed twice, or two family members both donated and it was flagged as suspicious. It's easy to over-contribute. The candidates just have to refund the monies as soon as they discover the error."

"So it's suspicious if he's *never* had any over-contributions?"

Zachary nodded slowly. "That's what I'm wondering. But I could be off base. Would you check next week, when you're back to work?"

"I'll find out," Heather agreed. "He's an interesting man. Self-made rather than old family money. One of these 'I pulled myself up by my own bootstraps' types."

"Hmm." Zachary thought about his meeting with Neufeld. He had never said anything either way, but Zachary had assumed that he was from old money like most of the politicians he knew of. "How did he make his money? I would expect someone like that to still show some of the signs of coming from the working class. Less expensive suits and watches. Maybe an old car. An old wife."

Mrs. Neufeld looked much younger than her husband, but could have had work done. Which would be another sign that his wealth ran deep, and he wasn't just an upstart.

Heather laughed at this. "I'll look into that. I think he had a construction business."

She didn't seem to clue in to the possibility of "construction business" being the equivalent of "mob ties."

Had Edie gotten herself cross-threaded with someone in the mob? Either the senator himself, or someone who had come into the campaign office to talk to him? The mob could be pretty swift to act, not needing actual proof of any violation. The mere suggestion that Edie would be trouble for the campaign might have been met with swift justice—or injustice.

"Be careful," Zachary warned. "Don't post anything about him or leave any trail. Don't ask anyone any questions. If you look into his business, only do it through the public databases, where you cannot be tracked."

Heather's forehead creased. "Be careful of what?"

"If this guy has ties to organized crime, I don't want him hearing a rumor that you have been asking questions about him. Don't do anything traceable."

"You think he has ties to organized crime?"

"Maybe. I don't want to find out the wrong way."

"Okay." She nodded. "I'll be careful. I'll go incognito, not ask anything in forums, and wipe my trail."

He'd trained her well. Zachary smiled. "Good. Well…" Kenzie came into the room. "Merry Christmas. Hope you have a good day with Grant!"

He turned the phone so that she could see Kenzie as well.

"Merry Christmas, Heather," Kenzie echoed.

Zachary terminated the call.

35

Despite her threats, Kenzie did let Zachary drive the car to Burlington to have dinner with her parents. He'd slept a couple of hours, as she'd suggested, so he was not in danger of falling asleep at the wheel on the way there.

They'd called Mr. Peterson and Pat before leaving. Both seemed well and contented, enjoying the special time together and looking forward to spending some time with Pat's mother and sister, who he had only recently been reconciled with.

Pat's father dying had cleared the way for him to reconnect with his family. Zachary had no idea how Gretta and Suzanne could have agreed not to have any contact with Pat until that point. Pat was a great guy, talented in many areas and very warm and caring, and Zachary didn't see how Pat's father could have bullied everyone into following his dictates just because Pat was gay. As if isolating themselves from him and preaching their bigoted beliefs would somehow convince Pat to give up his identity and return to them at some point, agreeing to align himself with their convictions. They had missed out on a lot of years with a great man.

Kenzie shifted in her seat. She looked at the cars around them, studying them suspiciously, jumping if a car suddenly shot by them. She watched behind them for a few minutes.

"Are you okay?" Zachary asked.

"I'm fine."

"You seem nervous."

"I'm fine," she repeated more firmly.

Zachary looked in the rearview mirror, analyzing and cataloging the vehicles behind them. "We are not being followed," he told her.

Kenzie's head snapped around and she looked at him. "What?"

"You seem concerned that someone might be tailing us. So I told you—there isn't."

Kenzie scowled, looking back over her shoulder again. "There are too many cars. How could you be sure?"

"Experience. Hypervigilance. Being aware of everything going on in the cars around me."

"You can't watch all of them."

He shrugged. "Most of them. Some, I know I don't have to worry about. I can eliminate the cars with families or those that drop back and never speed up again. The ones that take exit ramps and don't show up again further down the road. Vehicles that pass often slow down again later, so I try to stay on top of them. A tail car will often pass, hoping you'll discount it."

Kenzie looked at all the vehicles around them. "You can't keep track of all of these."

He shrugged and stepped on the gas. They zipped past several cars. Zachary kept his speed up for a couple of miles, then slowed to closer to the speed limit and pulled over a couple of lanes. Kenzie's face was white and pinched. She held on to the door handle on her side.

"What are you doing? You're just going to attract attention or get a speeding ticket?"

"Did you see any other cars speed up when we did?"

"No… but they could be hanging back farther."

"Yeah, but once we got out of sight, they would need to speed up to stay with us. And no one did."

"There could be another car following us that you didn't know about."

Zachary shook his head. "You don't need to worry," he assured her. "I've been doing this for a lot of years. It's second nature."

"It isn't like you've never been followed. What about the bomb? Someone followed you home."

"I don't think so. I think she looked through their computer system to see what address they had delivered packages to before."

"She could have followed you."

Zachary sighed. As much as he would like to talk Kenzie into believing him and understanding she was safe, she wasn't going to listen to logic and reason.

He knew how anxiety worked. It didn't matter whether it were logical or not. A fear could be completely nonsensical. That didn't take it away. Once the brain decided something was a danger, no amount of arguing would fix it.

"I'll protect you," he assured her. "You're safe with me."

She pressed her lips together in a thin line. "I don't need protecting. I'm just fine." She shrugged her shoulders, the movement stiff and jerky. "It's the highway on Christmas Day. What's going to happen? As long as you drive safely, nothing is going to happen to us."

"No," Zachary agreed. But he knew she was anxious no matter what she said about it. He couldn't talk her out of it; he couldn't make her feel better, and there was nothing he could do about it. Hopefully, the anxiety she was feeling because of the kidnapping a year before would fall away once they got to her mother's house and Kenzie saw that everyone was okay.

"Do you want the radio on?" he suggested, hoping music might help.

"No."

They drove some time in silence.

"If you want it on, you can put it on," Kenzie told him.

"No, it's okay."

"It won't bother me if you want it on."

Zachary just shook his head. He could zone out with the highway driving, it didn't make any difference to him whether the radio was on or not.

Kenzie reached over and turned it on. She scanned through the stations, finding channel after channel of Christmas music. She finally clicked it off again and looked out the window. Once more, she craned her head around to look behind them and watch the following cars.

It was a long, tense drive. Kenzie didn't seem to mind Zachary driving a little faster than she would usually tolerate, so the trip took less time, but it felt like it took twice as long.

Eventually, they pulled off into the long driveway leading up to the house. Kenzie watched behind them for some time, but no one else turned onto the driveway. She turned around to face forward, and her eyes flicked around the courtyard beside the house for any cars that didn't belong, but there was no one else parked there. Lisa's and Walter's vehicles were in the garage, out of sight, or else Walter wasn't there yet.

Kenzie pasted a smile on her face but didn't look at all happy and relaxed like she should be for a holiday dinner with her family. Zachary hurried around the car to her side to walk her to the door, as her parents would expect him to. He hit the button on his key fob to lock the doors and arm the car several times while they waited for Lisa to answer the door. Kenzie pushed his hand toward his pocket. He pressed it a couple more times while it was in his pocket, though he had to be careful not to hit the wrong button and either unlock the car again or hit the alarm button and irritate everyone with the horn honking. He tugged at his collar and cuffs, uncomfortable in the crisp shirt, tie, and suit.

The door opened. Kenzie's mother nodded graciously to them and pulled the door open the rest of the way to invite them in.

"MacKenzie," she greeted in her melodious voice, and bussed Kenzie's cheeks, "Merry Christmas, my dear!"

Kenzie gave her shoulders a squeeze, but her head was swiveling around. "Merry Christmas, Mom. Is Dad here?"

"Yes, I told you he would be."

Kenzie's shoulders dipped in relief. She glanced over at Zachary, her look warning him to keep any comments about her anxiety to himself. Zachary smiled as reassuringly as he could, giving her a brief nod.

"And Zachary," Lisa turned her attention to him, taking him by the hands first and then pulling him in for a quick hug and a whisper of a kiss across his cheeks. "I'm so glad that you are doing better this year. How are you feeling?"

"Pretty good. Very good for this time of year."

"I'm so glad to hear it."

Zachary bent down to scratch the ears of Lola, the dog that Lisa had saved from being put down in the name of science to further research the novel virus Kenzie had discovered had caused a number of deaths in the area.

"Hi, Lola," he greeted, petting and scratching the dog, who lapped up the attention. "How are you doing? Are you enjoying the holidays too? Does Lola get turkey or any special treats for Christmas?"

"She's always spoiled," Lisa informed him with a repressed smile. "That doesn't stop in the month of December."

Zachary chuckled.

Lisa helped Kenzie off with her coat to reveal the blazer and form-fitting blue dress she was wearing. Lisa's white cocktail gown sparkled under the lights. She handed Kenzie's coat to a maid standing by discreetly. Zachary slid off his coat and handed it to her as well. He pulled in his stomach and straightened and settled the suit, hoping it would become more comfortable, but it still rubbed and chafed like it belonged to someone else.

They walked to the study, where Walter had been sitting by the fire. He stood up and gave Kenzie a hug and peck on the cheek. "Merry Christmas, sweetheart. So glad you could come." He turned to Zachary. "And you too, young man. You don't know how pleased I am that you are feeling better this year. We didn't dare hope that you would be able to come see us today. I'm really glad. For both of you." He looked back at Kenzie.

"Thanks, Dad. Yes, I'm thrilled, too. It's nice to have him home for Christmas. We had a nice Christmas Eve." She looked at Zachary for his confirmation and, maybe, permission to share more about how he had done this year in contrast to previous years.

"It was better than I had even hoped," Zachary contributed. "Not just being able to stay home, but to enjoy some time with Kenzie, too. Even though I have been able to be home other years… it's never very pleasant. Lots of anxiety and… very dark thoughts."

"Is it your meds then, your therapy, or something you did differently this year?" Lisa inquired.

Zachary was trying hard to help shake off the stigma of mental illness by discussing it openly, just as he might if he had a heart condition or a broken bone. He appreciated the effort that Lisa and Walter put into normalizing it. They all knew that it took effort and finesse, but society would never get to the point where it was natural to discuss mental health and illness if some of them didn't push out of their comfort zones to address it.

"I would say it is mostly the meds," Zachary said. "I haven't felt this stable on a med protocol for a long time. Maybe ever. The side effects are not too bad, and it has helped to keep me on an even keel. This time of year is still hard… I am still fighting the depression and anxiety and being able to see beyond… the season."

"And he's been doing therapy, and our couple's therapy, and he's done better about taking anxiety pills or sleep aids when he needs them," Kenzie contributed, making sure they knew that Zachary was working on it proactively as well. "He really does work hard to stay…" She shook her head, losing track of the word she wanted to use.

"Sane?" Zachary suggested with a laugh. Walter and Lisa laughed as well, and the conversation moved on. Walter acted as the barman, offering Zachary a Coke and the ladies their usual drinks.

Dinner with Kenzie's family always felt like a bit of an ordeal. Zachary was very conscious of everything he did and whether he had acted appropriately or might have done something to embarrass Kenzie or his hosts. It was a long, drawn-out affair with pre-dinner drinks and conversation, followed by each course of the meal and postprandial drinks or coffee. Walter and Lisa were very good at dinner conversation and did not allow any long, awkward pauses, but Zachary always felt exhausted by the time it was finished.

He wasn't sure how he was going to feel after a sleepless night and his concern over Kenzie's anxiety. She seemed to be relaxing somewhat, relieved to see her father there and apparently in good health. She had tried to explain to Zachary how she had felt when she had arrived the previous year to find her mother there with a stranger, and Walter conspicuously absent. It had been very awkward and uncertain, with things only getting worse as Kenzie had been unable to raise any response from her father and Lisa had refused to explain what was going on.

The glass of wine in Kenzie's hand was probably helping. She didn't drink much but occasionally had a glass or two of wine when she was feeling particularly stressed. She would probably nurse the glass of wine most of the evening, and she was, he assumed, planning on Zachary driving home, so she didn't need to worry about her blood alcohol level.

After some time talking over drinks, they moved into the dining room, and the catering staff Lisa had engaged for the evening bussed the lavish dinner dishes to the table.

"So, are you working on anything interesting right now?" Walter asked Zachary.

"Well, I am working on an interesting case right now," Zachary said, "but nothing I can really talk about. You know how it is." He shrugged.

Walter dealt with politicians all the time; he certainly knew how some matters had to be handled with discretion. Walter nodded. "Of course, of course."

"I met someone you might know the other day," Zachary said, as if it were an entirely different matter. "Do you know Senator Neufeld?"

"Oh yes, of course," Walter agreed. He raised his brows at Zachary as he put a small slice of turkey on his plate. "How long has he been senator now? About ten years?"

"Yes, about that."

"So, not really the newcomer anymore but, of course, that's how people think of him. Not from one of the old Vermont families, he's bound to be considered an upstart. We're not always kind to newcomers around here."

"You don't know anything about his family?" Zachary asked.

"The family he came from? No, nothing. I have met his wife, of course. I don't know whether they plan to have any children."

"Children?" Kenzie echoed. "How old is his wife?"

"Just a young thing," Walter said, and looked at Zachary. "Thirty? Maybe thirty-five?"

Zachary nodded, though he really had no idea. He had been unsure whether Mrs. Neufeld was young or if she just looked that way.

"Oh, okay." Kenzie nodded.

There was a glance from Lisa to Kenzie. Zachary wouldn't have wanted to put it into words, but he suspected it had something to do with Lisa wondering whether Kenzie was planning to provide her with grandchildren. Kenzie was reaching that age at which she needed to make a decision before it was too late. Zachary thought she was somewhat open to the idea of children, but she certainly hadn't suggested she was ready to "try."

Kenzie glared at her mother and then at Zachary, as if he had been encouraging discussion of children and her fertility. Zachary lifted his hands in silent protest. He hadn't said anything about her having children, or even mentioned the possibility of the senator possibly having children. That had been Walter.

"I think he was in the concrete business," Walter said, speaking about the senator. "Maybe construction, too." He met Zachary's eyes, saying nothing but warning him with his eyes.

Zachary nodded. "That's what I heard. Heather was doing a little background, and—" He suddenly realized that he had given away that the senator was part of his case, and broke off. He cleared his throat. "It's always interesting to hear where people came from."

"It is," Walter agreed. He rubbed his chin, considering. "You ought to be careful of those Italians." He tapped the side of his nose.

"Neufeld?" Kenzie said. "That doesn't sound Italian."

"German, I think," Walter confirmed. "But there have been Neufelds associated with Italy."

Kenzie shook her head as if she had no idea what he was talking about. And it was probably best to keep things that way. If she thought Walter was warning Zachary against getting involved with powerful, possibly mob-connected politicians, her anxiety level was not going to continue to go down.

"He worked a few years ago with a lawyer named Cousins," Zachary said, figuring that if Walter was familiar with Senator Neufeld, he might as well get any additional information he could. There was a lot of word-of-mouth that Heather was not going to be able to access as she worked on the senator's background. If Walter was tuned in to those sources, Zachary might as well benefit from them. "Brent Cousins."

"Brent Cousins," Walter echoed, his tone going up. He laid down his fork beside his plate. "I didn't know Neufeld had anything to do with Brent Cousins."

"That's the rumor. Back when he was campaigning ten years ago he was Neufeld's lawyer."

Walter dabbed at his lips with his cloth napkin. He had barely touched anything on his plate. Kenzie had been worried about Walter's weight loss over the last year. Was he sick or just watching what he ate? He had been overweight before, but was trim and healthy-looking now. He didn't look like someone who was sick or had lost weight due to chemotherapy or something of that nature.

"Cousins is what we in the business would call a black hat," Walter said slowly. "I wouldn't accuse him of doing anything criminal or unethical, but I would be concerned about being associated too closely with him. There are some people you just don't want to get mixed up with."

Kenzie looked back and forth between Zachary and her father.

"What's this all about?" she asked. "We're not supposed to be talking business over Christmas dinner. Look at everything Mom had prepared for us today. Don't ruin it with talk about politicians and what color of hat they wear."

Walter gave a rumbling laugh. He sipped his drink and then stabbed a couple of creamed baby potatoes. "Everything looks fabulous, Lisa. As it always does."

"You would think that I cooked it myself," Lisa said in a teasing, confidential tone to Zachary, leaning toward him slightly. "Walter knows very well I didn't cook a thing at this table."

"But you ordered it," Zachary returned. "That takes skill."

"It does indeed," Lisa agreed. "Now MacKenzie is right—no more shop talk at the table. This is too good to waste with talk about unsavory characters. You have three hundred and sixty-four other days to do that."

Zachary nodded his head. "Yes, ma'am."

Lisa and Kenzie steered the rest of the dinner conversation away from work, not even discussing the family foundation, which they had been trying to get Kenzie more involved in.

After dinner and apple pie, they retired to the library for a tiny cup of coffee and more conversation. Zachary was wishing for a bigger or stronger cup of coffee, feeling sluggish and foggy after the big meal. He walked around the library looking at the titles on the spines of the book as if he might be interested in reading one of them, when nothing could be further from the truth. Put one of those big volumes in his lap in one of the buttery-soft leather chairs in the library, and he would be asleep in thirty seconds.

He caught a movement out of the corner of his eye and saw Kenzie reaching for her phone. She caught herself and looked at her parents, trying to decide whether to incur their wrath. She pulled the phone from her blazer pocket and looked at the screen.

"I'm sorry; I hope you'll excuse me for a minute," Kenzie said, turning her back to them and putting the phone up to her ear as she walked out into the hallway where she would have more privacy to speak to the caller.

36

Walter's and Lisa's eyes followed Kenzie out of the room. Lisa raised a penciled eyebrow, clearly not impressed by Kenzie taking a call when her attention was supposed to be on them. It was Christmas Day with her family, a day that only came once a year. They were trying to spend more time together, getting to know each other better as independent adults. Forgiving past wrongs and misunderstandings.

Conversation didn't resume immediately after Kenzie left the room. They were all a little awkward dealing with each other in her absence. Zachary was still just learning who these people were and how to deal with them. And there were dangers in dealing with Walter without Kenzie present, as he often had an agenda of his own that wasn't apparent to Zachary.

Zachary caught a couple of phrases from Kenzie's conversation in the hallway. Startled, he glanced at Walter.

"Is that a work call?" Walter asked in surprise. "I didn't think she was on call today."

"She shouldn't be getting any callouts," Zachary confirmed. Not unless there was a catastrophic event. Or if something else unexpected happened. The last time Kenzie had been called in on a day she was supposed to have off, it was because Dr. Wiltshire had broken his hand and was unable to go to a scene that, for political reasons, required immediate personal attention. It wasn't one of those routine cases where the medical examiner's office could attend the scene virtually via video chat and clear the scene that way.

"She's talking to Dr. Wiltshire," Walter insisted.

Zachary nodded. And that in itself was odd, because Dr. Wiltshire was still on medical leave waiting for his hand to heal. Dr. Cook was standing in for him, and had assured Kenzie that she would not have to come in on Christmas Day.

"Maybe he's just calling to say Merry Christmas," Lisa suggested.

That was a possibility. He and Kenzie were pretty close. But Kenzie's tone hadn't sounded like it was just a holiday greeting. She sounded concerned. But maybe that was natural. She was still worried that his hand might be too badly injured for him to return as the medical examiner.

The call only lasted for a few minutes, but Walter, Lisa, and Zachary were unable to get another conversation going while they waited for Kenzie to return.

Eventually, Kenzie said goodbye and returned to the library. She shot Zachary a look that he couldn't interpret, then smiled reassuringly at everyone.

"Everything is fine," she said lightly.

"Was that Dr. Wiltshire?" Walter demanded..

Kenzie nodded. "Yes. Just called to say Merry Christmas."

"You want to be careful about having a personal relationship with him," Walter warned.

Kenzie frowned, her brows drawing down. "What? What are you talking about? It's not a *personal* relationship," she said, with another look at Zachary as if he might be upset by this. "It's a professional relationship. He's my boss."

"Not right now. Right now he is on leave."

Kenzie rolled her eyes. "He's still my boss. Dr. Cook is only temporary. I still need to talk to Dr. Wiltshire sometimes. If I have something I need him to look at. To keep him up to date on an ongoing case, to ask questions or ask for input on a complicated situation."

"That's Dr. Cook's responsibility."

"Dr. Cook is a young doctor. He doesn't have the same experience as Dr. Wiltshire. Sometimes I need more than Dr. Cook can provide. Or I want a second opinion." Kenzie shook her head. "I don't see how it concerns you. Why would you care?"

"I care about anything that could affect the health or safety of my daughter."

They were all silent for a moment, considering this. Zachary exchanged looks with Kenzie. Her health or safety? How could talking to Dr. Wiltshire on the phone about an ongoing case or to wish him a Merry Christmas have to do with Kenzie's health or safety?

"Dad," Kenzie protested, "what are you talking about? How could talking to Dr. Wiltshire hurt me?"

"Dr. Wiltshire has enemies," Walter said slowly. "A fact which should be obvious to you from the nature of his injury."

Kenzie blinked at him. "The nature of his injury? What do you mean by that? He broke his hand."

"How?"

"Well… I don't know. He hasn't actually told me about it. He implied that it was sustained while golfing."

"Golfing," Walter repeated.

"Well, he hasn't said exactly how. I imagine that it's just as easy to hurt your hand while golfing as it is punching a wall. You get frustrated and swing into a tree. Or something happens with one of the golf carts, or tripping and falling, catching himself wrong."

"Is that the kind of injury he had? Punching a wall and trying to catch yourself from a fall wouldn't give you the same kind of injury, would they?"

"Well, no," Kenzie admitted. "Punching a wall would likely give you boxer's fractures, and catching yourself from a fall maybe a broken wrist, depending on how you caught yourself."

Walter looked at her and didn't push the question further. Kenzie shook her head. "His injury looks more like a crush injury.

Not that I examined his x-rays. That's just from seeing the bruises and the external fixator the surgeon put him in."

"A crush injury. From golfing."

"He still could have swung into a tree or had an accident with a golf cart. Maybe somebody ran over it. He said it was too embarrassing to talk about, I got the feeling it was sort of a freak accident."

She and Zachary had talked about it a couple of times. Zachary remembered how angry she had been when Dr. Cook had said that it was rumored to have been inflicted by a debt collector for some gambling debt. She insisted that she had never known Dr. Wiltshire to show any interest in sports, poker, or casinos. She was sure that he was not a gambling addict.

So how had he sustained the injury? A fall? An accident? A baseball bat?

Kenzie put her hands on her hips, confronting her father angrily. "So just how do *you* think he broke his hand?" she demanded. "Since you seem to know all about it."

"I don't know for sure," Walter said, "but I understand he has been mixed up with some… unsavory types."

Kenzie continued to glare at him. "Some unsavory types," she repeated. "What, you mean like the unsavory types you were mixed up with a year ago? The Russians?"

A shocked silence followed the accusation. Walter did not turn red and shout at Kenzie. That wasn't in his nature. Whether he was angry or not, Zachary couldn't tell. But he was definitely affected by what she had said. From what Kenzie had told him, Walter had agreed to help the Russians by lobbying against a bill in the legislature. But when he realized they were organized crime, he had tried to back out, resulting in Kenzie being kidnapped as leverage against him. And it had worked, as within hours he had agreed to do whatever it was they wanted him to.

Walter walked over to the sideboard and poured himself two fingers of Scotch, even though they had all been drinking after-dinner coffees rather than alcohol.

"Yes," he said eventually. "That's exactly what I mean."

Kenzie stared at him. She had turned as pale as a ghost. "You don't mean to say that Dr. Wiltshire is mixed up with the Russians?"

He sipped his drink. "You don't think so?"

"No," Kenzie protested faintly. "He couldn't be. He would never do anything for those mobsters."

"You've never seen him buckle to political pressure? You've never had any leaks or irregularities associated with the Medical Examiner's Office?"

She shook her head, but she didn't say no. Zachary knew she'd had some concerns over the past year or two. Some of them had been related to Dr. Wiltshire, and some of them had only been attributable to "a leak," but there were too many possible sources of the leak for them to narrow down who had been leaking information. Kenzie shook her head, unable to believe that Dr. Wiltshire could be responsible for anything questionable.

But that hand injury.

She had told Zachary about how bad it was; how ugly the bruising and how extensive the surgery required to try to repair it. Although Kenzie was hopeful Wiltshire would be able to rehabilitate his hand after the bones had all healed, he could hear the doubt in her voice. The worry that he would never again be able to return to the work he loved. He had been a mentor to her, and Kenzie hated the thought of his being forced into retirement due to the injury.

"If the Russians were the ones who injured his hand, then that means he was *not* cooperating with them," Kenzie pointed out. She swallowed and stared at Walter, waiting for his reaction.

Walter nodded his agreement.

A mixture of emotions washed over Kenzie's face. She eyed the glass in Walter's hand and, although Zachary had never seen her drink anything but a glass of wine or bottle of beer, he was sure she was considering asking him to pour her a glass of Scotch as well.

37

"I can't believe that Dr. Wiltshire would have anything to do with the Russians," Kenzie said in the car on the way home, shaking her head.

"Well, like you said, if they punished or tortured him by breaking his hand, that means he wasn't doing what they wanted him to."

"But the leaks and other things… he must have responded to pressure before. Then he tried to stop. Told them no, he wouldn't go any further."

Zachary pursed his lips. "Maybe," he agreed, "or maybe not. That could have been their first attempt to get him to work with them."

"But if Dad thought that he had already been working for them before or had heard rumors of him being involved… I mean, he *is* the one who would know. He's the one who is in that world."

Zachary grunted. She might have a point there.

"And someone in the medical examiner's office has been leaking information," Kenzie said. "Or maybe in the police department. It's hard to know which because information passes back and forth between them."

"But Dr. Wiltshire might have been trying to plug the leak rather than being the one leaking the information."

Kenzie shook her head in frustration. "Why wouldn't he just go to the police? And why wouldn't he go to them about his injury if he wasn't working for the Russians? Why would the Russians injure him instead of killing him, unless they had enough leverage over him to know that he wouldn't go to the police and could be persuaded to keep working for them?"

"Well…" Zachary gave up on trying to find a way to excuse Wiltshire or to show that they might be unjustly assuming he had been doing something illegal or unethical. "Okay. Maybe."

They drove in silence for a while.

"Why did he call you?" Zachary asked eventually. "Was it really just to say Merry Christmas?"

"Why else would he call me?" Kenzie snapped back.

"Okay. I just wondered… you gave me a look when you came back from talking to him. Like you had something to tell me, or I had done something wrong."

She slumped back in her seat, rubbing her head. She groaned. "I do not want to get caught in the middle of all this stuff. I don't. Why do the Russians have to come here, thinking that they can run everything the way that they want and get wealthy off slave labor, illegal drugs, and cryptocurrency?"

"Because they can," Zachary suggested.

Kenzie moaned again.

"Okay," she said eventually. "He did call for a reason other than just to wish me a Merry Christmas, but I was not going to bring it up in front of Walter."

Zachary swallowed. He focused on the dark road ahead of him, trying to get his brain to stay focused on that rather than worrying about what Dr. Wiltshire had called about. He wanted Kenzie to say it was just one of her cases, but he knew by how she had looked at him after the call that it was not. It was something far more personal.

"It's about *your* case," Kenzie said. "About you asking questions about something that is 'none of your business.'"

"I only ask questions about cases that I am paid to investigate. That means it literally is my business. My business is sticking my nose where it is sometimes not wanted."

"Well, congratulations, then. You've done a great job," she said sarcastically.

Zachary took a deep breath, held it, and let it out slowly. He couldn't let her anxiety and anger over whatever had happened to Dr. Wiltshire take over his mood. They were separate people. She could be angry without his taking it personally or getting angry as well.

"So that was the message? Stop poking my nose into other people's business?"

Kenzie nodded. "He heard something about you asking questions about Senator Neufeld and his people. Wanted to make sure that you knew that there are some heavy hitters associated with the senator who would not appreciate you implying that the senator or anyone associated with him is involved in anything shady."

Zachary tapped his steering wheel as he drove. "Except that making threats that indicate he does have something to do with organized crime implicates him rather than clearing him of suspicion."

Kenzie gave a laugh. "Yeah. Figure that one out. 'If you keep implying that the senator has something to do with leg breakers, we're going to break your legs.'"

Zachary chuckled. He pretended that it was all a joke, something silly, not something to be concerned about. The call had come from Dr. Wiltshire, who was not a threat to him. The Russians would not show up at Kenzie's house looking for him. The senator and his people did not know where Zachary lived. He was already taking all the appropriate precautions to ensure no one could follow him, and he had good security for his car and the house. They had been through enough before that they had learned what lengths they needed to go to in order to protect themselves. Zachary even had an explosives sniffer now, to be used to check out any deliveries, expected or unexpected, before opening them.

But despite his assurances to his conscious mind, his primitive brain was already looking for danger. Had they been followed? Who knew that they had been at Lisa's house? Kenzie had probably told Dr. Wiltshire where they were.

He couldn't just breathe away the tight knot of anxiety that formed in his stomach, taking up all the space previously occupied by Christmas dinner and threatening to expel it. He knew that his security systems were not as foolproof as he would like to think. They had been circumvented before. He was still healing from the multitude of small cuts received when the small package bomb had blown up. A year ago, Kenzie had been kidnapped off the street when she had gotten out of her car. Zachary, too, had been abducted by someone who knew where to find him when he was nowhere near Kenzie's house.

No one was safe from random attacks. Even the protection forces surrounding kings and presidents could be breached.

"Are you okay?" Kenzie asked after a long period of silence.

They were almost home. Soon, they would be back to the house, and they would both feel safer indoors with their security alarm armed. It was hardwired to the security company. No matter what happened, they would be alerted to anything happening at the house and would be there within minutes.

"Um, yeah. I'm fine," Zachary assured her. "It's, um, something to think about, but I don't think we have anything to worry about. I'm not investigating the senator; he was just adjacent to the investigation. I went to him directly. I wasn't sneaking around asking other people about him. We talked, and he seemed perfectly okay with that."

"You're not investigating him?"

He *hadn't* been. He hadn't actually thought that the senator had had anything to do with Edie Dwayne's death. Now, what was he to think? Who had the senator called when Zachary had left there? Or had someone else called in the big guns to complain about Zachary's investigation? Could it have been anyone but Senator Neufeld? Could he be beyond reproach and someone else was protecting him or directing operations around his senatorship without his knowledge?

"I'm... I asked him some questions and Heather was going to look a little bit into his background." He didn't tell her that Heather had already been running background. How could anyone know about that? Zachary had already walked Heather through what she needed to do to remain anonymous on the internet searches. Had she logged into a database that had required Zachary's username? Something that the Russians were party to?

"Your dad said it was the Russians, right?" he asked Kenzie. "It is definitely the Russians that Wiltshire got mixed up with?"

Kenzie considered, reviewing the conversation in her head. "I'm not sure he did," she said finally. "I'm sure that was what he meant, but I'm not sure he said it explicitly."

"Could it have been another crime cartel? Someone *like* the Russians but not the Russians?"

"I have no idea." She shook her head. "I don't think so. Does it matter? What difference does it make?"

"It doesn't, I guess... It's just good to know your enemy. I want to know who Neufeld is in bed with, and you don't find that kind of thing in a database. You don't want to know who Dr. Wiltshire is colluding with?"

She grunted something he didn't hear clearly, but he didn't really need to. Kenzie was probably feeling overwhelmed. She had already been worried about her dad and about the Russians who had kidnapped her and maybe him the previous year. It couldn't have done her good to hear that Dr. Wiltshire had been injured by them and was passing messages on for them.

"You saw him, didn't you?" Zachary asked.

Kenzie turned her head to look at him, even though it was dark and she probably couldn't see his face any better than he could see hers, hidden in the shadows.

"Dr. Wiltshire?" she asked doubtfully, unsure what he was asking. She must have thought him completely off his head. He knew very well that she had been talking to Dr. Wiltshire on the phone; she had not seen him face to face.

"No, I mean..." He tried to remember all of what she had told him about all that had happened to her while he had been in the hospital. She hadn't told him anything while he'd been in the psych ward. Hadn't spilled a word of what had happened to her while he'd been trying to get back on track and adjust to the new medications they had put him on. "I mean, you saw the oligarch, didn't you? You saw the guy in charge of the Russian cartel?"

"Yes." She sounded like she was speaking through gritted teeth. "What difference does that make?"

"You can identify him."

"I didn't see him do anything illegal. I just saw a Russian at the hotel. I knew that's who he was, but I don't have any proof. I don't know his name or where he moved his base to after the hotel was quarantined." She thumped her head back against the headrest. "I basically have nothing," she told him. "And he knows what I look like, where I work, and apparently how to put pressure on me."

Zachary put his hand lightly on her knee. Rather than swiping it away, she put her hand on top of his and intertwined their fingers. Neither said anything. Zachary knew there was nothing he could say that would make her feel better. What was he supposed to do? Promise to take care of her? She knew he would do his very best to protect her, no matter what it cost him. But that didn't make him stronger than the Russian mob.

"This has been a great Christmas," Kenzie growled.

Zachary sighed and didn't argue with her.

38

It would have made sense for Zachary to drop the investigation. He could call Oliver and say that he had run into nothing but dead ends and didn't have anything else to pursue in connection with Edie's death. Presume that it must have been just what Sheriff Taylor said—an accidental shooting out on a lonely road where Edie Dwayne had been sitting in her car by herself, waiting... for what?

If he did that, would it change anything? It wouldn't heal Dr. Wiltshire's broken hand. It wouldn't heal the trauma that Kenzie felt in the wake of her abduction, or what Walter had suffered, whether he himself had also been kidnapped or just had to make a deal with his daughter's kidnappers to buy her freedom.

It wouldn't change the fact that Jeff, Terry, and Marissa had grown up without their mother and that Oliver now sat by the fireplace alone.

And in all likelihood, it wouldn't change whether the Russians thought Zachary needed to be taught a lesson. Either they would come after him or they would not. Would they wait to see if he did as he was counseled and stay out of it? Probably not. If the warning had come from Dr. Wiltshire personally rather than the Russians, a call made out of his affection for Kenzie and concern for what would happen if Zachary continued to investigate, then the Russians knew nothing about the warning. They would not be waiting to see if it made him back off. They might be watching to see who he talked to after his visit to the senator, but they would not know what other steps he was taking.

There was no way they would know what research Heather was doing or if Zachary had found anything in the boxes of personal items from Oliver's house. They probably didn't even know that Heather did work for him.

Zachary had not seen anyone following him when he had come back from Oliver's. And no one had followed him to Oliver's or had any reason to think that Oliver would have a stack of papers to give to Zachary. They knew Zachary had talked to the senator because someone at his office or in his network of friends and allies had passed the word along. That was what had triggered the report to the Russians and Dr. Wiltshire's warning to back off.

As long as Zachary didn't go back to the senator's office or talk to anyone in his circles about what had happened to Edie Dwayne, he would be safe. The senator and the Russians would have no idea what he was doing and would think he had gone quiet.

So Zachary was confident that retrieving the boxes from the trunk of his car was safe and would not have any dangerous repercussions.

He waited until after Kenzie had left the house, promising she would only be at the Medical Examiner's office for a couple of hours. He didn't want to have to explain the logic of his actions to her. He *might* have left her with the impression that he wasn't going to investigate any further. He had not shared any identifying names from the case with her when he had described it, always mindful of keeping his clients' names and business confidential, so she would not think anything when she saw the boxes with Edie Dwayne's name on them.

Kenzie wouldn't know what case he was investigating. And if she thought it was just paperwork, she wouldn't be worried that it was something that would spur the Russians into action. *Not*

telling her anything about what he was doing would be more reassuring than explaining his actions.

Zachary started with an overview of the boxes, setting them all
out on the floor and removing the lids. He wanted to make sure
that there wasn't any mold or rodent damage to any paperwork in
the boxes, and he wanted to see how much paper there was to go
through. Oliver hadn't had much recollection of what was in the
boxes he had put away ten years before. It could all just be clothes
and old college textbooks, with no personal filing, journals, or
anything else that would be helpful to the investigation.

If that were the case, he intended to simply catalog everything
for Oliver. He would ensure it was all neatly sorted, put back away,
and labeled. In the future, if Oliver wanted to look at the boxes, or
if his children wanted to see what their mother had left behind, it
would be easy to find. It was the least Zachary could do for Edie
Dwayne, especially if he were not able to find anything that led to
her killer.

Zachary opened the boxes and the smell of old, dusty papers
rose to his nose. He was pleased to see that at least half of the space
in the boxes was filled with files, printed pictures, scrapbooks, and
books that might be journals. A treasure trove of information. He
dumped everything out of the boxes and refilled them first with the
non-paper items, taking inventory and pictures of the items as he
loaded them up. With the unimportant items out of the way, he
was left with several stacks of files, papers, pictures, and books. He
remembered how long it had taken him to go through all the
personal records on the Godfrey file, and there hadn't been
anywhere near as much. He needed to pare it down or make it
more manageable. He tried to sort the papers, pictures, and notebooks into rough chronological order.

The files were ordered by subject rather than date. Zachary did
not need to look through everything. Just the subjects that might
relate to the campaign office or other areas of Edie's life where she
might have run afoul of someone violent. Somehow, he didn't think
that her children's report cards or utility statements would be

important in the case. No one had shot Edie over homework or electricity usage.

That pared down the information that Zachary had to process considerably. But there was still a lot of work to be done.

Zachary knew his ability to read and process written information was much more limited than the ability of a computer system to do the same thing. Especially where cursive writing was involved, and all the notebooks were filled with Edie's well-formed, flowing handwriting.

The best thing to do was to use his tools. Zachary didn't have a dedicated scanner, so he used his phone, carefully taking a picture of each page of the notebooks, relevant files, and loose papers directly into a data processing app he paid a monthly subscription fee for. He opened a new vault and started scanning all the information in. The software would OCR all the information it could, both text and handwriting, and he would be able to search for particular terms, which was much more efficient than trying to read through all the papers and books stacked in front of him. Even at his best pace, it would take him several days to separate documents that might be important from those that were not.

He turned the TV on so that he would have something to watch and listen to while he was doing the tedious work of scanning the information into his database one page at a time.

It was afternoon before he had scanned all the information into his phone. He nursed a headache, gritty eyes, and a sore wrist from holding the phone steady through the repetitive scanning. He needed to invest in a dedicated scanner that he could just run stacks of paper through. And maybe one of those setups that could scan the pages of a book, too. He had enough money in the bank to invest in some equipment to make his life a bit easier.

39

"You look like you've been busy," Kenzie commented, coming in from the kitchen. Zachary evaluated her quickly, wondering whether he had been so intent on what he was doing that he had not even noticed her return. But she was just hanging up her coat, so she had just arrived home.

"Hey." Zachary looked at his phone to see what time it was. "You were longer than you expected to be."

"I was," Kenzie acknowledged. "But you don't look like you missed me."

"Of course I missed you… I've just been busy."

She nodded. "What's all of this?"

"Paperwork," Zachary told her vaguely. "Some stuff I've been needing to catalog."

"Well, I don't know about spending your holiday doing something like that, but…"

"Is spending the holiday with dead people better?" Zachary asked.

Kenzie laughed. "Well… I guess that depends on your perspective. My work was probably more interesting than yours was… but mine was more messy."

She brushed her hands together as if trying to rid them of dust. "I'm going to have a nice long shower. Then maybe a movie together? If you're just cataloging, you probably don't mind watching a movie at the same time?"

"Not at all. In fact, that's what I've been doing." He nodded toward the TV.

"Good. Sounds like a plan."

After scanning all the books and papers he had set aside, Zachary transferred them with care into a box, keeping them in date order. Then he sat at his computer and typed search terms into the vault.

One of the program's benefits was that even if it had not finished indexing a vault, he could tell it what to look for, and it would scan for just those letter shapes, looking for a match.

All the hits for Neufeld were either mismatches or just routine entries in Edie's notebook. It looked like she'd kept notes of what she was doing throughout the day in a hardback journal. But the notes were composed of a few keywords, sometimes with dates, times, or dollar amounts. Enough to trigger Edie's memory of something she was supposed to do or a message she was supposed to pass on to someone else in the office, but not enough for Zachary to understand what she had been writing about, and when it was something related to work and when it was something for her family or to do with a call from the school.

He searched for other possible trigger terms:

- Russia
- Bill
- Cryptocurrency
- Oligarch

He even tried some names that he hoped not to find in the vault:

- Kirsch
- Maxim

• Wiltshire

Nothing was turning up any useful results.

Maybe Edie hadn't found anything. Maybe it *was* just an accident. Maybe he was looking for ghosts where there were none.

"What is it?" Kenzie asked, turning to look at Zachary.

"Huh? Sorry, what?"

"What's with all the sighing and grumbling? You sound like a bored dog."

"Oh." Zachary's cheeks warmed. "I didn't realize I was doing that. Sorry."

She glanced at his screen but didn't lean in closer to see what he was trying to search. "You're not finding what you're looking for?"

"No. I didn't know if I would. I wasn't sure whether there was anything in there to find."

She raised her brows. "Why not just skim through to see if the type of information you needed was here, instead of processing everything before you were even sure?"

Zachary shifted uncomfortably. "I can't just skim through it," he told her. "It would take me longer to do that than to scan the pages."

"Oh." Kenzie thought about that. "Well... okay, I guess that makes sense."

"Best to use the tools at my disposal."

"Yeah. I didn't even think about you not even being able to skim through the papers to find what you were looking for. I've seen you process paperwork before, like the stuff you did in the Bircher kidnapping case, that took a lot of detailed compilation to sort out."

"Detailed," Zachary agreed. "Comparing each line on the logs and cross-referencing them. Not skimming."

"Isn't the detailed work harder?"

Zachary thought about it and tried to figure out how to explain it to her in a way that would make sense.

"In a log or list... each line and each field is equal in importance. You have to read each one with the same care and attention."

"Yes, sure," Kenzie agreed.

"But when you are reading a book full of random notes, or a file, or a journal… all the words don't have equal importance. Neither does each page. Or each file."

"What do you mean?"

"In school, when I was working with the resource room teacher…" Zachary's ears got hot at his admission that he was one of the stupid kids who needed extra help and attention from the resource room. The kids at school hadn't stopped at calling him stupid. They'd always had much more inflammatory words for those who were too stupid to get by in the normal classes.

"Uh-huh," Kenzie prompted when Zachary stalled, thrown back into his feelings of anger and inadequacy over his inability to perform at school.

"She taught me to skim textbooks by looking at the bolded headings. Not all the text on the page, but the black headlines."

"Right," Kenzie agreed, nodding.

"So those words were more important than the other, non-bolded text."

"Yes," Kenzie agreed again. "That makes sense."

"And she taught me to look at the captions for the photos and charts to see what they were talking about, because it was easier for me to understand what was going on if I could put pictures together with the words on the page."

"Uh-huh."

"And then if I was trying to answer a question in the textbook about what was in the chapter…" Zachary sighed, remembering how hard it was to go through each step to find the information he then needed to copy into his notebook with his stilted, awkward handwriting. "After I found the right heading, I didn't want to read all the text, because it took a long time, and I was only looking for one small piece. So I would take the longest word from the question and try to find it in the section."

"And that sentence would hopefully contain your answer," Kenzie offered.

"Yeah. And if not that one, then the next one…"

"Right."

"That's skimming. Or scanning. They are different, but I don't remember how."

"Sounds like a good skill to have," Kenzie encouraged. "Good for your teacher for walking you through it."

"But in these papers," Zachary motioned to the piles of papers and books, "Every word and sentence is of equal importance. I have to read every word on every page to see if it has something to do with my case. I can't read just one sentence per page or look for one word on every page in these hundreds of pages. But the computer system can do that. It can show me wherever that word shows up."

"Huh." Kenzie nodded. "I see. Skimming comes easily to me, because I can pick out a few words on a page to check its relevance without having to read every single word."

Zachary nodded. That was a process that seemed like magic to him. Being able to snapshot the page with her brain and then just look for the most important information on the page or quickly process it to see what it was about. How did someone do that without reading every letter of every word on every page?

"Well, sorry you didn't find what you were looking for," Kenzie sympathized. "That's a lot of work to do and come up empty." She looked at the boxes. "Did you have to scan everything in all of these boxes?"

"No, they weren't all papers. With the files, I just pulled the important files based on the folder's subject."

"Ah, that's good."

Zachary looked at the box of files he had skipped. Would it be worth scanning all those papers on the chance that they might contain what he was looking for? He pursed his lips, thinking about the process.

"So if you were skimming these files," he said slowly, "would you be able to tell quickly if the files were all what they said they were or if there were any papers on another topic mixed in with them?"

"Well, yes. Sure."

Zachary could pull out any pages from the utilities folder that were not the same bill format as the rest. He could find anomalies like that. But to be able to quickly flip through a file and see if all the letters were on the topic they were supposed to be was something that would be a long and painstaking search for him.

He raised his brows at Kenzie, wondering how she felt about spending time doing research the day after Christmas.

40

"Okay," Kenzie said, pulling a handful of files out of the box and looking at the labels on top. "This looks like typical household maintenance stuff: bills, repairs, kids' school stuff…"

Zachary nodded. "That's why I didn't think any of it was relevant. But if there are things in the folders that are not what it says they are…"

"Do you really think that's a possibility?" Kenzie opened the first folder and leafed through it. She put it aside and opened the next one.

"I don't know. Probably not. Why would she think she had to hide the nature of papers in her own filing system? Who did she think was going to be in her house looking at it? Her husband didn't even look at it when she died. He just started his own filing system."

"Did she know she was in danger? Did she think that someone might be looking for it?"

"I have no idea what she thought. To find that out, I would have to read all of this." Zachary gestured to the pile of notebooks and other papers he had already scanned.

Kenzie looked at the pile for a second, then back down at the files she had pulled out. "Well, let's see. It will only take a few minutes to look."

Zachary watched Kenzie leaf through each file in sequence, looking for anything that was out of place or not what it appeared to be. He marveled at her ability to quickly scan and process each page. Was it all just for show? Could she really know what was on each page without reading through it carefully? It wouldn't take her as long as it would take him, of course, but she seemed to be able to take in the whole page in a glance, taking less than a second per page.

He might have to employ her in some of his other cases. What would be a full day's work for him might take her only an hour. Or ten minutes. If Heather could do the same thing, then he needed to give her more of his work to preview. She could narrow down what he needed to look at.

Kenzie frowned and paused, looking at the backside of a page. Zachary watched her eyes go back and forth as she leaned in and read the page more carefully. He waited for her to decide it was nothing and keep going, but she shook her head and held it out to him.

"This does not look like homework or a report card."

Zachary flipped it to look at the other side, which was a picture apparently drawn by Jeff. He looked at the side Kenzie had been studying. A list of numbers. Dollar signs. Donations to the campaign, he decided.

"Edie took her son to the office with her sometimes," he explained. "When it was a professional day at the school and she still needed to be there. He liked to play office while he was there. I guess she gave him some recycling paper to draw on while he was there."

Kenzie nodded. She was looking at the back of the next page in the folder. She pulled it out and handed it to him. More donations. A woman's handwriting next to the list, pointing to a couple of the larger donations.

Where are these?

Deposited into wrong account?

Zachary looked at the numbers again and reached for his phone to scan them. Kenzie looked at the next page in the folder and handed it to him again.

Each page had Jeff's pictures on the front and campaign print-outs on the back, sometimes with handwritten notations, which he could only assume had been made by Edie. In some cases, there was a second comment made by a different hand responding to a query Edie had made.

There were six pages in total. Zachary took pictures of the front and back of each, thinking about what he read. He opened the web browser on his phone and started searching, then decided he needed a bigger screen and switched to his computer.

"What are you looking up?" Kenzie asked.

"Political donation rules. These amounts are way over what a candidate is allowed to receive."

"Let me see," Kenzie cuddled close to Zachary on the couch so that she could see his screen at the same time as he was looking at it.

Zachary scrolled through the statute, frowning in concentration. "Can they really only accept $1,500 per person?"

Kenzie nodded, reading with him. "From individuals," she agreed. "But it says that the amount they can receive from a political party is unlimited so, if the donors give to the party—"

"Then the party can give it to the candidate," Zachary filled in. He looked at the printouts and notes on the backs of the pictures again. "And people can donate however much they want to the party?"

"No... further down..."

Zachary scrolled, and Kenzie's finger stabbed at the screen. "There."

"Ten thousand," Zachary read. "Well, that's a bit more than the $1,500 limit. And some of these look like several related parties donated."

Kenzie nodded. "That's a common way for people to try to get around the limit. I'm not sure if it is actually legal, But they're less likely to get caught."

Zachary shook his head. "Some of these donations are still too high even for that." He read through the handwritten notes again. "And those are the ones that appear to be missing from the bank account."

"Well, that makes sense, doesn't it? They couldn't accept checks that big, so they probably returned them to the donors."

"Right."

Or not.

If Senator Neufeld had possible mob ties, his lawyer was known to be a black hat, and the accountant had disappeared, voluntarily or not, then maybe the money had not been returned to the party or the donor.

"What if they put it into another account?"

"Well, that would be breaking the rules. That would be against the law."

"Right," Zachary agreed.

"You think they were breaking the law?"

Zachary shrugged. Kenzie looked at him. "Wait a minute, I thought you were going to drop this investigation. This is the case involving the senator."

Zachary looked down at the pages in his hands. "New facts have come to light."

"You can't go after this guy. Dad told you. It could be dangerous. You don't want to be involved with this."

"They don't know I'm looking at these papers. No one knows they exist. Not even the widower. He never looked at anything. He just boxed it all up."

"Someone must know that it exists. Or suspect that it might."

"Why?" Zachary considered his own question. "Because I was warned off? Because Wiltshire called you to tell me to stay away from it? Someone must be afraid that I'm going to find something. Maybe not this, but something."

Kenzie nodded.

"But they don't know I have this," Zachary repeated. "I'm not out interviewing the senator or everyone he knows. I'm looking at some old files. Ten-year-old personal files. Household management.

Schoolwork. No one cares about that. They can't see what's going on in this house."

"No," Kenzie admitted. She looked around. "I just can't help feeling... vulnerable. These Russian mobsters... we know how violent they can be. They don't have any fear of punishment. If they get caught, they go to prison to club fed, not a gulag. The only person they fear is the oligarch or whoever is immediately over their heads. These are dangerous people. If they are at all involved with the senator... I don't want you to be involved with it. I don't want you to take the chance."

Zachary looked into her eyes, wide and round with fear. She didn't need the extra anxiety. She was already dealing with enough on her own without worrying about him, too.

He stacked the papers, tapped the edges square, and handed them to her. Kenzie took them back tentatively, as if expecting a further argument or protest from him. But Zachary said nothing. Kenzie slid the papers back into the children's art folder she had taken them from and closed it. She slid the folders back into the box without looking at them any further.

"It's Christmas," Zachary said. "Or still the holidays, anyway. We should be relaxing."

"And instead, we've both ended up working," Kenzie said with a laugh. "Does either of us actually know how to relax?"

"Debatable. Give me a few minutes to get the rest of this packed up, and then we can go for a walk or watch a movie." He looked at the TV, remembering that he was supposed to be watching the movie she had picked out. "Or order in a second Christmas dinner from the chicken place. They have stuffing, you know."

Kenzie laughed again. "What about garlic bread? Do they have garlic bread?"

Zachary licked his lips. "I'm hoping they do!"

Kenzie turned off the movie that they had both lost interest in. "Maybe we'll put something else on later. Dinner sounds good. I'll order it."

"With garlic bread."

"And we have pie for dessert," she reminded him. "So don't gorge on the garlic bread."

Zachary waited until she went into the kitchen to make the order and take the pie out of the freezer. He put the rest of the notebooks and papers into the remaining boxes.

The papers on the political donations were on his phone. He could look at them whenever he wanted to.

41

Zachary did not heed Kenzie's warning not to gorge on garlic bread. By the time he had finished both the traditional Christmas dinner (with garlic bread) and the bakery pie heated in the oven, he was so full that it hurt to move. He flopped on the couch in front of his computer, checking his inbox to see whether anything important or interesting had come up.

Kenzie finished putting the leftovers away in the fridge and joined him, holding her hand over her stomach. She had apparently not listened to her own warning either. Zachary grinned at her. "Good stuff, huh?"

"I am never ordering that again. Ooh."

"Next time, we just won't have pie, too," he suggested. "We'll leave the pie for later on."

Kenzie shook her head, moaning again. She sat on the couch, then stretched out to ease the pressure on her stomach, putting her feet into Zachary's lap.

"Hey, do you want to look at one more thing today?" Zachary asked, clicking the attachments on the email he had received from the Middleton Sheriff's Office.

Kenzie groaned. "I couldn't do one more thing."

"No?" Zachary was disappointed. "I guess it will wait until tomorrow."

Kenzie opened her eyes and looked at him. "What is it?"

"Autopsy report and photos."

"I can't get up." Kenzie motioned for him to hand her the computer, and he did.

He moved off the couch and knelt on the carpet beside her so he could see the screen as she reviewed the report.

"I need more time and space," Kenzie told him, giving him a playful shove. But Zachary stayed where he was.

Kenzie scrolled through the short autopsy report. There wasn't very much there of value. It said what Zachary expected it to— death by a single gunshot wound.

Kenzie examined each of the pictures. Zachary saw nothing unusual as he looked at them. He had viewed a number of autopsy pictures, and everything looked pretty normal.

"See anything?" he prompted.

Kenzie shook her head. "It's all pretty straightforward."

"You would have ruled it accidental?"

Kenzie opened the scene sketches and photos. "At a glance, yes. I would have to get deeper into it, though, make some calculations."

Zachary looked at her hopefully. Would she be able to find something in the autopsy that would prove or disprove Sheriff Taylor's theory?

"If you weren't told that the shot had come from the trees," Zachary touched them on the screen, "Where would you think that it had come from?"

"Hard to say. No witnesses or cameras. Estimating just from the bullet and body itself is tough." Kenzie scrolled through the report, looking for the various bits of information she required. "It was a .22, which could be either a handgun or a rifle. Not a lot of penetrating power. It went through the window, which would have slowed it down even more. If it was a long shot, it would have lost velocity traveling that distance."

She looked at the distances and all other details of the scene sketch, then turned back to the autopsy photos and details of the injury Edie Dwayne had received. A crease appeared between her brows.

"What?" Zachary asked eagerly.

"They didn't do any measurements of the trajectory of the shot."

"And they should have, right?"

"Without the proper measurements, I can only estimate from the pictures, and that's a challenge. You need an expert to look at it to be sure. And even then... photographic evidence isn't as good as direct measurements taken at the time of the autopsy. The same goes for the scene sketch." She switched her view again. "The distances are estimated. It should have been photographed and measured."

"We can go back and do that part."

"You know exactly where the car was ten years ago? And there haven't been any other changes to the landscape? There may be more trees now than there were. Or conversely, some might have been cut down or removed. I know you've done accident recon-struction, so you know how much stuff you have to guess at. How a difference in a few inches can make a difference to the outcome."

"Well... yeah," Zachary admitted. He often ran multiple scenarios when helping with accident scene reconstruction, selecting different distances based on witness testimony and acci-dent scene photos. They could do that with Edie's shooting; try several different scenarios to see how the injury matched up with what was shown in the autopsy photographs.

"You need an expert," Kenzie repeated. "But this does not look like a long-distance shooting."

"What?" Zachary perked up immediately. "It *doesn't*? What do you see?"

"From what I can see, the bullet wound is very small and neat, very round. The autopsy photo seems to indicate a straight, level path."

Zachary nodded his understanding. He knew it had not been a contact shot because there was no scorching or stippling. Besides which, it had gone through a window. But he didn't know a lot more about calculating the distance of a shot.

"If this bullet had come from over three hundred yards away," Kenzie tapped the scene sketch on the screen, "The bullet would be on a downward arc. It would have dropped several inches from when it was fired and would be pointing down. The hole would be larger and more ragged, and the bullet path into the body would be downward, not level. Someone standing outside the car, shooting directly into the car, the bullet goes straight across, nice and level, no drop and no arc."

Zachary stared at the small, neat bullet wound when Kenzie put it back up on the screen. The changes that Kenzie was talking about would have been subtle. Something that would be more easily read by an expert. But he imagined an expert would be able to tell the difference between a bullet that had been fired from the road just outside the car and the trees off in the distance.

It had never made sense to him that Edie would just have pulled over to the side of the road and been sitting there, unmoving, waiting until that bullet struck her. Why would she be sitting there, listening to the gunfire in the distance, when she was expected at home? She needed to return home to make supper for her children.

But if she had been shot from right outside the car, he could build a picture in his mind showing the scenario. Edie had pulled over to talk to someone. Maybe they had asked her for help. Maybe the meeting had been prearranged. Two cars stopping side by side on the road. Edie shot either from the other car through a rolled-down window or by a gunman who had gotten out of the car to walk closer and perform the execution.

Not an accident.

An accident didn't explain why she had stopped there.

The only way it made sense was if it was murder.

42

Zachary wanted to pick Jeff's brain about what he might have seen or heard at the campaign office a decade ago. He had only been a boy, but he had the clearest memory of any of the children of the events around Edie's death.

Jeff might not have heard anything at the campaign office. There was no guarantee that anything shady or illegal had been discussed around Jeff.

No one else in the campaign office had been killed. Only Edie. She had known something. And she had been silenced. Zachary remembered Jeff's hesitation at the end of their interview. That look like he had something else to tell Zachary, but couldn't decide whether to do it or not. Eventually, he had decided not to. Zachary needed to change his mind about that.

A phone call would not be good enough. It would be too easy for Jeff just to hang up. Zachary needed a face-to-face meeting. He had to tell Jeff that the accident had been no accident after all. Maybe then, Jeff would be willing to share what else he knew.

He drove back to Jeff's dorm in Randolph Center. They were still on their winter break. Zachary was a little surprised that the Dwayne kids hadn't gone home for Christmas. But maybe they'd all gotten together for Christmas dinner on a different day. It wasn't

229

like they needed to disclose their holiday plans to Zachary. But he thought most college kids made plans to go home for Christmas. Unless they had a girlfriend or boyfriend. And Jeff didn't seem to have a significant other.

The campus was quiet. There were a few security guards around, but no one challenged Zachary or his right to be there. Considering he had no business there, security was pretty lax. With most of the students having gone home for the holiday, maybe they didn't think they needed to do anything.

Zachary thought about Jeff's beloved dog Rosie and how she had inspired him to be a vet tech. Or maybe he had loved Rosie because he was so suited to veterinary care. If Rosie had still been alive, would Jeff have gone home for the holiday? What if his mother had still been alive? Would all the children have gathered around for a Christmas celebration? Or would they take it for granted that she would always be there?

A guard in the lobby of Jeff's building nodded to Zachary and didn't ask him for identification, tell him to sign in, or ask him who he was there to visit.

Oddly, the halls of the dorm felt more like Christmas to him than the dinner at Lisa's house. Zachary had spent most of his Christmases while in foster care at Bonnie Brown, an institution for children who were difficult to manage. Fighters, runaways, and delinquents of all sorts mixed with those who, like Zachary, suffered from trauma, abuse, mental illness, learning disabilities, or developmental disabilities. When they had not transferred him to Bonnie Brown for the holidays, he had ended up running away or attempting suicide. A house that could be burned to the ground by a Christmas candle and paper decorations was danger-ous. The bare, institutional halls of the dorm were familiar and calming.

Zachary reached Jeff's dorm room and knocked on the door.

There was no answer. It would serve Zachary right if Jeff had gone off with a friend for the holidays or if he were off running errands, skiing, or doing something else that would keep him from his dorm for an extended length of time. Of course Zachary should have called ahead to make arrangements. But he hadn't wanted to give Jeff the opportunity to make excuses.

He knocked again. Jeff's roommate had probably gone home for Christmas. Maybe Jeff had his earphones on and was listening to podcasts or music and couldn't hear the door. Zachary knocked one more time, as sharply as he could, and thought he heard a response from within. But it wasn't a clear invitation to enter or to stay out.

He tried the handle, but it was locked. Zachary leaned closer to the door and shouted.

"Jeff? Are you there? Can you unlock the door?"

He was growing uneasy. What if something had happened to Jeff? What if he had told someone else what he'd been reluctant to give to Zachary? What if he had told the wrong person about having talked to Zachary about the weeks before his mother's death? Had word gotten back to the senator or his staff?

Or was Jeff depressed, maybe triggered by Zachary questioning him about something traumatic that was best left in the past?

As a private investigator, Zachary did his best to obey the law. He couldn't expect the police to come down on his side if he were pestering private citizens, breaking into their homes, or any of the other things that were the fodder of popular PI TV shows. But that didn't mean that he didn't know his way around a set of lock picks or occasionally employ questionable practices when there was no way around it.

He could go downstairs to get the guard or to find the resident manager to check in on Jeff. He could call the police and request a welfare check. But all those things would take time, hours even, and he thought he'd heard a response from within the room. If Jeff were there and he was hurt or in distress, there wasn't time to find someone else and convince them to let him into the room.

Zachary glanced up and down the hall, but there was no one nearby to help him or to catch him doing something he shouldn't. He delved into his pocket and pulled out a slim zip-up case of tools. He selected a pick and torsion wrench and went to work.

There was a reason he practiced lock picking even when it

wasn't something he implemented regularly. That was all the more reason to practice, making sure he didn't get rusty. He didn't need to be standing at the door for twenty minutes trying to get it unlocked.

In thirty seconds, he was in the room.

It looked pretty much the same as it had the last time he had been there. Except that Jeff lay sprawled on the floor, paper white, in a pool of dark blood. Zachary knelt over him, feeling for a pulse, and then turning him over to assess the injury, a great gash in his throat that had already bled a shocking amount. Zachary shouted for help but didn't know if there was anyone nearby who would be able to hear him. He pressed one hand over Jeff's bloody throat and tried to operate his phone with the other hand, skating across it with bloody smears that hampered his ability to work the touch screen. He shouted at the phone, trying to get it to dial emergency services. When it finally worked, he managed to change it to speaker and shouted his location and the urgency of his request.

The dispatcher's voice came back to him in calm, measured tones, going through her script one point at a time, methodically getting whatever information she could from him. Zachary looked around for something to hold or tie around Jeff's throat to stanch the bleeding.

He grabbed the scarf around his own throat and nearly throttled himself trying to jerk it off with one hand. He folded it several times and pressed it into the cut, holding it firmly in place and hoping it would do the job.

There were noises from the hallway as the students who were still there over the winter break started to realize something was happening.

What is it?

Someone was shouting.

"Any help?" Zachary called out. "Can anyone help me?"

He didn't look away from Jeff as someone hovered in the doorway, peeking inside to see what was going on. Swearing, pushing back, withdrawing. People didn't want to see that. People couldn't stand the sight of blood. He was going to be on his own for a while, at least until the ambulance arrived, and who knew how long that would be.

"Let me in," someone growled. A female voice. The woman fought her way through the people who crowded around the doorway. "Get out of the way. I'm trained in first aid. Make a path."

Zachary didn't turn his head but, in a moment, she was at his side, evaluating the situation.

"Did you call 9-1-1?"

"They're still on the phone," Zachary advised, nodding toward his phone on the floor a couple of feet away.

"Where is he hurt? Can I see?"

"His throat has been cut. I'm not going to move the scarf. I want to keep the pressure on."

"Yes," she agreed. "Keep it on. Is he breathing?" She took Jeff's hand to feel for a radial pulse rather than getting her fingers close to Jeff's damaged neck.

"Yes. So far." Zachary had been worried about putting pressure on Jeff's neck, worried about interfering with his breathing. But he knew there wasn't anything any of them could do if Jeff bled out before help arrived. He worried now that the pressure on the injury would act like a sleeper hold, stopping the blood from getting to Jeff's brain. But what else could he do?

"Did you see who did this?" the girl asked as she sat beside Zachary, trying to help where she could. She monitored Jeff's pulse, put a pile of textbooks under his feet to raise them above his head, and murmured soothingly that they were doing everything they could; he was going to be all right.

"No. I just got here and found him like this."

"It's crazy! Who would do such a thing? He didn't do it to himself, did he?"

Zachary shook his head. He looked around for the blade that had been used and didn't find it. It couldn't very well be a self-inflicted wound if there was no weapon in the room.

The dispatcher spoke occasionally to ask if there was any change in Jeff's condition and to give them an update on the ambulance's ETA. It seemed to take forever. Then they could finally hear the wailing of the ambulance and, eventually, the babble of voices as the paramedics were directed toward the room, everyone trying to tell them what was going on at the same time, whether or not they actually knew anything.

The room was small, too small for a victim and four attendants. The woman who had offered her first aid assistance exited to give them some room, and one of the paramedics entered and knelt next to Zachary to see what they were dealing with. She reported information back to her partner, who relayed it to the hospital. Zachary continued to hold the makeshift bandage in place until they finally took over, with one paramedic taking his position, allowing Zachary to exit and the other paramedic to enter.

Zachary found the police waiting in the hallway, expecting a statement from him. Zachary did his best to fill them in on the little he knew, leaving out the part about the room being locked. He said the handle had turned in his hand, which it had, but not until after he'd picked the lock.

"Do you have any idea who did this?" one of the cops asked.

Zachary shook his head. "I didn't see anyone coming out of there, and he was unconscious already when I found him, so he didn't say anything."

He did not say he suspected the Russians or someone from the senator's office. He knew when to keep his mouth shut.

"Had you planned to come over and see him today? Did he know that you were coming?"

"No, I just stopped in. Jeff wasn't expecting me."

"Is it possible that this was a suicide attempt?"

"No. I can't see anyone being able to do that to himself. And I couldn't see the blade that was used anywhere. Whoever did this, he must have taken it with him."

The cops took turns clearing people out of the doorway and looking in to see how things were going with Jeff.

Eventually, they were ready to move him, and Zachary stood back out of the way as they transferred Jeff to a gurney and took him down the hall to the elevator. Zachary looked around, unsure what to do next. There was a huge pool of blood on the floor.

Students peeked in to look at it and then withdrew again, pale or retching.

"Will you be going to the hospital?" one of the cops asked Zachary. "We will need your name and contact information."

Zachary gave them the needed information and then walked down to his car. When he reached the lobby, he saw more cops there talking to the security officer. Giving him hell, Zachary hoped, for letting anyone walk in there without getting their identification and finding out what they were there for. What good was there in having a security guard if all he did was watch people go in and out? Didn't that sort of defeat the idea of security?

"It's the holidays," Zachary heard the guard protest. "No one is supposed to be here. I'm just supposed to be here to deter kids from breaking in or damaging property. No one is supposed to be here."

Zachary shook his head and walked outside. His hand was shaking so badly when he reached his car that it took several attempts to position his thumb over the correct button to disarm the alarm and unlock the doors. He sat down and leaned back, and the shaking started in earnest.

His legs shook. A quaking started deep down inside of him in the middle of his belly and spread outward to the rest of his body. Tears began to run down his cheeks.

For a while, he just let himself go. He couldn't stop it even if he tried, and hoped that it would pass faster if he didn't fight it, just letting his body work through the crash following the adrenaline rush and the realization of what he had just done.

He looked at his hands, still smeared with blood. He should have washed it off before leaving. But where? In Jeff's room? There was no sink, and it wouldn't be right for him to stay in the room and contaminate the crime scene. There must be public restrooms in the building, but Zachary couldn't go back in and look for one.

He opened the glove box, found some napkins, and did his best to wipe off most of the sticky blood. He had wipes and other supplies in the trunk, but his legs were too shaky to get out and get them, and he wanted to get to the hospital to be on hand to hear how Jeff was when the doctor came out to talk to his father.

Oliver.

Oliver didn't even know yet. Zachary wiped the screen of his phone and looked for Oliver's number. He closed his eyes as it rang, trying to think of how to explain what had happened to Jeff. And how could he say that everything would be okay when Oliver asked him? He thought of Jeff's white face and the dark pool of blood on his floor and had to take several deep breaths to calm himself down and keep from throwing up.

"Zachary, did you have a good Christmas Day?" Oliver asked cheerfully, unaware of anything that had happened.

"I'm at Jeff's," Zachary told him, short-circuiting any small talk. "He's been hurt. You need to get here as soon as you can. To the medical center."

"What do you mean he's been hurt?" Oliver demanded, off balance. "What happened?"

"Someone attacked him in his dorm room. I came here and found him bleeding. The paramedics have taken him to the medical center. Can you get here? Do you need someone to drive you?"

"I can drive myself. But I don't understand what happened."

"I don't know. We'll have to talk when you get here. Hopefully, he'll be awake and be able to tell you."

"Was it a mass shooting? I'm always scared to death that something is going to happen to them when they are away to school. Was he shot? Is anyone else hurt?"

"He wasn't shot. He was cut. I don't think anyone else was hurt. Not as far as I know."

He couldn't tell Oliver his suspicions about something illegal going on out of the senator's campaign office. About his suspicions that something had happened that had gotten Edie killed.

And now his son? Zachary prayed that Jeff would recover quickly. They would stitch up the cut and give him blood. He would be just fine.

"Can I meet you there?" he asked Oliver. "Will you come?"

"Of course I'll come. You'll be there too? You won't leave him alone?"

"He won't be alone," Zachary assured him. He wouldn't be able to be with Jeff all the time, but someone would be monitoring him. He wouldn't be by himself.

"Okay. I'll be there as quickly as I can."

"Drive carefully. Don't take risks. We don't want you to be in an accident." He would have offered to drive out to get Oliver and bring him back to the medical center, but that would have left Jeff unattended for much longer, and Zachary wanted to be right there, to know that he was safe and hold vigil for him until his dad could get there.

It wouldn't be right for Oliver to lose his son, too. He couldn't lose his son like this. Zachary had to make sure.

43

When he reached the medical center, Zachary took the go bag from his trunk and used the restroom nearest the parking lot to wash the remaining blood off his hands. He swapped his bloody clothes for the clean set in his bag. He felt much better once he was cleaned up. No need to walk into the emergency room looking like he was the one who was hurt. And he didn't want to be covered in Jeff's blood when he met Oliver. Oliver didn't need that first impression branded on his memory. He needed Jeff to be okay when he got there. For him to be clean, stitched up, and looking normal. He would learn enough of what had happened from the media and what the police told him. And Zachary's carefully edited version.

Like Sheriff Taylor, Zachary wanted to spare Oliver's feelings as much as possible. He could understand Taylor's desire to downplay it and not upset Oliver and his family with something that couldn't be changed.

Approaching the triage desk in the emergency room, he explained that he was there with Jeff Dwayne and would be waiting to talk to the doctor once they had some news. The nurse looked him over, nodded, and didn't demand to know his relationship with Jeff. Maybe she had already been told to expect him.

He sat in the waiting area, elbows on his knees, head down, and just waited for the time to pass. He didn't have the energy to do anything on his phone, even to check the time.

"Excuse me, sir?"

Zachary looked up at the man who had addressed him, hoping to see a cheerful doctor there to tell him that everything had gone fine and that Jeff was in recovery and could talk to him.

But it was a cop. Not in uniform, so probably a detective. He displayed a shield on his belt in case Zachary doubted his identification.

"Deputy James, sir. You came in with the boy?"

Zachary nodded. "How is he doing, do you know?"

"They're working on him. Don't know anything yet."

Zachary wiped his face with his hands, pressing palms for a moment over gritty eyes before dropping them down again.

"What can I do for you?"

"Well, I would like to hear everything you can tell me about what happened today, and anything leading up to it. Any ideas at all you might have." He took a step back from Zachary. "If you would come with me, we'll go somewhere more private to talk."

"His dad is coming in. I called him."

"We'll keep an eye out for him. I imagine he'll call or text you if he can't find you."

Zachary got to his feet. "Yeah. I guess so."

He followed the deputy to an exam room. One with a closing door, not just curtains. The deputy nodded to the examination table with its strip of sanitary white paper.

"Sorry, it's not the most comfortable digs." He sat down on a wheeled stool.

Zachary boosted himself up onto the table and tried to be relaxed and calm about the interview. The cop wasn't there because he thought Zachary had done something wrong; he just needed the background and what Zachary had seen and heard. He was coming into the situation blind. He was probably worried about the safety of the other students in the dorm.

"Your name?"

Zachary went through all his personal information and showed James his driver's license to confirm his identity and address.

"And what were you doing in Randolph Center today?"

"I was here to see Jeff. I wanted to ask him some more questions about… the case that I'm investigating."

"A case you are investigating?" James repeated. "You're not a cop."

"No. A private investigator. Jeff's father hired me to look into the case of his wife's death ten years ago. The police already closed it, wrote it off as an accident. In Middleton, not here."

"His wife's death."

Zachary nodded.

"And what does this have to do with the kid?"

"Well… maybe nothing. Maybe he saw or heard something that someone didn't want him to talk about."

The cop stared at him for a minute, then started jotting notes in his notebook. "What makes you think that?"

"I was going to talk to him about what had happened to his mom and what he might have witnessed… and suddenly this happens to him."

"What makes you think it is related?"

"I don't like coincidences."

The deputy grunted. "Neither do I. Who knew you were coming here?"

"No one knew I was coming today, not even Jeff. But I talked to him on Thursday. This was my second time talking to him, because I have reason to believe that he might know more than he told me. And I was told on Friday to back off of the case."

"Who told you that?"

Zachary considered his answer. He had already been the target of violence and had still stepped forward to warn Jeff to stay out of trouble. Zachary didn't want to get him in worse trouble if the warning had been in spite of the Russians rather than on their behalf.

"It was anonymous," he said. "Something passed on to me through several proxies. I'm not sure where it originated."

"Am I to take it that you have made progress on this case and had discovered that it might not, in fact, have been an accident?"

Zachary nodded. "There is that possibility. That's why I wanted to ask Jeff some more questions."

"You must know who is behind it."

"No. I needed to talk to Jeff," Zachary repeated firmly. He wasn't about to start throwing around accusations that the senator was somehow involved in the attack on Jeff.

James studied him, skeptical. "Tell me what happened today," he said finally. "From the time you arrived at the campus. You didn't tell Mr. Dwayne that you were coming today? How did you know he would be here rather than home for Christmas?"

"I was at his dad's on Christmas Eve. He wasn't there. His dad said he wouldn't be home for the holidays. I don't know what Jeff's plans were, but he wasn't home."

"Go ahead."

"Well... there's not much to tell. I walked into the dorm. Nodded to the guard. He didn't ask for any identification or have me sign in. I didn't see anyone on my way up to Jeff's room. Everything was quiet, deserted. I guess most of the students went home for Christmas or had something else to do."

James nodded.

"I got up to Jeff's room and knocked and called out a few times. I heard a noise inside, but he didn't answer the door. I was worried about him. I opened the door and found him like that, in a pool of blood."

"The door was unlocked?"

"I was able to get in without breaking the door down," Zachary said. "If I had waited for the police to check on him, he might not have been alive when help arrived."

James opened his mouth to ask the question again, then changed his mind. "So when you opened the door, he was down."

"Yes."

"There was no one else in the room?"

"No."

"And you hadn't passed anyone in the hallway?"

"No. It was all quiet. I was surprised at how many people showed up when I shouted out for help. I wouldn't have guessed anyone else was on the floor."

"They come out of the woodwork when there is a tragedy," James observed dryly.

"Where did you park when you arrived at the dorm?"

Zachary described the location of his car as best he could. He would need to draw it out to give James the exact location, but the deputy seemed satisfied with his verbal description.

"Did you see anyone else outside?"

Zachary closed his eyes and tried to replay everything he had seen when he got out of his car. Of course he had been looking around for anyone suspicious, as he always did when he parked. He had not seen anyone suspicious. No killer coming out of the dorm with a dripping knife. No one running. No one who avoided looking at him or was startled to see him there.

Whoever had cut Jeff's throat had not been obvious when he left. Maybe he had gone out a back door. He had not been covered with blood spray or Zachary or the security guard would have noticed.

Had he seen a man? A woman? Anyone who wasn't a young adult, other than the guard?

"I don't know," he said, shaking his head. "I wish I could point you in the right direction. There was a man walking past the building when I arrived. But I don't know whether he had been inside and was leaving or was just walking across the campus and crossing in front of the building. He didn't look suspicious. No blood, no weapon, casual and calm."

"There was little disturbance at the scene. No sign of a struggle. No actions that would have suggested anger or retribution, trying to get back at him for cheating on a girlfriend, or some other teenage drama. The only thing that argues against it being a professional job is the fact that the boy was still alive when you got to him."

"There was a lot of blood."

James nodded. "There was. And from what the doctors are

saying, he would not have lasted long without intervention. If you hadn't been there right away, he would have bled out quickly. Which is why I am thinking that his attacker must have been in the building at the same time as you, or immediately before. You reached him within minutes or seconds. Lucky for him, not so lucky for the attacker."

"What about surveillance cameras? There seemed to be a good number of them around. Did any of them catch him? Or her?"

"You noticed a lot of surveillance cameras?"

Zachary shifted, making the paper crinkle beneath him. "I am a private investigator. It's my business to notice things like that. I have evaluated the security measures in a number of buildings. I notice where the cameras are and what direction they are pointed in. They didn't look like dummy cameras, so they must have gotten something."

"We are checking into it. Of course, everyone who knows anything is currently on vacation, so people who know how the system works have to be called in. I was hoping we would have some eyewitness testimony in the meantime."

Zachary shook his head, "I think the security guard would have a better idea of who was in and out of there than me. He was sitting there watching people come and go. I just went in and didn't see anyone on the way in. Except this one guy who walked by the building outside, and I'm afraid that if I accuse him, he'll turn out to be a professor. I don't think he is a viable suspect. I wouldn't want to waste anyone's time chasing him."

"Well, we may want you to look at some pictures or do a sketch anyway. Since so far we don't have anywhere else to go."

Zachary shook his head. It would be a waste of time.

"You said that he made a noise when you were outside the room. Was he conscious when you entered? Did he say anything?"

"No. He was already passed out. I didn't get any kind of response from him. I don't know if the noise he made was in response to my shouting and knocking on the door or if I was just lucky to have heard a random groan when I was in the hallway.

Either way… I'm glad I didn't just walk away and decide to try again later."

"I'm sure his dad will be happy about it, too," James agreed.

Zachary pulled out his phone and looked at the screen, hoping to see a call or a text from Oliver. It wouldn't be too much longer until he reached the hospital. Zachary wouldn't have any news for him on how Jeff was doing, but at least he would be close by when the doctor came out to say that they were finished stitching Jeff up and he was going to be just fine.

That would be a relief. Zachary wanted so badly to hear those words. He didn't consider the possibility that the young kid who wanted to be a veterinary tech and work with dogs and other animals would never be able to achieve his goal. Oliver didn't deserve to lose another family member.

"Where is he coming from?" James asked.

"Middleton."

"He'll be here soon."

Zachary nodded. "I told him to go slow and not to get into a car accident."

"Hopefully, he listened to you."

44

Zachary couldn't tell Deputy James much, so their interview quickly petered out. Zachary told him in generalities about the death of Mrs. Edie Dwayne, how she had been shot apparently at random while she sat on the side of a deserted road. He didn't include any details such as where Edie had been working at the time, what her son might know, or why the police had deemed it an accidental death when there was evidence pointing in the other direction.

"All of this happened ten years ago?" James asked with a shake of his head. "I don't see how that could have anything to do with this attack. This kid would just have been a boy at the time. He couldn't have anything to do with it. Unless the killer is some whack job who thinks he has been given a mission to kill the whole family. I mean, you never know, but killers don't usually leave a ten-year gap with nothing happening in between. Unless he was in prison during the break."

"That's a possibility." Zachary had been wondering why there was a ten-year gap between Edie's death and the phone calls to Oliver claiming that it was not an accident. Was it something as simple as the perpetrator having been in prison during the gap?

But then, why come back and draw attention to his crime?

Why point out what he had done ten years earlier and start people looking into it again? And why attack Jeff, who had been a child at the time? Did it have something to do with Zachary talking to him?

They didn't have long to wait. Oliver didn't park his car in the lot, abandoning it instead in front of the emergency room entrance with a skidding, protesting squeal of tires.

Hospital security stepped forward to tell Oliver that he couldn't leave his car there and would have to go find a parking space. The deputy waved him off, indicating that he would handle it. Oliver spotted Zachary and dashed up to him.

"Zachary. How is he? Please tell me he's okay."

"I don't know anything yet. I'm sure the doctor will be out any minute to tell you."

"How bad is it?" Oliver's face was white. "You have to tell me now. I'm here. You have to let me know how dire it really is."

"If Mr. Goldman had not gotten there when he did, you would have lost him," James told Oliver. "They said that he would have lost too much blood by the time someone could have gotten to him."

Oliver grabbed Zachary and pulled him close, squeezing him in a bear hug. Zachary allowed himself to be held for a minute. It actually felt good after all the waiting and uncertainty. But then he squirmed and pulled his way out of Oliver's grip.

"I'm just glad I got there in time," he said, slapping Oliver on the back. "I'm glad that I could do something for him."

"What happened?" Oliver demanded. "I don't understand how he was hurt."

"If you want to come with me," Deputy James said, "I'll explain it to you the best I can."

"Give me your keys," Zachary offered. "I'll move the car. Then I'll be back, and… hopefully, we'll be able to get something from the doctors about his current condition."

Oliver patted his pockets for his keys, which were already in his hand. Zachary took the keys gently from him. He didn't mind taking a short break from the hospital atmosphere to regroup. A few minutes of fresh air, doing a service for Oliver, and then, hopefully, the good news that Jeff would be fine.

James nodded his approval and escorted Oliver away, presumably back to the room where Zachary had disclosed what he had seen—or not seen.

Zachary waited outside the emergency room doors after parking the car. There was no one else out there, but there were plenty of cigarette butts on the pavement and in nearby plant pots and ashtrays to show that it was a popular place for the smokers to stand as they regrouped and got their nicotine fix. At times like this, Zachary almost wished that he smoked, so that he would not look strange standing there by himself, just thinking, with nothing in his hand. He just needed a few more minutes away from the hospital to clear his mind.

He pulled out his phone. Just about as good an excuse for standing off by himself instead of sitting in the waiting area. He hit the speed dial for Kenzie's cell phone and waited for a few rings to see if she would be able to answer. If she were in the midst of a dissection, she would not. And it was the post-Christmas rush, so he assumed she would have several autopsies to do over the next few days.

"Zachary, hi."

Zachary breathed out, relieved. Glad to hear a familiar voice and to be able to talk to her for a few minutes.

"Hi. I was just wondering how your day was going. Things are probably pretty busy."

"Ah, you know it," Kenzie said. "Always a bit busier this time of year."

"But you sound okay," Zachary observed.

She didn't sound stressed by the workload. She had been expecting the increase in arrivals and had taken things easy for the past week in preparation. Working didn't stress her out nearly as much as dinner with her parents or the anniversary of her abduction.

"Yes, it's fine. All in a day's work."

"Will you be working late today, then? Not pressuring you to get off at a specific time. Just wondering what it looks like."

"It looks like… probably a late day today. Maybe for a couple of days. Then, if all goes well and we don't have too many New Year fatalities, things should get back to normal again."

"Sounds good. Have you heard anything from Dr. Wiltshire? About how his hand is healing and when you'll get him back?"

"Too early to tell. Right now, it's a matter of waiting for the bones to heal. Everything is being held immobile. So then when the bones are healed, he has to rehab the muscles that haven't had anything to do for weeks and see if there is any nerve damage."

"You don't sound too optimistic about it," he observed, trying to interpret her tone.

"I just keep thinking about the amount of damage… It's very extensive. I know he's had the best surgeons consulting and working on it, so he has the best chances anyone could hope for. But I'm worried it won't be enough. He'll have too much damage to be able to work here any longer. He still has all that knowledge and he'll have basic functionality for sure… but whether he'll have the skill to work with the bodies anymore… I just don't know."

"Can he still work there as the boss? Directing things, showing you want to do, signing off the paperwork, all that kind of thing?"

"I don't know. And I don't know whether he'll want to. Maybe he'll want to teach or consult with the FBI or something."

"Or retire."

"I hope not." Kenzie sighed. "He is really good at what he does. I would hate to see him just put on a shelf."

"Yeah."

There was a page over the hospital system, which was broadcast outside the doors as well as inside. Kenzie made a noise.

"What was that?"

"Just a page."

"Where are you?"

Zachary realized that this wouldn't be a casual conversation any longer. He wouldn't be able to use the call with Kenzie as an escape from the real world.

"Uh… at the hospital in Randolph Center."

"Where? What are you doing there? Are you okay?"

"I'm fine. Nothing to do with me. Just… a witness."

"You're interviewing a witness at the hospital?"

"If he wakes up."

"What is he in the hospital for? You didn't tell me you were going to be there today."

"Well, I certainly wasn't expecting to be. I… went to talk to him at his residence and found that he had been attacked. So now I'm just waiting to find out how soon he'll be okay."

He knew he was trying to manipulate his own emotional responses with the "how soon he'll be okay" instead of "if he'll be okay." Because *of course* Jeff was going to be okay. He couldn't die. It wouldn't be fair to his father. And it wouldn't be fair to Zachary, who had just tried to save his life. If Jeff didn't recover, Zachary would blame himself for the rest of his life for not getting to the dorm ten minutes earlier.

"How badly was he hurt? What happened?"

Zachary hesitated, not wanting to say it out loud. Not wanting to jinx it somehow.

"He was… his throat was cut. He bled a lot before I got there."

"Oh, man." Kenzie was quiet, not sure what to say for a while. "That's terrible. But… some people do recover from injuries like that. I've seen it many times."

The "many" was probably an exaggeration. And she probably hadn't seen it herself. Since the patients she saw were the ones who had not made it. She might have treated someone who had been injured while in medical school, but certainly not since she had started work at the Medical Examiner's office.

"I'm just waiting for the news that they've fixed him all up," Zachary told her, keeping his tone optimistic.

"Great. I'm sure you'll hear something soon. Thank goodness you got there when you did."

"Yeah. Thank goodness."

If he'd gotten there any later, Jeff might have been dead or have already lost too much blood.

And if he had gotten there any earlier, Zachary might have run into the would-be killer himself. If he'd sustained similar injuries, he and Jeff might both have died.

"Be careful," Kenzie warned. Perhaps her mind was running in the same paths as Zachary's was. "I always worry about you."

"I'm at the hospital. The police are around. I couldn't be safer."

"Good. I'll see you tonight, then. Have supper without me if you get hungry. We'll spend some time together once I get home."

"Okay," Zachary agreed, even though his real response was that he would wait for her and not have supper without her. She wanted to hear that he would look after his own needs first, so he let her think he was in full agreement. Then she wouldn't worry so much.

With a sigh, he put the phone back in his pocket and walked back through the Emergency doors.

45

Zachary looked around for Oliver or Deputy James, but couldn't see either of them. So they were either still talking or had found Jeff and were sitting with him in whatever room or hallway they had parked him in after his surgery. He went up to the triage nurse, who was too busy to deal with him for some time. He waited patiently, not wanting to interrupt the flow of the new patients who arrived.

Another nurse happened by. She touched Zachary's arm. "Weren't you here with the boy who got his throat cut?"

"Yes, that's right. I went out to park his dad's car for him, and I don't know where he's gotten off to. Is Jeff out of surgery? Is his dad with him or still talking to the cop somewhere?"

"Let's find out, shall we?" She took him to another desk and sat down to look at the computer monitor. She tapped the keys. "Jeff... Dwayne. Is that right?"

"Yes."

"Okay, yes, looks like he is out of surgery. He has already been transferred to a unit. Let's write it down for you." She picked up a slip of paper and wrote the unit and room number for him. "You need to go down this hall. There is a bank of elevators. Take it up to the second floor. You'll be able to see the signs showing you which way each unit is when you get off the elevators. If you have trouble finding your way, stop at any of the nursing stations and ask for help."

"Thanks so much." Zachary gave her a warm smile. "I really appreciate you stopping to help me."

"Good luck. I'm glad to see that he made it out of surgery okay. And he isn't even in ICU, which is pretty amazing when you think about the shape he was in when he arrived."

"A testament to the skill of your doctors."

"And the resilience of youth."

Zachary nodded. He picked up the paper and followed her directions to find the unit to which Jeff had been transferred.

Oliver was in the hallway and saw Zachary coming. "Zachary! I was wondering what had happened to you!" he said cheerfully. "Was beginning to think that you might have decided you liked my car and decided to take it for a test drive."

Zachary smiled. "No, sorry to be so long. I had to take a call." He looked toward the room, wondering why Oliver wasn't inside holding Jeff's hand and waiting for him to open his eyes. "I was surprised they got him in a room so fast. Sometimes, you can wait hours, even days, to be moved to a room."

"Better here," Oliver said, "not like the big city hospitals. They are small enough to give patients individual attention. A very nice change from the red tape and bureaucracy you see in other hospitals."

"That's great. And where's Deputy James? Did he already leave?"

"He's in there with Jeff right now. Finding out if he can remember anything from the attack."

Zachary's heart throbbed. "He's already awake? And he's able to talk?" He hadn't been sure whether Jeff would even be able to speak after having his throat slit.

"I guess there wasn't enough damage to the trachea or vocal cords or whatever to affect his voice. I thought he would have to be on a ventilator, maybe breathing through a hole in his chest, but…" Oliver shook his head. "He's breathing normally, and they said it didn't damage his windpipe. The damage was to the blood vessels. He would have bled out, not suffocated."

Zachary hadn't been able to examine the damage that had been done while he'd been trying to save Jeff's life. But he supposed he hadn't heard any whistling or sucking noises through Jeff's throat. He'd been able to tell that Jeff was breathing and to focus just on stopping the bleeding and hoping that he wasn't cutting off the blood flow to Jeff's brain.

"And there's no... permanent damage? He's awake and lucid. He can talk and remember what happened...?"

"He's talking to Deputy James right now. I don't know how much he remembers, but he seems to be perfectly normal. Thanks to you and your quick action."

"It was only by chance that I was there in time to help him."

That probably wasn't the most comforting thing for Zachary to say to the grieving father. Though it was hard to think of Oliver as a grieving father or even an anxious parent when he was grinning so widely.

"It was meant to be," Oliver corrected. "You were meant to be there at that time to help him. I am sure of it."

"Well, I'm glad I was."

Deputy James exited Jeff's room, still speaking through the door to Jeff, and then he turned and looked at Oliver and Zachary.

"Ah, there you are. He's all yours." James nodded to Zachary. "Thank you again for your time and for being there to help perform the rescue today."

Zachary kept his mouth shut and didn't protest again that it had just been chance that he had been there. Fate had put him there, and all he had done was follow the first aid training he had been given years before. He just nodded.

"Was he able to give you a description of the person who attacked him?"

James sighed. "Unfortunately, no. It's not unusual for someone who has been assaulted to have no memory of the incident or what happened immediately before it. And from the position of the wound, I suspect he was grabbed from behind and his throat slit without his ever seeing who it was."

"How did the attacker get in?"

"The same way as you. Walked past the security guard. Door left unlocked. Just walked in and attacked the boy while he was sitting on his bed studying or listening to music, his back to the door."

Zachary said nothing about the door being locked when he arrived. Obviously, the killer had locked it on his way out, not planning for anyone to find Jeff there until it was much too late.

He rubbed the back of his neck. "I'm sorry not to be able to offer any eyewitness testimony of who did it, either. Did you get any physical evidence? Fingerprints? Skin under Jeff's fingernails."

"Unfortunately, no. I'm afraid his attacker is not going to be caught in the near future. Maybe when he attacks again…"

"Or if they find anything on the security footage."

"Yes. Hopefully." James touched his temple in a brief goodbye salute to Oliver. He nodded his head at Zachary and walked off.

"Come on in," Oliver invited, grasping Zachary's sleeve. "Come and talk to Jeff so he can thank you."

Zachary was somewhat embarrassed and bashful to be presented to Jeff as the man who had saved his life and whom he needed to thank for the service.

"Anyone would have done the same thing," he assured the young man, his cheeks and ears getting hot. "I just happened to be in the right place at the right time."

"Thank you for doing that," Jeff told him earnestly. His voice was a little rough, slightly different in tone from when Zachary had talked with him previously. If there was no damage to his voice box, then perhaps his throat had been a little bruised by the manhandling or by the insertion of a breathing tube while he had been on the operating table.

Oliver grabbed one of the visitor chairs and pulled another over from the other side of the curtain, where there was a vacant bed. They didn't need to talk in whispers to avoid disturbing a roommate. Oliver pressed Zachary into the second chair.

"Sit here and let's talk for a bit," he told Zachary sternly. "I want to hear about everything you have found so far."

Zachary sat down. But he looked at Jeff rather than starting a narrative of his investigation.

"I was coming over today to ask you some questions."

Jeff nodded, waiting for Zachary to tell him what they were.

"I found some things in your mother's papers." Zachary pulled out his phone and showed Jeff one of the pictures he had drawn on the back of the used paper. "Do you remember doing this?"

"Doing what?" Jeff asked with a laugh. "Do I remember coloring some pictures? I drew a lot back then. I have no idea."

"Did you draw while you were at the campaign office? When Edie had to go in for something and you had a PD day so you didn't have school? It must have been hard for her to juggle everything, if you needed her at the same time as she needed to work on the campaign or take care of something that was going on at the office."

"Uh, yeah, sure. I would draw or play office. Whatever I could find to keep myself entertained. I liked playing office, I don't think I was ever really any trouble for her."

"Never," Oliver declared. "Jeff loved reading and drawing and would be happy doing it for hours. Not like some kids who could get into mischief if you left them alone for two minutes."

Jeff laughed. "Terry?"

"Not only him. Your sister was pretty good at getting into things, too. It was a relief when you came around and were so laid back. Just what the doctor ordered."

They both looked at Zachary, who raised his hands as if they had accused him of something. "I had behavioral problems," he said in his defense. "ADHD, PTSD, learning disabilities…"

"I'll bet you were a joy," Oliver said with a chuckle. Zachary was tongue-tied and didn't know what to say. Oliver didn't really want to know anything about Zachary's childhood. He was just trying to keep the conversation flowing.

"We won't get into that," Zachary said. "So… what can you remember from when you had to entertain yourself at the office?"

he prompted Jeff. "Can you remember who your mom might have talked to? Any of the conversations she had?"

Jeff rolled his eyes. "I was nine," he pointed out. "How many conversations do you remember from when you were nine?"

"A few of them," Zachary said. "Especially if one of my parents was upset with me for something. I remember some of those conversations quite clearly. Or if they were talking about me and I was eavesdropping and wasn't supposed to know what they were saying."

Jeff nodded slowly. He fingered the bandages on his neck as he thought about it.

"Well, I guess, yeah. I remember some sprinklings of conversations while I was there. But not a lot. And I don't know how it all fits together."

46

Zachary showed Jeff the picture of one of the back sides of the images on his phone. "Do you remember what you were drawing on?"

"Paper from the recycle bin," Jeff said, nodding as he remembered. "Mom was very big on reusing and not making waste. We only have one world. Don't screw it up. There wasn't any need to have a sketchbook or a writing tablet with all new paper in it when we had so much paper just sitting there in the recycle bin for anyone to take."

Oliver nodded his agreement. "Yes, Edie was very environmentally minded. She didn't like waste."

"Did you ever look at the information on the other sides of your drawing paper?" Zachary asked Jeff.

"No, why would I?" But Jeff studied the picture now, looking it over with interest. Then he shrugged. "It just looks like dry campaign stuff to me. Why are you asking?"

"Because the information on the backs of these pages shows that the campaign was taking more money than they were legally allowed to. And that some of that money was being diverted elsewhere."

Jeff swiped through the pictures thoughtfully.

"What are you talking about?" Oliver demanded. "The senator's campaign was dirty? They were taking illegal donations?"

"Someone was taking illegal donations. From what I can see on these few pages—that money was not making it to the campaign."

"Where was it going?"

"There is no way to tell from these few pages. I might have to look at the backs of other pages in Edie's files to see if I can figure out anything else. But this is what I wanted to talk to you about today," he told Jeff. "This is why I came to see you—to see if you remembered any of this."

"He was just a little kid," Oliver objected. "You can see that. He was just drawing pictures while his mom did a little bit of office work. He didn't know what he was drawing on."

"He may have seen or heard things." Zachary took the phone back and switched to one of the pages with Edie's question handwritten on it. He handed it back to Jeff.

"Is that your mother's handwriting?"

"I don't know. I think so. Dad?" Jeff held it out to Oliver, and he took it and squinted at the screen.

Oliver smiled. "Yes, that's Edie's writing. Even after all these years, it is still familiar. It still makes me think of the notes we used to write each other. Notes on the pad beside the phone to say where we would be when we went out, knowing the other person would be wondering. We always tried to keep each other informed. We were so busy working and driving kids back and forth to their lessons and school activities. That was how we communicated as we came and went."

Zachary was momentarily distracted by this. "And the day she died? Had she written anything on that pad to tell you what she planned to do? Did you look at it when you got home from school?" Zachary switched his attention to Jeff again. "When she wasn't home?"

"Yeah…" Jeff thought back, nodding. "But she hadn't written it down. There wasn't anything on the pad to say where she was.

Usually, there was a little note, saying how long she would be and where she had gone. Like Dad said. But there wasn't anything." He grimaced. "Maybe they would have found her faster if she had left a note,"

"It wouldn't have made any difference," Oliver pointed out. "It was too late to do anything for her. She was killed instantly by that stray bullet. Even if someone had been in the car with her, they wouldn't have been able to do anything to help." Oliver gazed at Jeff, giving a little shudder. "I'm glad none of you were in the car. That would have been horrible."

Zachary pictured the lonely stretch of road. Edie's body in the front seat of the car. A child in the back, unable to do anything to help her. No cell signal to call for help. No one around, except her killer.

If Kenzie was right and it had not been a stray bullet from the kids target shooting, then the killer would have seen a child sitting in the back seat. He would have killed Jeff as well as Edie, if he had been accompanying her that day.

Zachary still believed Jeff knew something meaningful, even if he hadn't been in the car with her that day. Why would someone have tried to kill him unless he knew something? Someone Zachary had talked to had been worried Jeff held the missing pieces of the puzzle. He was worried about the possibility of Jeff revealing what he knew, so he had tried to kill him.

The trouble was that Jeff didn't know what it was that he knew. And he didn't know who had come up behind him and slit his throat.

"Something was going on at the election office," Zachary said slowly. "Your mother had questions about how the donations were being handled. She was asking Mr. Baxter, the accountant, questions about where the donations were going. Why the campaign's official accounts did not reflect the donations that they knew the campaign had received."

Jeff's brows drew down. He nodded slowly. "She and Mr. Baxter talked."

"Do you remember them talking about the donations?"

"I don't know. I remember them talking. I don't remember them arguing or having any kind of fight or disagreement. Just talking about office stuff. Boring money stuff. It didn't mean anything to me, so I can't recall any details. I can't tell you what any of it was about."

"We have a record," Zachary said, tapping his phone to indicate the pictures. "We know what it was about."

"But you don't know how it was resolved," Oliver said. "She might have had questions and there were simple answers. If they weren't actually arguing, if Edie was just asking Baxter questions, then that doesn't prove anything."

"Were there others around who knew what was going on?" Zachary asked Jeff. "Who at the office would know the answers? Baxter isn't around. We are trying to trace him, and then maybe I could ask him, but he apparently went to Scotland to retire, and I haven't been able to find him yet."

"I don't know. Mom did stuff on the computers. The other ladies mostly just stuffed envelopes and gossiped. I don't think they knew anything that was going on, just their individual jobs. Mr. Baxter... or sometimes the lawyer was there."

"What about the senator?" Zachary pictured himself sitting in the senator's office and tried to replay their conversation. Had the senator known what was going on in his own campaign office? Had he been a party to it? Or had his staff been doing something behind his back?

"The senator wasn't there very much. But the office was pretty much run by his wife," Jeff advised.

Zachary had difficulty fathoming how someone as young as Cathy Neufeld could have kept everything running in the campaign office. He was waffling again about whether she were as young as she looked. If she were only thirty or thirty-five, then she had to have been twenty or twenty-five when Edie had died. It was very young to take on all the responsibility for the campaign. And she was quite a bit younger than the senator himself.

"What was she like back then?" he asked Jeff. "She must have been very young. What did you think of her?"

"Young?" Jeff shook his head. "They all seemed ancient to me. Mrs. Neufeld was a battle-ax."

Zachary's confusion must have shown. Oliver laughed. "The senator's *first* wife," he advised. "Not the new one."

47

Everything fell into place. Zachary laughed at himself, trying to make the puzzle piece fit where it clearly didn't. The old Mrs. Neufeld and the new Mrs. Neufeld. The previous wife, the old Mrs. Neufeld, ran the campaign office like a military installation, and the new Mrs. Neufeld, much younger and prettier, was arm candy for the senator to take to balls and events.

The wife who had gotten him elected, ousted for the younger, pretty model. How many times had he seen that scenario play out in politics, business, and Hollywood? He should have clued in a long time ago. In Zachary's defense, the new Mrs. Neufeld was acting as Senator Neufeld's executive secretary rather than living a life of leisure in his mansion, so he could be excused for not realizing that the Mrs. Neufeld who had run the campaign office was not the same Mrs. Neufeld as the one who now ran his district office.

"Okay, so tell me about the *old* Mrs. Neufeld," Zachary said, pulling out his notepad. "What is her name?"

"Shirley. She is doing charity work now, as far as I know." Oliver rubbed his forehead, concentrating. "I'm trying to remember what cause I heard she was championing…" He shook his head. "Not that it matters, I suppose. She was a very strong, capable woman. Still is, of course. She had a degree from Harvard. MBA, if I'm not mistaken. Not something very many senators' wives have, at least not here in Vermont."

Very capable. Zachary jotted down the MBA. He would definitely need to interview Shirley Neufeld. Or would that have negative consequences? He was afraid that it was his interview with Senator Neufeld that had prompted the warning from Dr. Wiltshire to watch himself and drop the investigation for his own safety. And perhaps what had prompted the attack on Jeff.

If Shirley Neufeld resented her ex-husband for dumping her for the younger Cathy Neufeld, she might be more than willing to help Zachary with his investigation.

Unless she had been involved in diverting fraudulent donations. If she had run the campaign office and the campaign had been involved in fraudulent transactions, then it was more than likely that she had been involved. And she would not be eager to reveal the fact to Zachary.

They would need to run background on her. See where she had come from and what she was doing now. Find out a little more about whether there had ever been any suggestion that she had been involved in illegal activities.

"What was she like?" Zachary directed the question at both Oliver and Jeff. They would, he assumed, both have slightly different viewpoints. Jeff had been closer to her in her day-to-day work, but had a child's perspective. Oliver had probably known more about her but would only have seen her more public persona.

"Calling her an old battle-ax probably isn't fair," Oliver said, correcting his earlier comment. "She was focused, capable, and knew what she was doing. She didn't suffer fools. I don't think she dominated her husband. Not in public, anyway. But she definitely believed it was her place to work at his side and to see that he was elected. I don't think there was ever any doubt in her mind that he *would* be elected. He wanted to be senator, and she was going to make sure he got what he wanted."

"A good person to have in your court if you have ambitions," Zachary suggested.

"Absolutely. I'm sure if he'd wanted to be elected President, she would have done everything in her power to ensure that he was."

That would have been significantly more difficult than just getting him elected senator. But maybe she could have done it. Zachary got the impression Shirley Neufeld wasn't the type to back down from any challenge.

Zachary looked at Jeff, who frowned at the question.

"I don't know. I was scared of her. They had kids, but they were older. High school at that time, I think. As far as I was concerned, they were grown up. She wasn't the motherly type. A lot of the women who worked at the campaign office had kids in school, and they were like substitute mothers or aunts. If Mom had to go out for a few minutes to get stamps at the post office or something like that and I had to stay behind or didn't want to go with her, she could just leave me there and if I needed anything, I could ask one of them."

He looked at Oliver, who nodded at this. It had apparently not concerned him that Edie had occasionally left Jeff at the campaign office while she ran errands.

"But Mrs. Neufeld, I would never have asked her for anything," Jeff declared. "I always felt like she was more like… the principal. Or a prison warden. Someone to be avoided."

"Did she ever talk to you? Get after you for something?"

"If she ever thought I had stepped over the line. Oh, yeah. She would let me know it. Call me out. Probably talk to Mom about it, too. And if Mom thought I had done something I shouldn't at the campaign office and embarrassed her or gotten into some kind of mischief, I'd get grounded. Or worse."

A disciplinarian. The one who ran the office and knew everything that was going on. Would it have been possible to run a fraudulent campaign without her knowing about it?

"Was she ever around when your mom had a conversation with Mr. Baxter about donations not being accounted for properly?"

"I don't know if I ever heard any conversations about donations at all," Jeff protested. But then he shook his head, arguing with himself. "Actually…" he closed his eyes, "yes… I think she did. I was just doing my thing… you know, punching holes in paper, drawing my pictures, pretending to write letters or memos. I didn't like Mr. Baxter." He looked up at Zachary.

"You were uncomfortable around him," Zachary summarized. "He offered you candy, and maybe other gifts or favors and, because of that, you saw him as a dangerous stranger. Someone who might victimize you, even though your mom said it was okay."

"She liked him. They didn't argue." Jeff looked at his father, then back at Zachary, trying to focus on the memories, analyzing them, evaluating them with a young adult's viewpoint rather than a child's. "If they talked about the donations… *when* they talked about the donations, it wasn't like she was accusing him of something."

48

Jeff was in the kneehole of the unused desk with a stack of recycled paper and his colored pencils. The little space was his "office." Private, with walls all around him, no one would know that he was there unless they were looking for him and knew that was his favorite place to work. He knelt with his paper on the floor, in a position his mother insisted could not be comfortable or good for his back or knees, but which felt perfectly natural for Jeff.

"I just can't understand it," Mom told Mr. Baxter. "I know donations are coming in that haven't been entered into the system. Mrs. Neufeld says that everything is being properly accounted for and that it isn't any of my business. I don't know if I should do something about it. If I should tell Mr. Neufeld. I would look pretty stupid if it's all above board and Mr. Neufeld already knows all the details. I don't want to look stupid in front of him."

"I think you're just not seeing the full picture." Mr. Baxter's voice was smooth and intimate in a way that always made Jeff's skin crawl.

It wasn't that he did or said anything wrong, but Jeff always felt like it was there, just underneath the surface, like in a horror movie where the person was possessed by an alien that would come out if threatened. There was something creepy and slimy under Mr. Baxter's skin.

"You hear the pledges people make when they call in," Mr. Baxter continued, "but you don't see how it plays out. You're only seeing part of the picture. If the donation is too large for a donation to the campaign, then it actually gets made out to the party. Then, the party can pass it through to the campaign. But the amounts won't necessarily match. They'll take a certain percentage for administrative handling and only cut a check to the campaign once a month. So you don't see it flow through, with one pledge to match one check that the campaign receives."

"I know all of that," Mom said. "But there is a *lot* more being pledged than what the campaign ever receives, from individuals or the party."

"Of course. People say they will send in a certain amount... and then they don't. We have a lot of pledges that fall through. It's the nature of the job. People get excited or feel strongly about one of the party's platforms and promise that they're going to fund it... but when it comes down to it, they have other commitments, a spouse or someone else in the organization says they can't give that much, or they get distracted by another platform or cause. Or," a note of humor entered Mr. Baxter's voice, "they don't even have the money they say they will give. Someone who only makes forty thousand a year can't commit twenty thousand to a political or charitable campaign, no matter how strongly they feel about it. Or a hundred thousand. Sometimes people call and promise thousands when they don't have a penny in the bank."

"I suppose. But I know a lot of the donors, and they are legitimate. I guess... it is just because I don't see the whole picture," she conceded.

"It is all very heavily regulated," Mr. Baxter told her in his oily voice. "You don't see how carefully everything is handled. But it is all processed through certain channels to ensure that we are not in violation of any of the political donation statutes or generally accepted accounting principles. You don't need to worry about it.

You stay on top of the phones and administrative work, and Mrs. Neufeld and I will take care of the donations and accounting."

Jeff scowled. Mr. Baxter sounded like he was talking to a child, rather than to Mom, who knew lots of things and was not a child or silly woman like he saw on TV shows. She had gone to college and he shouldn't talk to her like she didn't know what she was talking about.

But Mom didn't protest the way he talked to her. She walked around the desk and peeked around it into the kneehole to check on Jeff.

"I have to go over to the store to pick up some things for the party tonight," she told Jeff. "Do you want to come with me or do you want to stay here?"

The "party" was not a fun one that kids would enjoy. No clown, superhero, or cake. No games or movie. It was just adults standing around with glasses in their hands, making boring comments about Mr. Neufeld and the election. The food wasn't even any good. Fruit and cheese, weird looking finger food made of things like mussels, raw fish, or blood-red meat.

He didn't have any desire to stand around while Mom picked up the platters of food and any last-minute decorations they needed for the hall.

"I'll stay here."

"Okay. You be good, and talk to one of the campaign ladies if you need anything. All right?"

Jeff nodded. "I'm just going to work in my office," he told her, pointing to the stapler and hole punch he had liberated from the assembly room. "I have very important work to do."

She smiled. "Okay, bud. I'll see you when I get back. Then we'll go home for some supper. I'm going to be out tonight to look after the party, but Dad will be home. You guys can watch baseball or something."

"Okay," Jeff agreed.

She blew him a kiss and then left to take care of her errands.

Jeff started working on a picture of a tank Transformer, imagining how it would tower over the trees when it stood up. It would have guns on its arms and on top of its head, or out its eyes. Planes would fly around it and get shot down. They wouldn't be able to take it down.

"That woman is going to be a problem."

This was not Mr. Baxter's smarmy voice, but the lawyer's. Cousins. Jeff thought Cousins was a weird name. He had cousins on his father's side of the family, who they called the Dwayne cousins, and cousins on his mother's side, who were called the Brown cousins. What were Mr. Cousins's cousins called? Did he have Cousins cousins?

Jeff snorted and shook his head. *Cousins cousins.*

"Everything is under control." This time, it was Mr. Baxter's voice, but not the indulgent, fatherly tone he used when talking to Mom. It was a cringing, whining tone. "You don't need to worry about Edie. She's not going to say anything. I've explained it to her. She understands."

"She is asking too many questions. I don't like it."

"The only person she's talking to about it is me. I've warned her that if she starts asking other people questions and it leaks out, it could make it look like there are problems where there aren't any. If rumors get out there are problems with the donations, people will assume it is true, without any proof. She believes in Neufeld's campaign and she won't do anything to harm it."

"All it takes is one comment to the wrong person."

"I know. I've made sure she understands that. I've made sure she won't talk to anyone else about it. Not even her husband."

"You can't stop a woman from talking to her husband," Cousins said in a loud, disapproving tone, as if this were the worst news he'd ever heard. It made Jeff jump. He peeked out through a knot in the kneehole panel at Cousins, worried that he might hit someone or throw something. "This has got to stop," Cousins insisted. "We need to put a lid on this."

"There is nothing to worry about," Baxter insisted, holding his hands up as if to halt Cousins. "I promise you. Everything is under control."

"I told you when you hired that woman that there was going to be a problem. But you've got a crush on her or something, and wouldn't listen to reason. Now look at the position you've put us in!"

"Everything is handled," Baxter repeated. "You don't need to worry about her saying anything."

"We are going to need to take additional measures to ensure it."

"You can't do that," Baxter protested. "Just leave Edie and her family alone."

49

There was silence after Jeff's recounting of his memories of the conversations at the campaign office. Zachary wrote down a few notes before the thoughts could run right out of his mind, and tried to think of all the new pieces of information that Jeff's story offered. And whether his conclusions were defensible. Jeff had been nine years old. It had happened a decade earlier. How accurate were his memories? What had been rewritten or recast in the years since it had happened? If they were able to identify the culprit who had killed Edie or who had ordered her killed, and part of Jeff's story was needed to establish his guilt, would his story be considered credible? Would a jury believe him? Would a lawyer be able to cast doubt on his testimony?

"You really didn't like Mr. Baxter," Oliver observed, sounding surprised by this.

Jeff looked at him sharply. "No, I didn't," he agreed, sounding like this was the beginning of an argument they'd had before. He sounded like he was ready to batten down and defend his position. Ready for the attack.

But Oliver didn't argue it, didn't say that he thought that Mr. Baxter was a wonderful guy and that Jeff had disliked him for no reason, as sometimes children do. Children can be put off by anything about a person. A smell. Weird clothes. Words that had unintentionally hurt. Maybe just a bad vibe. In Zachary's experience, children tended to be much more discerning than adults. Adults felt like they had to like everyone, or at least be civil or find something good to say about everyone. Children didn't have those social compunctions yet. If they didn't like a person, they didn't like him.

And Jeff had not liked Mr. Baxter.

Zachary hadn't met Baxter, so he didn't know how he would feel about him, but he hoped that he would have been as discerning as a nine-year-old.

"He liked your mom," Oliver pointed out. "You said that he defended her and didn't want anything to happen to her, so why are you holding a grudge against him? Why wouldn't you like him?"

Jeff looked at Zachary, as if he didn't know what to say. Zachary could see that he didn't believe his father would believe anything he had to say about his instincts toward Baxter, or the fact that he had offered him candy or other treats. Oliver would just say that he was being a nice guy. Jeff's instincts told him otherwise.

Zachary didn't say anything. Nothing he said would help either one of them come to a better understanding or settle the issue of whether Baxter had been good or bad.

But where was he now?

"I just wished he was gone," Jeff said, sounding uncomfortable. He rubbed the bony ridges over his eyes with both hands, looking tired. He probably didn't have much energy after losing so much blood, and his body was still trying to clear the effects of the anesthetic. It would be a few days before he was feeling like himself again. He lowered his hands to his lap again, and looked at Zachary. "I wished he was gone, and then he was."

Zachary looked at him. "What?"

"I always felt guilty about it. For years. I didn't even understand why I felt so guilty about him being gone. Because I wanted him to be gone. I guess I sort of thought... I wished it, and it came true, and I felt like I was responsible for making him disappear."

"Did he disappear?" Zachary asked, looking from Jeff to Oliver.

"Was he actually a missing person? Because my assistant and I have been trying to track him, and haven't been able to find any sign of him."

"No, I never heard anything about him being missing," Oliver dismissed. He put his hand on Jeff's knee, patting him comfortingly. "You certainly didn't have anything to do with him going away. He retired, left the country. I think he came into some land in Ireland."

"Scotland is what I was told," Zachary said. "Did you ever have any contact with him, either right before he left or any time afterward?"

"I didn't know him personally." Oliver rubbed the bridge of his nose. "I just knew him because both he and Edie worked at the campaign office. She never had anything bad to say about him." Oliver shot a look at his son here. "I think… he just wasn't cut out for small town Vermont living. It can be pretty isolating. It isn't for everyone."

"So you don't know that he did go to Scotland. Who really knew him? Was he friends with anyone?"

"I don't know. He wasn't from around here. I never knew where he came here from. They said he went to Ireland—Scotland—but he didn't have an accent. He was American."

Someone who had come to Vermont to escape scrutiny somewhere else? Zachary wondered if Baxter was an alias. Maybe they couldn't find him because that wasn't his real identity. He might have warrants out for him in another jurisdiction by another name. He might have gone underground to avoid being caught again.

Was it an important piece of the puzzle or a distraction? Zachary didn't want to spend hours or days looking for the man and trying to put together his history just to find out that he had nothing at all to do with the crime he was trying to solve, the death of Edie Dwayne.

The two of them had been friends or, at least, work acquaintances. One of them had died. Possibly been murdered. The other had disappeared.

Might have disappeared.

Might have run away and hidden.

Might just have been someone who had worked at the campaign office, minding his own business, and gone on to retire to Scotland after inheriting a property.

"You said that you wished he was gone, and then he disappeared," Zachary said to Jeff.

"Yeah."

"When?"

Jeff shrugged. "I don't know."

"Was it after the discussion that you told us about? You wished that day that he was gone?"

"Yeah, maybe. I think so."

"And how soon after that was he gone?"

"I never saw him again."

Zachary looked at Oliver, who raised his brows and shrugged, unable to confirm or deny whether it was true.

"Do you know when he went to Scotland?" Zachary pressed. "Was it before or after Edie died?"

"I don't know... I guess I became aware of it afterward, but I have no idea when it was that he left. Like I said, I didn't know him personally. So I don't know when he left."

Zachary looked at Jeff, whose eyes were at half-mast, close to sleep. "Jeff? Do you know how soon after that conversation between Baxter and Cousins your mother was killed?"

Jeff's eyes closed, then opened. They fluttered a couple of times, and he pushed himself up into a more upright position. He was trying to stay awake, but he was clearly fading.

"I don't know for sure. I think it was soon after that. There was a big party, Mom had gone to get the platters and everything for it... I don't remember much about what happened around then. It's one of the last memories that I have of her. One of the strongest."

50

Zachary shook hands with Oliver before leaving. Jeff was asleep, so he didn't say goodbye to him. Oliver planned to stay with him. He wasn't going to go back home because Jeff was sleeping and come back later when he woke up. He intended to camp out there for as long as he needed to. The other kids would be coming to see Jeff and to let him know that they were rooting for him.

"Thank you so much for going to see him," Oliver squeezed Zachary's hand again. "I can never thank you enough for being there when he needed you and saving his life. I'll be indebted to you for as long as I live."

Zachary shook his head and tried to make noises like it was nothing. Anyone else would have done the same. But it was false modesty. It might only have been a coincidence that he had been there when Jeff needed him the most, but he had been the one to get the door open and had put everything he had into keeping Jeff alive until the paramedics could get there and provide their expert care. Maybe anyone would have tried to do the same, but Zachary had done it and was proud of himself.

There was no time to deal with the information he had gathered from Oliver and Jeff. He didn't know what time Kenzie would be getting home. He knew she would be late, but he didn't know how late she would be and didn't want her to have to wait for him.

So he headed for home. He would have to deal with the search for Baxter and a deeper look into his history later. And he needed to talk to the old Mrs. Neufeld.

But he would have time for one phone call before he got home. And maybe for another call or two after he got home, depending on when Kenzie got home. Zachary looked up Sheriff Taylor's phone number before heading out and initiated a call with him. He might have to leave a message, but there was a chance that Taylor would answer.

"Ian Taylor," the sheriff's gruff voice greeted. "You'd better not be a telemarketer."

Zachary laughed. "Can I offer you a new cell phone plan?" he teased.

"Who is this?" Taylor asked, chuckling.

"Zachary Goldman. We talked about—"

"Edie Taylor. Yeah. I'm not quite that senile yet."

"I have another question for you."

"Mom said you got copies of the pictures and such from the police files."

"Yes, I appreciate her pulling those for me. They were very helpful."

"In proving that it was an accident, I hope," Taylor offered.

Zachary didn't confirm this or correct him. Some questions were best left unanswered.

"I was wondering about something that came up during my discussions with people who knew or worked with Edie. Do you remember Baxter? Ronnie Baxter?"

"Sure, I remember him. Bookkeeper or accountant fellow. Lived here for a few years."

"Do you know why he left?"

"I don't recall. Probably never knew. People come and go. It's their own business."

"There was never a missing person report filed for him?"

"For Ronnie Baxter?" Taylor's tone seemed genuinely surprised. "No, no missing person report."

"No one missed him?"

"Missed him? You're making it sound like he disappeared, but I'm sure that was not the case. People come and go all the time. I don't remember why he left, but he didn't disappear."

"Someone told me that he retired to Scotland."

"Retired? Seems like he was a mite young for retirement. But sometimes people look younger than they are. Or they say they're retiring when they're starting a new career. Cops often retire and take their pension, but then they go on to open a bar or set up a fruit stand."

"So far we haven't been able to find any trace of Ronnie Baxter when he left here. Not in the United States or in Scotland. It seems like he just vanished."

"Well..." Taylor chuckled. "I'm sure nothing happened to him. I would have heard something about it. He just moved on. Happens all the time. Sometimes, people leave possessions or other people behind, but grown adults are allowed to leave whenever they like. If there is no indication of violence or that they are vulnerable adults, we just let them go. If we investigated every time someone moved out of town..."

"I'm not saying that you should. I'm just curious about what happened to him. Maybe there's a friend or family member that I should talk to. Do you know if he was close to anyone?"

"I have no idea. He wasn't here for more than a few years, and I don't recall him having any drinking buddies. He was more of a loner."

"No friends at all?"

"I'm sure he had friends, but I don't know who they were."

"Were there ever any concerns about him being a pedophile or predator?"

"What?" Taylor's voice rose. "Pal, you'd better be careful about what accusations you make. You can't go around accusing people of stuff like that."

"I didn't accuse anyone of anything," Zachary shot back. "I

asked whether there was ever any suggestion that he was. Jeff Dwayne had some disturbing things to say about him."

That made it sound like Jeff's feelings about Baxter were much more concrete than they were, but that was Zachary's intention. Little would put a cop's back up more than the possibility of a child predator going free.

"Are you kidding me?" Taylor demanded. "Oliver and Edie never said anything about him. He wasn't even on my radar."

"I don't think Jeff ever said anything to them at the time. He was pretty young, and Baxter never did much more than to try to nurture a relationship with him. It was still in the early stages of grooming. Giving him presents. Making friends with Edie. Getting nice and close."

Taylor muttered a curse under his breath. "Well, then, I'm glad he disappeared, wherever it was he went. Best not to have sickos like him in Middleton."

"The question is, did he go on and take up a new alias in another town? Stateside? Over to Scotland? Or did something happen to him like Edie's 'accident'?"

"Edie's death *was* an accident," Taylor affirmed.

"Possibly," Zachary agreed. No point in antagonizing Taylor about it. But he couldn't bring himself to anything more than it being a possibility. At this point, homicide seemed much more likely. They wouldn't know for sure without a witness or an expert testifying about the trajectory of the bullet and indications of the distance of the shooter. Zachary trusted Kenzie's judgment, even though she had said that they needed an expert.

"It was," Taylor assured him. "What happened to her was tragic, but it was not a big conspiracy."

51

"How is your young witness?" Kenzie asked almost as soon as she saw Zachary. "Did he... how did the surgery go?"

"A complete success." A smile came to Zachary's lips as soon as the question had cleared Kenzie's lips. "In fact, we had a good talk at the hospital before I headed home."

"He was able to talk? That *is* a good result. I'm amazed he was even awake. You must have been there to help him within a minute or two of the attack."

"The police must think so. The detective kept asking me if I had seen anyone or passed anyone in the hallway. But I didn't see anyone else. His attacker must have exited a different direction than I entered."

"The boy was lucky. And no damage to his windpipe?" Kenzie frowned, thinking about it. "That would suggest a professional hit to me. Most of the cases I know of where the victim has survived, the windpipe was slashed rather than the carotid. A jealous lover or crazed killer who didn't really know what they were doing. If the carotid was cut but not the windpipe, that's the opposite. That's not a crazed attack. That was skilled. Targeted."

Zachary looked at Kenzie and thought about that. He had tried not to think too much about how Jeff had come to be hurt. Violence sometimes happened at colleges. Attackers who were jealous lovers, heavy drinkers, drug users, or in the early stages of a yet undiagnosed mental illness. It was lucky that Jeff had been the only person attacked.

But if Kenzie was right and it hadn't been a random or crazed attack, that confirmed the theory that Edie had been targeted. Not only that, but the killer had been worried Jeff knew something that would identify him. The attack on Jeff was no more random than the attack on Edie.

He had been thinking it ever since he had discovered Jeff bleeding out in his dorm room, but he had been hoping that he was wrong. That it would turn out to be an inexpert attack, an accident. A college kid hopped up on bath salts.

He could understand why Taylor wanted Edie's death to be a random accident. It was much easier to deal with than a professional hit. If it were random, Zachary wouldn't need to go any deeper into the investigation.

"This is a dangerous man, Zachary," Kenzie warned, her eyes worried. "This isn't something you can fool around with."

"I'm not fooling around."

"Do you know who it is? Who attacked him?"

"I have an idea."

There were still too many possibilities. Zachary was sure that even if Senator Neufeld was involved somehow, he hadn't been the person to attack Jeff. That had been a professional. Someone who had been hired. And he wasn't yet sure whether Neufeld himself was the one behind everything. The corruption might be somewhere else in his organization. Jeff's recounting of the conversation he'd heard between Baxter and Cousins had not included the senator. If it were a clear, untainted memory, there was no evidence that the senator had been aware of the conversation. If Cousins was the one who had ordered Edie Dwayne killed, or done it himself, he may have been acting alone.

Cousins might have been working alone or with someone else. He may or may not have been acting under direction from the senator.

There were more questions than answers.

"You should turn this over to the police," Kenzie told him.

"The police are working on it. I've told them everything I could. They are talking to witnesses, pulling recordings, all that kind of thing. They'll find out who it was."

"I don't want *you* investigating it. I don't want you getting hurt."

Zachary looked for a way to reassure her that he was not in any danger. No one knew he was investigating it. He had plenty of security. There was no way for anyone to come up on him unaware.

But none of those reassurances would be true, and she would read it in his face. Zachary cleared his throat, casting around for a way to explain why he had to stick with it until he could put the culprit behind bars and not just hope that the police would be able to figure it out on their own.

"The only way to be safe is to catch this guy."

"And put yourself in harm's way?" Her voice rose in objection.

"I'm not trying to put myself in harm's way. I'm trying to protect myself and others. Believe me, I don't want to end up as someone's target. I'm not putting myself out there as bait. I'm being as careful as I can be."

Kenzie shook her head. "I don't believe it."

And there was no way to reassure her that he had no intention of baiting the killer.

They didn't talk about it the rest of the night or the next morning. Zachary knew that Kenzie didn't want him to continue with the investigation, and Kenzie knew that Zachary would anyway. There was no common ground. No way that either of them could persuade the other.

Kenzie went to the medical examiner's office in the morning, and Zachary did a few searches to find out what he could about the old Mrs. Neufeld—Shirley Neufeld—and where to find her.

She was not hard to find. After her separation and divorce from the senator, she had fallen out of favor with the press, and probably no one was trying to follow her to get her picture or a statement about life with the senator anymore. That part of her life was over; no one cared about the old connection.

She was in Burlington. The drive there took a couple of hours. The weather and the roads were good despite the time of year. The weather between Christmas and New Year's Day could be nasty, but it was holding out so far.

He didn't have Shirley Neufeld's office address and didn't know whether she worked. She might be volunteering somewhere or working under her maiden name, sitting at home by the fireplace, painting, or writing her memoirs.

It was the winter break, so he hoped that even if she usually worked, he might find her at home.

She lived in an outlying area, and Zachary figured when he looked at the GPS map that it would be a wealthy area, possibly with security gates in front of every property. It wasn't as exclusive as he had feared, but he was still driving by nicer homes than he envisioned anyone he knew would ever live in. Other than Kenzie's parents, of course. The Kirsch family mansion could compete with any of the houses Zachary was seeing.

The GPS led him through several winding roads until he was finally in front of a seven-figure mansion with walls filled with glittering windows. There was a number on the fence at the edge of the property that matched the one Zachary had tapped into the GPS. Zachary looked the house over for a few minutes, idling at the access road, before forcing himself to move ahead. He wasn't going to find out very much sitting there at the curb. He could find a place to surveil the house where the homeowner would be less likely to notice him, but all he would find out was how many people worked there and when the senator's ex-wife was home.

Right now, he didn't need her schedule. He needed to know what kind of a person she was and whether she was the type who would have ordered a hit on a mother of three if it would benefit her and her husband. He was already afraid of what the answer might be.

52

Zachary drove up the driveway to the house. He anticipated that he would be met at the door. There were enough surveillance cameras pointed at the road and the entrance for Mrs. Neufeld and her staff to know of every approach to the house before a visitor, invited or uninvited, reached it.

So he was surprised when he reached the door and it didn't open. He rang the doorbell and waited for a while longer. Maybe Mrs. Neufeld was on a holiday trip and the staff had been given the time off.

But he didn't want to assume, so he waited a while longer, rapped hard on the door with his knuckles, and waited again.

Eventually, he thought he could hear stirrings from within, though it was hard to know for sure with the heavy front doors. These were not the typical hollow-core doors one might find in many middle-class Vermont communities.

The door clicked and opened just far enough for the woman on the other side to look out. Her eye applied to the crack between the door and the frame, she spoke in a low, whispery voice.

"Yes? Who are you?"

"My name is Zachary Goldman. I'm looking for Shirley Neufeld?"

"What for?"

"Is she at home, ma'am? Is that you?"

"Who wants to know?"

"My name is Zachary Goldman," he repeated.

She stared at him through the crack.

"If I could come in, I could explain better. If the lady of the house is in, we could have a discreet conversation..."

"I don't support any causes that do door-to-door solicitations."

"No, ma'am. I wanted to talk to you about what happened ten years ago."

She stared at him without saying anything for what seemed like a long time. Zachary focused on a knothole in the door, staring at it and staying absolutely still.

Eventually, the door opened farther. Still not all the way open, but only enough to admit him. It was more like he was sneaking inside and trying to avoid being seen.

There was a great hall with a sparkling chandelier and a long, curving staircase, like something off a movie set. Everything was silent and still. If there were anyone else in the house, Zachary would be hard-pressed to identify their location.

The woman who had answered the door took him to a library grander than the study at Lisa Cole Kirsch's house, which Zachary had thought pretty amazing. She indicated that he should take a black leather chair and poured a Scotch without asking. Zachary settled himself into the seat and tried to make himself comfortable.

The woman, who he assumed was the old Mrs. Neufeld, appeared to be in her sixties, with deep lines running from her nose to her mouth like a smoker. Her forehead was permanently creased with several lines. Her dark hair was in a short, severe style. Her eyes glittered with intelligence and she studied him curiously.

She handed him the crystal tumbler of Scotch and poured herself another, sitting in another of the club chairs. The room was slightly cool, as if the fireplace should have been in use. And perhaps it would have been if he had announced his intention to show up there.

"And who, exactly, are you?" she demanded without first introducing herself, "Zachary Goldman."

"I am investigating a series of events that took place ten years ago. This would have been around the time you were helping your husband in his senatorial campaign."

"Are you." She looked disapproving. "What do you know about anything that happened back then?"

Zachary set the tumbler on a side table close to the chair. He didn't feel unsafe there, but he was spooked by the silence of the old house. People had repeatedly told him that Mrs. Neufeld was the one who had run her husband's campaign. She had been the one to get him elected. If there had been any fraud going on, she had probably known about it. Maybe been the benefactor of it.

Maybe he should have brought someone with him. If not the police, then at least someone who could account for what had happened to Zachary once he arrived there, so he didn't go missing like Mr. Baxter.

But he didn't have any evidence that she had done anything she shouldn't have. For him to proceed with his investigation, he had to know more about her. How she operated. The kind of person she was. What she would tell him about the campaign ten years ago and whether it was truthful or not.

"I'm sorry to barge in on you like this," he apologized. "I know I should probably have called ahead. This is probably not the best time for a visit."

Her shoulders lifted and fell. "It's quiet. It's the holidays. I'm not busy with a lot of other things. Why not?"

"Great. I guess you know that ten years ago when you were running the campaign for your husband's election—"

"Ex-husband," she corrected icily.

"Sorry, of course. Your ex-husband's campaign."

"What about it?"

"You know that while you were running that campaign, a woman who did some of the administrative work for the campaign was killed in what was determined at that time to be an accidental shooting."

Her eyes were steady. She didn't look away from him or pretend that she didn't know what he was talking about.

"Yes. I remember that. What about it?"

"Do you remember the woman's name?"

The senator had disclaimed all knowledge. Zachary wanted to know just how much Mrs. Neufeld remembered or was willing to admit to. Maybe he wanted to know that Edie was remembered and not just tossed to the side as something worthless and unimportant.

"Edie," Mrs. Neufeld said. "Edie Dwayne."

"Yes. She was a big fan of the senator."

"Many of us were," Mrs. Neufeld said dryly. "And many of us were disappointed."

"I am sorry to hear about your divorce," Zachary told her. "I'm sorry things didn't turn out for you."

"They turned out for the senator just how he wanted them to," she said cuttingly. "And once he had everything he wanted politically, he cleaned house."

Out with the old and in with the new. He got rid of the woman who had helped him to be elected and replaced her with a younger, prettier model. One that was easier on the eyes and looked better in publicity photos. Not a cover model and not a ditz, but one that the senator had determined would look better at his side than this aging, lined, work-worn woman.

"I'm sorry," Zachary repeated.

She gave a nod. Stiff, almost regal.

"Do you remember what happened to Edie?" Zachary asked, returning to the previous topic.

"She was shot, like you said."

"She was. The sheriff at the time... might have misjudged the situation when he decided it was an accident right away. It might have been better if he had spent a little more time investigating what had happened there and made sure that all the forensics matched up with his theory."

"Oh?" she was unconcerned. "What do you mean by that?"

"It doesn't look like it *was* an accident." Zachary didn't have any qualms about repeating a fact he didn't know to be true, as if it were. What he wanted was her reaction. Her knowledge. How she expected him to treat the information that he had discovered.

53

"I find that hard to believe," Mrs. Neufeld offered. "Certainly the sheriff at the time was no rocket scientist. He was a country cop who… to be as generous as possible… was not as 'on his game' as perhaps he should have been."

"He was drinking," Zachary suggested.

Mrs. Neufeld's eyebrows went up, perhaps surprised by his knowledge. "He was."

"And so he missed some things that he might have seen if he had been sober and not thinking so much about what he had lost."

"That may be," Mrs. Neufeld agreed. "And… how does this bring you to my door today?"

"Well, that's just the beginning. I am investigating Edie Dwayne's death and, since she worked at your husband's campaign office, that has led me to what was going on with the campaign prior to and shortly after her death."

"Oh?"

"The disappearance of Mr. Baxter, for one thing. Around the same time as Mrs. Dwayne was killed."

"I don't believe Mr. Baxter disappeared. I think, if you look into it, you will find that he left the country."

"That was the rumor. But there has been no sign of him in the

US or Scotland in the past ten years. Seems a little suspicious, doesn't it?"

"Not really. Sometimes people like to get away from life." She raised her brows at Zachary. "Perhaps they want to be away from callers showing up on their doorsteps, people who expect them to be home at all hours and on holidays, who want pictures or interviews or other things. It can be quite exhausting to be in the public eye."

"I'm sure it can," Zachary agreed, not apologizing for being there. "But he hasn't just changed to an unlisted phone number and address."

"Perhaps not. I barely knew the man. He wasn't very... memorable."

"And Edie? You must have dealt with her quite a bit as she did all the administrative work for the office."

"Not *all* of the administrative work," Mrs. Neufeld corrected.

"Sorry, a good amount of the administrative work for the office. You must have known her, since you were basically running the campaign, and she was part of the limited support staff."

"I knew who she was, of course. But we didn't know each other personally. We were not friends. She was just there when I needed things done for the campaign."

"You knew she had children."

"Yes, of course. Many of our office staff did. Some people are 'joiners.' They will get involved in whatever organization or event needs them. A political campaign, the PTA, Brownies, a community picnic. They tended to know each other because they had kids in the same classes or school."

"She had three children."

Mrs. Neufeld looked unmoved by the information.

"She sometimes brought her youngest child, Jeff, to the campaign office if he had the day off school."

The woman looked as though she would deny knowledge of this. But she had already said that she knew Edie Dwayne and that she knew she had children. Of course she would know if Edie sometimes brought her son to work.

"We tried to provide a good environment for working mothers. People like the senator might not understand that mothers are sometimes left without childcare when their children don't have school." She shook her head. "I can't say I remember Jeff specifically, but the women did sometimes bring children around when they were working. As long as the children did not disrupt the office, I had no problem with that."

"Jeff was attacked in his college dorm yesterday. It would appear that someone did not want him to talk about what he remembered from his time at the campaign office."

"What makes you think it was anything to do with the campaign?"

"The timing, for one. I just talked to him about his mother and the campaign office before the holidays and, when I went back to ask him further questions, he had been attacked to prevent him from saying anything else."

"That seems like a leap."

"But I got to Jeff in time, and the doctors were able to repair the damage. He was able to talk to us about what he remembered."

Mrs. Neufeld's eyes flashed. "Well, that's very good."

Zachary looked at her steadily, waiting for any change in her expression. She gave no sign. Not a woman to play poker with.

"What can you tell me about your lawyer? Brent Cousins?"

"He's not my lawyer any longer."

"Does he still work for your husband?"

"My *ex*-husband?" Her voice was icy over having to correct him again.

"Right, sorry. Your ex-husband."

"I wouldn't know. I don't have anything to do with his affairs anymore."

"Was Cousins still your ex-husband's lawyer when the two of you separated?"

"Mr. Cousins is very loyal to the senator. *Very* loyal."

"The kind of guy who would do anything for him?" Zachary guessed.

"Yes, I would say so."

Zachary sat there breathing, thinking about it. He knew Shirley Neufeld was intentionally pointing him toward Brent Cousins and the senator. But was it because they were guilty? Or because she wanted someone to take the fall? Or just because she wanted to get back at her ex-husband for how he had treated her?

"What can you tell me about Cousins?"

"What do you want to know?"

Zachary considered the possibilities. "Does he own a gun?"

"How would I know that?" Her lips curled in amusement.

"I don't know. *Does* he?"

"A lot of people own guns, Mr. Goldman."

"Does he own a 22? Or did he ten years ago?"

She shrugged. "It's entirely possible."

"Do you know where he was the night that Edie Dwayne was killed?"

"How would I know that?"

"You worked closely together. You probably had some idea of his schedule." Zachary leaned forward, resting his elbows on his knees. "From a conversation that Jeff Dwayne heard, Cousins was threatening to do something to harm Edie. And Baxter was begging him not to."

"Ronnie Baxter did like Edie, you know. He might have had a bit of a crush on her."

"You didn't know he was a pedophile?"

She blinked at him, recoiling in genuine astonishment. "What?"

"I suspect that the reason he wanted to get close to Edie had nothing to do with *her*. He wanted access to Jeff."

Mrs. Neufeld turned her head away, looking disgusted. "I can't believe there was someone like that in my campaign office. If I had known... there is no way I would have allowed him there. No way."

"*Your* campaign office?"

"My husband's campaign office."

"Your ex-husband's campaign office."

"He wasn't my ex-husband at the time."

"You considered it your office. From what everyone I've talked to has said, you were the one who ran everything in that office. You're the one who made the decisions. The assignments."

Shirley Neufeld nodded her head almost imperceptibly as Zachary made this statement.

"So, were you also the one who told Cousins to take care of Edie Dwayne? Did you tell him that you thought she had become too much of a liability and wanted him to take her out?"

She shook her head, jaw tightening. "Of course not. Why would I do that? I liked the women who worked at the campaign office. They were very hard workers, very loyal. And Edie was the best. Why would I want anything to happen to her? Her death meant that I had to take everything on myself. Everything. Do you know what kind of a burden that was? I didn't have any reason to wish Edie Dwayne dead. Why would I do something like that?"

"Because she knew about the missing donations. The monies that were being diverted from the campaign. She knew that something fraudulent was going on, and she asked too many questions. You were afraid that you would all be exposed."

Mrs. Neufeld shook her head slowly. "I don't know what you are talking about. There was no fraud. The books of account for political campaigns are examined very closely. They are independently audited. There are statutory requirements in place. Someone can't just trample all over those rules, it would be discovered in a heartbeat."

"Well, with a crooked accountant and lawyer and all the right people in on it... it seems like it might be possible. Unless someone inside the campaign office made a stink, of course. If someone in the campaign office blew the whistle on what was going on, then not only would the house of cards come tumbling down, but your husband would also lose the election."

"Ex-husband."

"Not back then."

Back then, she had wanted nothing more than to ensure his win. Back then, she had been loyal to him and had done everything in her power to make sure that he would win. Zachary didn't know whether the missing money had gone to line someone's pocket or if it had actually gone into applying pressure and bribes in the appropriate places to make sure that Neufeld won. But the fraud had gone undetected by anyone other than Edie Dwayne, and then she had to die.

Then they couldn't trust her to stay there even a day longer. They had to find a way to get rid of her quickly and cleanly.

Mrs. Neufeld picked up her tumbler and took a couple of large swallows, showing no more reaction to the alcohol than she would have to apple juice. Ice clinked in her glass. "I assume you have evidence of all of this?"

"I'm not ready to show you my hand yet. I was hoping to get your cooperation."

"Because you believe I am no longer loyal to my ex-husband?"

"Why would you be? You got him elected, and he tossed you out like last week's newspaper. You did all the work, while he stood around looking pretty. It was your organization, your money, your influence," he looked at her after each phrase to make sure that his answers were correct and hitting home, "and after all that you did to set him up as the king, he decided to take a new queen."

Zachary didn't point out the superlatives. Younger, sexier, more beautiful. He was sure Shirley Neufeld already heard each one of those words every time she looked at the new Mrs. Neufeld. Every time she considered why her husband had betrayed her like he had. They were ringing in her ears now without Zachary even saying one of them.

"So I think… you decided to reach out."

"Reach out?"

"Oliver Dwayne was still living in the same house. His old phone number had not been disconnected. You decided to reach out and let him know that everything was not as it had seemed. That Edie Dwayne was not killed in an unfortunate accident. You wanted him to know what had really happened."

The corners of her mouth twitched. Not a smile or a frown. Just a very slight contraction of the muscle in the corner of her mouth.

54

Back at home, Zachary filled Kenzie in on his discoveries and theories. He couldn't keep the details to himself. He had to tell Kenzie everything. Just telling her bits and pieces wasn't working for him. It was too hard to keep track of what he had told her and what he was trying to keep a secret. He would just have to trust that she would keep it all confidential.

"You think that Mrs. Neufeld—the old Mrs. Neufeld—was the one making anonymous calls to your client?" Kenzie demanded. "The calls that prompted him to hire you to look into this whole mess?"

Zachary nodded. "Who else had a motive to expose what had been done ten years ago? Who profits from Oliver finding out that his wife was murdered instead of being killed in a freak accident? He humiliated her by tossing her aside for a younger woman, and now she wants to ruin him. What better way than exposing the campaign fraud and the murder committed to cover it up?"

"Not a woman you want to cross," Kenzie observed.

"No. And the senator should have known that. He should have realized she would retaliate and that he had a lot to hide."

"That's assuming he knew about the campaign fund fraud and the murder," Kenzie pointed out.

"Yeah. But I really can't imagine that he didn't. I know he didn't have much to do with the running of the campaign office, but I can't imagine he was completely ignorant as to what was going on. I don't think it was a scheme just cooked up by Mrs. Neufeld, the lawyer, and the accountant without the senator knowing about it."

"But if you want him to be charged in any of this, you have to have some kind of proof. And so far…"

"So far, I don't have much," Zachary admitted. "The testimony of a boy who was nine years old at the time, and which *doesn't* point to the senator, only to the lawyer. A bullet trajectory that doesn't match the scenario that the ex-sheriff proposed. The attempted murder of the one witness to the plot to kill his mother."

"You need more. And you need to tell the police what you have discovered so far. You can't keep pursuing this on your own. If Mrs. Neufeld had wanted to get you out of the way… you put yourself right in the path of danger, without any kind of backup. You can't do that." Her expression was tight, clearly not happy with his continued investigation.

"But she isn't the one who killed Edie Dwayne. She wanted someone investigating the case."

"You didn't know that. You still don't know that. You just *think* you know."

Zachary didn't see the point in trying to argue it. He and Kenzie would never see everything from the same perspective. She would always think he was being too reckless. And he would always think that she needed too much proof before accepting the truth.

"And I thought the caller was a man," Kenzie said. "Or did you just say that to throw me off?"

Zachary chuckled. "I said that the caller used a voice changer. You can change your voice from female to male with the click of a button. The original calls were made using a voice changer, too. But I think that caller probably was male. But I don't know whether it was the senator or Cousins. Or even Baxter, if he was intent on keeping Edie out of danger. He might have thought that if he could keep her out of the way with anonymous threats… and then Cousins wouldn't have to do anything."

"But Edie didn't stop because of the threatening messages."

Zachary shook his head and sighed. "I don't think it would have made any difference whether she had or not, I think once she was on to the campaign fund fraud, it was too late. They had to eliminate her because they knew they would never be able to keep her quiet forever."

"So is that it? Are you finished with this case?"

Zachary made a list on his fingers, trying to remember each loose end he still had to tie up.

"Getting the Sheriff's Office in Middleton to reopen the Edie Dwayne death and to get a specialist to look at the bullet trajectory to confirm that it was an execution-style killing rather than a stray bullet from target-shooting kids. Which will hopefully help assuage ex-Sheriff Taylor's guilt over it."

"You think that he'll feel better because he got it wrong?" Kenzie looked at Zachary like he was crazy.

"No, I think he'll feel better that it wasn't the kids he had previously warned to stay away. The kids that he had not arrested for reckless shooting before."

"Because he should have arrested them instead of just warning them to keep quiet?"

"Because I think that one of his kids was part of that group, and he has always worried it was his own son who had fired the bullet that killed Edie Dwayne."

"His own son?"

"He knew those kids. He knew they had been there. He didn't want to ruin anyone's life by arresting them. It seemed like a small thing if they just promised never to go back there or to shoot toward the public road again. I saw pictures of his kids in his house. They would have been the right age."

"You think that's why he was so insistent that it was just an accident?"

"Yes. He couldn't see past the guilt that he might have let his own kid kill a woman because he'd gone easy on them."

Kenzie shook her head. "Okay, so you have to get the Sheriff's Office to reopen the case and look at the new evidence. But will there ever be enough there for a conviction? You still don't know who it was that killed her."

"It's down to a pretty small number of people unless they hired someone from out of town to do their clean-up work." He moved to the next finger to tick off another point: "I'm crowd sleuthing Ronnie Baxter's location."

"What is crowd sleuthing?"

"I've uploaded details to a 'justice project' board that amateur sleuths from all around the world look at and try to solve. The power of having thousands of people looking for clues or answers rather than just two or three. Anyone from all around the world can look at Ronnie Baxter's picture, name, known history, and rumors, and try to find him. Some of them will run searches in other countries. Some of them will look for facial recognition searches in the wild. Some of them will look for legal name changes or known aliases. They might find a criminal record or someone who knew him as a juvenile. And then they'll try to figure out where he went when he left Vermont. Did he really go to Scotland? Did he inherit land there? Hide under another name? They might come up with something. We might be able to find him. If he didn't want Edie killed, maybe he'll be willing to talk to the police."

"If he's alive."

Zachary nodded soberly. "I honestly doubt he is. I think he and Edie were both killed. But finding two bodies out on that road might have looked suspicious, so they got rid of Baxter and said that he had gone away to take over the family farm in Scotland as cover."

Kenzie nodded. "There are lots of places in Vermont to hide a body. Lots of wilderness areas where no one will ever find it."

"Maybe one of my crowd sleuths will be able to match a John Doe to Ronnie Baxter. There are some professionals on the boards as well as amateurs."

"What else do you still need to do to close the case?" Kenzie asked. "I really want this one off your plate. You are in danger as long as you are investigating it. Some of the people involved are heavy hitters. You know that my dad and Dr. Wiltshire both warned you against dealing with Senator Neufeld or this lawyer…"

"I'd like to know who it was that killed Edie… but I'll have to leave that to the police and hope that they can tie the evidence to someone. Maybe match the bullet to another crime."

"Didn't they already do ballistics on it?"

"Yes… and no match." Zachary shrugged. "I don't know. I'm hoping there is other evidence that they'll be able to do something with once they reopen it. And then… I want to know if the senator was involved. If he knew what was going on, either before or after Edie's death. When I talked to him, he put on a good show of not knowing anything… but he didn't even 'know' things that he should have."

"That will be up to the police to find out," Kenzie said, eager to have him hand everything off and close the case. "They have more resources than you do, and you don't want to get involved with something political. Senator Neufeld is a heavy hitter. Let someone else take the flak for that."

"The police won't get any answers from him."

"They *might*," Kenzie insisted. "You never know. You should have Heather prepare the final bill for Mr. Dwayne, so there is a clean break between your investigation and the police reopening the case. No overlap."

"I will," Zachary assured her. "I'll call her in the morning."

He wasn't sure he actually would, but Kenzie would sleep better thinking everything was taken care of to her liking.

55

Z achary had been up for several hours when Heather called. He wasn't expecting a call from her but, on the other hand, there were several things that he was supposed to follow up on for her. Approving client bills and following up on delinquent payments. Reviewing the skips she had done before passing them on to the companies he had contracted with, other bits and pieces he had let slide while he'd been investigating the Dwayne case or taking time off for the holidays.

No one had assumed that he would be able to keep working up until Christmas Eve or any time after then into the new year so, even though he hadn't been looking at his new emails, he knew Heather would have let him know if there were anything urgent for him to take care of.

But there was a lot to do that he hadn't been focused on.

He swiped to answer the call. "Hi, Feathers. Hey, I know you're waiting for a bunch of things from me—"

"It's okay. I'm not calling about anything outstanding," she cut him off before he could get into a lengthy excuse about what was holding him up.

"Oh. Okay. Well... good morning."

Heather laughed. "Morning, Zachy. Though it's probably more like noon for you. How long have you been up?"

He didn't even bother looking at the system time on his computer. "A while," he admitted.

"I never have to worry about waking you up in the morning, no matter how early I call you. So I'm calling about a hit from one of your crowd sleuths."

Zachary's heart sped. He hadn't been expecting anything so soon. He tamped down his excitement over the news. It wasn't necessarily anything earth-shattering. One of the reasons that he'd asked Heather to manage the crowd sleuthing was that he imagined there would be dozens or even hundreds of possible clues to follow up on, and most of them would lead nowhere.

"That's great. Anything… promising?"

"I wouldn't be calling you if there wasn't. Someone remembered a John Doe that turned up ten years ago near George Montgomery Bird Sanctuary."

Zachary thought about it, then shook his head. "Where is George Montgomery Bird Sanctuary?"

"It's in Quebec, across the border."

A body showing up not only outside Vermont but in another country would go a long way to explaining why no one had ever connected John Doe to Ronnie Baxter.

So would the fact that Ronnie Baxter had never been reported missing. If there was nothing for the Quebec authorities to match their John Doe to, and the body had no identification on it, how were they to connect it to an accountant who was supposed to have gone to Scotland to live?

"In Quebec," Zachary repeated. "How sure are they that it's Baxter?"

"The timing is right. Found within a week of Edie Dwayne's death. Body still recognizable, and I can tell you the picture they published of the John Doe looks remarkably like Ronnie Baxter."

"How was he killed?"

"Twenty-two to the head. Close range."

"Bingo. Do they have ballistics?"

"Yes. I've suggested they send them on to Middleton Sheriff's Office for comparison to the bullet taken from Edie Dwayne's body."

"It's going to be a match."

"Probably," Heather agreed. "But unless you can put it together with a weapon or a person, that doesn't get us that much closer to the killer."

"But it will help us get the file reopened. If she was killed with the same gun as a body that was dumped in Quebec, that doesn't sound so much like a stray bullet from target shooting practice."

"No," Heather agreed, a smile in her voice. "I thought you would be pleased."

"I am! I didn't expect to get any results that quickly if the online sleuths managed to find anything at all."

"Well, that actually isn't all of it."

Zachary turned the phone to speaker mode and put it down, resting his fingers on the keys of his laptop so that he could make a few notes while Heather talked. "What else?"

"We have a list of possible aliases and charges or reports against Ronnie Baxter before his arrival in Vermont. There are probably a few that are false leads. But a number of them are repeated several times by different sleuths, and the mugshots and timeline look right."

"So he was a known offender. That's why he showed up in Vermont without any history."

Jeff's gut feeling that Baxter was not someone to be trusted had been accurate.

"That's right."

"Pedophile or fraud?"

"Both. He'd only done short stints, when he was convicted. He usually managed to plead down. Do a few months and then be out on the street again. Looks like he lost his credentials, but none of his employers actually checked to see."

"Not surprising. I don't think employers usually check with the governing boards."

"They just assume that everything is legit," Heather agreed.

"Maybe talk to a couple of references, previous employers. But none of them said anything about the charges against him?"

"He probably had fake references. Not hard to do. Either that, or they couldn't talk because he hadn't been convicted, or because they'd signed a confidentiality clause so that it wouldn't get back to their clients that they had hired someone who hadn't been qualified or had committed fraud."

"I guess." Heather agreed. "Everyone covering their own backsides."

Zachary chuckled. "That's the way it works. If you could email me a list of those aliases and whatever backup you have to go with them, that would be great. I don't know if we will do anything with them, but I'd like to at least show them to Jeff to let him know that he wasn't just imagining things. He felt like... maybe he had judged Baxter harshly just because Baxter creeped him out, and he really was just a nice guy after all."

"I'm glad he can't do anything to hurt anyone else."

"Yeah." Zachary shifted uncomfortably and tried to suppress his own visceral reaction to the thought of the pedophile. His heart rate sped and his gut twisted. But Baxter hadn't done anything to Zachary, or to Jeff. And he would never have the chance to hurt another kid again.

"Did you read the backgrounds I sent you? You didn't say if you wanted anything more..."

Zachary cleared his throat. "No, I've been..."

"That's okay. Just let me know if you want anything else after you've read through them."

After hanging up, Zachary navigated to his email inbox and opened a view showing all his emails from Heather. The email attachment on Ronnie Baker was sparse, A picture she had managed to dig up on him and a couple of paragraphs about his time in Middleton. But no threads before or after that.

The profile on Brent Cousins was more fulsome, but Zachary stopped at the top, his eyes riveted on the profile picture Heather had attached. He had seen that face somewhere recently, but it took him a few minutes of reviewing before he could remember where.

He had been waiting to speak to Senator Neufeld after he'd met with Zachary.

Zachary turned his head when he heard Kenzie's voice from the bedroom, sharp at first and then raised in concern. She wasn't talking to him, so he assumed she must be on the phone. He had not expected her to be up for another hour or two. But then she was out of bed, walking around the bedroom, turning on the water in the bathroom, getting ready for her day even though it was much earlier than usual. He walked down the hall to the bedroom and then poked his head into the en suite bathroom to check on her.

"Did you get a call out?" he asked, seeing her combing her hair in front of the mirror.

She jumped and looked at him, eyes wide and startled.

"Hey, sorry, I didn't mean to scare you. I just heard you on the phone, and then it sounded like you were getting ready."

"Yeah. No. I'm up, but it wasn't a call-out. It was... Dad."

Zachary studied her face, trying to divine everything he could. Had something happened to Walter? Or to Lisa?

"What is it?"

"He wanted me to come—wanted us to come..." She shook her head. "I don't know what's going on. He's at Senator Neufeld's house."

"Senator Neufeld's house? What's he doing there?"

"I don't know. I couldn't get much coherent over the phone. Do you mind? If we go over there and see what's going on?"

"Of course not," Zachary said. "Whatever you need."

"He sounded worried and kind of... scattered. And you know Dad, he's never like that. He's always calm."

Zachary nodded. Often unnaturally calm. And acting as if he knew what was going to happen six moves ahead, like a chess master. He was very smart, like Kenzie, and had a lot of experience in politics and arranging a way for everything to come out the way he wanted it to in the end.

"What can I do? I'll get us some coffee to go. Do you want breakfast?"

"No. I don't think I could eat anything anyway. I'll just get dressed and go. If we get hungry on the road, we can grab something at a gas station."

"Okay."

Zachary hurried to the kitchen to get the coffee and brewed a fresh pot to fill up their to-go mugs. While the machine was popping and gurgling, he returned to the living room to pack a bag. He already had his refilled go bag in the car. But he added everything else he could think of that they might need if there were some kind of trouble. If Walter was upset, then there must be trouble. Zachary added a camera. Memory cards and USB drives. Microfiber cloths to wipe down fingerprints or clean up liquids. Several pairs of gloves. Garbage bags. He packed it all quickly into a soft-sided briefcase and poured the fresh coffee into the mugs when Kenzie came out of the bedroom.

"Thanks." Kenzie took a mug from him and sipped it, probably burning her mouth. "Appreciate it."

They didn't discuss it much on the way. If Kenzie had known something concrete, she would have told him, but all she had was the fact that Walter had called for their help and that she thought there was trouble. It was at the senator's house, and she had already told Zachary to stay away from him. Walter himself had warned against getting involved in the senator's or Brent Cousins's affairs, so what was he doing over there at the house, and what had he gotten himself into?

Zachary drove as fast as he dared, keeping an eye on the traffic and making sure that he wasn't being too aggressive. He didn't want to attract the cops and have to sit and wait for them to write up a speeding ticket. For once, Kenzie didn't tell him to slow down or eye the speedometer as if he were guilty of all seven deadly sins.

She was obviously worried about what Walter had gotten himself into.

56

Z achary already had the senator's address, so he hadn't needed to look it up before leaving the house. He found it on his phone using voice commands while he drove. Kenzie was white knuckling the emergency brake and door handle, so he eased his foot off the gas a little. Eventually they exited the highway and had to slow down for the smaller and smaller country roads, until they reached the driveway for the senator's home.

Unlike his ex-wife's new house, the senator's did have an iron gate barring entry to the driveway. But the two sides of the gate hung open, inviting them in. Zachary didn't even have to try anything shady.

Walter was sitting on a low stone wall around a raised garden at the front of the house. How long had he been out there waiting for them? It had been a couple of hours since his call to Kenzie; surely he hadn't been sitting outside on the frozen stone since then?

He had his face in his hands, but sat up taller and let his hands fall to his lap when he heard the car approaching. He didn't get to his feet as Zachary expected him to.

Kenzie had her door open before the car came to a complete stop, and Zachary mashed the brake the rest of the way to the floor, worried she would be knocked off balance by the motion of the car.

Zachary opened his door and jumped out, following close behind Kenzie to be ready for any trouble. Their feet crunched through the gravel and snow.

"Dad!" Kenzie hurried over to him and grabbed him in an embrace. "Dad, you're freezing! How long have you been out here? What's going on?"

"I didn't want to stay in the house."

"What's going on?"

He looked toward the imposing mansion and sighed. "Oh, MacKenzie..."

"What is it, Dad?"

Walter looked at Zachary. "I warned you to stay out of trouble."

"Is this because of something I did?" Zachary asked worriedly.

"No. I just mean... I told *you*... why didn't I listen to myself?"

"Oh, Dad." Kenzie rubbed his back. She was looking around, eyes sharp, trying to figure out what was happening. "What's wrong? Tell me what's going on."

Walter sighed heavily again. "We'd better go back in," he said, pushing himself to his feet. He struggled to get up and then swayed on his feet momentarily, getting his legs under him again. He walked to the door like an old man instead of the healthy, vigorous man Zachary had come to know. Kenzie held his arm, checking his face worriedly several times.

The door was unlocked and he led them in. The house was quiet. No sign of any servants, the senator, or his wife. Who had let Walter in? Had the door been open when he got there?

"She said he wanted to meet with me," Walter told them. "I came over... she said to come right in. That he would be in his study."

They followed Walter in. He had obviously been to the senator's home before and knew his way around it well enough to go directly to the study rather than having to wander around calling out and checking doors. The house was silent. It was clear that the senator wasn't home.

Walter opened the heavy study door. He looked like he would

stop Kenzie from going in, but then he stopped himself from denying her entrance.

The senator *was* at home. He was sitting at his desk as Walter had assumed he would be. The only problem was, his upper body sprawled on the desk motionless. The sharp smell of vomit filled the room. Ignoring it, Kenzie hurried across the room to the dead man with a cry of alarm. Her fingers went quickly to his neck to feel for a pulse. She drew back, fingers red with blood. Zachary unzipped his bag and pulled out a wipe for her. As she wiped the blood off, Zachary pulled out a pair of gloves and a garbage bag. He handed her the gloves and opened the bag for her to deposit the wipe into and dropped it to the floor.

"He's dead?"

Kenzie nodded. She finished snapping the gloves on and lifted the senator's head briefly to look at the gaping, bloody wound across his throat. She set his head back down in the position it had been in. She indicated the coffee mug and water glass on the desk. "Don't touch those. He vomited; I wouldn't be surprised if he was poisoned before his throat was cut."

She looked at Walter. "You found him here like this?"

Walter nodded. He was looking pale and somewhat green.

"Why didn't you call the police?"

"I thought you needed to be here... and I thought..." His eyes flicked to Zachary. "I wanted to make sure that there wasn't anything... related to your investigation."

Zachary shook his head. "I haven't been here. I have no idea how much work he did from home. What notes he might have had. If he ever recorded or wrote anything down about what happened to Edie Dwayne's murder." He stopped himself, then continued. "Or Ronnie Baxter's."

"Baxter?" Kenzie repeated, "But you don't know that he—"

"He was killed around the same time as Edie. His body was dumped in Quebec."

Kenzie's eyes were wide and curious, but she stayed focused on the job at hand. They would have time to discuss Ronnie Baxter later.

"Did you touch anything?" she asked Walter sternly. "Doorknob," she said, looking back at the study door. "The door itself? Did you knock? Ring the bell? Did you touch anything else?"

"No, I don't think so."

Zachary walked around the room, his hands in his pockets, glancing over anything that might be of interest. There were notes in the Moleskine notebook beside Neufeld's body. Zachary got closer to try to read the scribbled notes. He took out his camera and snapped a few photos. He didn't think that he should turn the pages of the notebook, even with gloves on, so he didn't. He just considered the words he had seen on the page as he walked around the room, then left the study to check out the rest of the house.

"Zachary!" Kenzie called after him, "You should stay in here."

He ignored her. He knew there wouldn't be much time to search the rest of the house. She would call the police within minutes, and the police would respond quickly to a call to the senator's residence. Zachary was surprised there were no on-site security cops. Not even a butler or doorman to check people at the door, making sure that they were expected and not carrying any weapons.

Maybe the senator thought that he was safe there because it was remote and there were locked gates to discourage visitors. Only the gates hadn't been closed. Had he unlocked them for someone? His killer? Or had the killer left them open when he had left?

"Zachary?"

He figured Kenzie would probably stay in the same room with the corpse. She wouldn't want to explore the rest of the house, unless there were another corpse to check on. She would not want to release the scene until the proper officials arrived. She would monitor it until she was sure it was properly controlled.

The senator and his wife had separate bedrooms. Not unusual. Some people preferred to sleep alone. Some people snored, or thrashed, or had nightmares. Zachary frequently moved out to the couch to sleep if he knew he was keeping Kenzie awake. She didn't need his disruptive nightmares when she had work the next morning.

Nothing was obviously missing or disturbed in the senator's

bedroom or closet. Mrs. Neufeld's room, however, was another story. Clothes had clearly been removed from the closet; some had been dropped to the floor and abandoned there. Luggage had been removed from the closet. Of course, her toothbrush, makeup, and other sundries had been removed from the bathroom. Zachary put on gloves and checked the rest of the bathroom drawers and cabinets, then went through the drawers in the bedside table and other pieces of furniture in Cathy Neufeld's room.

There was another book in the bedside table drawer, similar to the one on the senator's desk. Zachary took it out and opened it, wondering whether it was another of the senator's books, and he kept several around the house so that there would always be one handy if he had a thought he wanted to record.

But it was obviously not the senator's.

Zachary took pictures of the last few pages of the notebook as well as the first inside page. He slid the book back away where he had found it.

His phone started vibrating, and he took it out to see Kenzie's number. He answered it. "Kenz?"

"You need to come back here," she said, voice tight, "the police are going to be here anytime, and you need to be here when they arrive."

"Okay. I will be."

He sped up his search of the rest of the house. There were sirens in the distance. By the time they arrived in front of the house, he was back in the study with the others. He put his own gloves into the garbage bag and stood near the door, as if he had been too freaked out by the body to get any closer.

Walter was sitting in one of the club chairs, looking frail and sick.

There was a racket as the police cars pulled up and entered the house, shouting out warnings and queries.

57

"In here," Kenzie called, standing in the doorway, partway into the hall so they would be able to see her. She didn't hold up her hands or do anything to indicate that she felt like she didn't belong exactly where she was.

"The rest of the house has not been cleared," she advised. "I'm sure there's no one else here, but I haven't checked."

A couple of cops stayed with them and gawked at the senator's body while the rest fanned out throughout the house to make sure they were, in fact, alone and that there were no other bodies to be discovered.

"Tell us what happened here," instructed a detective who put himself in charge. "Who are you and when did you get here?"

Kenzie took charge, introducing herself as Assistant Medical Examiner in Roxboro and giving Walter's and Zachary's names.

"How did you come to be here? This is well out of your jurisdiction, and the medical examiner doesn't usually find the bodies before the police."

Kenzie explained about Walter being invited over and then calling Kenzie when he found the body.

"What have you touched?"

They managed to bypass any questions that would require

Zachary to tell what he had been doing in the rest of the house, letting everyone think that he had been in the same room as Kenzie and Walter the entire time.

The detective could clearly see that Walter was not doing well, only asking him a few preliminary questions and then leaving him alone. He asked Kenzie a number of questions about the state of the body and she answered him, but said that he should get official answers from his own medical examiner.

"Where is the rest of the household? His wife? Staff?"

"There wasn't anyone else here when we got here. Dad, you talked to someone; was it his wife? Did she say where she was going?"

Walter shook his head. "I don't understand. I came here to talk to him... she said to go right in. He was expecting me, so why...?"

He looked inadvertently over at the body and shook his head, choking up. Kenzie patted her shoulder.

"Sorry, Dad, we'll get you out of here as soon as possible."

"You might try his lawyer," Zachary told the cop. "Brent Cousins. He was meeting with the senator earlier in the week. They've worked together for years. Maybe he'll have some insight into what was happening in the senator's life."

The cop wrote down the name. "Brent Cousins. We'll be sure to give him a call."

"Do you need anything else?" Kenzie asked the detective. "I'm sure you'd like us out of your crime scene."

He sighed, arms folded grumpily over his chest. "I know where to find you. So I suppose you can go. I'll be in touch. It would be nice if you could stay around long enough to liaise with our medical examiner."

"I don't think I want to be here when your medical examiner arrives. He isn't going to be happy to find me on the scene. Best if we don't have to butt heads with each other."

"Fine. Thank you for calling us and holding the scene until we could get here. And for any other help you can give us."

She nodded and stripped off her gloves, disposing of them before she left the room. They walked Walter out.

"Buttheads?" Zachary joked, "You said buttheads."

Kenzie shook her head. "What are you, twelve?"

He snickered. Kenzie looked at Walter's car, parked in the driveway in front of Zachary's. "I'm going to drive Dad. Are you staying in town, Dad, or do you want me to take you to Mom's?"

"I can drive," he muttered.

"No, you can't. I don't want you to be in an accident. Mom's? A hotel? Where do you want me to take you?"

"Take me to Lisa's," he sighed, "but don't tell your mother… she's going to have a fit over this!"

"I can't exactly not tell her. She'll want to know why I'm driving you. And she'll want to know why you look like that."

He straightened up, standing a little taller. "Look like what?"

"That's a bit better. You can work on your story while we drive over there. But I don't think you'll be able to keep the fact from her that the senator was murdered. It's going to be all over the news."

He slumped down again. Kenzie opened the passenger door for him.

"She's going to want to know everything," Walter groaned.

Kenzie gave Zachary a little wave. "I'll see you over there. Don't get there twenty minutes before me."

"How would I do that?"

"I want to talk to you about your little tour before the police got there, too."

Zachary did his best to look innocent. "Just making sure the rest of the house was secure."

"Mm-hmm."

He climbed into his car and waited for Kenzie and Walter to get settled before he backed up and turned around, navigating around the various police cars. His travel mug was still in its holder, and he had a sip of coffee, but it was barely warm despite being in an insulated mug. He probably had time to get some more coffee before going to Lisa's house. Then he wouldn't beat Kenzie there.

.   .   .

He arrived at the mansion just behind Kenzie. She gave him a frown as she climbed out of Walter's car. She walked up to his door, and he buzzed the window down. "Are you going in? Or are you coming right back?"

"I'm just going to say hello, then I'll be back. Dad has agreed that he will have to talk to Mom about what happened, and I don't want to be around for that part. I don't want to have to answer her questions, and I don't want to hear what he tells her."

"Walter might put a little spin on it."

She nodded. "Exactly. But I can't drop him off and not say hello, so I'll be just a minute."

"We have dinner reservations."

Kenzie had been turning away from him, but she turned back, scowling. "What? What are you talking about? We have reservations where?"

"I don't know. Wherever you like. But we have reservations, so we can't stay here. For dinner."

"Oh." Kenzie's expression cleared and she laughed. "Yeah. Thanks."

He nodded and raised the window. He watched Kenzie walk to the front door with Walter. She stopped at the door to talk to her mother, looking over her shoulder at Zachary a couple of times while she did so. He could see her shaking her head several times. Then she finally turned around and returned to the car.

She opened the door and slid into her seat. "Thank goodness for those dinner reservations. I don't know if I could have gotten away without them."

Zachary waited until she was belted in, then turned the car around the little court and returned the way they had come.

"Coffee's fresh," he told her, pointing to her mug. "And I didn't know if you would be hungry after all of that, so I got you a muffin, too. If you don't want it now, you can have it whenever you need it."

"I'm starving."

Unlike many people, Kenzie was not grossed out by dead bodies. While her father and other witnesses might be too queasy to eat anything after seeing a murder victim, it didn't hurt Kenzie's constitution. She carefully pulled the plastic wrap open and bit into the fresh muffin.

"This is awesome. Thanks. I didn't want to have to go all the way back home before I could eat. But gas station food…"

"We could stop somewhere else, you know. Get whatever you feel like."

"No, this is good. I wanted something, but didn't want to have to stop."

She ate her muffin, washed it down with coffee, then leaned back into her seat, sighing. "That hit the spot. Now… what exactly were you doing taking a tour of the house before the police got there?"

"There could have been another body, you know. Mrs. Neufeld. Security staff. Maid. Anyone. Or the murderer might still be in the house. It was important to have a look around."

"But you didn't find any other bodies or our murderer. So why did it take so long to get back to the study? And isn't it stupid to go looking around the house for a murderer all by yourself? Unarmed? Instead of waiting for the cops?"

"Well…" Zachary cleared his throat. "Maybe I didn't think that part through very carefully. I can be…"

"Impulsive," she finished. "Yeah, I think you might have mentioned that before."

"Did you find anything interesting?"

He nodded. "Mrs. Neufeld has split."

"She's gone? You mean permanently? How do you know?"

"Clothes, suitcase, toiletries. She's gone."

"Why would she leave? Do you think she is the one who called Walter? He didn't say for sure who it was, I wasn't sure whether that was who he meant had called him, but I'm pretty sure it was."

"I suspect so."

"Why would she do that?" Kenzie's tone was skeptical. "You don't think she's the one who killed the senator, do you? Women don't usually slash their husband's throats."

"He was poisoned first, you thought."

"Women *do* poison their husbands," she admitted. "Then what? She got too impatient and finished him off? Someone else came in and did that?"

"I don't know. She left a notebook. She might have explained there, but I couldn't read it."

"We can look at it together," she said, familiar with his learning disabilities and how difficult it was for him to read handwriting.

"Need to download a translator app."

"What?" She turned her head, staring at him.

"It's in Cyrillic."

"Russian? Really?" Kenzie shook her head. "She's Russian?"

"Let's check."

58

Zachary called Heather on speaker. He waited for the call to ring through as he merged onto the highway.

"Hi, Zachy."

"Hey. You're on speaker with Kenzie."

"Oh, hi, Kenzie."

"Hi."

"Heather, I didn't get a chance to look at the background on Senator Neufeld before I left this morning. Did you get much on his wife?"

"First wife or second wife?"

"Second wife."

"Not a lot. We were looking at events ten years ago, and she wasn't in the picture yet, so I didn't spend much time on her."

"Do you have her name? Pre-marriage?"

"Catherine... hang on a sec and let me look it up. It was Russian."

Zachary glanced aside at Kenzie.

"Catherine Ivanov," Heather told him after tapping a few computer keys.

"She didn't sound Russian. No accent."

"No. American-born."

"Okay. So she has parents here?"

"Yes."

"Any idea if they are involved with any of the... Russian crime families or oligarchs in this part of the country?"

There was a long pause. "Zachary, I don't even know how I would look that up."

"No." Zachary laughed. "Sorry. Something for us to ask the police about. They can follow it up on their end."

"Do we think now that she is... involved in something shady? Does the senator know?"

"The senator doesn't know anything anymore. You'll hear about it on the news later today. He was murdered."

Heather gasped. "Oh, I didn't know. And you think it as his wife?"

"I think she was likely involved. We'll see what the police have to say after they investigate it."

After a few more exchanges, he terminated the call with Heather.

"The Russians," Kenzie said, shaking her head. "It must be a coincidence. Not everyone who is Russian is a criminal. There are plenty of honest, hard-working Russian immigrants who have never broken the law..."

It sounded more like she was trying to reassure herself than trying to tell him that Catherine Ivanov Neufeld had not been Russian or had not been involved in any crime.

"Do you think it's a coincidence that she called Walter?" Zachary asked. "Did he know the Neufelds well?"

"I don't know. He knows everyone in politics, but how well? I can't tell you that."

"Why would she call him to ensure that he was the one to find the body?"

Kenzie sipped her coffee, not answering him for a long time.

"You think that she wanted him to find the body so that he would toe the line and not do anything to cross the Russians?"

"I don't know," Zachary admitted. "It's possible. Maybe the senator had been working for the Russians and then decided he wasn't going to listen to them anymore. Maybe this was a warning to your dad not to do the same. I don't know why else she would have called him. Did he say anything else in the car?"

"Not much. He was just… like he was when we came up to the house. Pale. In shock. Scared."

Not the way she was used to seeing him.

"If he's still lobbying for the Russians…" Kenzie started. Then she stopped.

Zachary glanced over at her. "You're not going to stop him. And he's not doing anything illegal by signing a contract or helping them, so the police won't have anything to say about it. If this is what happens when someone tries to fight back against the Russians, then he's better off just doing it. Trying to get them the votes they need when they ask for it. That's why Catherine Neufeld called him. She wants him to know that *no one*, no matter how high they rank, backs out of a contract with them."

"A lesson they thought they had already taught him a year ago," Kenzie said quietly. Her abduction. Walter's possible abduction. Walter had agreed to lobby against the bill he had previously agreed to, even if he had decided that the group he was working for were not people he wanted to be associated with. Walter wasn't willing to risk Kenzie's life.

And now, he'd had another glimpse of what would happen if he didn't do exactly what they wanted.

59

Zachary had prepared his final report for Oliver. There were still some holes in it, answers that he hadn't been able to get but that hopefully, the police would be able to provide as they reopened the investigation into Edie Dwayne's death and tried to sort out what had happened at the senator's mansion. While Edie's death had gone largely unnoticed by the public ten years earlier, just a short, sad announcement in the local news, the senator's death was big news and there would be plenty of pressure from the public to solve it.

Would they reveal the involvement of the Russians or try to keep that part quiet? If they vilified a specific racial or cultural group, there could be a big backlash. Pressure could still be brought to bear against the police and political leaders, even if Senator Neufeld was out of the picture. There was enough money flowing into Vermont's economy from the Russian oligarch's cryptocurrency to make anyone seriously consider whether they dared mention Catherine's origin or alliances. She had left her notebook behind. Was that an oversight or a taunt? Maybe she fully expected them to have it translated and, in so doing, find out how she and her family had influenced the senator and his decisions over the last couple of years.

Digging more deeply into the organizations Zachary knew had been donating to the senator's campaign ten years ago—the ones who had not made it into the official books—Zachary had not been able to find out very much. Shell corporations out of Delaware, one of the jurisdictions that allowed owners and directors to hide behind the name of an agent. Offshore accounts that he couldn't trace. Perhaps the police would be able to, but they would first have to have a reason. The Russians? Or other influencers?

Zachary didn't know whether the companies that had put him into office in the first place had been Russian, or whether the Russians had put Catherine in his path later and used her to pressure and manipulate him.

Had Zachary's investigation prompted the senator to look more closely at the first Mrs. Neufeld? Maybe he had been unaware that Edie Dwayne's death had been a murder and that his wife had been involved in diverting monies. The few words Zachary had found scribbled on the last page of his notebook suggested a crisis of conscience.

I didn't know
Edie Dwayne
Shirley
Catherine

Perhaps Zachary's visit had prompted him to look at what had happened in the past, and that led to his looking at his current situation and realizing he was being manipulated by his new wife. Had he decided to put a stop to it?

And then Catherine and her clan had put an end to him.

But so far, Zachary had no proof of any of that. Maybe Catherine had decided she didn't want to be his Girl Friday anymore. Maybe she had decided she wanted an even more lavish lifestyle and her husband could not provide that. Not alive, anyway. Or maybe he had just chewed his food too loudly. There was nothing to indicate why she had left.

Zachary looked into the hospital room and found Oliver there, visiting with Jeff. The TV was on, and they both seemed more interested in the show than in talking to each other.

Oliver's eye caught Zachary's movement in the door, and he turned his head to look at him.

"Oh, Zachary, come in. How are you?" He shook his son's arm. "Put that on mute, why don't you? Mr. Goldman is here to talk to us."

Jeff turned the TV off. Zachary wondered whether Oliver had been the one who had wanted it turned on in the first place.

"Hello, Mr. Goldman."

"Just Zachary is fine. How are you feeling?"

Jeff rubbed his bandaged throat with careful fingers. "I'll be glad when they say I can go home. It's hard to sleep here, with everyone coming in to check on me all the time, and the paging and people walking and talking all night long."

Zachary nodded. He'd had enough experience with hospitals to know what Jeff was talking about.

"I brought you this," Zachary offered Oliver an envelope with his report. "My part in the investigation is done. The police are going to reopen Edie's case and look at it again, especially in light of Mr. Baxter being killed with a bullet from the same gun as Edie and then dumped in Quebec. That doesn't indicate an accidental shooting."

"No," Oliver agreed, grimacing. "I would say not."

His expression was a mixture of emotions. Relief that things would be set right and Edie would get justice. Sadness over her loss and the fact that he had let it go for ten years without insisting that her death be properly investigated. Concern for Jeff as he looked at him and patted his leg.

"Ronnie Baxter was not a good man," Zachary told Jeff. "You were right about that. But he did defend your mother, which is probably what got him killed."

Jeff swallowed and nodded. "At least he's not out there hurting anyone." His cheeks were pink with embarrassment. He looked at Oliver. "And he never touched me. He never got that far."

"I'm sorry that we didn't know. Didn't recognize him for what he was."

"It wasn't your fault. You didn't even know him. And Mom..."

"Men like that are very convincing," Zachary said. "They learn very quickly how to manipulate people, how to make them think that they are trustworthy and that any suspicions they do have are unfounded. Baxter was not new at it. He'd had lots of experience."

There was a tap at the door. They all turned to look and, instead of a nurse or doctor there to examine Jeff or take his vitals, it was ex-Sheriff Taylor. He nodded at them.

"Sorry to barge in. I can come back another time. I didn't realize I would be interrupting anything."

Oliver rose to his feet. "Zachary and I were just going to wander down to the coffee machine and go over this report," he said, holding up the envelope Zachary had given him. "Jeff could use a break from having to look at this same old face. Doesn't need Dad hanging over him like an old woman all the time."

Zachary stood and followed Oliver out the door, making space for the ex-lawman to sit down to visit with Jeff.

"Everything is pretty straightforward," Zachary said, indicating the report in the envelope. "But we can go over it."

"Not necessary. Just a polite excuse to get out of the room so Jeff can have some privacy."

"Sheriff Taylor isn't actually a law enforcement officer anymore. He isn't interviewing Jeff about what happened…?"

"No. Just a neighbor stopping in to say hello. His kids were close to Marissa and Terry in age, so our families knew each other well. Jeff is the baby, younger than any of them."

Would Taylor tell either of them about his alcoholism after his wife had left him? How it may have contributed to the lack of an investigation into Edie's death?

Or maybe they already knew that. It was a close-knit community. They may all have known about it at the time or it may have come to light in the years since.

"I'll bring your boxes back to you sometime when you're out at the house. Everything has been sorted. If you want to look through them now… I don't think anything in there will hurt too much."

Oliver nodded. "Thank you for that. I appreciate all you have done."

"Edie was trying to do the right thing."

"She always did."

They stopped at the coffee machine to get four cups of fresh coffee, settling them into a tray to take a couple back to Jeff and Taylor.

They walked in a circle around the floor, through a couple of other units in addition to Jeff's, trying to ensure that Taylor had plenty of time to chat before they returned.

There was a loud crack like a firecracker, making Zachary flinch and duck behind a pillar to protect himself. Oliver laughed, teasing him for his nervousness. Zachary grabbed him and pulled him behind the pillar as well.

"Zachary," Oliver protested.

"That was a gunshot."

"It couldn't have been. It was just... someone dropping a binder on a desk or something. This is a hospital. No one would be—"

Zachary's brain was running through the possibilities, rabbiting from one to another, trying on theories and discarding them more quickly than he could have put them into words. One possibility jumped to the forefront.

Jeff.

Someone had already made an attempt on Jeff's life. They might not be able to prove who it was or that it was related to the investigation into his mother's death, but they all knew it was.

Only Zachary and Oliver knew what Jeff had been able to recall so far. No one else knew who his testimony might implicate.

He might not have even told Oliver and Zachary everything he remembered.

What if Taylor's alcoholism had been triggered by more than just his wife leaving him? Maybe his lackluster investigation into Edie Dwayne's death had been more than an assumption that kids, maybe his own son, had been responsible for Edie's death. Maybe he'd had a hand in it.

Zachary ran toward Jeff's hospital room.

Oliver was slower. "Zachary?"

Zachary had a head start, but running was not a strength. He had been doing a lot more walking in the past year, even when climbing stairs when he could but, since his spinal cord injury a few years before, he had never been able to run without tripping over his own feet. This time, he didn't even think about it. He had saved Jeff's life once. Had he left him alone in the room with a killer?

When Oliver realized Zachary was running in earnest, that he really was concerned with Jeff's safety and believed the noise had been a gunshot, he was hard on Zachary's heels.

"It wasn't him!" Oliver insisted, puffing behind Zachary but gaining on him. "It wasn't a gunshot!"

Only a second or two could have passed between the noise and Zachary starting his run back toward Jeff's room. Zachary could hear raised voices. Shouting, worried babble, but no screams or hysteria.

Zachary was worried that they would not be able to get back to the room. There would be security guards already rushing to the room, barring anyone from getting in there. He wouldn't be able to get close.

But there hadn't been enough time. If there were security guards on the floor, they were not quick enough to recognize the noise as a gunshot and, if they were stationed on another floor, the staff would have to call them first.

Oliver passed Zachary on the last turn. Zachary tripped, banged into the wall, and nearly fell face-first, but at the last minute, he managed to regain his balance and followed Oliver into the hospital room.

60

Taylor stood, gun still drawn and held in both hands, pointed not at Jeff, but at the man on the floor. He was face down. But Zachary knew who it would be as he and Oliver rolled the man over while Taylor kept his gun pointed directly at the man's center mass.

Brent Cousins.

Of course, that made more sense. Zachary's brain immediately started telling him all the reasons that Taylor couldn't have been the one who had killed Edie or gone after Jeff.

He had walked into the hospital room in full sight of all the staff. He had let Oliver and Zachary see him. It would have been useless to come to the hospital to kill Jeff with so many witnesses. They would have had him dead-to-rights for murder.

Zachary had never gotten a bad vibe from him. His instincts were not flawless, of course, but they were well developed. Taylor had never set off any alarm bells. He had been open with Zachary and provided him with the information he needed, including tips on how to get the information that the police department had archived.

If he had been the killer or somehow involved in the plot, it would have been easier to say that he didn't have copies of any notes or remember anything specific about the investigation. He could have blocked Zachary from accessing the police files, telling his mother to lose them or find a reason to reject his information request.

And Taylor was in AA. That wasn't to say that someone in AA could not be a murderer or be dishonest but, with the amount that Zachary knew about AA, he didn't believe someone who went to his meetings regularly and was working on not just staying sober, but improving himself, making amends, and being a positive influence in the lives of others was likely to be a cold-blooded killer.

"He's dead," Zachary confirmed to ex-Sheriff Taylor. Even so, he pushed Cousins's gun farther away from him as if he might come back to life and grab it and again threaten them.

Nurses and others who had heard the shot congregated in the doorway, looking in and chattering with each other. One nurse came in and knelt by Zachary to examine Cousins and to confirm Zachary's diagnosis. She was a small, compact woman with a no-nonsense buzz cut. Maybe an army medic before becoming a nurse. No stranger to gunfire and death.

There were pages being called out over the PR system. Security. Code Silver.

"Brent Cousins," Oliver said, looking down at him. "Why would he come here?" He looked over at Jeff, lying wide-eyed in the bed, shocked by everything that had happened. But safe and sound. No new injuries. Zachary had been expecting to find him with a bullet hole in his chest and arterial blood soaking into the bedsheets.

"He wanted to eliminate the last known witness," Zachary said, taking a few deep breaths to try to calm his thumping heart. "He didn't know what Jeff might know, but he wasn't willing to risk that Jeff might be able to testify against him."

"What about the other kids?" Oliver demanded, his face pale. "Should I call them? What if…?"

"The other kids didn't know anything about Cousins, did they?

They were at school or could look after themselves at home. Jeff was the one who was too young to leave on his own. So he was the only one who spent any time at the campaign office."

Jeff nodded his agreement. "The others got to stay home and watch TV or play on the computer. I had to go with Mom to help at the office."

He bent over the side of the bed to look down at the man who lay on the floor. "He just walked in here like he didn't think he could get caught. Was he really going to kill me?"

Zachary didn't like to confirm to Jeff that he had been the intended victim, but it was obvious that for the second time in a week, Jeff had been targeted by someone who had fully intended to take his life.

"At least it's over now," he told Jeff.

"Is that really the end of it?" Oliver demanded. He looked at his son, helpless in the hospital bed. If Taylor hadn't been there to react with deadly force, the outcome would have been very different.

Security started to arrive, yelling out orders for everyone to put up their hands, targeting Taylor as the shooter and acting as if he were a dangerous criminal.

"He was defending Jeff," Zachary told one of the security guards, who was determined to put them all in restraints until the real cops could arrive. "The dangerous shooter is the one on the floor, not Sheriff Taylor."

"Sheriff?" one of them sneered. "Sheriff of what? He's got no jurisdiction here."

"He didn't do anything wrong," Jeff echoed. "He was just defending me. I would be dead if he hadn't shot Mr. Cousins!"

Zachary submitted to his hands being restrained behind his back with flexicuffs, followed by a brief, inexpert pat down to make sure that he wasn't carrying any weapons. He was allowed to sit cross-legged on the floor to await the police, which hurt his tailbone.

· · ·

When everything was sorted out and they were released from their restraints, Zachary looked around, shaking his head. The second time he'd been at a scene the police and medical examiner had to be called to in as many days. It had certainly been an unexpectedly intense case.

"Do you think that's the end of it?" Oliver asked anxiously. "Tell me you don't think anyone else will be coming after my son."

"No, I don't think so. I think… this is the end of it. Ronnie Baxter is gone. Brent Cousins. The senator. Somebody should keep an eye on Mrs. Neufeld—both Mrs. Neufelds, if they can find Catherine—but I think she was more interested in exposing Senator Neufeld than in hurting anyone physically. If she can keep whatever money she got out of the scam in her offshore bank accounts, I don't think there's any need to fear her."

"You think all of this was because of money?" Oliver asked. "Killing my Edie and trying to kill Jeff, and everything else that happened in between? You think it was all for money?"

"Money and power. Shirley also wanted the senator to be elected. But when he got rid of her…"

"What drama people have in their lives," Oliver said, shaking his head. "Can you imagine how stressful it would be to marry for money and power? How you would feel if you suddenly felt it all starting to slip away…?"

Zachary nodded, thinking about it. There were certainly no guarantees when marrying for love. People fell out of love, broke their vows, left their marriages, or, more heartbreaking, died. But marry for beauty, and it was bound to fade with age. Marry for money or power… either one was a precarious perch.

"Will you be keeping an eye on things?" he asked Taylor, who was watching the police proceedings with something like nostalgia. "I know you're not always in town and you don't exactly live on Oliver's street, but…"

"Keep an ear to the ground?" Taylor asked.

"Yeah. You still have contacts who are positioned to know what's going on in the county?"

Taylor nodded his agreement. "We'll look after the Dwaynes," he promised. "And if either of the Mrs. Neufelds show up... they won't get far."

Zachary hoped it was true. Neither one should have any reason to go after Oliver or his family, but it was difficult to trust that people would always behave rationally. Not after all the evidence he'd seen that said otherwise.

EPILOGUE

Zachary and Kenzie watched the extensive TV coverage of the death of Senator Neufeld and a brief mention of the death of an armed gunman in the Randolph Center medical clinic.

Kenzie had clearly been upset by the reports surrounding the senator's murder. She poured herself a glass of wine in the kitchen and was riffling through the contents of the freezer. He assumed she was looking for a comforting pint of ice cream. Possibly with chocolate sauce and sprinkles.

"Have you talked to your dad?" he asked. "Checked in to see how he's doing?"

"No," Kenzie admitted. "I don't want to hover over him. I know I'm not his parent."

"I doubt he'd mind you just checking in."

"It isn't like he's going to tell me anything about the Russians and what precautions he's taking to protect himself." She shook her head. "How can he protect himself? Either he does what they ask, or he gets taken out like the senator?"

"I think you'd feel better if you knew he was okay."

Kenzie closed the freezer door with a sigh. "I know," she agreed. "I'm just afraid of what I'm going to hear. He's so stubborn."

Zachary tried to keep a straight face, and not say anything stupid about the apple not falling far from the tree or the pot calling the kettle black.

Kenzie glared at him. "That's enough out of you."

"I didn't say anything."

"And you'd better not."

"Do you want me to give you some space?" he asked when she pulled out her phone to make the call. Normally, when she called her parents, she retreated to the bedroom to talk to them privately.

"No. Let's do this together."

She returned to the living room and sat down, tapping Walter's number on her phone and putting the call on speaker.

The phone rang a few times before it was picked up. But the voice that answered was not Walter's.

"MacKenzie?" Lisa's voice asked.

Kenzie frowned at her phone, looking at the screen to ensure she had called the correct number and hadn't slipped down a row to call her mother.

"Mom? Is everything okay? I was calling Dad. Did you pick up his phone?"

"Yes. He isn't taking any calls at the moment."

"What's wrong? Why isn't he taking any calls?"

Walter was not the type who could go a day without talking on the phone. Zachary doubted he could go for more than an hour without talking to one of his friends or political acquaintances. Other than over dinner, when phones were banned.

"I don't want you to overreact," Lisa warned.

"What?" Kenzie's voice rose. "Of course I'm going to overreact when you start the conversation that way! What's wrong with Dad?"

"Your father is fine. You can talk to him in a few minutes, if you like."

"If he's fine, why isn't he answering any calls?"

"With everything that has happened, we have been talking about the possibility of his retirement."

"What?" Kenzie's voice was slightly less panicked this time. "I can't believe that Dad would ever even consider it. He lives to lobby."

"I know he does, dear. But this past year has been very difficult for him. The new forces that are in play... people that he doesn't want to be involved with... it is getting harder and harder to choose which issues he wants to be involved with and to take what he believes to be the most ethical stand."

In other words, the Russians were pressuring him, and if he didn't do what he was told, bad things happened. Kenzie was kidnapped. He was sent to find the body of an old friend. Whether or not the threats were explicit, he understood what those things meant. He was no fool.

"So he's going to retire?" Kenzie asked. "What if they don't want him to? How is that going to stop them from pressuring him?"

"They may not have any choice," Lisa said slowly. "People get older and... are less able to perform the tasks they once thrived on."

"I've asked Dad if he's sick," Kenzie told her mother worriedly. "He always says he's just fine. Is he sick? What is it?"

"An incident like the one on Wednesday at the senator's house can be quite a shock to the system. It could result in an adverse medical event. A heart attack or stroke, for example."

Kenzie's eyes were wide and alarmed. Zachary couldn't reconcile Lisa's calm and measured tone with her words. He couldn't understand her being so calm if Walter had suffered a stroke after being sent to find the senator's body.

He had not looked good. Neither of them had trusted him to drive himself home afterward. But Zachary had figured he would recover quickly enough.

"What happened?" Kenzie demanded. "A stroke? Why didn't you call me?"

"I told you that your father is fine," Lisa repeated. "But to the rest of the world... he has suffered a nervous collapse. Possibly a stroke. He may never be the same. He might be forced to retire from the job he loves so much."

They were all silent for a few long seconds. Zachary held Kenzie's hand.

They had wondered how Walter was going to pull away from the influence of the Russians without sacrificing himself or his family. Now they had the answer.

It wouldn't take long for the word to spread. Walter Kirsch was in the hospital or a private clinic. Maybe there would be an official announcement from Lisa Cole Kirsch that he had decided it was time to slow down and enjoy life. Smell the roses, direct his family foundation, occasionally join Lisa at dinners and fundraisers. But he would no longer be a regular at the Capitol, shaking hands and championing bills.

Any inquiries to his doctors would be discreetly turned away. Doctor-patient confidentiality. But there would be some signs that he was recovering from an illness. Maybe Walter would walk with a cane for a few months. Wear dark glasses. Be seen with a white-suited attendant. It wouldn't take much to convince the public—including the Russians—that Walter could not work as he had for so many years.

"Can I talk to Daddy, Mom?"

"Of course, dear. Give me a minute to take him his phone."

Did you enjoy this book? Reviews and recommendations are vital to making a book successful.

Please leave a review at your favorite book store or review site and share it with your friends.

Don't miss the following bonus material:
Sign up for mailing list to get a free ebook
Read a sneak preview chapter
Other books by P.D. Workman
Learn more about the author

UNLOCK ACCESS TO
ZACHARY GOLDMAN'S CASE FILES!

Get a peek inside Zachary's case
files and see what other
intriguing tales are in store!

SCAN TO UNLOCK OFFER

books.pdworkman.com/sign-up-zg

PREVIEW OF SHE ONCE VANISHED

PREVIEW CHAPTER 1

Although Zachary was a private investigator, there wasn't usually any cloak-and-dagger involved. That was for spies, not private investigators, and even the spies he knew didn't use that sort of thing. But his new client had insisted on absolute privacy, and Zachary understood why.

His client had checked in at a motel under a name that was not his own, probably paying cash. Even so, the motel manager had probably taken down his license plate number so he would have a way to trace him if he trashed the room or ran up long-distance charges. If the car was a rental, that was one more hurdle to overcome to find out who the man who had asked to meet Zachary really was.

Zachary knew who he was supposed to meet. They exchanged several emails before graduating to a phone call so that Zachary could talk to him in real-time and try to get his questions answered.

But Zachary would not take on the case until he knew for sure that the man was who he purported to be. It would not do for a private investigator to be hoodwinked by accepting a retainer from someone who was not who he said he was. A public scandal would not be good for business. People liked to think the person they were hiring knew what he was talking about.

Zachary parked down the street from the motel and walked in. If the new client had any shadows—reporters, law enforcement types, or rabid fans—Zachary did not want his car to be identified or targeted.

No one seeing Zachary would give him a second look. In fact, most would avoid taking even a first look. He was on the short side and had to work to keep his weight in the healthy zone. His hair was dark and buzzcut short, the epitome of easy to care for. He usually had several days' growth of beard, making him look scruffy and unkempt.

People did not like being approached by a scruffy, possibly homeless man. They would cross to the other side of the street to avoid him. They would not look at him very closely and if asked to describe him, they probably wouldn't be able to. That was how he kept his anonymity. Not with dark glasses, a hat, and a trench coat. Just social stigma.

He watched for anyone suspicious on the street. People hanging around who didn't belong. Sitting in their cars for more than a minute or two. Anyone who was obviously watching the motel.

Everyone seemed to be minding their own business. No one watched Zachary's progress as he made his way down the street, pausing occasionally by garbage cans as if he might be looking for bottles or discarded food.

Eventually, he had reached the motel. He looked at each car in the parking lot. No one was sitting in any of them. No one smoking and studiously looking in the other direction. Nothing of any note.

Zachary knocked on the door he had been told to, though there was no car in the parking spot assigned to that room. He'd been told to knock loudly, which seemed to contradict the client's wish to remain unnoticed, but Zachary followed his instructions anyway.

A curtain twitched two motel rooms down. Zachary stood still, watching it, waiting for the door in front of him to open. Instead, the door two rooms down opened, and a young man stuck his head out the door.

"Mr. Goldman. Come down here."

Zachary joined him. The man shut, locked, and chained the door. He closed the blinds and pulled the curtain straight so that there was no way for anyone outside to see in. The stale air inside the motel room was tinged with a faint scent of bleach and cigarette smoke.

The man turned to look at Zachary. He removed dark glasses, which probably made him half-blind in the dim motel room.

"Well, you wanted to see me face-to-face," he told Zachary. "Are you satisfied?"

Zachary was mildly surprised that the man *was* who he said he was. That he had told the truth about moving to Vermont and wanting to hire an obscure private investigator and have him investigate a case that, as far as the police were concerned, was not a crime. The file had been closed and life went on for the rest of the world. For everyone except Dain Porter and Elysse Allan.

Zachary held his hand out to Dain Porter to shake.

"Good to meet you, Mr. Porter."

"Dain. And may I call you Zachary?"

He nodded. He always preferred that his clients call him by his first name. Mr. Goldman was just too formal.

"Have a seat."

The motel room was provisioned with a small table and two straight wooden chairs, and Dain and Zachary both sat down. Dain stood again to fill a cup of coffee from the small motel room carafe. "Can I get you one?"

"Sure." Zachary could always use another cup of coffee.

Dain brought both cups over to the table and sat down again. He looked around as if he thought he might have forgotten to do something else. Traffic hummed in the distance and there were occasional voices or the sounds of footsteps from the other motel rooms. Then he brought his gaze back to Zachary, studying him for a moment as if he wasn't sure he could trust him.

"I'm not much to look at," Zachary told him. "But you wouldn't want me attracting attention."

"No," Dain agreed. He looked at the window, confirming that

no one could look in at them. This was what he had become. Someone who was hunted everywhere he went. He always had to be on the alert. Always looking over his shoulder, and in front of him, and on his flanks. He could never be sure that he hadn't been seen and recognized.

"I didn't see anyone suspicious," Zachary confirmed. "I don't think you were followed."

"No. Of course not. That's good."

"I appreciate you meeting with me in person. I know this is probably not what you had in mind when you first emailed me."

"No, that's true. I figured I'd just be able to email you, and you would take the case." He gave a crooked smile. "But I appreciate that you didn't. I appreciate that you respected my privacy enough to ensure that it was actually me and not someone else using my name."

"I suppose I could just have verified it was you via a video chat, but with all of the technology available these days... it wouldn't be that hard to fake a video."

Dain nodded. "I've seen some pretty convincing deep fakes. I appreciate your caution."

"Good. Now that I know it is you, and you know my rates..."

Dain pulled out his phone. He tapped the screen a few times, and then Zachary's vibrated in his pocket. He pulled it out to see the notification that the e-transfer from Dain had been auto-deposited into his account.

That was the second matter taken care of.

"Thank you. So... why don't you tell me exactly what you hope to get from this investigation?"

Dain rolled his eyes. He had, of course, already told Zachary what he wanted him to investigate. He didn't see why he should go through it all again. But Zachary wanted to be clear on exactly what Dain wanted him to find out. What he wanted Zachary to do was no small undertaking. Zachary needed to know the exact parameters and when Dain would consider the job complete. What if what Zachary discovered *wasn't* what Dain had hoped to find? What if the truth was something quite different?

"I want you to find out what happened to Elysse when she disappeared," Dain said firmly. "What *really* happened, not the story she told the world."

"What do you think happened?"

Dain looked away. "I don't know. I wish I did. But the story Elysse told when she got back didn't make any sense. It didn't fit. She would never do something like that."

Zachary nodded slowly. It was easy for one partner in a relationship to be wrong about who their partner was. It happened all the time. People who thought they knew each other found themselves incompatible. Or they discovered that their partner had been pretending and wasn't who they said they were. People kept secrets, some of them buried deep, until one day they wouldn't stay buried any longer.

"Why don't you tell me what you know?" he told Dain. "The full story from your point of view."

"You already know my story; it was all over the media."

"The media adds or omits things, gets things wrong. I want to hear it directly from you. Everything."

PREVIEW CHAPTER 2

"It's not that complicated," Dain sighed, raking a hand through his hair as frustration flickered across his face. "We had an argument. Elysse stomped off. It wasn't the first time she'd done that. I knew that she would cool down, and then she would come back, we would make up, and… happily ever after."

"Or at least until the next fight."

Dain shrugged. "No relationship is perfect. People argue. Couples have different opinions. Personalities. Elysse and I are both… passionate people. We love each other. We have arguments. Sometimes yell at each other. And then it blows over. We make up… just as passionately."

He actually blushed.

Zachary chuckled. "So that's the summary, the short story. I'd like to hear more. If you want me to be able to figure out what happened, I need all the nuances, the little things that happened along the way. More about your relationship, your plans, and how they went off the rails."

Dain rubbed a hand over his face. "That seems like a waste of time. I know what happened when we were together; I want to know what happened when she left."

"How far have you gotten on that in the last six months?"

"*I'm* not a private investigator," Dain snapped. "If I was, I wouldn't have needed to hire you. I would have just figured it all out on my own."

"Well, I *am* a private investigator and I need more information than you have given me. How did the two of you meet?"

"Why do we need to go back that far?"

"I need background. I need more details about your relationship. I need to start building a profile of Elysse that is not just based on her Instagram feed."

Dain sighed. "Remember before Instagram was a big thing? We knew each other in school. Grew up together. Small community in Oregon. She was this cute girl who attended some of the same classes as me. Back when we were both awkward and gawky, before she was a social media influencer."

"And you liked each other back then?"

"Sometimes yes and sometimes no." Dane laughed. "You know kids... boys and girls fight, don't want anything to do with each other in the younger grades. And then you start to grow up and the hormones and social pressure take over. Then suddenly, you're looking at each other in a totally different light."

"And eventually, the two of you got together."

Dain nodded. "We started going out together... getting more serious... going steady... then her Instagrammer life took over. Suddenly, she's one of the most recognizable people on the planet. She has millions of followers. Everything she posts is an instant hit. What started out as being something fun ended up taking over her life. She spent every waking minute planning her next post, getting it just right, obsessively monitoring her views."

"That must have been hard on the relationship."

"It took over the relationship. Instagram became her boyfriend. I was just this guy who showed up in some of the shots. But people loved the relationship stuff. She had to post about us some of the time if she wanted to keep her views up."

Zachary nodded encouragingly.

"I just… sometimes I wished we could go back to the way it was. To be able just to be boyfriend and girlfriend in a small town, this little rural place… like it was idyllic. Of course, it wasn't really; there are always challenges. You want to do different things and have to consider each other's feelings, and their backgrounds, and their families. But it seemed like it was a lot simpler before she became a famous' influencer.'"

"I have heard that it can be very stressful."

Zachary didn't know a lot of famous social media figures, but he did know one, Brittany "the bombshell" Blake. He had misjudged her initially, thinking that she had it all made. He thought she had a life of leisure, with everyone worshipping her, and all she had to do was post a few pictures. He hadn't realized how hard she had to work to look good, stay healthy, and make all the appearances that her fans expected. He had thought she was snobby and stuck up when she was really down to earth, thoughtful, and cared about other people. Her fans had rescued them from a dire situation, and she had also helped Zachary on another case since then.

He wouldn't ever judge someone by their popularity again. Being famous did not equate with a life of leisure and luxury.

"It was incredibly stressful," Dain agreed. "You don't know how many times I thought about leaving. Just let Elysse live her life online, being the darling of social media, and live my life outside the spotlight, without all those expectations. Only… I love her. How could I leave her because she's too popular? It sounds… ridiculous and shallow."

"I'm sure that wasn't the reason you thought about leaving."

"No. Not exactly, but that was what it would look like. For the rest of my life, I would be the guy who left Elysse Allan. I would be the villain. The jerk who broke Elysse Allan's heart." He grimaced and looked away.

"And what you got instead was…"

"For five days, I was the guy who murdered Elysse Allan."

Dain swallowed hard. He stared at the window as if he could see it all playing out before him.

"Everyone was so sure of themselves. I was the one who reported her missing! I was the one looking for her, insisting that the police follow up on her disappearance. But the police and everyone else made me the prime suspect. They decided that I had murdered her and dumped her body somewhere it might never be discovered."

She Once Vanished, Book #19 of the *Zachary Goldman Mysteries* series by P.D. Workman
can be purchased at pdworkman.com

ABOUT THE AUTHOR

P.D. Workman is a USA Today Bestselling author and multi-award winner, renowned for her prolific output of over 100 published works that span various genres. With a knack for crafting page-turners, Workman captivates readers with everything from cozy mysteries like the Auntie Clem's Bakery series to gripping young adult and suspense novels.

A prolific reader and writer since childhood, P.D. Workman crafts emotionally powerful stories that don't shy away from hard topics. Her books tackle mental illness, addiction, abuse, and trauma with raw honesty and compassion, giving voice to the often unheard. If you crave authentic, character-driven page-turners that hit deep and stay with you long after the final page, you're in the right place.

With each new release, fans eagerly anticipate another thrilling blend of thought-provoking storytelling and relatable characters that define P.D. Workman's brand as an author of unforgettable page-turners—gripping tales that leave a lasting impact long after the last page is turned.

> P. D. Workman, does not shy from probing the deep psychological scars of childhood trauma, mental illness, and addiction. Also characteristic of this author, these extremely sensitive issues are explored with extensive empathy, described with incredible clarity, and portrayed with profound insight.
>
> — —KIM, GOODREADS REVIEWER

Some of Workman's titles have been translated into Spanish, French, Portuguese, German, and Italian.

Workman began writing at an early age and is a prolific reader as well as writer. She is also passionate about teaching and learning, expresses her creativity through art and cooking, and loves exploring the Calgary parks and green spaces where the Parks Pat Mysteries are set. She was a legal assistant for many years and has done extensive charitable work.

Workman was born and raised in Alberta, Canada, and is married with one adult son.

Please visit P.D. Workman at pdworkman.com to see what else she is working on, to join her mailing list, and to link to her social networks.

If you enjoyed this book, please take the time to recommend it to other purchasers with a review or star rating and share it with your friends!

tiktok.com/@pdworkmanauthor

facebook.com/pdworkmanauthor

x.com/pdworkmanauthor

instagram.com/pdworkmanauthor

amazon.com/author/pdworkman

bookbub.com/authors/p-d-workman

goodreads.com/pdworkman

linkedin.com/in/pdworkman

pinterest.com/pdworkmanauthor

youtube.com/pdworkman

Find P.D. Workman's books at

PDWORKMAN.COM

Scan the QR code below